HARD TIMES

FOR THESE TIMES

CHARLES DICKENS

HARD TIMES

FOR THESE TIMES

INTRODUCTION BY WILLIAM W. WATT

Holt, Rinehart and Winston

NEW YORK · CHICAGO · SAN FRANCISCO
TORONTO · LONDON

Eighth Printing, April, 1964

Introduction copyright © 1958 by William W. Watt
Typography Design by Stefan Salter
Printed in the United States of America
Library of Congress Catalog Card Number: 58-7847
29255-0218

INTRODUCTION

Hard Times was announced in *Household Words* on March 11, 1854, as a "new tale by Mr. Charles Dickens to be published weekly . . . and completed in five months." When the first three chapters appeared in the issue of April 1, the author, who had not been seriously at work on the book before January, was still struggling in midstream. Dickens was used to what he called "the great disadvantages which attend a detached and desultory form of publication." But not since 1841 had he tried a novel in weekly, not monthly, installments, and *Hard Times* was to be by far the shortest of his novels—less than a third as long as any of the four preceding it. He had to arrange the material so that it would "divide well" into twenty lengths of about five double-column pages, each installment containing enough excitement to keep the reader's interest alive for a week. He had to plan the whole so that, without any evident stalling or corner-cutting en route, the last installment would appear on schedule. And he had to finish the book before August in spite of an unusual number of distractions, any one of which might have given a less energetic writer an acceptable excuse for failing to meet the deadlines. The editorial work on *Household Words*—of which he was the dedicated "conductor"; the inevitable theatricals and parties—compulsory for a man to whom hard play was as important as hard work; the continual spate of correspondence; the domestic logistics required to move his entire ménage—wife, sister-in-law, nine children (with two friends), nurse, governess, and twenty-seven pieces of luggage—from London to Boulogne in mid-June, slowing down his sprint on the homestretch to seventy-two words in five days: perhaps these involvements were all standard order of Dickens procedure. But considering that he had been persuaded by the publishers to write the book to buoy up the sinking sale of the magazine—in spite of a resolution to write no more fiction for a year after the completion of *Bleak House* in the previous fall; considering further that his estrangement from the inadequate invalid whom he had married was hastening to a climax: it is a testimony to Dickens' amazing creative energy that *Hard Times* got written at all. Only Dickens, who had apparently never doubted that his energy was infinite, could have wondered in the fall of 1854 why he was more tired than he had ever been in his life.

Of course he was partly repeating himself in *Hard Times*—as all prolific writers do. There is more truth in Taine's generalization that this novel is "an abstract of all the rest" than in Wagenknecht's assertion that Dickens got "completely away from his own material and method." Gradgrind and Bounderby—particularly Josiah—belong in the same gallery with other hardheaded men of business: Ralph Nickleby, Scrooge, Jonas Chuzzlewit, Mr. Dombey, Murdstone, and the Smallweeds. Sissy and Louisa, as children, touch the same heartstrings as all the tender wanderers lost in a world of uncomprehending adults, from Oliver Twist to Pip. Sissy in particular echoes a Cinderella theme that runs through the novels; and she and Rachael as adults have affinities with a type of Victorian saint whom Dickens had portrayed before (in Agnes Wickfield or Esther Summerson), a paragon not unlike the mythical Lady with the Lamp in the Crimea who so offended Lytton Strachey. Mr. M'Choakumchild's schoolroom, for all its special Manchester flavor, is not too remote from Dr. Blimber's Academy (*Dombey and Son*), where the tender plants—as helpless as the passive pitchers—are forced to bloom before their time; and it has an echo of the more brutal Dotheboys Hall (*Nicholas Nickleby*), in which the "practical mode of teaching" requires that after the "third boy" has defined a horse he must proceed at once to the stable to rub down the horse of Mr. Squeers. Dickens had dealt with the dangers of a people's revolution in *Barnaby Rudge*. In sketching the interminable legal convolutions of divorce he was merely touching on a major theme of *Bleak House*. The theme of the broken clown dates back nearly twenty years to the gayer pages of *Pickwick*. And that ubiquitous Gothic gimmick—the mysterious stranger—had popped in and out of Dickens' novels long before Mrs. Pegler began her perennial visits to Coketown.

In many ways *Hard Times* is an expanded version of the second Christmas story, *The Chimes*. Gradgrind is a full-length Filer (see page xvii). Bounderby, with his blustering about turtle soup and venison, is at least a first cousin of Alderman Cute, who is perpetually threatening to "put down" all alleged pleasures or other offenses among the common people. Though Stephen Blackpool is less resigned to his fate than the more cheerful Trotty Veck and less rebellious than Will Fern, his plight is not unlike theirs: he is haunted, like Trotty, by the specter of helpless poverty and hunted, like Will, for a crime of which he is innocent.

This is not to say that Dickens in *Hard Times* is merely boiling a pot full of leftovers from his own table. It is only to indicate that readers, both in his day and in ours, who have found the book so utterly atypical have a hard case to prove. Dickens is always Dickensian, and if every character in Dickens is not "like a character out of Dickens," it is because even some of his best friends have failed to see his variety.

Generally speaking, *Hard Times* is in the direct line of his development as a novelist. Beginning with *Pickwick Papers* (1836-1837), in which the tone is dominantly playful, the atmosphere pre-Victorian, and the structure episodic, he gradually became more seriously concerned with Victorian social problems and more skillful in constructing a well-built novel. In *Oliver Twist* (1837-1839), *Nicholas Nickleby* (1838-1839), *The Old Curiosity Shop* (1840-1841), *Barnaby Rudge* (1841)—which, despite its eighteenth-century setting, is a tract for the times—and *Martin Chuzzlewit* (1843-1844), he tended to be more concerned with attacking isolated evils without surrendering his license as primarily a public entertainer who enjoyed the meandering freedom' of the old-fashioned picaresque novel. But in *Dombey and Son* (1846-1848) he proved his ability to erect a complex social and narrative structure on a single serious theme, the sin of Pride; and in *Bleak House* (1852-1853) he contrived an infinitely elaborate network to show how a whole society can be involved in the moral and mental confusion symbolized in the fog-webbed Court of Chancery. *David Copperfield* (1849-1850), Dickens' effort to exorcise the deep-rooted memories of his childhood and young manhood, is off the main line. *Hard Times*, though on a smaller scale, reveals the serious social purpose and tight plotting of *Dom-*

bey, Bleak House, Little Dorrit (1855-1857), and *Great Expectations* (1860-1861).

2

To look first at the raw materials, Dickens' shortest novel is his only full-scale treatment of both the evil practices of Victorian industrialism and the economic and ethical theories by which they were rationalized. The ruthless exploitation represented by Josiah Bounderby of Coketown was evil enough in itself. But what especially annoyed Dickens was that such excesses were solemnly sanctified by the code of Gradgrindism, an offspring of the marriage of the laissez faire of the orthodox economists and the pleasure principle of the utilitarians.

As most schoolboys used to know, between the 1770's and the 1840's England was transformed from an essentially agricultural island into the most powerful industrial nation of the world. Between 1769 and 1785 appeared five machines that were to revolutionize cotton manufacture: Watt's steam engine, Arkwright's water frame, Hargreaves' spinning jenny, Crompton's mule, and Cartwright's power loom. Their usefulness was immensely increased by a number of improvements in transportation: the spreading network of canals, the improved roads of Telford and McAdam, and—most important of all—the railroads. Although the crude birth rate apparently did not increase appreciably until the end of the nineteenth century, the great migration of industry from country to town mushroomed the industrial centers of the midlands overnight.

With the spread of smoking factories and bigger businesses came the rise of the middle-class manufacturer and merchant to a position of political and social power and the inevitable separation of the Heads of industry from the Hands. Not long before 1832, the pivotal year of middle-class emancipation, Gradgrind Senior, unrepresented in Parliament, would have lived over his shop with his apprentices; Bounderby would probably not have known what a Powler was. By 1854 Dickens could picture Thomas Gradgrind, M.P., as retired in middle life from the hard facts of wholesale hardware, and, between sessions of sifting other facts in the great parliamentary dustbin, going home to apply them to his family at his country house on the outskirts of Coketown. At the same time Josiah Bounderby, Esquire, still bumptiously active as "banker, merchant, manufacturer, and what not," could patronize a lady housekeeper—or perhaps one should say a housekeeping lady—who had been married to a man who was a Powler on one side and a Scadgers on the other.

But, as usual, human welfare had not kept pace with material prosperity. Illth—to use a favorite word of Ruskin's—had spread more rapidly than wealth. Significant legislative reforms in the two decades after 1832, supported by genuinely practical men who were by no means as shortsighted as Gradgrind or as hardhearted as Bounderby, had brought some solace to the industrial worker by the time of the Great Exhibition of 1851 in the Crystal Palace. Repeal of the Corn Laws in 1846, the continued improvement in methods of manufacture and transportation, the opening of new frontiers in the Western Hemisphere and in Australia—all contributed toward a genuine gain in national prosperity. Undoubtedly the average industrial worker would have been slightly better off—economically speaking—in 1854 than at the depth of the "hungry forties": the era of Carlyle's *Past and Present* (1843), Mrs. Browning's "Cry of the Children" (1843), Tom Hood's "Song of the Shirt" (1843), Disraeli's *Sybil* ("two nations, the rich and the poor"—1845), Friedrich Engels' *Condition of the Working Class* (1845), and Mrs. Gaskell's *Mary Barton* (1848)— not to mention the darker passages of Dickens' first two Christmas stories: *A Christmas Carol* (1843) and *The Chimes* (1844). But Dickens was not to be taken in by averages. He knew that middle-class prosperity had not even begun to trickle down to Stephen Blackpool—who was not a statistical digit but a human being who would bleed if you pricked him—and that there were thousands essentially like him. He knew something of their inhuman habitations and their appalling working conditions. And he was not to be diverted—by consoling statistics or war in the Crimea or "the great Forge-bellows of puffery at work" exalting the Crystal Palace as a symbol of England's material prosperity— from doing something about it.

In 1838, after his first sight of Manchester, he had vowed some day to "strike the heaviest blow in [his] power" for the victims of exploitation in the cotton mills. During the first four years of

Household Words he had fought their battle again and again both as author and conductor. Now in *Hard Times* he was gathering his strength for what he might have called—in the current fistic phraseology of which he was so fond—a "settler."

3

In its general outlines Coketown could be any smoky mill town in the industrial midlands of England in the middle of the nineteenth century. This anonymity was clearly a part of Dickens' intention. On March 11, 1854, three weeks before the first installment in *Household Words,* he complained to a writer in the *Illustrated London News* who had asserted that the new novel was to be concerned with the current strike in Preston, where Dickens had gone in search of background at the end of January. Dickens insisted that some chapters were written before he made the trip or thought about the strike there. His story, he maintained, had "a direct purpose in reference to the working people all over England." Moreover, he had learned from sad experience that if he picked a specific locale from the map of England his readers would insist on fitting his characters to individuals whom the author had never seen or heard of in his life. Twelve years later, writing to his sister-in-law in regard to the impending production of Boucicault's play *A Long Strike,* he let the cat out of the bag:

Might it not ease the way with the Lord Chamberlain's office, and still more with the audience, when there are Manchester champions in it, if instead of "Manchester" you use a fictitious name? When I did Hard Times I called the scene Coketown. Everybody knew what was meant, but every cotton-spinning town said it was the other cotton-spinning town.

If everybody in 1854 knew that Coketown was Manchester, it was not because Dickens is concerned with the local particulars of life in any mill or tenement. It was because the economic philosophy of Gradgrind is clearly a parody of some of the doctrines of the Manchester School. This label was, and still is, loosely applied to a group of ideas intimately associated with a body of influential Manchester citizens in the middle of the nineteenth century.

Although Dickens is not directly dealing with their doctrine of Free Trade or their victory over the Corn Laws, under the leadership of Cobden and Bright, he is very much concerned with the broad foundation of their philosophy: the gospel of laissez faire. If they were not a hundred per cent against any government regulation of enterprise (Cobden, for example, is clearly on the record for restricting the hours of child labor), they were generally opposed to all interference with the freedom of employers to worship the gods of Supply and Demand in their own way. Thus throughout the 1830's and 1840's the Manchester School had become associated in the public mind with stubborn opposition to all the proposals by which enlightened legislators were attempting to make factory labor endurable for human beings.

At the beginning of Book Two Dickens touches directly on laissez faire with characteristic hyperbole:

Whenever a Coketowner felt he was ill-used—that is to say, whenever he was not left entirely alone, and it was proposed to hold him accountable for the consequences of any of his acts—he was sure to come out with the awful menace, that he would "sooner pitch his property into the Atlantic."

And Stephen Blackpool, in his respectful defiance of Bounderby, simply states Dickens' objection to the doctrine:

Nor yet lettin' alone will never do 't. Let thousands upon thousands alone, aw leading the like lives and aw faw'en into the like muddle, and they will be as one, and yo will be as anoother, wi' a black unpassable world betwixt yo, just as long or short a time as sitch-like misery can last.

Although the phrase "laissez faire" was not widely publicized in England until 1848, when it was used as a chapter heading in John Stuart Mill's *Principles of Political Economy*, the general doctrine was not, of course, the private property of the Manchester School; it had been a fundamental maxim of economic theory since the seventeenth century. When Dickens named the younger brothers of Tom and Louisa *Adam Smith* and *Malthus* Gradgrind, he showed at least a superficial knowledge of economic history. For it was Adam Smith who wrote the classic statement of the rationale of laissez faire (*The Wealth of Nations,* 1776); and it was Thomas

Malthus who, by arguing that poverty and starvation were unavoidable evils to prevent overpopulation, gave the orthodox economists and their eminently practical parrots a pseudoscientific basis for refusing to improve the lot of the working man (*Essay on Population*, 1798). If Dickens had wished to add another manchild to the unhappy Gradgrind clan, he might have named him after David Ricardo, propounder of the iron law of wages (*Principles of Economics and Taxation*, 1817). An even more appropriate choice would have been Ricardo's friend Jeremy Bentham.

Bentham did not originate utilitarianism, the doctrine with which his name is inevitably linked, but he expounded it at length in two major works: *Principles of Morals and Legislation* (1789) and *Deontology* (1834). His gospel was popularized in Victorian England by the *Westminster Review* (which he founded in 1823), by his friend James Mill (1773-1836), and—in significantly altered form—by the latter's famous son, John Stuart Mill (1806-1873). Although neither Bentham nor the Mills are mentioned in *Hard Times*, the spirit of utilitarianism haunts Coketown (as it haunted Manchester) and is especially at home at Stone Lodge.

Whatever its distortion by Gradgrind, Benthamite Utilitarianism (or Benthamism) began life as an ethical theory growing out of its author's sincere effort to discover a practical way of discriminating between good and bad laws. Bentham argued that the only object that any man pursues is his own pleasure, that if he takes into consideration the happiness of others, it is to keep his own happiness from being interfered with by the sanctions of society. Thus in pursuing his own pleasure, he adds to the general happiness, and in pursuing the general happiness, he promotes his own pleasure. A motive is good if it brings happiness to the person involved; an action is right if it achieves the greatest good (or happiness) of the greatest number of people. The greatest happiness formula has been traced back to the seventeenth century, but Bentham, a mountain of energy with a passion for figures, buried the simple formula under a complex "hedonistic calculus" for "scientifically" determining the consequences of an act in terms of pleasure. To keep from introducing too many variables into the picture, he stubbornly refused to allow any differences in the *quality* of pleasures. This leads logically to his notorious equation: quantities of pleasure being equal, pushpin [a trivial child's game] is as good as poetry.

The industrialists of the Manchester School and their apologists were not all thoroughly indoctrinated with Bentham's philosophy. But just as a later generation of industrialists distorted Darwin in defense of their fitness to survive in the economic struggle according to their own ruthless methods, the Manchester men made a natural selection of what suited them in utilitarianism. Obviously, they argued, if the collective good of society depends in the long run on each individual's pursuing his own pleasure as he sees fit, any interference with the right of the individual to pursue his own economic interest, any break in the iron curtain of laissez faire or tampering with the laws of Supply and Demand is treason to the hard facts of living—or at least making a living.

As it turns up in the code of Gradgrindism, the utilitarian pleasure principle is nothing more than a license permitting—or even encouraging—unrestricted selfishness. Tom and Bitzer, the two star pupils of Mr. M'Choakumchild, are well grounded in self-interest from early youth. The Whelp's ambition is to become "that not unprecedented triumph of calculation which is usually at work on number one"; and at the end of the book when Gradgrind Senior implies that there may be other motives in life than the individual's own pleasure, Bitzer cuts him off:

"I beg your pardon for interrupting you, sir . . . but I am sure you know that the whole social system is a question of self-interest. What you must always appeal to, is a person's self-interest. It's your only hold. We are so constituted. I was brought up in that catechism when I was very young, sir, as you are aware."

And, of course, it is Sissy Jupe's selflessness which makes her a failure in the Gradgrind course in economics:

. . . after eight weeks of induction into the elements of Political Economy, she had only yesterday been set right by a prattler three feet high, for returning to the question, "What is the first principle of this science?" the absurd answer, "To do unto others as I would that they should do unto me."

4

Of course Girl number twenty was doomed to fail from the very first days at school, when she confessed her inability to define a horse and blushingly admitted that she might carpet a room with representations of flowers. Later, when she put her trembling finger squarely on the statistical fallacy in Mr. M'Choakumchild's "stutterings" on national—or natural—prosperity, she was obviously past hope. For Dickens saw in the utilitarianism of the Manchester School not only a brazen egoism but also a total immersion in facts and figures and an aesthetic blindness that squeezed all the poetry from life.

Here again, though he may have been exaggerating, he was not inventing. The typical reforms of the two decades following the Reform Bill of 1832 were not the result of hit-or-miss humanitarianism; they followed widespread investigations by Parliamentary Committees and Royal Commissions which enshrined their findings in mountains of "blue books" cluttered with statistical tables. Local inquiries supplemented those on a national basis. After the establishment of the first English Statistical Society, in Manchester in 1834, similar organizations broke out all over England. The year 1836 saw the beginning of the practice of selling parliamentary blue books to the public. Compiling, publishing, and reading statistics about the condition of England assumed the proportions of a national fad. In a few years' time the treatment of national affairs had been transformed—to use G. M. Young's phrase— "from a polemical to a statistical basis, from Humbug to Humdrum."

Although Dickens has been accused of a good deal of "cockney ignorance" about political economy, nobody could fairly accuse him of maintaining that all statistics are useless stutterings. As conductor of *Household Words* he insisted that his contributors support their arguments with facts; and the numbers of that magazine, though replete with fancy and whimsy, are so regularly filled with numerical data that the index contains a special section under the heading *Statistics*. But the statistics are not always treated with a solemn Gradgrindian reverence: take this, for example, from "A Few Facts about Matrimony" based on the report of the Registrar-General for 1850:

The average annual number of weddings is about one hundred and twenty-three thousand. It would help a winter's night's amusement to decide how many pounds weight of California produce must be wasted for the rings? How many garlands of orange blossoms for the hair and bonnets of the brides?

When statistical averages were used to conceal human misery or evade the solution to human problems, Dickens' amusement turned to anger. He had given his readers a sketchy preview of his attitude in the character of Filer, whom he refused to excise from *The Chimes* to please Forster. Filer could prove anything by tables, including the fact that poor Trotty Veck was violating the laws of political economy by enjoying his favorite dish, tripe, even at Christmas time:

"But who eats tripe? . . . Tripe is without an exception the least economical and the most wasteful article of consumption that the markets of this country can by possibility produce. The loss upon a pound of tripe has been found to be, in the boiling, seven-eighths of a fifth more than the loss upon a pound of any other animal substance whatever. Tripe is more expensive, properly understood, than the hothouse pine-apple. Taking into account the number of animals slaughtered yearly within the bills of mortality alone, and forming a low estimate of the quantity of tripe which the carcasses of those animals, reasonably well butchered, would yield, I find that the waste on that amount of tripe, if boiled, would victual a garrison of five hundred men for five months of thirty-one days each, and a February over. The Waste, the Waste!"

Perhaps in the interval between *The Chimes* and *Hard Times* Dickens had made a special note of the fact that the first International Statistical Congress—proposed at London during the Exhibition of 1851—had been held in Brussels in 1853 under the guiding spirit of the pioneer Belgian statistician, Adolphe Quételet. It was that distinguished census taker who argued that statistics on the average man (*l'homme moyen*)—including the annual number and age distribution of marriages—were governed by the strictest scientific laws. Perhaps Dickens was annoyed by a new rationalization of poverty in terms of Malthusian arithmetic or a fresh batch of blue books on his desk. At any rate, by the beginning of 1854 he was ready to give the digit-worshippers the full satiric treatment.

In a letter to Charles Knight (January 30, 1854) Dickens gives an advance sample of the acid with which he was to etch the picture of Gradgrind trying to unlock the problems of the human heart with a statistical key:

My satire is against those who see figures and averages, and nothing else—the representatives of the wickedest and most enormous vice of this time—the men who, through long years to come, will do more to damage the real useful truths of political economy than I could do (if I tried) in my whole life; the addled heads who would take the average of cold in the Crimea during twelve months as a reason for clothing a soldier in nankeens on a night when he would be frozen to death in fur, and who would comfort the labourer in travelling twelve miles a day to and from his work, by telling him that the average distance of one inhabited place from another in the whole area of England, is not more than four miles. Bah!

Like his addiction to facts and figures Gradgrind's aesthetic limitations also have a utilitarian flavor. Obviously if a learned man reduced poetry to the same level as pushpin, it was easy for his practical followers to try to eliminate it completely from their lives on grounds of uselessness:

"We were peeping at the circus," muttered Louisa, haughtily, without lifting up her eyes, "and father caught us."

"And, Mrs. Gradgrind," said her husband in a lofty manner, "I should as soon have expected to find my children reading poetry."

Literature and the other arts could hardly be expected to thrive in a cult whose gods had consciously set out to discount not only fancy and imagination but all the traditional virtues of the human heart: love, honor, reverence, kindness, conscience, unselfish generosity.

Though not all as blind as Gradgrind, utilitarian critics shared a common tendency toward aesthetic astigmatism. As Buckley points out, the editors of the *Westminster Review* "found on the whole very little 'utility' in the literature of their time. One reviewer went so far as to warn his readers against all purposeless composition:

'Ledgers,' he remarked with perfect reason, 'do not keep well in rhyme, nor are three deckers built by songs, as towns were of yore. . . . Literature is a seducer; we had almost said a harlot. She may do to trifle with; but woe be to the state whose statesmen write verses, and whose lawyers read more in Tom Moore than in Bracton.' "

Akin to this general attitude—which was not, of course, the private monopoly of the Manchester School—was a widespread aesthetic literalness among the middle-class critics of the period. Successful ornaments were to be literally faithful to nature; illusions were not to be taken as anything but illusions; verisimilitude was the rule. Buckley reminds us that Redgrave condemned a table in the Crystal Palace supported by swans "not so much because the piece was graceless and cumbersome, as because he himself was perplexed to know 'why swans should make their nests under a table at the risk of having their necks broken by everyone seated at it.' " One can hear Gradgrind reducing it to his own irrefutable logic: "Girl number twenty, your definition of a swan. . . . Would you design a table supported by swans? . . . Would you have swans making their nests under your dining room table?" Buckley also cites an eminently sensible critic of a somewhat later vintage as laying down the simple principle that "nothing within doors should suggest that one is out of doors." Nothing such as flowers on the carpet or graminivorous quadrupeds on the wallpaper.

Gradgrind also had the middle-class faith in education which is one of the hallmarks of Victorian England. But it had to be education in accordance with a system that conforms closely to the utilitarian ideal. The system was Gradgrind's, but Josiah, though he himself had done all right as a graduate of the school of hard knocks, was willing to concede that his own education would not fit everybody and followed along at a distance.

There was apparently no limit to the number of subjects in the Gradgrind curriculum providing they could be reduced to facts and figures. At least M'Choakumchild was a master of facts-in-general. "Orthography, etymology, syntax, and prosody, biography, astronomy, geography, and general cosmography, the sciences of compound proportion, algebra, land-surveying and levelling, vocal music, and drawing from models, were all at the ends of his ten chilled fingers." The list, which does not end here, is obviously indiscriminate; it contains a few subjects (biography? vocal music? drawing? prosody?) which might prove traitors to the Gradgrind camp. The reader is led to infer elsewhere that, next to his special interest in putting down fancy and spreading the gospel of Manchester political economy, Gradgrind is mainly interested in natural science, the study of which he would limit largely to collecting specimens and memorizing nomenclature. In *Hard Times* at least Dickens reflects a widespread suspicion of the growing emphasis in Victorian England on science and scientific education; he too is guilty of the prejudice that turns up in various forms in the works of Carlyle, Newman, Ruskin, and Arnold. The world of fancy and imagination, the world of wonder —these realms, Dickens appears to say, are a monopoly of the arts: one can "never wonder" about science.

Whatever the inconsistencies about the curriculum, Dickens is stubbornly consistent about other aspects of the schooling which he associated with the Manchester utilitarians. He objected to the rigid conformity of a system which, paradoxically, was intended to serve a philosophy of rugged individualism: M'Choakumchild "and some one hundred and forty other schoolmasters, had been lately turned at the same time, in the same factory, on the same principles, like so many pianoforte legs." He objected to the appalling quantity of miscellaneous information that was poured into the little pitchers. He was annoyed by an inquisitorial classroom method which—paradoxically again under a system that pretended to exalt reason—made no allowance for unorthodox answers arrived at by reason rather than by rote: a letter to W. H. Wills (January 26, 1854) reveals that Dickens' satire of classroom procedure was intentionally patterned after the Educational Board's questions for the examination of teachers. Finally, Dickens despised any educational plan that left no room for fun. Here was the closest link between the philosophy of the Gradgrind schoolroom —or the antiseptic "barber shop" at Stone Lodge—and the plight of Stephen Blackpool. The middle-class child who was forbidden the useless wonders of Jack the Giant Killer or the Circus was the victim of the same monstrous philosophy that denied the industrial worker the right to enjoy himself when he was not bound to his loom. The utilitarian philosopher and the evangelical champion of Sabbatarian blue laws may have started from different premises, but they were agreed to squeeze the joy out of life. Every busy little bee was to improve each shining hour—in school and out—and grow up to be a paragon of busyness, like Bounderby, to whom all relaxation was evil idleness. Though he was one of the busiest writers that ever lived, Dickens was no fanatical worshiper of the Victorian gospel of work. No amount of earnest Victorian education or industry could atone for the murder of innocent fun. "The English are, so far as I know, the hardest-worked people on whom the sun shines. Be content if, in their wretched intervals of pleasure, they read for amusement and do no worse. They are born at the oar, and they live and die at it. Good God, what would we have of them!" The passage is from another letter to Knight (March 17, 1854), but Dickens makes the point in his novel in much the same words (see page 58). In part *Hard Times* is an apology for idlers; there are moments when the reader might suspect that Dickens would be willing to dispense with poetry if the world could have its fill of pushpin.

Although John Stuart Mill's autobiography was not published until 1873, it is not inconceivable that Gradgrind's pedagogical method was based on hearsay evidence about James Mill's notorious system for developing his son from an infant prodigy into the perfect utilitarian philosopher. The Mill curriculum was, of course, more impressive in its quality. And James Mill's rigid dialectic was certainly calculated to make his son an independent thinker, not a passive pitcher filling up with unrelated facts. But the isolation from other children, the proscription of fun, above all the insistent emphasis on the rational workings of the mind—all these were calculated to dry up the wellsprings of human feeling and produce in John Stuart Mill in his early twenties a crisis not unlike Louisa's. The younger Mill—never doomed to be a Bitzer or a Whelp—required strong drafts of Wordsworth and Carlyle to effect a partial cure. Louisa found salvation—or at least the inspiration to become a sort of all-England aunt—in the loving kindness of Sissy Jupe. Obviously the parallel must not be pushed too far.

5

The career of the younger Mill reveals what any reader of *Hard*

Times might suspect: that Dickens' satire of Manchester theory and practice was an oversimplification. Far from practicing pure self-interest, the utilitarians had a social conscience that helped to promote many of the significant reforms of the early Victorian period, with most of which Dickens was in hearty agreement. It was one of the paradoxes of what Dodds has called "The Age of Paradox" (the 1840's) that the ranks of economic orthodoxy contained "men who, while in the act of proclaiming that happiness for all, or at least for the greatest number, could best be achieved by laissez faire, spent their days and nights trying to put legislative hedges around the garden of unrestricted competition." Long before 1854 Mill had seen the need for modifying laissez faire and was hard at work undermining the hedonistic calculus to admit differences in the *quality* of pleasure.

Dickens knew that there were middle-class businessmen in Victorian England who were not like Gradgrind or Bounderby: he had portrayed a number of them sympathetically—for example, the sugary Cheeryble brothers in *Nicholas Nickleby* or Rouncewell in *Bleak House*. He would certainly have been the first to admit that his whole attitude toward organized labor was not summed up in the bemuddled Stephen Blackpool or in that travesty of a labor organizer, the spellbinding Slackbridge: he is on record elsewhere in defense of labor's right both to organize and, if necessary, to strike. In fact it is probable that he left the strike out of *Hard Times* partly because he didn't know enough to depict one and partly because, like Stephen, he had given a solemn promise to a woman, Mrs. Gaskell, that he wouldn't strike.

Some critics have asserted that *Hard Times* not only oversimplifies the Victorian picture and Dickens' view of it but offers no "message" except—as George Orwell puts it: "If men would behave decently the world would be decent." Obviously Dickens furnishes no easy practical solution to the problems he deplores, not even anything as tangible as Carlyle's Hero Worship or Matthew Arnold's Culture. He does not argue, like Carlyle, that medieval serfdom was preferable to Victorian industrial bondage: he was constantly annoyed by chatter about "the good old times." He is certainly—in *Hard Times* and elsewhere—as impatient with institutional cures as he is with laissez faire. But even if it is

assumed that all the positive suggestions in the book can be reduced to Orwell's common denominator—the pleas for better
relations between employer and employee, for more humane
divorce laws, for more Christian love and charity, for more poetry,
fancy, fantasy, imagination, nonsense, or fun—is the Golden Rule
too trite to be the central theme of a great novelist? And isn't
there a positive value in a powerful warning?

Although Dickens is not often ranked as one of the Victorian
"prophets," *Hard Times* still has an embarrassing amount to say
to our more enlightened generation. Laissez faire and brutal industrial exploitation may not be major issues in America today.
The patriarchal father and the self-made humbug may belong to a
dying race. Cooperation between employer and employee, collective bargaining, paternalistic schemes for the workers' welfare,
recognition of labor's right to organize and strike—all these, if not
everywhere attained, are such common features of modern industry that to call *Hard Times* "sullen Socialism"—as Macaulay
once did—now seems not only inaccurate but grossly reactionary.
It might be argued that in our society both employer and worker
have more leisure than they know how to spend and more entertainment than they can possibly enjoy. But as long as people
worship statistics, or put a higher value on "getting the facts"
than on reasoning intelligently from them, or give such words as
practical, utilitarian, and *functional* an honored place in the
gallery of clichés, or encourage educational curricula that exalt
technology or business administration above the subtle essences of
the humanities, or deprecate poetry as useless nonsense, or con-
demn nursery rhymes or fairy stories as unfit for child minds, or
chorus, "I don't know anything about Art, but I know exactly
what a horse looks like"—as long as these things are, *Hard Times*
will have a living message.

6

In the last analysis, of course, *Hard Times* is not a parliamentary
blue book, a blueprint for action, or merely a tract; it is a serious
novel—one of the most serious that Dickens ever wrote—and must
be judged in terms of its success as a work of art.

Dickens was acutely aware of the special limitations of an unusually short novel—at least for Victorian fiction—served up over a period of less than five months in a series of weekly installments. He wrote to Forster in February, 1854:

The difficulty of the space is CRUSHING. Nobody can have an idea of it who has not had any experience of patient fiction-writing with some elbow-room always, and open places in perspective. In this form, with any kind of regard to the current number, there is absolutely no such thing.

On April 18, halfway through the book, he wrote to Wills:

I am in a dreary state, planning and planning the story of Hard Times (out of materials for I don't know how long a story), and consequently writing little.

In November, three months after the book appeared, he wrote again of the "perpetual trouble" given him by "the compression and condensation necessary for that disjointed form of publication."

Such external evidence should be enough to disillusion the many readers who still assume that Dickens was a great untutored genius, uninterested in the art of the novel, who, almost unconsciously, poured out his prolific installments with one hand on his public's pulse, or purse, and the other clutching an even-flow, ever-flow pen. The internal evidence reveals how carefully he considered both the moral and the social structures of *Hard Times*.

The events are fitted neatly into a three-part extension of the Biblical moral: "Whatsoever a man soweth, that shall he also reap." In the first book (Sowing) Dickens prepares the seedbeds: Gradgrindism is carefully planted in the school and at Stone Lodge, and the seeds are blown abroad in Bounderby's bank and factory and around the blackened streets of Coketown. By the end of Book One they have taken root—with varying degrees of firmness—in Bitzer, Tom, and Louisa, but have found no friendly soil in Sissy or her friends of the Horse-riding. Book Two (Reaping) and Book Three (Garnering) portray the evil harvest: the growth of the class "grind" into a malignant labor spy; the hardening of the Whelp into a sycophantic crook; the failure of

Louisa's marriage and her perilous approach to adultery; and Stephen's flight and death—his only way out of the muddle perpetuated, if not created, by the system.

Parallel with the degeneration of the students of Gradgrindism is the fall of the master and his crude, half-tutored colleague Bounderby. At the end of Book One, with Louisa's marriage to Josiah, both the father and the husband are at the summit of triumph. By the end of the novel, Gradgrind—baffled by the breakdown of Louisa and the revelation of Tom's true character—has finally admitted the failure of the system; the unregenerate Bounderby, ignominiously shown up by two old ladies, is a failure and a phony in everybody's eyes but his own. Each book reaches a dramatic climax in the progress of Gradgrind's disillusionment: Book One, with Louisa's futile outburst against the system in her father's study on the eve of her marriage; Book Two, with her return through the storm to face him with the dramatic evidence of the failure of the marriage; and the third book with the spectacle of the fugitive Whelp in blackface confronting his father with the clinching evidence from the shabby center ring of Sleary's Horse-riding.

Finally, there is, of course, a direct ratio between the extent of each character's infection with Gradgrindism and his exposure to the antidotes of fancy and kindness represented by Sissy, the pupil of M'Choakumchild voted least likely to succeed. Jane, who grows up after her father has entered Parliament and her mother has been reduced by facts to a mumbling vegetable, is clearly the prize exhibit of the value of Sissy's magic treatment. Louisa, who has befriended Sissy and weakly resisted Gradgrindism until her marriage, is cured first among those seriously infected. Gradgrind Senior, who has seen in a glimpse early in the book that "there is something in that girl [Sissy] which could hardly be set forth in tabular form," but who does not really begin to see Sissy's virtues until after Louisa's return in the storm, is finally contrite before the curtain comes down. The Whelp, never closely associated with Sissy, is not redeemed until the epilogue, when Death cuts short his penitence. Bitzer, who has chased "Girl number twenty" after school for not knowing the facts about quadrupeds, and Bounderby, who has blustered from the start against the admission of a stroller's child to school, are unredeemed. And, of course, it is Sissy's influence that gives Harthouse—a willing ally if not a direct victim of Gradgrindism—his only moment of comparative decency in the novel.

A reader who needs any further proof of Dickens' artful planning might consider the relative intricacy of the social structure in the book. The industrial proletariat is represented at its most degraded by Stephen's drunken wife and at its decent best by Stephen and Rachael; the Victorian middle class is typified in its shortsighted but well-meaning materialism by Gradgrind and his family, in its boorishness and selfishness by Bounderby, in its hard-earned self-respect by Mrs. Pegler; the aristocracy in its shabby-genteel snobbery by Mrs. Sparsit and in its enervated dilettantism by Harthouse. Considered as a separate subgroup, Harthouse, Sparsit, and Bounderby represent three distinct varieties of social pretense, a fascinating school for snobbery. Sleary and the happy denizens of the Horse-riding defy convenient classification. Economically they belong to the Victorian proletariat, but they represent also the special aristocracy of the arts, if not the more snobbish levels of that aristocracy. They have about them a natural affinity for democracy, a deep-grained aversion to snobbery; there is something in Sleary and Childers and Kidderminster that doesn't love a wall. And both directly and through their ambassadress they speak a language of the imagination and the heart that knows no class barriers.

Dickens is careful to show how Gradgrindism, like the toils of Chancery in *Bleak House* and the Circumlocution Office in *Little Dorrit,* indiscriminately involves all classes of society. If Gradgrind supplies the motive power for the whirling wheel, Bounderby is sitting squarely in the center, and others are drawn in toward him by centripetal force: Stephen and Rachael through Blackpool's earnest efforts to solve the dilemmas of his marriage and his job; Louisa through a reluctant marriage; Tom and Bitzer through their nefarious endeavors to put the lessons of Gradgrindism into practice; Mrs. Pegler by her natural desire to see her successful son; Mrs. Sparsit by force of economic circumstance; Harthouse out of boredom and a vague desire to dabble in the hard facts puddle; and Sissy because her father wants her to have a respectable education. That the paths of these characters should cross and recross is credible enough. Only occasionally—as in the big dramatic scene where almost everyone suddenly appears from the wings to be on the stage for the unveiling of Mrs. Pegler and the unmasking of her son, or in the fortuitous discovery of the Old Hell Shaft by Sissy and Rachael on a quiet Sunday walk—might the reader feel that the long arm of coincidence is being strained unduly. It is never, as elsewhere in Dickens and often in Hardy, torn completely out of the socket.

In fitting the pieces of *Hard Times* into the tight format of twenty weekly issues of *Household Words,* Dickens managed to achieve a symmetrical structure without sacrificing probability. In view of all the evidence, it is hard to see how Lord David Cecil, like other critics, could argue seriously that Dickens had "no sense of form."

If he was less successful in his efforts to find a consistently credible narrative style, it was partly because in *Hard Times* Dickens the journalist and Dickens the artist were not always at peace with each other. It is not that art and propaganda don't mix but that he wasn't always careful about mixing them. A propagandist from the start, he had contrived in his earlier novels to gild the philosophic pill in such a way that many readers could choose to ignore it if they didn't like the taste. There is no ignoring Gradgrindism. In *Hard Times* the frustrated crusader of *Household Words* is always smoldering volcanically beneath the surface and occasionally bursting out of the crater. When Dickens blends his attack on Gradgrindism with his dramatic base, as in the opening chapters in the schoolroom or the closing scenes where the wheel comes full circle in the Circus, he gives a beautiful demonstration of how smoothly his comic art can serve a didactic purpose. When he puts his own lessons directly into the mouths of his characters, there is a clear distinction between, for example, the anguished outpourings of Louisa (Book I, Chapter Eleven and Book II, Chapter Twelve), the muddled but perceptive plaints of Stephen (Book II, Chapter Five), and the wheezy folk philosophy of Mr. Sleary (Book III, Chapter Eight). His panoramic pictures of Coketown—at the beginning of Book I, Chapter Five or Book II, Chapter One—illustrate his special talent for combining setting and satire: he simultaneously creates both atmosphere and attitude, view and point of view. But when

Dickens rings down the curtain on a simple love scene between two millworkers by striding on stage and haranguing his audience with a threatening sermon that he has already preached in more subtle ways through half the book, he has ripped off the artist's mask and we see only the bare face of the soapbox orator:

> It was but a hurried parting in the common street, yet it was a sacred remembrance to these two common people. Utilitarian economists, skeletons of schoolmasters, Commissioners of Fact, genteel and used-up infidels, gabblers of many little dog's-eared creeds, the poor you will have always with you. Cultivate in them, while there is yet time, the utmost graces of the fancies and affections, to adorn their lives, so much in need of ornament; or, in the day of your triumph, when romance is utterly driven out of their souls, and they and a bare existence stand face to face, Reality will take a wolfish turn, and make an end of you.

As a journalist, Dickens was not only a crusader but a reporter. He had a reporter's conscience about documenting his narrative with authentic facts; he wanted desperately to *realize* his characters for readers who were accustomed to losing them in a statistical morass. Moreover, as Ford has convincingly shown, the mid-Victorian public demanded verisimilitude. But at the same time he had an old ham's love for theatrical effects, a caricaturist's talent for neglecting the shadings, and a poet's natural tendency to view reality in symbolic, not literal terms. The mixture is evident in the notorious case of Krook in *Bleak House*. Dickens' journalistic conscience and his duty to his literal-minded readers would not let him rest the case for Krook's fatal explosion on the symbolic grounds clearly prepared in the book; instead he had to append a gratuitous note in the preface insisting that actual deaths by spontaneous combustion are on the record.

In the same way Dickens tried to achieve a measure of literal realism in *Hard Times*. He traveled to Preston to see what a strike was like; he wrote to Mark Lemon for a list of "slang terms among the tumblers and circus-people"; he tried patiently to reconstruct Stephen's Lancashire dialect down to the last apostrophe; he attempted a phonetic mimicry of Sleary's asthmatic wheezing. But these are only minimum concessions to verisimilitude. The noisy labor meetings in the book bear no resemblance to the quiet scene that Dickens found during the strike in Preston; they are demonstrations crudely staged by Dickens to motivate Stephen's flight. Stephen's dialect would probably not appeal to Professor Henry Higgins, and Dickens supplies no explanation of why Rachael, playing her saintly role against the same backdrop, should speak with a more evident veneer of cultivation. And there is an inevitable correlation between an asthmatic wheeze and a conthithtent lithp only in a world in which the Emperor of Japan juggles five washbasins for recreation. The point is that in *Hard Times* Dickens made no pretense of documenting his tale throughout with photographic, tape-recorder realism.

Such documentation would have been out of place in a novel devoted to drawing odious comparisons between Fact and Fancy. Dickens is intent on showing that—even in darkest Coketown, where all the surfaces shout Fact, Fact, Fact—life can be viewed with the fanciful eye of childhood. M'Choakumchild is a "dry Ogre" or a Morgiana pouring hot oil onto the forty thieves; Gradgrind in his observatory conjures up a memory of Bluebeard; Bounderby is an explosive monster who blows up like a soap bubble; Stephen's wife is an "evil spirit"; even the factories can be Fairy Palaces at night; and Sissy is the "good fairy" who carries the magic bottle and is out to see that—with the help of some gratuitous crystal gazing—it will all end more or less happily ever after. Dickens' songs of innocence were psychologically motivated by his subconscious desire to sugarcoat the bitter memories of his own childhood: a genuine self-made man, he tried always to suppress the dark recollection of his labor in the blacking warehouse; Bounderby, the self-made humbug who boasted openly of having once sold empty blacking bottles, was an intruder in his Paradise. At times the dreamworld of childhood is an incongruous mixture of fairyland, Eden, and Heaven in which one might find Wordsworth, Blake, Rousseau, and Andrew Lang walking happily hand-in-hand with the neighborhood Sunday school teacher:

The dreams of childhood—its airy fables; its graceful, beautiful, humane, impossible adornments of the world beyond: so good to be believed in once, so good to be remembered when outgrown, for then the least among them rises to the stature of a great Charity in the heart, suffering little children to come into the midst of it, and to keep with their pure hands a garden in the stony ways of this world, wherein it were better for all the children of Adam that they should oftener sun themselves, simple and trustful, and not worldly-wise. . . .

But such confused and cloying peterpantheism serves to remind the reader that *Hard Times* cannot be measured by the straight rule of realism. If the reader finds a field near Coketown peopled with childlike circus people so out of this world that they have "a special inaptitude for any kind of sharp practice," he should be no more surprised than at finding Oberon and Titania in a wood near Athens. And Bounderby and Bottom both appear monstrously absurd in such enchanted realms. It is a tribute to Dickens' genius that the world of *Hard Times* is so real without being realistic.

Dickens' approach to reality had always been partly allegorical, but in *Hard Times* the symbolism is sustained with remarkable consistency. The jungle of Coketown is typified throughout by two forbidding animal symbols: the smoke entwines like monstrous serpents and the pistons of the steam engines trumpet like melancholy elephants. The color imagery is calculated: the buildings of Coketown are brick- or blood-red and coated with deathly black; the undertaker's ladder—"the one poor ghastly pomp of the neighborhood"—is black; Stephen is a Blackpool; the circus people have the pink and white freshness of childhood, whereas the young victims of Gradgrindism, notably Bitzer, have the contrasting pallor of premature age; Gradgrind works in an observatory blue with blue books perfecting a philosophy that seals his children in what Tom calls a "jaundiced jail." Not only do Gradgrind and Bounderby have symbolic names—like others in the book and throughout Dickens—but they live in a world of hardness. In *Hard Times* a hardware merchant retires to Stone Lodge to study hard facts, while a graduate of the school of hard knocks, with a metallic laugh and a brassy speaking trumpet of a voice, lives in a house and works in a bank, both of which have a brazen door latch and a brazen door handle. The elements of nature are carefully keyed into Dickens' symbolic scheme. Bounderby, always flying storm warnings, runs the gamut in a single chapter (Book II, Chapter Five), all the way from a light breeze to a hurricane. The fire at which Louisa stares also smolders within her, eventually flaming out in her interview with her father on the wedding eve.

The rainstorm which gathers with Mrs. Sparsit's gloom as she spies in the bushes breaks out in its full fury when Louisa bursts into Stone Lodge to confront Gradgrind with the failure of her marriage. Stephen in his flight leaves the smoke of Coketown in the fresh dawn; and the star at which he gazes from the depths of the Old Hell Shaft—a single symbol for all the horrors of the mining industry—not only clears the muddle of his mind and the bitterness in his heart but leads him—on a Sunday evening in autumn—to "the God of the poor."

Dickens does not limit his affection for the symbolic metaphor to the narrator. He supplies Mrs. Sparsit with a talent for not only creating the image of the long staircase but sustaining it in her imagination through three suspenseful chapters. Aware that this is a rather unexpected achievement for a member of the anti-fancy league, he apologizes to the reader:

> Now, Mrs. Sparsit was not a poetical woman; but she took an idea in the nature of an allegorical fancy, into her head. Much watching of Louisa, and much consequent observation of her impenetrable demeanour, which keenly whetted and sharpened Mrs. Sparsit's edge, must have given her as it were a lift, in the way of inspiration.

He makes no apology when, dropping all pretense of echoing a human voice, he fills Louisa's mouth with a torrent of confused metaphors:

> "How could you give me life, and take from me all the inappreciable things that raise it from the state of conscious death? Where are the graces of my soul? Where are the sentiments of my heart? What have you done, O father, what have you done with the garden that should have bloomed once, in this great wilderness here?"
>
> She struck herself with both her hands upon her bosom.
>
> "If it had ever been here, its ashes alone would save me from the void in which my whole life sinks . . . Would you have doomed me, at any time, to the frost and blight that have hardened and spoiled me? Would you have robbed me—for no one's enrichment—only for the greater desolation of this world—of the immaterial part of my life, the spring and summer of my belief, my refuge from what is sordid and bad in the real things around me, my school in which I should have learned to be more humble and more trusting with them, and to hope in my little sphere to make them better?"

Louisa's education, though it denied her the pleasures of good poetry, should have had the advantage of protecting her from bad. The reader might be forgiven for asking where, in an education devoted to facts, even pseudo facts, she developed a taste for such fustian.

Whatever its faults, the symbolic method of *Hard Times* had distinct advantages for Dickens. He did not know Manchester as he knew London, and there were definite limits to his understanding of Victorian industry. He could not have documented Coketown with journalistic detail as Arnold Bennett was later to realize the Five Towns. He needed a method that would permit him to give the essential color of his material without his concerning himself with every stitch. Writing with less than a third of his usual elbow room, he found that he could rely heavily on the symbolic shorthand that he had used throughout the Christmas stories but less consistently in the novels.

If he had tried to pour the raw material into a longer series of larger molds, he might have done more to motivate the estrangement between Louisa and Sissy or the refusal of Stephen to join the union. He might have given Gradgrind a bigger role in Book Two —perhaps developing in some detail the influence of the hard facts philosophy in the national dustbin of London or the political tie-up there between the middle-class Mammonism of a Gradgrind and the upper-class dilettantism of a Harthouse. He might have done more to show, not merely suggest, the growth of Sissy's influence at Stone Lodge during the absence of the patriarchal father, perhaps letting the reader in on the secret of what happened to Adam Smith and Malthus Gradgrind. He might, if he had done more leg work in Manchester, have given an idea of Bounderby's workaday job to indicate that no man becomes the titan of an industrial and financial empire by merely blowing off steam. At considerably more pains than he took he might even have drawn a picture of the infant Victorian labor movement that is something more than a comic cartoon. All these additions could have been clear gain.

On the other hand, he would probably have provided a more intricate plot acted on a more lavish series of sets and peopled with a more generous array of characters, some of them merely eccentric extras, lovable or hatable but expendable. He would probably have yielded far more often to his love for wearying repetition and divagation. He would almost certainly have devised more big scenes of sentimental melodrama to set beside the tear-jerking wake of Stephen and Rachael at the bedside of the drunken derelict. In short, he would have baked the jumbo plum pudding novel that most of his readers expected of him.

But such a book would not have had the taut structure, the dramatic pace, the symbolic economy, and the single-minded dedication to a serious purpose which make *Hard Times* both a powerful criticism of the Victorian industrial world and an intriguing example of Dickens' mature art.

Lafayette College
March, 1958

WILLIAM W. WATT

BIOGRAPHICAL OUTLINE

(Based on Edgar Johnson's *Charles Dickens: His Tragedy and Triumph*)

1812   Charles Dickens born at Portsea on the Channel coast February 7, son of John Dickens, an improvident Navy clerk memorialized as Micawber in *David Copperfield*.

1814   Moved with his family to London.

1817   Moved to Chatham, a shipbuilding town near the cathedral city of Rochester.

1821   Began schooling under William Giles, supplementing his schooling with a vast amount of reading, including the *Arabian Nights* and *Tales of the Genii*, the novels of Fielding, Smollett, and Defoe, *Don Quixote* and *Gil Blas*, the *Tatler*, *Spectator*, and *Idler*, Goldsmith's *Citizen of the World*, and Mrs. Inchbald's *Collection of Farces*.

1822   Moved back to London (Camden Town), interrupting schooling.

1824   Worked in a blacking warehouse pasting labels on bottles of shoe polish. Two weeks after the job began, his father was imprisoned for debt in the Marshalsea. Charles lived alone in a lodging house after his mother and the other children moved in with father, who was released after three months. The events of the year were later recalled in *David Copperfield* and *Little Dorrit* and colored his entire view of life.

1827   Left school for good after two and a half years at Wellington House Academy to become an office boy for an attorney's firm.

1828   Became a free lance reporter for the law courts in Doctors' Commons.

1829   Met his first love, Maria Beadnell, with whom he carried on a romantic affair for four years.

1832   Became a reporter for two newspapers: the *True Sun* and the *Morning Advertiser*.

1833   Contributed a series of sketches of London life to the *Monthly Magazine*, some of them under the pseudonym "Boz." Became a regular parliamentary reporter for the *Morning Chronicle*.

1835   Contributed sketches to the *Evening Chronicle* and other periodicals. Fell in love with Catherine Hogarth.

1836   Published his first book, *Sketches by Boz*. Married Catherine Hogarth, who eventually bore him ten children.

1836/37 Published *The Posthumous Papers of the Pickwick Club* in monthly parts, originally intended merely as text to accompany sporting prints by Robert Seymour. Starting slowly, it soon became a best-seller, making him famous at 24. In the fall of 1836 he left the *Morning Chronicle* to become editor of a monthly, *Bentley's Miscellany*. Met John Forster, his biographer.

1837   Was profoundly affected by the death of Catherine Hogarth's younger sister, Mary (the "little Nell" of *The Old Curiosity Shop*), whose idealized memory was to haunt his books.

1837/39 Published *Oliver Twist* in monthly parts in *Bentley's Miscellany*.

1838/39 Published *Nicholas Nickleby* in monthly parts. Visited Manchester (1838) and was shocked by living and working conditions of the factory hands.

1840   Resigned as editor of *Bentley's Miscellany* after prolonged argument with Richard Bentley. Began *Master Humphrey's Clock*, a weekly miscellany, out of which grew two weekly serials: *The Old Curiosity Shop* (1840-41) and *Barnaby Rudge* (1841).

1842   Made a five month lecture tour of the United States, arguing boldly for international copyright and the abolition of slavery. After his return published *American Notes*, in which he was strongly critical of many aspects of American life.

1843/44 Continued his satire of America in *Martin Chuzzlewit*, published in monthly parts. Published his first two Christmas stories: *A Christmas Carol* (1843) and *The Chimes* (1844).

1844/45 Spent most of a year in Italy (July, 1844 to June, 1845).

1846/48 Published *Dombey and Son* in monthly parts. Edited (1846-7) a new Radical newspaper, the *Daily News*.

1848   Barnstormed for five months in England and Scotland as director and actor with his own amateur theatrical troupe. Wrote a series of articles for the *Examiner*, including serious comments on social problems.

1849/50 Published *David Copperfield* in monthly installments, his own favorite among his books. Began *Household Words*, "conducted by Charles Dickens," (March 30, 1850).

1851   Lost his father and his daughter, Dora Annie, within two weeks.

1852/53 Published *Bleak House* in monthly parts. Gave his first public benefit readings from his books (1852).

1854   Published *Hard Times* in weekly parts in *Household Words* (April 1 through August 12).

1855/57 Published *Little Dorrit* in monthly parts. Produced and acted in Wilkie Collins' melodrama, *The Frozen Deep*, in which Ellen Ternan, who later became his mistress, played a small part (1857).

1858   Became separated from his wife after years of incompatibility. Gave his first professional readings.

1859/60 Published the last number of *Household Words* (May 28, 1859). Started as conductor of *All the Year Round* (April 30, 1859), which began, in its first issue, with the weekly serial, *A Tale of Two Cities*.

1860/61 Published *Great Expectations* in weekly parts in *All the Year Round*.

1864/65 Published *Our Mutual Friend* in monthly parts. On returning with Ellen Ternan from a Paris vacation (June 9, 1865) was in a railway accident, from the shock of which he never fully recovered.

1867/68 Despite rapidly failing health, made a triumphal five month tour of America (November-April), where his readings did much to heal old wounds.

1869   Broke down after giving 74 of a hundred farewell readings in England, Scotland, and Ireland.

1870   Gave a final series of readings in London. Stood for an hour and a half during private audience with Queen Victoria. Began *The Mystery of Edwin Drood* in monthly parts in April. Died from a paralytic stroke on June 9, leaving it unfinished. Was buried in Westminster Abbey.

TEXTUAL AND BIBLIOGRAPHICAL NOTE

The text of this edition is that of *The Nonesuch Dickens* (edited by Arthur Waugh, Hugh Walpole, Walter Dexter, and Thomas Hatton, London, 1938). I have made a few slight alterations for consistency in punctuation and spelling, mostly in the dialect of Stephen Blackpool. The right hand running heads supplied by the author himself for the Charles Dickens Edition, London, 1868, have been retained as side heads in this edition.

Other works by Dickens are listed in the Biographical Outline on pages xxxv-xxxviii.

The standard nineteenth century biography is by Dickens' close friend John Forster: *The Life of Charles Dickens* (3 vols., London, 1872-4); edited and annotated by J. W. T. Ley, London, 1928. The indispensable modern biography is Edgar Johnson's *Charles Dickens: His Tragedy and Triumph* (2 vols., New York, 1952). A readable short life is Dame Una Pope-Hennessy's *Charles Dickens, 1812-70* (London, 1946).

Significant critical estimates of Dickens are by: G. K. Chesterton (*Charles Dickens: A Critical Study,* London, 1906 and *Appreciations and Criticisms,* London, 1911); George Santayana ("Dickens," in *Soliloquies in England,* London, 1922, reprinted in *Essays in Literary Criticism of George Santayana,* ed. Irving Singer, New York, 1956); George Gissing (*Critical Studies of the Works of Charles Dickens,* New York, 1924); Edmund Wilson ("Dickens: The Two Scrooges," in *The Wound and the Bow,* Boston, 1941, reprinted in *Edmund Wilson: Eight Essays,* Doubleday Anchor Books, Garden City, 1954); Lionel Stevenson ("Dickens's Dark Novels, 1851-1857," *Sewanee Review,* 1943, 51:398-409); George Orwell ("Charles Dickens," in *Dickens, Dali, and Others,* New York, 1946, reprinted in *A Collection of Essays by George Orwell,* Doubleday Anchor Books, Garden City, 1954); and Dorothy Van Ghent ("The Dickens World," *Sewanee Review,* 1950, 58:419-38). George H. Ford (in *Dickens and His Readers,*

Princeton, 1955) discusses the changing aspects of novel-criticism since 1836 with special reference to Dickens' works.

Critical essays on *Hard Times* are by: Bernard Shaw (Introduction to *Hard Times* in the Waverley Edition of Dickens, London, 1912); F. R. Leavis (*"Hard Times:* An Analytic Note," in *The Great Tradition,* London, 1948, reprinted as a Doubleday Anchor Book, Garden City, 1954); and Edgar Johnson (in Volume Two of his biography, pages 801-819). Commentaries on *Hard Times* by Dickens' contemporaries are the laudatory footnote in Ruskin's *Unto this Last* (*Cornhill Magazine,* August, 1860, 2:159) and more extensive reviews in the *Westminster Review* (October, 1854, 62:318-21) and the *Atlantic Monthly* (March, 1877, 39:353-58).

In addition to the essays, novels, and poems mentioned in the Introduction (page xi), the student especially interested in Victorian attitudes on economics and business ethics might consult Herbert Spencer's *Social Statics* (London, 1851), a defense of laissez faire, and Ruskin's *Unto this Last* (*Cornhill Magazine,* August-November, 1860, 2:155-166, 278-286, 407-418, 534-564), a powerful attack on the classical economists. Two late Victorian books on more specialized subjects relevant to *Hard Times* are: Arnold Toynbee's *Lectures on the Industrial Revolution in England* (London, 1884, available in a Beacon paperback edition, Boston, 1956); and Sir Leslie Stephen's *The English Utilitarians* (3 vols., London, 1900). Of the many broader treatments of the Victorian period, the following throw considerable light on Dickens and *Hard Times:* J. L. and Barbara Hammond, *The Bleak Age* (London, 1934, reprinted as a Pelican Book, London, 1947); G. M. Young, *Victorian England: Portrait of an Age* (New York, 1936, reprinted as a Doubleday Anchor Book, Garden City, 1954); Humphrey House, *The Dickens World* (Oxford, 1941); *Ideas and Beliefs of the Victorians* (London, 1949); Jerome Buckley, *The Victorian Temper* (Cambridge, Mass., 1951); and John W. Dodds, *The Age of Paradox: A Biography of England 1841-1851* (New York, 1952).

CONTENTS

Introduction   vii
Biographical Outline   xxxv
Textual and Bibliographical Note   xxxix

BOOK THE FIRST
SOWING

CHAPTER

ONE   The One Thing Needful   1
TWO   Murdering the Innocents   2
THREE   A Loophole   8
FOUR   Mr. Bounderby   13
FIVE   The Key-Note   20
SIX   Sleary's Horsemanship   25
SEVEN   Mrs. Sparsit   38
EIGHT   Never Wonder   45
NINE   Sissy's Progress   50
TEN   Stephen Blackpool   58
ELEVEN   No Way Out   63
TWELVE   The Old Woman   70
THIRTEEN   Rachael   75
FOURTEEN   The Great Manufacturer   83
FIFTEEN   Father and Daughter   88
SIXTEEN   Husband and Wife   95

BOOK THE SECOND
REAPING

ONE   Effects in the Bank   101
TWO   Mr. James Harthouse   114

CHAPTER

THREE The Whelp   121
FOUR Men and Brothers   126
FIVE Men and Masters   134
SIX Fading Away   140
SEVEN Gunpowder   152
EIGHT Explosion   164
NINE Hearing the Last of It   176
TEN Mrs. Sparsit's Staircase   184
ELEVEN Lower and Lower   188
TWELVE Down   197

BOOK THE THIRD
GARNERING

ONE Another Thing Needful   202
TWO Very Ridiculous   208
THREE Very Decided   217
FOUR Lost   225
FIVE Found   234
SIX The Starlight   242
SEVEN Whelp-Hunting   252
EIGHT Philosophical   263
NINE Final   269

HARD TIMES

FOR THESE TIMES

BOOK THE FIRST

SOWING

CHAPTER ONE

THE ONE THING NEEDFUL

"Now, what I want is, Facts. Teach these boys and girls nothing but Facts. Facts alone are wanted in life. Plant nothing else, and root out everything else. You can only form the minds of reasoning animals upon Facts: nothing else will ever be of any service to them. This is the principle on which I bring up my own children, and this is the principle on which I bring up these children. Stick to Facts, sir!"

The scene was a plain, bare, monotonous vault of a schoolroom, and the speaker's square forefinger emphasised his observations by underscoring every sentence with a line on the schoolmaster's sleeve. The emphasis was helped by the speaker's square wall of a forehead, which had his eyebrows for its base, while his eyes found commodious cellarage in two dark caves, overshadowed by the wall. The emphasis was helped by the speaker's mouth, which was wide, thin, and hard set. The emphasis was helped by the speaker's voice, which was inflexible, dry, and dictatorial. The emphasis was helped by the speaker's hair, which bristled on the skirts of his bald head, a plantation of firs to keep the wind from its shining surface, all covered with knobs, like the crust of a plum pie, as if the head had scarcely warehouse-room for the hard facts stored inside. The speaker's obstinate carriage, square coat, square legs, square shoulders,—nay, his very neckcloth, trained to take him by the throat with an unaccommodating grasp, like a stubborn fact, as it was,—all helped the emphasis.

"In this life, we want nothing but Facts, sir; nothing but Facts!"

The speaker, and the schoolmaster, and the third grown person present, all backed a little, and swept with their eyes the inclined plane of little vessels then and there arranged in order, ready to have imperial gallons of facts poured into them until they were full to the brim.

CHAPTER TWO

MURDERING THE INNOCENTS

THOMAS GRADGRIND, sir. A man of realities. A man of facts and calculations. A man who proceeds upon the principle that two and two are four, and nothing over, and who is not to be talked into allowing for anything over. Thomas Gradgrind, sir—peremptorily Thomas—Thomas Gradgrind. With a rule and a pair of scales, and the multiplication table always in his pocket, sir, ready to weigh and measure any parcel of human nature, and tell you exactly what it comes to. It is a mere question of figures, a case of simple arithmetic. You might hope to get some other nonsensical belief into the head of George Gradgrind, or Augustus Gradgrind, or John Gradgrind, or Joseph Gradgrind (all supposititious, non-existent persons), but into the head of Thomas Gradgrind—no, sir!

In such terms Mr. Gradgrind always mentally introduced himself, whether to his private circle of acquaintance, or to the public in general. In such terms, no doubt, substituting the words "boys and girls," for "sir," Thomas Gradgrind now presented

Thomas Gradgrind to the little pitchers before him, who were to be filled so full of facts.

Indeed, as he eagerly sparkled at them from the cellarage before mentioned, he seemed a kind of cannon loaded to the muzzle with facts, and prepared to blow them clean out of the regions of childhood at one discharge. He seemed a galvanizing apparatus, too, charged with a grim mechanical substitute for the tender young imaginations that were to be stormed away.

"Girl number twenty," said Mr. Gradgrind, squarely pointing with his square forefinger, "I don't know that girl. Who is that girl?"

"Sissy Jupe, sir," explained number twenty, blushing, standing up, and curtseying.

"Sissy is not a name," said Mr. Gradgrind. "Don't call yourself Sissy. Call yourself Cecilia."

"It's father as calls me Sissy, sir," returned the young girl in a trembling voice, and with another curtsey.

"Then he has no business to do it," said Mr. Gradgrind. "Tell him he mustn't. Cecilia Jupe. Let me see. What is your father?"

"He belongs to the horse-riding, if you please, sir."

Mr. Gradgrind frowned, and waved off the objectionable calling with his hand.

"We don't want to know anything about that, here. You mustn't tell us about that, here. Your father breaks horses, don't he?"

"If you please, sir, when they can get any to break, they do break horses in the ring, sir."

"You must'nt tell us about the ring, here. Very well, then. Describe your father as a horsebreaker. He doctors sick horses, I dare say?"

"Oh yes, sir."

"Very well, then. He is a veterinary surgeon, a farrier, and horsebreaker. Give me your definition of a horse."

(Sissy Jupe thrown into the greatest alarm by this demand.)

"Girl number twenty unable to define a horse!" said Mr. Gradgrind, for the general behoof of all the little pitchers. "Girl number twenty possessed of no facts, in reference to one of the commonest of animals! Some boy's definition of a horse. Bitzer, yours."

The square finger, moving here and there, lighted suddenly on

Bitzer, perhaps because he chanced to sit in the same ray of sunlight which, darting in at one of the bare windows of the intensely
whitewashed room, irradiated Sissy. For, the boys and girls sat on
the face of the inclined plane in two compact bodies, divided up
the centre by a narrow interval; and Sissy, being at the corner
of a row on the sunny side, came in for the beginning of a sun-
beam, of which Bitzer, being at the corner of a row on the other
side, a few rows in advance, caught the end. But, whereas the
girl was so dark-eyed and dark-haired, that she seemed to receive
a deeper and more lustrous colour from the sun, when it shone
upon her, the boy was so light-eyed and light-haired that the
self-same rays appeared to draw out of him what little colour he
ever possessed. His cold eyes would hardly have been eyes, but
for the short ends of lashes which, by bringing them into immediate contrast with something paler than themselves, expressed
their form. His short-cropped hair might have been a mere
continuation of the sandy freckles on his forehead and face. His
skin was so unwholesomely deficient in the natural tinge, that he
looked as though, if he were cut, he would bleed white.

"Bitzer," said Thomas Gradgrind. "Your definition of a horse."

"Quadruped. Graminivorous. Forty teeth, namely twenty-four
grinders, four eye-teeth, and twelve incisive. Sheds coat in the
spring; in marshy countries, sheds hoofs, too. Hoofs hard, but
requiring to be shod with iron. Age known by marks in mouth."
Thus (and much more) Bitzer.

"Now girl number twenty," said Mr. Gradgrind. "You know
what a horse is."

She curtseyed again, and would have blushed deeper, if she
could have blushed deeper than she had blushed all this time.
Bitzer, after rapidly blinking at Thomas Gradgrind with both
eyes at once, and so catching the light upon his quivering ends of
lashes that they looked like the antennæ of busy insects, put his
Always in knuckles to his freckled forehead, and sat down
training again.

The third gentleman now stepped forth. A
mighty man at cutting and drying, he was; a government officer;
in his way (and in most other people's too), a professed pugilist;
always in training, always with a system to force down the general throat like a bolus, always to be heard of at the bar of his

little Public-office, ready to fight all England. To continue in fistic phraseology, he had a genius for coming up to the scratch, wherever and whatever it was, and proving himself an ugly customer. He would go in and damage any subject whatever with his right, follow up with his left, stop, exchange, counter, bore his opponent (he always fought All England) to the ropes, and fall upon him neatly. He was certain to knock the wind out of common sense, and render that unlucky adversary deaf to the call of time. And he had it in charge from high authority to bring about the great public-office Millennium, when Commissioners should reign upon earth.

"Very well," said this gentleman, briskly smiling, and folding his arms. "That's a horse. Now, let me ask you girls and boys, Would you paper a room with representations of horses?"

After a pause, one half of the children cried in chorus, "Yes, sir!" Upon which the other half, seeing in the gentleman's face that Yes was wrong, cried out in chorus, "No, sir!"—as the custom is, in these examinations.

"Of course, No. Why wouldn't you?"

A pause. One corpulent slow boy, with a wheezy manner of breathing, ventured the answer, Because he wouldn't paper a room at all, but would paint it.

"You *must* paper it," said the gentleman, rather warmly.

"You must paper it," said Thomas Gradgrind, "whether you like it or not. Don't tell *us* you wouldn't paper it. What do you mean, boy?"

"I'll explain to you, then," said the gentleman, after another and a dismal pause, "why you wouldn't paper a room with representations of horses. Do you ever see horses walking up and down the sides of rooms in reality—in fact? Do you?"

"Yes, sir!" from one half. "No, sir!" from the other.

"Of course, No," said the gentleman, with an indignant look at the wrong half. "Why, then, you are not to see anywhere, what you don't see in fact; you are not to have anywhere, what you don't have in fact. What is called Taste, is only another name for Fact."

Thomas Gradgrind nodded his approbation.

"This is a new principle, a discovery, a great discovery," said the gentleman. "Now, I'll try you again. Suppose you were going to carpet a room. Would you use a carpet having a representation of flowers upon it?"

There being a general conviction by this time that "No, sir!" was always the right answer to this gentleman, the chorus of No was very strong. Only a few feeble stragglers said Yes: among them Sissy Jupe.

"Girl number twenty," said the gentleman, smiling in the calm strength of knowledge.

Sissy blushed, and stood up.

"So you would carpet your room—or your husband's room, if you were a grown woman, and had a husband—with representations of flowers, would you?" said the gentleman. "Why would you?"

"If you please, sir, I am very fond of flowers," returned the girl.

"And is that why you would put tables and chairs upon them, and have people walking over them with heavy boots?"

"It wouldn't hurt them, sir. They wouldn't crush and wither, if you please, sir. They would be the pictures of what was very pretty and pleasant, and I would fancy——"

"Ay, ay, ay! But you mustn't fancy," cried the gentleman, quite elated by coming so happily to his point. "That's it! You are never to fancy."

"You are not, Cecilia Jupe," Thomas Gradgrind solemnly repeated, "to do anything of that kind."

"Fact, fact, fact!" said the gentleman. And *Matters of fact* "Fact, fact, fact!" repeated Thomas Gradgrind.

"You are to be in all things regulated and governed," said the gentleman, "by fact. We hope to have, before long, a board of fact, composed of commissioners of fact, who will force the people to be a people of fact, and of nothing but fact. You must discard the word Fancy altogether. You have nothing to do with it. You are not to have, in any object of use or ornament, what would be a contradiction in fact. You don't walk upon flowers in fact; you cannot be allowed to walk upon flowers in carpets. You don't find that foreign birds and butterflies come and perch upon your crockery; you cannot be permitted to paint foreign birds and butterflies upon your crockery. You never meet with quadrupeds going up and down walls; you must not have quadrupeds represented upon walls. You must use," said the gentleman, "for all these purposes, combinations and modifications (in primary colours) of mathematical figures which are susceptible of proof and demonstration. This is the new discovery. This is fact. This is taste."

The girl curtseyed, and sat down. She was very young, and she looked as if she were frightened by the matter of fact prospect the world afforded.

"Now, if Mr. M'Choakumchild," said the gentleman, "will proceed to give his first lesson here, Mr. Gradgrind, I shall be happy, at your request, to observe his mode of procedure."

Mr. Gradgrind was much obliged. "Mr. M'Choakumchild, we only wait for you."

So, Mr. M'Choakumchild began in his best manner. He and some one hundred and forty other schoolmasters, had been lately turned at the same time, in the same factory, on the same principles, like so many pianoforte legs. He had been put through an immense variety of paces, and had answered volumes of head-breaking questions. Orthography, etymology, syntax, and prosody, biography, astronomy, geography, and general cosmography, the sciences of compound proportion, algebra, land-surveying and levelling, vocal music, and drawing from models, were all at the ends of his ten chilled fingers. He had worked his stony way into Her Majesty's most Honourable Privy Council's Schedule B, and had taken the bloom off the higher branches of mathematics and physical science, French, German, Latin, and Greek. He knew all about all the Water Sheds of all the world (whatever they are), and all the histories of all the peoples, and all the names of all the rivers and mountains, and all the productions, manners, and customs of all the countries, and all their boundaries and bearings on the two and thirty points of the compass. Ah, rather overdone, M'Choakumchild. If he had only learnt a little less, how infinitely better he might have taught much more!

He went to work in this preparatory lesson, not unlike Morgiana in the Forty Thieves: looking into all the vessels ranged before him, one after another, to see what they contained. Say, good M'Choakumchild. When from thy boiling store, thou shalt fill each jar brim full by-and-by, dost thou think that thou wilt always kill outright the robber Fancy lurking within—or sometimes only maim him and distort him!

CHAPTER THREE

A LOOPHOLE

MR. GRADGRIND walked homeward from the school, in a state of considerable satisfaction. It was his school, and he intended it to be a model. He intended every child in it to be a model—just as the young Gradgrinds were all models.

There were five young Gradgrinds, and they were models every one. They had been lectured at, from their tenderest years; coursed, like little hares. Almost as soon as they could run alone, they had been made to run to the lecture-room. The first object with which they had an association, or of which they had a remembrance, was a large black board with a dry Ogre chalking ghastly white figures on it.

Not that they knew, by name or nature, anything about an Ogre. Fact forbid! I only use the word to express a monster in a lecturing castle, with Heaven knows how many heads manipulated into one, taking childhood captive, and dragging it into gloomy statistical dens by the hair.

No little Gradgrind had ever seen a face in the moon; it was up in the moon before it could speak distinctly. No little Gradgrind had ever learnt the silly jingle, Twinkle, twinkle, little star; how I wonder what you are! No little Gradgrind had ever known wonder on the subject, each little Gradgrind having at five years old dissected the Great Bear like a Professor Owen, and driven Charles's Wain like a locomotive engine-driver. No little Gradgrind had ever associated a cow in a field with that famous cow with the crumpled horn who tossed the dog who worried the cat who killed the rat who ate the malt, or with that yet more famous cow who swallowed Tom Thumb: it had never heard of those celebrities, and had only been introduced to a cow as a graminivorous ruminating quadruped with several stomachs.

To his matter of fact home, which was called Stone Lodge, Mr. Gradgrind directed his steps. He had virtually retired from the wholesale hardware trade before he built Stone Lodge, and was now looking about for a suitable opportunity of making an arithmetical figure in Parliament. Stone Lodge was situated on a moor within a mile or two of a great town—called Coketown in the present faithful guide-book.

A very regular feature on the face of the country, Stone Lodge was. Not the least disguise toned down or shaded off that uncompromising fact in the landscape. A great square house, with a heavy portico darkening the principal windows, as its master's heavy brows overshadowed his eyes. A calculated, cast up, balanced, and proved house. Six windows on this side of the door, six on that side; a total of twelve in this wing, a total of twelve in the other wing; four and twenty carried over to the back wings. A lawn and garden and an infant avenue, all ruled straight like a botanical account-book. Gas and ventilation, drainage and water-service, all of the primest quality. Iron clamps and girders, fireproof from top to bottom; mechanical lifts for the housemaids, with all their brushes and brooms; everything that heart could desire.

Everything? Well, I suppose so. The little Gradgrinds had cabinets in various departments of science too. They had a little conchological cabinet, and a little metallurgical cabinet, and a little mineralogical cabinet; and the specimens were all arranged and labelled, and the bits of stone and ore looked as though they might have been broken from the parent substances by those tremendously hard instruments their own names. And, to paraphrase the idle legend of Peter Piper, who had never found his way into their nursery, if the greedy little Gradgrinds grasped at more than this, what was it for good gracious goodness' sake, that the greedy little Gradgrinds grasped at!

Their father walked on in a hopeful and satisfied frame of mind. He was an affectionate father, after his manner; but he would probably have described himself (if he had been put, like Sissy Jupe, upon a definition) as "an eminently practical" father. He had a particular pride in the phrase eminently practical, which was considered to have a special application to him. Whatsoever the public meeting held in Coketown, and whatsoever the subject of such meeting, some Coketowner was sure to seize the occasion of alluding to his eminently practical friend Gradgrind. This always pleased the eminently practical friend. He knew it to be his due, but his due was acceptable.

He had reached the neutral ground upon the outskirts of the town, which was neither town nor country, and yet was either spoiled, when his ears were invaded by the sound of music. The clashing and banging band attached to the horse-riding establishment which had there set up its rest in a wooden pavilion was in full bray. A flag, floating from the summit of the temple, proclaimed to mankind that it was "Sleary's Horse-riding" which claimed their suffrages. Sleary himself, a stout modern statue with a money-box at its elbow, in an ecclesiastical niche of early Gothic architecture, took the money. Miss Josephine Sleary, as some very long and very narrow strips of printed bill announced, was then inaugurating the entertainments with her graceful equestrian Tyrolean Flower-Act. Among the other pleasing but always strictly moral wonders which must be seen to be believed, Signor Jupe was that afternoon to "elucidate the diverting accomplishments of his highly trained performing dog Merrylegs." He was also to exhibit "his astounding feat of throwing seventy-five hundred-weight in rapid succession backhanded over his head, thus forming a fountain of solid iron in mid-air, a feat never before attempted in this or any other country, and which having elicited such rapturous plaudits from enthusiastic throngs it cannot be withdrawn." The same Signor Jupe was to "enliven the varied performances at frequent intervals with his chaste Shakespearean quips and retorts." Lastly, he was to wind them up by appearing in his favourite character of Mr. William Button, of Tooley Street, in "the highly novel and laughable hippo-comedietta of The Tailor's Journey to Brentford."

Thomas Gradgrind took no heed of these *The touch* trivialities of course, but passed on as a practical *of Nature* man ought to pass on, either brushing the noisy insects from his thoughts, or consigning them to the House of Correction. But, the turning of the road took him by the back of the booth, and at the back of the booth a number of children were congregated in a number of stealthy attitudes, striving to peep in at the hidden glories of the place.

This brought him to a stop. "Now, to think of these vagabonds," said he, "attracting the young rabble from a model school."

A space of stunted grass and dry rubbish being between him and the young rabble, he took his eyeglass out of his waistcoat to look for any child he knew by name, and might order off. Phenomenon almost incredible though distinctly seen, what did he then behold but his own metallurgical Louisa, peeping with all her might through a hole in a deal board, and his own mathematical Thomas abasing himself on the ground to catch but a hoof of the graceful equestrian Tyrolean Flower-Act!

Dumb with amazement, Mr. Gradgrind crossed to the spot where his family was thus disgraced, laid his hand upon each erring child, and said:

"Louisa! ! Thomas! !"

Both rose, red and disconcerted. But, Louisa looked at her father with more boldness than Thomas did. Indeed, Thomas did not look at him, but gave himself up to be taken home like a machine.

"In the name of wonder, idleness, and folly!" said Mr. Gradgrind, leading each away by a hand; "what do you do here?"

"Wanted to see what it was like," returned Louisa, shortly.

"What it was like?"

"Yes, father."

There was an air of jaded sullenness in them both, and particularly in the girl: yet, struggling through the dissatisfaction of her face, there was a light with nothing to rest upon, a fire with nothing to burn, a starved imagination keeping life in itself somehow, which brightened its expression. Not with the brightness natural to cheerful youth, but with uncertain, eager, doubtful flashes, which had something painful in them, analogous to the changes on a blind face groping its way.

She was a child now, of fifteen or sixteen; but at no distant day would seem to become a woman all at once. Her father thought so as he looked at her. She was pretty. Would have been self-willed (he thought in his eminently practical way) but for her bringing-up.

"Thomas, though I have the fact before me, I find it difficult to believe that you, with your education and resources, should have brought your sister to a scene like this."

"I brought *him*, father," said Louisa quickly. "I asked him to come."

"I am sorry to hear it. I am very sorry indeed to hear it. It makes Thomas no better, and it makes you worse, Louisa."

She looked at her father again, but no tear fell down her cheek.

"You! Thomas and you, to whom the circle of the sciences is open; Thomas and you, who may be said to be replete with facts; Thomas and you, who have been trained to mathematical exactness; Thomas and you, here!" cried Mr. Gradgrind. "In this degraded position! I am amazed."

"I was tired, father. I have been tired a long time," said Louisa.

"Tired? Of what?" asked the astonished father.

"I don't know of what—of everything, I think."

"Say not another word," returned Mr. Gradgrind. "You are childish. I will hear no more." He did not speak again until they had walked some half-a-mile in silence, when he gravely broke out with: "What would your best friends say, Louisa? Do you attach no value to their good opinion? What would Mr. Bounderby say?"

At the mention of this name, his daughter stole a look at him, remarkable for its intense and searching character. He saw nothing of it, for before he looked at her, she had again cast down her eyes.

"What," he repeated presently, "would Mr. Bounderby say?" All the way to Stone Lodge, as with grave indignation he led the two delinquents home, he repeated at intervals "What would Mr. Bounderby say!"—as if Mr. Bounderby had been Mrs. Grundy.

CHAPTER FOUR

MR. BOUNDERBY

NOT being Mrs. Grundy, who *was* Mr. Bounderby?

Why, Mr. Bounderby was as near being Mr. Gradgrind's bosom friend, as a man perfectly devoid of sentiment can approach that spiritual relationship towards another man perfectly devoid of sentiment. So near was Mr. Bounderby—or, if the reader should prefer it, so far off.

He was a rich man; banker, merchant, manufacturer, and what not. A big, loud man, with a stare, and a metallic laugh. A man made out of a coarse material, which seemed to have been stretched to make so much of him. A man with a great puffed head and forehead, swelled veins in his temples, and such a strained skin to his face that it seemed to hold his eyes open, and lift his eyebrows up. A man with a pervading appearance on him of being inflated like a balloon, and ready to start. A man who could never sufficiently vaunt himself a self-made man. A man who was always proclaiming, through that brassy speaking-trumpet of a voice of his, his old ignorance and his old poverty. A man who was the Bully of humility.

A year or two younger than his eminently practical friend, Mr. Bounderby looked older; his seven or eight and forty might have had the seven or eight added to it again, without surprising anybody. He had not much hair. One might have fancied he had talked it off; and that what was left, all standing up in disorder, was in that condition from being constantly blown about by his windy boastfulness.

In the formal drawing-room of Stone Lodge, standing on the hearthrug, warming himself before the fire, Mr. Bounderby delivered some observations to Mrs. Gradgrind on the circumstance of its being his birthday. He stood before the fire, partly because it was a cool spring afternoon, though the sun shone; partly because the shade of Stone Lodge was always haunted by the ghost of damp mortar; partly because he thus took up a commanding position, from which to subdue Mrs. Gradgrind.

"I hadn't a shoe to my foot. As to a stocking, I didn't know such a thing by name. I passed the day in a ditch, and the night in a pigsty. That's the way I spent my tenth birthday. Not that a ditch was new to me, for I was born in a ditch."

An autobiography   Mrs. Gradgrind, a little, thin, white, pink-eyed bundle of shawls, of surpassing feebleness, mental and bodily; who was always taking physic without any effect, and who, whenever she showed a symptom of coming to life, was invariably stunned by some weighty piece of fact tumbling on her; Mrs. Gradgrind hoped it was a dry ditch?

"No! As wet as a sop. A foot of water in it," said Mr. Bounderby.

"Enough to give a baby cold," Mrs. Gradgrind considered.

"Cold? I was born with inflammation of the lungs, and of everything else, I believe, that was capable of inflammation," returned Mr. Bounderby. "For years, ma'am, I was one of the most miserable little wretches ever seen. I was so sickly, that I was always moaning and groaning. I was so ragged and dirty, that you wouldn't have touched me with a pair of tongs."

Mrs. Gradgrind faintly looked at the tongs, as the most appropriate thing her imbecility could think of doing.

"How I fought through it, *I* don't know," said Bounderby. "I was determined, I suppose. I have been a determined character in later life, and I suppose I was then. Here I am, Mrs. Gradgrind, anyhow, and nobody to thank for my being here, but myself."

Mrs. Gradgrind meekly and weakly hoped that his mother—

"*My* mother? Bolted, ma'am!" said Bounderby.

Mrs. Gradgrind, stunned as usual, collapsed and gave it up.

"My mother left me to my grandmother," said Bounderby; "and, according to the best of my remembrance, my grandmother was the wickedest and the worst old woman that ever lived. If I got a little pair of shoes by any chance, she would take 'em off and sell 'em for drink. Why, I have known that grandmother of mine lie in her bed and drink her fourteen glasses of liquor before breakfast!"

Mrs. Gradgrind, weakly smiling, and giving no other sign of vitality, looked (as she always did) like an indifferently executed transparency of a small female figure, without enough light behind it.

"She kept a chandler's shop," pursued Bounderby, "and kept me in an egg-box. That was the cot of *my* infancy; an old egg-box. As soon as I was big enough to run away, of course I ran away. Then I became a young vagabond; and instead of one old woman knocking me about and starving me, everybody of all ages knocked me about and starved me. They were right; they had no business to do anything else. I was a nuisance, an incumbrance, and a pest. I know that very well."

His pride in having at any time of his life achieved such a great social distinction as to be a nuisance, an incumbrance, and a pest, was only to be satisfied by three sonorous repetitions of the boast.

"I was to pull through it, I suppose, Mrs. Gradgrind. Whether I was to do it or not, ma'am, I did it. I pulled through it, though nobody threw me out a rope. Vagabond, errand-boy, vagabond, labourer, porter, clerk, chief manager, small partner, Josiah Bounderby of Coketown. Those are the antecedents, and the culmination. Josiah Bounderby of Coketown learnt his letters from the outsides of the shops, Mrs. Gradgrind, and was first able to tell the time upon a dial-plate, from studying the steeple clock of St. Giles's Church, London, under the direction of a drunken cripple, who was a convicted thief, and an incorrigible vagrant. Tell Josiah Bounderby of Coketown, of your district schools and your model schools, and your training schools, and your whole kettle-of-fish of schools; and Josiah Bounderby of Coketown, tells you plainly, all right, all correct,—he hadn't such advantages— but let us have hard-headed, solid-fisted people—the education that made him won't do for everybody, he knows well—such and such his education was, however, and you may force him to swallow boiling fat, but you shall never force him to suppress the facts of his life."

Being heated when he arrived at this climax, Josiah Bounderby of Coketown stopped. He stopped just as his eminently practical friend, still accompanied by the two young culprits, entered the room. His eminently practical friend, on seeing him, stopped also, and gave Louisa a reproachful look that plainly said, "Behold your Bounderby!"

"Well!" blustered Mr. Bounderby, "what's the matter? What is young Thomas in the dumps about?"

He spoke of young Thomas, but he looked at Louisa.

"We were peeping at the circus," muttered Louisa, haughtily, without lifting up her eyes, "and father caught us."

"And, Mrs. Gradgrind," said her husband in a lofty manner, "I should as soon have expected to find my children reading poetry."

"Dear me," whimpered Mrs. Gradgrind. "How can you, Louisa and Thomas! I wonder at you. I declare you're enough to make one regret ever having had a family at all. I have a great mind to say I wish I hadn't. *Then* what would you have done, I should like to know?"

Mr. Gradgrind did not seem favourably impressed by these cogent remarks. He frowned impatiently.

"As if, with my head in its present throbbing state, you couldn't go and look at the shells and minerals and things provided for you, instead of circuses!" said Mrs. Gradgrind. "You know, as well as I do, no young people have circus masters, or keep circuses in cabinets, or attend lectures about circuses. What can you possibly want to know of circuses then? I am sure you have enough to do, if that's what you want. With my head in its present state, I couldn't remember the mere names of half the facts you have got to attend to."

"That's the reason!" pouted Louisa.

"Don't tell me that's the reason, because it can be nothing of the sort," said Mrs. Gradgrind. "Go and be somethingological directly." Mrs. Gradgrind was not a scientific character, and usually dismissed her children to their studies with this general injunction to choose their pursuit.

In truth, Mrs. Gradgrind's stock of facts in general was woefully defective; but Mr. Gradgrind in raising her to her high matrimonial position, had been influenced by two reasons. Firstly, she was most satisfactory as a question of figures; and, secondly, she had "no nonsense" about her. By nonsense he meant fancy;

and truly it is probable she was as free from any alloy of that nature, as any human being not arrived at the perfection of an absolute idiot, ever was.

The simple circumstance of being left alone with her husband and Mr. Bounderby, was sufficient to stun this admirable lady again without collision between herself and any other fact. So, she once more died away, and nobody minded her.

"Bounderby," said Mr. Gradgrind, drawing a chair to the fireside, "you are always so interested in my young people— particularly in Louisa—that I make no apology for saying to you, I am very much vexed by this discovery. I have systematically devoted myself (as you know) to the education of the reason of my family. The reason is (as you know) the only faculty to which education should be addressed. And yet, Bounderby, it would appear from this unexpected circumstance of to-day, though in itself a trifling one, as if something had crept into Thomas's and Louisa's minds which is—or rather, which is not—I don't know that I can express myself better than by saying—which has never been intended to be developed, and in which their reason has no part."

"There certainly is no reason in looking with interest at a parcel of vagabonds," returned Bounderby. "When I was a vagabond myself nobody looked with any interest at *me;* I know that."

"Then comes the question," said the eminently practical father, with his eyes on the fire, "in what has this vulgar curiosity its rise?"

"I'll tell you in what. In idle imagination."

"I hope not," said the eminently practical; "I confess, however, that the misgiving *has* crossed me on my way home."

"In idle imagination, Gradgrind," repeated Bounderby. "A very bad thing for anybody, but a cursed bad thing for a girl like Louisa. I should ask Mrs. Gradgrind's pardon for strong expressions, but that she knows very well I am not a refined character. Whoever expects refinement in *me* will be disappointed. I hadn't a refined bringing up."

"Whether," said Gradgrind, pondering with his hands in his pockets, and his cavernous eyes on the fire, "whether any instructor or servant can have suggested anything? Whether

Louisa or Thomas can have been reading anything? Whether, in spite of all precautions, any idle story book can have got into the house? Because, in minds that have been practically formed by rule and line, from the cradle upwards, this is so curious, so incomprehensible."

"Stop a bit!" cried Bounderby, who all this time had been standing, as before, on the hearth, bursting at *Bounderby's* the very furniture of the room with explosive *penetration* humility. "You have one of those stroller's chil- *and advice* dren in the school."

"Cecilia Jupe, by name," said Mr. Gradgrind, with something of a stricken look at his friend.

"Now, stop a bit!" cried Bounderby again. "How did she come there?"

"Why, the fact is, I saw the girl myself, for the first time, only just now. She specially applied here at the house to be admitted, as not regularly belonging to our town, and—yes, you are right, Bounderby, you are right."

"Now, stop a bit!" cried Bounderby, once more. "Louisa saw her when she came?"

"Louisa certainly did see her, for she mentioned the application to me. But Louisa saw her, I have no doubt, in Mrs. Gradgrind's presence."

"Pray, Mrs. Gradgrind," said Bounderby, "what passed?"

"Oh, my poor health!" returned Mrs. Gradgrind. "The girl wanted to come to the school, and Mr. Gradgrind wanted girls to come to the school, and Louisa and Thomas both said that the girl wanted to come, and that Mr. Gradgrind wanted girls to come, and how was it possible to contradict them when such was the fact!"

"Now I tell you what, Gradgrind!" said Mr. Bounderby. "Turn this girl to the right about, and there's an end of it."

"I am much of your opinion."

"Do it at once," said Bounderby, "has always been my motto from a child. When I thought I would run away from my egg-box and my grandmother, I did it at once. Do you the same. Do this at once!"

"Are you walking?" asked his friend. "I have the father's

address. Perhaps you would not mind walking to town with me?"

"Not the least in the world," said Mr. Bounderby, "as long as you do it at once!"

So, Mr. Bounderby threw on his hat—he always threw it on, as expressing a man who had been far too busily employed in making himself, to acquire any fashion of wearing his hat—and with his hands in his pockets, sauntered out into the hall. "I never wear gloves," it was his custom to say. "I didn't climb up the ladder in *them*. Shouldn't be so high up, if I had."

Being left to saunter in the hall a minute or two while Mr. Gradgrind went upstairs for the address, he opened the door of the children's study and looked into the serene floor-clothed apartment, which, notwithstanding its book-cases and its cabinets and its variety of learned and philosophical appliances, had much of the genial aspect of a room devoted to hair-cutting. Louisa languidly leaned upon the window looking out, without looking at anything, while young Thomas stood sniffing revengefully at the fire. Adam Smith and Malthus, two younger Gradgrinds, were out at lecture in custody; and little Jane, after manufacturing a good deal of moist pipe-clay on her face with slate-pencil and tears, had fallen asleep over vulgar fractions.

"It's all right now, Louisa: it's all right, young Thomas," said Mr. Bounderby; "you won't do so any more. I'll answer for its being all over with father. Well, Louisa, that's worth a kiss, isn't it?"

"You can take one, Mr. Bounderby," returned Louisa, when she had coldly paused, and slowly walked across the room, and ungraciously raised her cheek towards him, with her face turned away.

"Always my pet; ain't you, Louisa?" said Mr. Bounderby. "Good-bye, Louisa!"

He went his way, but she stood on the same spot, rubbing the cheek he had kissed, with her handkerchief, until it was burning red. She was still doing this, five minutes afterwards.

"What are you about, Loo?" her brother sulkily remonstrated. "You'll rub a hole in your face."

"You may cut the piece out with your penknife if you like, Tom. I wouldn't cry!"

CHAPTER FIVE

THE KEY-NOTE

COKETOWN, to which Messrs. Bounderby and Gradgrind now walked, was a triumph of fact; it had no greater taint of fancy in it than Mrs. Gradgrind herself. Let us strike the key-note, Coketown, before pursuing our tune.

It was a town of red brick, or of brick that would have been red if the smoke and ashes had allowed it; but as matters stood it was a town of unnatural red and black like the painted face of a savage. It was a town of machinery and tall chimneys, out of which interminable serpents of smoke trailed themselves for ever and ever, and never got uncoiled. It had a black canal in it, and a river that ran purple with ill-smelling dye, and vast piles of building full of windows where there was a rattling and a trembling all day long, and where the piston of the steam-engine worked monotonously up and down, like the head of an elephant in a state of melancholy madness. It contained several large streets all very like one another, and many small streets still more like one another, inhabited by people equally like one another, who all went in and out at the same hours, with the same sound upon the same pavements, to do the same work, and to whom every day was the same as yesterday and to-morrow, and every year the counterpart of the last and the next.

These attributes of Coketown were in the main inseparable from the work by which it was sustained; against them were to be set off, comforts of life which found their way all over the world, and elegancies of life which made, we will not ask how much of the fine lady, who could scarcely bear to hear the place mentioned. The rest of its features were voluntary, and they were these.

You saw nothing in Coketown but what was severely workful. If the members of a religious persuasion built a chapel there—as the members of eighteen religious persuasions had done—they made it a pious warehouse of red brick, with sometimes (but this is only in highly ornamental examples) a bell in a birdcage on the top of it. The solitary exception was the New Church; a stuccoed edifice with a square steeple over the door, terminating in four short pinnacles like florid wooden legs. All the public inscriptions in the town were painted alike, in severe characters of black and white. The jail might have been the infirmary, the infirmary might have been *The Coketown* the jail, the town-hall might have been either, *institutions* or both, or anything else, for anything that appeared to the contrary in the graces of their construction. Fact, fact, fact, everywhere in the material aspect of the town; fact, fact, fact, everywhere in the immaterial. The M'Choakum-child school was all fact, and the school of design was all fact, and the relations between master and man were all fact, and everything was fact between the lying-in hospital and the ceme-tery, and what you couldn't state in figures, or show to be pur-chaseable in the cheapest market and saleable in the dearest, was not, and never should be, world without end, Amen.

A town so sacred to fact, and so triumphant in its assertion, of course got on well? Why no, not quite well. No? Dear me!

No. Coketown did not come out of its own furnaces, in all respects like gold that had stood the fire. First, the perplexing mystery of the place was, Who belonged to the eighteen denomina-tions? Because, whoever did, the labouring people did not. It was very strange to walk through the streets on a Sunday morn-ing, and note how few of *them* the barbarous jangling of bells that was driving the sick and nervous mad, called away from their own quarter, from their own close rooms, from the corners of their own streets, where they lounged listlessly, gazing at all the church and chapel going, as at a thing with which they had no manner of concern. Nor was it merely the stranger who noticed this, because there was a native organization in Coketown itself, whose members were to be heard of in the House of Commons every session, indignantly petitioning for acts of parliament that should make these people religious by main force. Then came the Teetotal Society, who complained that these same people *would* get drunk, and showed in tabular statements that they did get drunk, and proved at tea parties that no inducement, human or Divine (except a medal), would induce them to forego their custom of getting drunk. Then came the chemist and druggist, with other tabular statements, showing that when they didn't get drunk, they took opium. Then came the experienced chaplain of the jail, with more tabular statements, outdoing all the previous tabular statements, and showing that the same people *would* resort to low haunts, hidden from the public eye, where they heard low singing and saw low dancing, and mayhap joined in it; and where A. B., aged twenty-four next birthday, and committed for eighteen months' solitary, had himself said (not that he had ever shown himself particularly worthy of belief) his ruin began, as he was perfectly sure and confident that otherwise he would have been a tip-top moral specimen. Then came Mr. Gradgrind and Mr. Bounderby, the two gentlemen at this present moment walking through Coketown, and both eminently practical, who could, on occasion, furnish more tabular statements derived from their own personal experience, and illustrated by cases they had known and seen, from which it clearly appeared—in short, it was the only clear thing in the case—that these same people were a bad lot altogether, gentlemen; that do what you would for them they were never thankful for it, gentlemen; that they were restless, gentlemen; that they never knew what they wanted; that they lived upon the best, and bought fresh butter; and insisted on Mocha coffee, and rejected all but prime parts of meat, and yet were eternally dissatisfied and unmanageable. In short it was the moral of the old nursery fable:

> *There was an old woman, and what do you think?*
> *She lived upon nothing but victuals and drink;*
> *Victuals and drink were the whole of her diet,*
> *And yet this old woman would* NEVER *be quiet.*

Is it possible, I wonder, that there was any analogy between the case of the Coketown population and the case of the little Gradgrinds? Surely, none of us in our sober senses and acquainted with figures, are to be told at this time of day, that one of the foremost elements in the existence of the Coketown working-people had been for scores of years, deliberately set at nought? That there was any Fancy in them demanding to be brought into healthy existence instead of struggling on in convulsions? That exactly in the ratio as they worked long and monotonously, the craving grew within them for some physical relief—some relaxation, encouraging good humour and good spirits, and giving them a vent—some recognized holiday, though it were but for an honest dance to a stirring band of music—some occasional light pie in which even M'Choakumchild had no finger—which craving must and would be satisfied aright, or must and would inevitably go wrong, until the laws of the Creation were repealed?

"This man lives at Pod's End, and I don't quite know Pod's End," said Mr. Gradgrind. "Which is it, Bounderby?"

Mr. Bounderby knew it was somewhere down town, but knew no more respecting it. So they stopped for a moment, looking about.

Almost as they did so, there came running round the corner of the street at a quick pace and with a frightened look, a girl whom Mr. Gradgrind recognized. "Halloa!" said he. "Stop! Where are you going! Stop!" Girl number twenty stopped then, palpitating, and made him a curtsey.

"Why are you tearing about the streets," said Mr. Gradgrind, "in this improper manner?"

"I was—I was run after, sir," the girl panted, "and I wanted to get away."

"Run after?" repeated Mr. Gradgrind. "Who would run after *you?*"

The question was unexpectedly and suddenly answered for her, by the colourless boy, Bitzer, who came round the corner with such blind speed and so little anticipating a stoppage on the pavement, that he brought himself up against Mr. Gradgrind's waistcoat and rebounded into the road.

"What do you mean, boy?" said Mr. Gradgrind. "What are you doing? How dare you dash against—everybody—in this manner?"

Bitzer picked up his cap, which the concussion had knocked off; and backing, and knuckling his forehead, pleaded that it was an accident.

"Was this boy running after you, Jupe?" asked Mr. Gradgrind.

"Yes, sir," said the girl reluctantly.

"No, I wasn't, sir," cried Bitzer. "Not till she run away from me. But the horse-riders never mind what they say, sir; they're famous for it. You know the horse-riders are famous for never minding what they say," addressing Sissy. "It's as well known in the town as—please, sir, as the multiplication table isn't known to the horse-riders." Bitzer tried Mr. Bounderby with this.

"He frightened me so," said the girl, "with his cruel faces!"

"Oh!" cried Bitzer. "Oh, An't you one of the rest! An't you a horse-rider! I never looked at her, sir. I asked her if she would know how to define a horse to-morrow, and offered to tell her again, and she ran away, and I ran after her, sir, that she might know how to answer when she was asked. You wouldn't have thought of saying such mischief if you hadn't been a horse-rider?"

"Her calling seems to be pretty well known among 'em," observed Mr. Bounderby. "You'd have had the whole school peeping in a row, in a week."

"Truly, I think so," returned his friend. "Bitzer, turn you about and take yourself home. Jupe, stay here a moment. Let me hear of your running in this manner any more, boy, and you will hear of me through the master of the school. You understand what I mean. Go along."

The boy stopped in his rapid blinking, knuckled his forehead again, glanced at Sissy, turned about, and retreated.

"Now, girl," said Mr. Gradgrind, "take this gentleman and me to your father's; we are going there. What have you got in that bottle you are carrying?"

"Gin," said Mr. Bounderby.

"Dear, no, sir! It's the nine oils."

"The what?" cried Mr. Bounderby.

"The nine oils, sir. To rub father with."

"Then," said Mr. Bounderby, with a loud short laugh, "what the devil do you rub your father with nine oils for?"

"It's what our people always use, sir, when they get any hurts in the ring," replied the girl, looking over her shoulder, to assure herself that her pursuer was gone. "They bruise themselves very bad sometimes."

"Serve 'em right," said Mr. Bounderby, "for being idle." She glanced up at his face, with mingled astonishment and dread.

"By George!" said Mr. Bounderby, "when I was four or five years younger than you, I had worse bruises upon me than ten oils, twenty oils, forty oils, would have rubbed off. I didn't get 'em by posture-making, but by being banged about. There was no rope-dancing for me; I danced on the bare ground and was larruped with the rope."

Mr. Gradgrind, though hard enough, was by no means so rough a man as Mr. Bounderby. His character was not unkind, all things considered; it might have been a very kind one indeed, if he had only made some round mistake in the arithmetic that balanced it, years ago. He said, in what he meant for a reassuring tone, as they turned down a narrow road, "And this is Pod's End; is it, Jupe?"

"This is it, sir, and—if you wouldn't mind, sir—this is the house."

She stopped, at twilight, at the door of a mean little public house, with dim red lights in it. As haggard and as shabby, as if, for want of custom, it had itself taken to drinking, and had gone the way all drunkards go, and was very near the end of it.

"It's only crossing the bar, sir, and up the stairs, if you wouldn't mind, and waiting there for a moment till I get a candle. If you should hear a dog, sir, it's only Merrylegs, and he only barks."

"Merrylegs and nine oils, eh!" said Mr. Bounderby, entering last with his metallic laugh. "Pretty well this, for a self-made man!"

CHAPTER SIX

SLEARY'S HORSEMANSHIP

THE name of the public house was the Pegasus's Arms. The Pegasus's legs might have been more to the purpose; but, underneath the winged horse upon the sign board, The Pegasus's Arms was inscribed in Roman letters. Beneath that inscription again, in a flowing scroll, the painter had touched off the lines:

Good malt makes good beer,
Walk in, and they'll draw it here;
Good wine makes good brandy,
Give us a call, and you'll find it handy.

The Pegasus's Arms

Framed and glazed upon the wall behind the dingy little bar, was another Pegasus—a theatrical one—with real gauze let in for his wings, golden stars stuck on all over him, and his ethereal harness made of red silk.

As it had grown too dusky without, to see the sign, and as it had not grown light enough within to see the picture, Mr. Gradgrind and Mr. Bounderby received no offence from these idealities. They followed the girl up some steep corner-stairs without meeting any one, and stopped in the dark while she went on for a candle. They expected every moment to hear Merrylegs give tongue, but the highly trained performing dog had not barked when the girl and the candle appeared together.

"Father is not in our room, sir," she said, with a face of great surprise. "If you wouldn't mind walking in, I'll find him directly."

They walked in; and Sissy, having set two chairs for them, sped away with a quick light step. It was a mean, shabbily furnished room, with a bed in it. The white night-cap, embellished with two peacock's feathers and a pigtail bolt upright, in which Signor Jupe had that very afternoon enlivened the varied performances with his chaste Shakspearean quips and retorts, hung upon a nail; but no other portion of his wardrobe, or other token of himself or his pursuits, was to be seen anywhere. As to Merrylegs, that respectable ancestor of the highly trained animal who went aboard the ark, might have been accidentally shut out of it, for any sign of a dog that was manifest to eye or ear in the Pegasus's Arms.

They heard the doors of rooms above, opening and shutting as Sissy went from one to another in quest of her father; and presently they heard voices expressing surprise. She came bounding down again in a great hurry, opened a battered and mangy old hair trunk, found it empty, and looked round with her hands clasped and her face full of terror.

"Father must have gone down to the Booth, Sir. I don't know why he should go there, but he must be there; I'll bring him in a minute!" She was gone directly, without her bonnet; with her long, dark, childish hair streaming behind her.

"What does she mean!" said Mr. Gradgrind. "Back in a minute? It's more than a mile off."

Before Mr. Bounderby could reply, a young man appeared at the door, and introducing himself with the words, "By your leaves, gentlemen!" walked in with his hands in his pockets. His face, close-shaven, thin, and sallow, was shaded by a great quantity of dark hair, brushed into a roll all round his head, and parted up the centre. His legs were very robust, but shorter than legs of good proportions should have been. His chest and back were as much too broad, as his legs were too short. He was dressed in a Newmarket coat and tight-fitting trousers; wore a shawl round his neck; smelt of lamp-oil, straw, orange-peel, horses' provender, and sawdust; and looked a most remarkable sort of Centaur, compounded of the stable and the play-house. Where the one began, and the other ended, nobody could have told with any precision. This gentleman was mentioned in the bills of the day as Mr. E. W. B. Childers, so justly celebrated for his daring vaulting act as the Wild Huntsman of the North American Prairies; in which popular performance, a diminutive boy with an old face, who now accompanied him, assisted as his infant son: being carried upside down over his father's shoulder, by one foot, and held by the crown of his head, heels upwards, in the palm of his father's hand, according to the violent paternal manner in which wild huntsmen may be observed to fondle their offspring. Made up with curls, wreaths, wings, white bismuth, and carmine, this hopeful young person soared into so pleasing a Cupid as to constitute the chief delight of the maternal part of the spectators; but in private, where his characteristics were a precocious cut-away coat and an extremely gruff voice, he became of the Turf, turfy.

"By your leaves, gentlemen," said Mr. E. W. B. Childers, glancing round the room. "It was you, I believe, that were wishing to see Jupe!"

"It was," said Mr. Gradgrind. "His daughter has gone to fetch him, but I can't wait; therefore, if you please, I will leave a message for him with you."

"You see, my friend," Mr. Bounderby put in, "we are the kind of people who know the value of time, and you are the kind of people who don't know the value of time."

"I have not," retorted Mr. Childers, after surveying him from head to foot, "the honour of knowing *you*,—but if you mean that you can make more money of your time than I can of mine, I should judge from your appearance, that you are about right."

"And when you have made it, you can keep it too, I should think," said Cupid.

"Kidderminster, stow that!" said Mr. Childers. (Master Kidderminster was Cupid's mortal name.)

Mr. Bounderby is instructed in terms of art "What does he come here cheeking us for, then?" cried Master Kidderminster, showing a very irascible temperament. "If you want to cheek us, pay your ochre at the doors and take it out."

"Kidderminster," said Mr. Childers, raising his voice, "stow that!—Sir," to Mr. Gradgrind, "I was addressing myself to you. You may or you may not be aware (for perhaps you have not been much in the audience), that Jupe has missed his tip very often, lately."

"Has—what has he missed?" asked Mr. Gradgrind, glancing at the potent Bounderby for assistance.

"Missed his tip."

"Offered at the Garters four times last night, and never done 'em once," said Master Kidderminster. "Missed his tip at the banners, too, and was loose in his ponging."

"Didn't do what he ought to do. Was short in his leaps and bad in his tumbling," Mr. Childers interpreted.

"Oh!" said Mr. Gradgrind, "that is tip, is it?"

"In a general way that's missing his tip," Mr. E. W. B. Childers answered.

"Nine oils, Merrylegs, missing tips, garters, banners, and ponging, eh!" ejaculated Bounderby, with his laugh of laughs. "Queer sort of company, too, for a man who has raised himself."

"Lower yourself, then," retorted Cupid. "Oh Lord! if you've raised yourself so high as all that comes to, let yourself down a bit."

"This is a very obtrusive lad!" said Mr. Gradgrind, turning, and knitting his brows on him.

"We'd have had a young gentleman to meet you, if we had known you were coming," retorted Master Kidderminster, nothing abashed. "It's a pity you don't have a bespeak, being so particular. You're on the Tight-Jeff, ain't you?"

"What does this unmannerly boy mean," asked Mr. Gradgrind, eyeing him in a sort of desperation, "by Tight-Jeff?"

"There! Get out, get out!" said Mr. Childers, thrusting his young friend from the room, rather in the prairie manner. Tight-Jeff or Slack-Jeff, it don't much signify: it's only tight-rope and slack-rope. You were going to give me a message for Jupe?"

"Yes, I was."

"Then," continued Mr. Childers, quickly, "my opinion is he will never receive it. Do you know much of him?"

"I never saw the man in my life."

"I doubt if you ever *will* see him now. It's pretty plain to me, he's off."

"Do you mean that he has deserted his daughter?"

"Ay! I mean," said Mr. Childers, with a nod, "that he has cut. He was goosed last night, he was goosed the night before last, he was goosed to-day. He has lately got in the way of being always goosed, and he can't stand it."

"Why has he been—so very much—Goosed?" asked Mr. Gradgrind, forcing the word out of himself, with great solemnity and reluctance.

"His joints are turning stiff, and he is getting used up," said Childers. "He has his points as a Cackler still, but he can't get a living out of *them*."

"A Cackler!" Bounderby repeated. "Here we go again!"

"A speaker, if the gentleman likes it better," said Mr. E. W. B. Childers, superciliously throwing the interpretation over his shoulder, and accompanying it with a shake of his long hair—which all shook at once. "Now, it's a remarkable fact, sir, that it cut that man deeper, to know that his daughter knew of his being goosed, than to go through with it."

"Good!" interrupted Mr. Bounderby. "This is good, Gradgrind! A man so fond of his daughter, that he runs away from her! This is devilish good! Ha! ha! Now, I'll tell you what, young man. I haven't always occupied my present station of life. I know what these things are. You may be astonished to hear it, but my mother ran away from *me*."

E. W. B. Childers replied pointedly, that he was not at all astonished to hear it.

"Very well," said Bounderby. "I was born in a ditch, and my mother ran away from me. Do I excuse her for it? No. Have I ever excused her for it? Not I. What do I call her for it? I call her probably the very worst woman that ever lived in the world, except my drunken grandmother. There's no family pride about me, there's no imaginative sentimental humbug about me. I call a spade a spade; and I call the mother of Josiah Bounderby of Coketown, without any fear or any favour, what I should call her if she had been the mother of Dick Jones of Wapping. So, with this man. He is a runaway rogue and a vagabond, that's what he is, in English."

"It's all the same to me what he is or what he is not, whether in English or whether in French," retorted Mr. E. W. B. Childers, facing about. "I am telling your friend what's the fact; if you don't like to hear it, you can avail yourself of the open air. You give it mouth enough, you do; but give it mouth in your own building at least," remonstrated E. W. B. with stern irony. "Don't give it mouth in this building, till you're called upon. You have got some building of your own, I dare say, now?"

"Perhaps so," replied Mr. Bounderby, rattling his money and laughing.

"Then give it mouth in your own building, will you, if you please?" said Childers. "Because this isn't a strong building, and too much of you might bring it down!"

Eyeing Mr. Bounderby from head to foot again, he turned from him, as from a man finally disposed of, to Mr. Gradgrind.

"Jupe sent his daughter out on an errand not an hour ago, and then was seen to slip out himself, with his hat over his eyes, and a bundle tied up in a handkerchief under his arm. She will never believe it of him, but he has cut away and left her."

"Pray," said Mr. Gradgrind, "why will she never believe it of him?"

"Because those two were one. Because they were never asunder.

Because, up to this time, he seemed to dote upon her," said Childers, taking a step or two to look into the empty trunk. Both Mr. Childers and Master Kidderminster walked in a curious manner; with their legs wider apart than the general run of men, and with a very knowing assumption of being stiff in the knees. This walk was common to all the male members of Sleary's company, and was understood to express, that they were always on horseback.

"Poor Sissy! He had better have apprenticed her," said Childers, giving his hair another shake, as he looked up from the empty box. "Now, he leaves her without anything to take to."

"It is creditable to you, who have never been apprenticed, to express that opinion," returned Mr. Gradgrind, approvingly.

"*I* never apprenticed? I was apprenticed when I was seven year old."

"Oh! Indeed?" said Mr. Gradgrind, rather resentfully, as having been defrauded of his good opinion. "I was not aware of its being the custom to apprentice young persons to——"

"Idleness," Mr. Bounderby put in with a loud laugh. "No, by the Lord Harry! Nor I!"

"Her father always had it in his head," resumed Childers, feigning unconsciousness of Mr. Bounderby's existence, "that she was to be taught the deuce-and-all of education. How it got into his head, I can't say; I can only say that it never got out. He has been picking up a bit of reading for her, here—and a bit of writing for her, there—and a bit of ciphering for her, somewhere else—these seven years."

Mr. E. W. B. Childers took one of his hands out of his pockets, stroked his face and chin, and looked, with a good deal of doubt and a little hope, at Mr. Gradgrind. From the first he had sought to conciliate that gentleman, for the sake of the deserted girl.

"When Sissy got into the school here," he pursued, "her father was as pleased as Punch. I couldn't altogether make out why, myself, as we were not stationary here, being but comers and goers anywhere. I suppose, however, he had this move in his mind —he was always half-cracked—and then considered her provided for. If you should happen to have looked in to-night, for the purpose of telling him that you were going to do her any little service," said Mr. Childers, stroking his face again, and repeating his look, "it would be very fortunate and well-timed; *very* fortunate and well-timed."

"On the contrary," returned Mr. Gradgrind. "I came to tell him that her connexions made her not an object for the school, and that she must not attend any more. Still, if her father really has left her, without any connivance on her part—Bounderby, let me have a word with you."

Upon this, Mr. Childers politely betook himself, with his equestrian walk, to the landing outside the door, and there stood stroking his face, and softly whistling. While thus engaged, he overheard such phrases in Mr. Bounderby's voice as "No. *I* say no. I advise you not. I say by no means." While, from Mr. Gradgrind, he heard in his much lower tone the words, "But even as an example to Louisa, of what this pursuit which has been the subject of a vulgar curiosity, leads to and ends in. Think of it, Bounderby, in that point of view."

Meanwhile, the various members of Sleary's company gradually gathered together from the upper regions, where they were quartered, and, from standing about, talking in low voices to one another and to Mr. Childers, gradually insinuated themselves and him into the room. There were two or three handsome young women among them, with their two or three husbands, and their two or three mothers, and their eight or nine little children, who did the fairy business when required. The father of one of the families was in the habit of balancing the father of another of the families on the top of a great pole; the father of a third family often made a pyramid of both those fathers, with Master Kidderminster for the apex, and himself for the base; all the fathers could dance upon rolling casks, stand upon bottles, catch knives and balls, twirl hand-basins, ride upon anything, jump over everything, and stick at nothing. All the mothers could (and did) dance, upon the slack wire and the tight-rope, and perform rapid acts on bare-backed steeds; none of them were at all particular in respect of showing their legs; and one of them, alone in a Greek chariot, drove six in hand into every town they came to. They all assumed to be mighty rakish and knowing, they were not very tidy in their private dresses, they

Sleary's company

were not at all orderly in their domestic arrangements, and the combined literature of the whole company would have produced but a poor letter on any subject. Yet there was a remarkable gentleness and childishness about these people, a special inaptitude for any kind of sharp practice, and an untiring readiness to help and pity one another, deserving often of as much respect, and always of as much generous construction, as the every-day virtues of any class of people in the world.

Last of all appeared Mr. Sleary: a stout man as already mentioned, with one fixed eye, and one loose eye, a voice (if it can be called so) like the efforts of a broken old pair of bellows, a flabby surface, and a muddled head which was never sober and never drunk.

"Thquire!" said Mr. Sleary, who was troubled with asthma, and whose breath came far too thick and heavy for the letter s, "Your thervant! Thith ith a bad piethe of bithnith, thith ith. You've heard of my Clown and hith dog being thuppothed to have morrithed?"

He addressed Mr. Gradgrind, who answered "Yes."

"Well, Thquire," he returned, taking off his hat, and rubbing the lining with his pocket-handkerchief, which he kept inside for the purpose. "Ith it your intenthion to do anything for the poor girl, Thquire?"

"I shall have something to propose to her when she comes back," said Mr. Gradgrind.

"Glad to hear it, Thquire. Not that I want to get rid of the child, any more than I want to thtand in her way. I'm willing to take her prentith, though at her age ith late. My voithe ith a little huthky, Thquire, and not eathy heard by them ath don't know me; but if you'd been chilled and heated, heated and chilled, chilled and heated in the ring when you wath young, ath often ath I have been, *your* voithe wouldn't have lathted out, Thquire, no more than mine."

"I dare say not," said Mr. Gradgrind.

"What thall it be, Thquire, while you wait? Thall it be Therry? Give it a name, Thquire!" said Mr. Sleary, with hospitable ease.

"Nothing for me, I thank you," said Mr. Gradgrind.

"Don't thay nothing, Thquire. What doth your friend thay? If you haven't took your feed yet, have a glath of bitterth."

Here his daughter Josephine—a pretty fair-haired girl of eighteen, who had been tied on a horse at two years old, and had made a will at twelve, which she always carried about with her, expressive of her dying desire to be drawn to the grave by the two piebald ponies—cried, "Father, hush! she has come back!" Then came Sissy Jupe, running into the room as she had run out of it. And when she saw them all assembled, and saw their looks, and saw no father there, she broke into a most deplorable cry, and took refuge on the bosom of the most accomplished tight-rope lady (herself in the family-way), who knelt down on the floor to nurse her, and to weep over her.

"Ith an infernal thame, upon my thoul it ith," said Sleary.

"O my dear father, my good kind father, where are you gone? You are gone to try to do me some good, I know! You are gone away for my sake, I am sure! And how miserable and helpless you will be without me, poor, poor father, until you come back!" It was so pathetic to hear her saying many things of this kind, with her face turned upward, and her arms stretched out as if she were trying to stop his departing shadow and embrace it, that no one spoke a word until Mr. Bounderby (growing impatient) took the case in hand.

"Now, good people all," said he, "this is wanton waste of time. Let the girl understand the fact. Let her take it from me, if you like, who have been run away from, myself. Here, what's your name! Your father has absconded—deserted you—and you mustn't expect to see him again as long as you live."

They cared so little for plain Fact, these people, and were in that advanced state of degeneracy on the subject, that instead of being impressed by the speaker's strong common sense, they took it in extraordinary dudgeon. The men muttered "Shame!" and the women "Brute!" and Sleary, in some haste, communicated the following hint, apart to Mr. Bounderby.

"I tell you what, Thquire. To thpeak plain to you, my opinion ith that you had better cut it thort, and drop it. They're a very good natur'd people, my people, but they're accuthtomed to be quick in their movementh; and if you don't act upon my advithe, I'm damned if I don't believe they'll pith you out o' winder."

Mr. Bounderby being restrained by this mild suggestion, Mr.

Gradgrind found an opening for his eminently practical exposition of the subject.

"It is of no moment," said he, "whether this person is to be expected back at any time, or the contrary. He is gone away, and there is no present expectation of his return. That, I believe, is agreed on all hands."

"Thath agreed, Thquire. Thtick to that!" From Sleary.

"Well then. I, who came here to inform the father of the poor girl, Jupe, that she could not be received at the school any more, in consequence of there being practical objections, into which I need not enter, to the reception there of the children of persons so employed, am prepared in these altered circumstances to make a proposal. I am willing to take charge of you, Jupe, and to educate you, and provide for you. The only condition (over and above your good behaviour) I make is, that you decide now, at once, whether to accompany me or remain here. Also, that if you accompany me now, it is understood that you communicate no more with any of your friends who are here present. These observations comprise the whole of the case."

"At the thame time," said Sleary, "I mutht put in my word, Thquire, tho that both thides of the banner may be equally theen. If you like, Thethilia, to be prentitht, you know the natur *Both sides of the banner* of the work and you know your companionth. Emma Gordon, in whothe lap you're a lying at prethent, would be a mother to you, and Joth'phine would be a thithter to you. I don't pretend to be of the angel breed myself, and I don't thay but what, when you mith'd your tip, you'd find me cut up rough, and thwear an oath or two at you. But what I thay, Thquire, ith, that good tempered or bad tempered, I never did a horthe a injury yet, no more than thwearing at him went, and that I don't expect I thall begin otherwithe at my time of life, with a rider. I never wath much of a Cackler, Thquire, and I have thed my thay."

The latter part of this speech was addressed to Mr. Gradgrind, who received it with a grave inclination of his head, and then remarked:

"The only observation I will make to you, Jupe, in the way of influencing your decision, is, that it is highly desirable to have a sound practical education, and that even your father himself (from what I understand) appears, on your behalf, to have known and felt that much."

The last words had a visible effect upon her. She stopped in her wild crying, a little detached herself from Emma Gordon, and turned her face full upon her patron. The whole company perceived the force of the change, and drew a long breath together, that plainly said, "she will go!"

"Be sure you know your own mind, Jupe," Mr. Gradgrind cautioned her; "I say no more. Be sure you know your own mind!"

"When father comes back," cried the girl, bursting into tears again after a minute's silence, "how will he ever find me if I go away!"

"You may be quite at ease," said Mr. Gradgrind, calmly; he worked out the whole matter like a sum: "you may be quite at ease, Jupe, on that score. In such a case, your father, I apprehend, must find out Mr.——"

"Thleary. Thath my name, Thquire. Not athamed of it. Known all over England, and alwayth paythe ith way."

"Must find out Mr. Sleary, who would then let him know where you went. I should have no power of keeping you against his wish, and he would have no difficulty, at any time, in finding Mr. Thomas Gradgrind of Coketown. I am well known."

"Well known," assented Mr. Sleary, rolling his loose eye. "You're one of the thort, Thquire, that keepth a prethiouth thight of money out of the houthe. But never mind that at prethent."

There was another silence; and then she exclaimed, sobbing with her hands before her face, "Oh give me my clothes, give me my clothes, and let me go away before I break my heart!"

The women sadly bestirred themselves to get the clothes together—it was soon done, for they were not many—and to pack them in a basket which had often travelled with them. Sissy sat all the time, upon the ground, still sobbing, and covering her eyes. Mr. Gradgrind and his friend Bounderby stood near the door, ready to take her away. Mr. Sleary stood in the middle of the room, with the male members of the company about him, exactly as he would have stood in the centre of the ring during his daughter Josephine's performance. He wanted nothing but his whip.

The basket packed in silence, they brought her bonnet to her, and smoothed her disordered hair, and put it on. Then they pressed about her, and bent over her in very natural attitudes, kissing and embracing her: and brought the children to take leave of her; and were a tender-hearted, simple, foolish set of women altogether.

"Now, Jupe," said Mr. Gradgrind. "If you are quite determined, come!"

But she had to take her farewell of the male part of the company yet, and every one of them had to unfold his arms (for they all assumed the professional attitude when they found themselves near Sleary), and give her a parting kiss—Master Kidderminster excepted, in whose young nature there was an original flavour of the misanthrope, who was also known to have harboured matrimonial views, and who moodily withdrew. Mr. Sleary was reserved until the last. Opening his arms wide he took her by both her hands, and would have sprung her up and down, after the riding-master manner of congratulating young ladies on their dismounting from a rapid act; but there was no rebound in Sissy, and she only stood before him crying.

"Good-bye, my dear!" said Sleary. "You'll make your fortun, I hope, and none of our poor folkth will ever trouble you, I'll pound it. I with your father hadn't taken hith dog with him; ith a ill-conwenienth to have the dog out of the billth. But on thecond thought, he wouldn't have performed without hith mahter, tho ith ath broad ath ith long!"

With that he regarded her attentively with his fixed eye, surveyed his company with his loose one, kissed her, shook his head, and handed her to Mr. Gradgrind as to a horse.

"There the ith, Thquire," he said, sweeping her with a professional glance as if she were being adjusted in her seat, "and the'll do you juththithe. Good-bye, Thethilia!"

"Good-bye, Cecilia!" "Good-bye, Sissy!" "God bless you, dear!" In a variety of voices from all the room.

But the riding-master eye had observed the bottle of the nine oils in her bosom, and he now interposed with "Leave the bottle, my dear; ith large to carry; it will be of no uthe to you now. Give it to me!"

"No, no!" she said, in another burst of tears. "Oh, no! Pray let me keep it for father till he comes back! He will want it when he comes back. He had never thought of going away, when he sent me for it. I must keep it for him, if you please!"

"Tho be it, my dear. (You thee how it ith, Thquire!) Farewell, Thethilia! My latht wordth to you ith thith, Thtick to the termth of your engagement, be obedient to the Thquire, and forget uth. But if, when you're grown up and married and well off, you come upon any horthe-riding ever, don't be hard upon it, don't be croth with it, give it a Bethpeak if you can, and think you might do wurth. People must be amuthed, Thquire, thomehow," continued Sleary, rendered more pursy than ever, by so much talking; "they can't be alwayth a working, nor yet they can't be alwayth a learning. Make the betht of uth; not the wurtht. I've got my living out of the horthe-riding all my life, I know; but I conthider that I lay down the philothophy of the thubject when I thay to you, Thquire, make the betht of uth: not the wurtht!"

The Sleary philosophy was propounded as they went downstairs; and the fixed eye of Philosophy—and its rolling eye, too—soon lost the three figures and the basket in the darkness of the street.

CHAPTER SEVEN

MRS. SPARSIT

A lady housekeeper

Mr. Bounderby being a bachelor, an elderly lady presided over his establishment, in consideration of a certain annual stipend. Mrs. Sparsit was this lady's name; and she was a prominent figure in attendance on Mr. Bounderby's car, as it rolled along in triumph with the Bully of humility inside.

For, Mrs. Sparsit had not only seen different days, but was highly connected. She had a great aunt living in these very times called Lady Scadgers. Mr. Sparsit, deceased, of whom she was the relict, had been by the mother's side what Mrs. Sparsit still called "a Powler." Strangers of limited information and dull apprehension were sometimes observed not to know what a Powler was, and even to appear uncertain whether it might be a business, or a political party, or a profession of faith. The better class of minds, however, did not need to be informed that the Powlers were an ancient stock, who could trace themselves so exceedingly far back that it was not surprising if they sometimes lost themselves—which they had rather frequently done, as respected horse-flesh, blind-hookey, Hebrew monetary transactions, and the Insolvent Debtors' Court.

The late Mr. Sparsit, being by the mother's side a Powler, married this lady, being by the father's side a Scadgers. Lady Scadgers (an immensely fat old woman, with an inordinate appetite for butcher's meat, and a mysterious leg which had now refused to get out of bed for fourteen years) contrived the marriage, at a period when Sparsit was just of age, and chiefly noticeable for a slender body, weakly supported on two long slim props, and surmounted by no head worth mentioning. He inherited a fair fortune from his uncle, but owed it all before he came into it, and spent it twice over immediately afterwards. Thus, when he died, at twenty-four (the scene of his decease, Calais, and the cause, brandy), he did not leave his widow, from whom he had been separated soon after the honeymoon, in affluent circumstances. That bereaved lady, fifteen years older than he, fell presently at deadly feud with her only relative, Lady Scadgers; and, partly to spite her ladyship, and partly to maintain herself, went out at a salary. And here she was now, in her elderly days, with the Coriolanian style of nose and the dense black eyebrows which had captivated Sparsit, making Mr. Bounderby's tea as he took his breakfast.

If Bounderby had been a Conqueror, and Mrs. Sparsit a captive Princess whom he took about as a feature in his state-processions, he could not have made a greater flourish with her than he habitually did. Just as it belonged to his boastfulness to depreciate his own extraction, so it belonged to it to exalt Mrs. Sparsit's. In the measure that he would not allow his own youth to have been attended by a single favourable circumstance, he brightened Mrs. Sparsit's juvenile career with every possible advantage, and showered waggon-loads of early roses all over that lady's path. "And yet, sir," he would say, "how does it turn out after all? Why, here she is at a hundred a year (I give her a hundred, which she is pleased to term handsome), keeping the house of Josiah Bounderby of Coketown!"

Nay, he made this foil of his so very widely known, that third parties took it up, and handled it on some occasions with considerable briskness. It was one of the most exasperating attributes of Bounderby, that he not only sang his own praises but stimulated other men to sing them. There was a moral infection of clap-trap in him. Strangers, modest enough elsewhere, started up at dinners in Coketown, and boasted, in quite a rampant way, of Bounderby. They made him out to be the Royal Arms, the Union-Jack, Magna Charta, John Bull, Habeas Corpus, the Bill of Rights, An Englishman's house is his castle, Church and State, and God save the Queen, all put together. And as often (and it was very often) as an orator of this kind brought into his peroration,

> "Princes and lords may flourish or may fade,
> A breath can make them, as a breath has made,"

—it was, for certain, more or less understood among the company that he had heard of Mrs. Sparsit.

"Mr. Bounderby," said Mrs. Sparsit, "you are unusually slow, sir, with your breakfast this morning."

"Why, ma'am," he returned, "I am thinking about Tom Gradgrind's whim;" Tom Gradgrind, for a bluff independent manner of speaking—as if somebody were always endeavouring to bribe him with immense sums to say Thomas, and he wouldn't; "Tom Gradgrind's whim, ma'am, of bringing up the tumbling-girl."

"The girl is now waiting to know," said Mrs. Sparsit, "whether she is to go straight to the school, or up to the Lodge."

"She must wait, ma'am," answered Bounderby, "till I know myself. We shall have Tom Gradgrind down here presently,

I suppose. If he should wish her to remain here a day or two longer, of course she can, ma'am."

"Of course she can if you wish it, Mr. Bounderby."

"I told him I would give her a shake-down here, last night, in order that he might sleep on it before he decided to let her have any association with Louisa."

"Indeed, Mr. Bounderby? Very thoughtful of you!" Mrs. Sparsit's Coriolanian nose underwent a slight expansion of the nostrils, and her black eyebrows contracted as she took a sip of tea.

"It's tolerably clear to *me*," said Bounderby, "that the little puss can get small good out of such companionship."

"Are you speaking of young Miss Gradgrind, Mr. Bounderby?"

"Yes, ma'am, I'm speaking of Louisa."

"Your observation being limited to 'little puss,'" said Mrs. Sparsit, "and there being two little girls in question, I did not know which might be indicated by that expression."

"Louisa," repeated Mr. Bounderby. "Louisa, Louisa."

"You are quite another father to Louisa, sir." Mrs. Sparsit took a little more tea; and, as she bent her again contracted eyebrows over her steaming cup, rather looked as if her classical counte-nance were invoking the infernal gods.

"If you had said I was another father to Tom—young Tom, I mean, not my friend Tom Gradgrind—you might have been nearer the mark. I am going to take young Tom into my office. Going to have him under my wing, ma'am."

"Indeed? Rather young for that, is he not, sir?" Mrs. Sparsit's "sir," in addressing Mr. Bounderby, was a word of ceremony, rather exacting consideration for herself in the use, than honour-ing him.

"I'm not going to take him at once; he is to finish his educational cramming before then," said Bounderby. "By the Lord Harry, he'll have enough of it, first and last! He'd open his eyes, that boy would, if he knew how empty of learning *my* young maw was, at his time of life." Which, by the by, he probably did know, for he had heard of it often enough. "But it's extraordinary the difficulty I have on scores of such subjects, in speaking to any one on equal terms. Here, for example, I have been speaking to you this morning about tumblers. Why, what do *you* know about tumblers? At the time when, to have been a tumbler in the mud of the streets, would have been a godsend to me, a prize in the lottery to me, you were at the Italian Opera. You were coming out of the Italian Opera, ma'am, in white satin and jewels, a blaze of splendour, when I hadn't a penny to buy a link to light you."

Gentility and Humility

"I certainly, sir," returned Mrs. Sparsit, with a dignity serenely mournful, "was familiar with the Italian Opera at a very early age."

"Egad, ma'am, so was I," said Bounderby, "—with the wrong side of it. A hard bed the pavement of its Arcade used to make, I assure you. People like you, ma'am, accustomed from infancy to lie on down feathers, have no idea *how* hard a paving-stone is, without trying it. No, no, it's of no use my talking to *you* about tumblers. I should speak of foreign dancers, and the West End of London, and May Fair, and lords and ladies and honourables."

"I trust, sir," rejoined Mrs. Sparsit, with decent resignation, "it is not necessary that you should do anything of that kind. I hope I have learnt how to accommodate myself to the changes of life. If I have acquired an interest in hearing of your instructive experiences, and can scarcely hear enough of them, I claim no merit for that, since I believe it is a general sentiment."

"Well, ma'am," said her patron, "perhaps some people may be pleased to say that they do like to hear, in his own unpolished way, what Josiah Bounderby, of Coketown, has gone through. But you must confess that you were born in the lap of luxury, yourself. Come, ma'am, you know you were born in the lap of luxury."

"I do not, sir," returned Mrs. Sparsit with a shake of her head, "deny it."

Mr. Bounderby was obliged to get up from table, and stand with his back to the fire, looking at her; she was such an enhancement of his position.

"And you were in crack society. Devilish high society," he said, warming his legs.

"It is true, sir," returned Mrs. Sparsit, with an affectation of humility the very opposite of his, and therefore in no danger of jostling it.

"You were in the tiptop fashion, and all the rest of it," said Mr. Bounderby.

"Yes, sir," returned Mrs. Sparsit, with a kind of social widowhood upon her. "It is unquestionably true."

Mr. Bounderby, bending himself at the knees, literally embraced his legs in his great satisfaction and laughed aloud. Mr. and Miss Gradgrind being then announced, he received the former with a shake of the hand, and the latter with a kiss.

"Can Jupe be sent here, Bounderby?" asked Mr. Gradgrind.

"Certainly." So Jupe was sent there. On coming in, she curtseyed to Mr. Bounderby, and to his friend Tom Gradgrind, and also to Louisa; but in her confusion unluckily omitted Mrs. Sparsit. Observing this, the blustrous Bounderby had the following remarks to make:

"Now, I tell you what, my girl. The name of that lady by the teapot, is Mrs. Sparsit. That lady acts as mistress of this house, and she is a highly connected lady. Consequently, if ever you come again into any room in this house, you will make a short stay in it if you don't behave towards that lady in your most respectful manner. Now, I don't care a button what you do to *me*, because I don't affect to be anybody. So far from having high connexions I have no connexions at all, and I come of the scum of the earth. But towards that lady, I do care what you do; and you shall do what is deferential and respectful, or you shall not come here."

"I hope, Bounderby," said Mr. Gradgrind, in a conciliatory voice, "that this was merely an oversight."

"My friend Tom Gradgrind suggests, Mrs. Sparsit," said Bounderby, "that this was merely an oversight. Very likely. However, as you are aware, ma'am, I don't allow of even oversights towards you."

"You are very good indeed, sir," returned Mrs. Sparsit, shaking her head with her State humility. "It is not worth speaking of."

Sissy, who all this time had been faintly excusing herself with tears in her eyes, was now waved over by the master of the house to Mr. Gradgrind. She stood looking intently at him, and Louisa stood coldly by, with her eyes upon the ground, while he proceeded thus:

"Jupe, I have made up my mind to take you into my house;

and, when you are not in attendance at the school, to employ you about Mrs. Gradgrind, who is rather an invalid. I have explained to Miss Louisa—this is Miss Louisa—the miserable but natural end of your late career; and you are to expressly understand that the whole of that subject is past, and is not to be referred to any more. From this time you begin your history. You are, at present, ignorant, I know."

"Yes, sir, very," she answered, curtseying.

"I shall have the satisfaction of causing you to be strictly educated; and you will be a living proof to all who come into communication with you, of the advantages of the training you will receive. You will be reclaimed and formed. You have been in the habit now of reading to your father, and those people I found you among, I dare say?" said Mr. Gradgrind, beckoning her nearer to him before he said so, and dropping his voice.

"Only to father and Merrylegs, sir. At least I mean to father, when Merrylegs was always there."

"Never mind Merrylegs, Jupe," said Mr. Gradgrind, with a passing frown. "I don't ask about him. I understand you to have been in the habit of reading to your father?"

"O yes, sir, thousands of times. They were the happiest—O, of all the happy times we had together, sir!"

It was only now when her sorrow broke out, that Louisa looked at her.

"And what," asked Mr. Gradgrind, in a still lower voice, "did you read to your father, Jupe?"

"About the Fairies, sir, and the Dwarf, and the Hunchback, and the Genies," she sobbed out; "and about——"

"Hush!" said Mr. Gradgrind, "that is enough. Never breathe a word of such destructive nonsense any more. Bounderby, this is a case for rigid training, and I shall observe it with interest."

"Well," returned Mr. Bounderby, "I have given you my opinion already, and I shouldn't do as you do. But, very well, very well. Since you are bent upon it, *very* well!"

So, Mr. Gradgrind and his daughter took Cecilia Jupe off with them to Stone Lodge, and on the way Louisa never spoke one word, good or bad. And Mr. Bounderby went about his daily pursuits. And Mrs. Sparsit got behind her eyebrows and meditated in the gloom of the retreat, all the evening.

CHAPTER EIGHT

NEVER WONDER

LET us strike the key-note again, before pursuing the tune.

When she was half-a-dozen years younger, Louisa had been overheard to begin a conversation with her brother one day, by saying "Tom, I wonder"—upon which Mr. Gradgrind, who was the person overhearing, stepped forth into the light and said, "Louisa, never wonder!"

Herein lay the spring of the mechanical art and mystery of educating the reason without stooping to the cultivation of the sentiments and affections. Never wonder. By means of addition, subtraction, multiplication, and division, settle everything somehow, and never wonder. Bring to me, says M'Choakumchild, yonder baby just able to walk, and I will engage that it shall never wonder.

Now, besides very many babies just able to walk, there happened to be in Coketown a considerable population of babies who had been walking against time towards the infinite world, twenty, thirty, forty, fifty years and more. These portentous infants being alarming creatures to stalk about in any human society, the eighteen denominations incessantly scratched one another's faces and pulled one another's hair by way of agreeing on the steps to be taken for their improvement—which they never did; a surprising circumstance, when the happy adaptation of the means to the end is considered. Still, although they differed in every other particular, conceivable and inconceivable (especially inconceivable), they were pretty well united on the point that these unlucky infants were never to wonder. Body number one, said they must take everything on trust. Body number two, said they must take everything on political economy. Body number three, wrote leaden little books for them, showing how the good grown-up baby invariably got to the Savings-bank, and the bad grown-up baby invariably got transported. Body number four, under dreary pretences of being droll (when it was very melancholy indeed), made the shallowest pretences of concealing pitfalls of knowledge, into which it was the duty of these babies to be smuggled and inveigled. But, all the bodies agreed that they were never to wonder.

There was a library in Coketown, to which general access was easy. Mr. Gradgrind greatly tormented his mind about what the people read in this library: a point whereon little rivers of tabular statements periodically flowed into the howling ocean of tabular statements, which no diver ever got to any depth in and came up sane. It was a disheartening circumstance, but a melancholy fact, that even these readers persisted in wondering. They wondered about human nature, human passions, human hopes and fears, the struggles, triumphs and defeats, the cares and joys and sorrows, the lives and deaths of common men and women! They sometimes, after fifteen hours' work, sat down to read mere fables about men and women, more or less like themselves, and about children, more or less like their own. They took De Foe to their bosoms, instead of Euclid, and seemed to be on the whole more comforted by Goldsmith than by Cocker. Mr. Gradgrind was for ever working, in print and out of print, at this eccentric sum, and he never could make out how it yielded this unaccountable product.

Coketown literature

"I am sick of my life, Loo. I hate it altogether, and I hate everybody except you," said the unnatural young Thomas Gradgrind in the hair-cutting chamber at twilight.

"You don't hate Sissy, Tom?"

"I hate to be obliged to call her Jupe. And she hates me," said Tom, moodily.

"No, she does not, Tom, I am sure!"

"She must," said Tom. "She must just hate and detest the whole set-out of us. They'll bother her head off, I think, before they have done with her. Already she's getting as pale as wax, and as heavy as—I am."

Young Thomas expressed these sentiments sitting astride of a chair before the fire, with his arms on the back, and his sulky face on his arms. His sister sat in the darker corner by the fireside, now looking at him, now looking at the bright sparks as they dropped upon the hearth.

"As to me," said Tom, tumbling his hair all manner of ways with his sulky hands, "I am a Donkey, that's what I am. I am as obstinate as one, I am more stupid than one, I get as much pleasure as one, and I should like to kick like one."

"Not me, I hope, Tom?"

"No, Loo; I wouldn't hurt *you*. I made an exception of you at first. I don't know what this—jolly old—Jaundiced Jail," Tom had paused to find a sufficiently complimentary and expressive name for the parental roof, and seemed to relieve his mind for a moment by the strong alliteration of this one, "would be without you."

"Indeed, Tom? Do you really and truly say so?"

"Why, of course I do. What's the use of talking about it!" returned Tom, chafing his face on his coat-sleeve, as if to mortify his flesh, and have it in unison with his spirit.

"Because, Tom," said his sister, after silently watching the sparks awhile, "as I get older, and nearer growing up, I often sit wondering here, and think how unfortunate it is for me that I can't reconcile you to home better than I am able to do. I don't know what other girls know. I can't play to you, or sing to you. I can't talk to you so as to lighten your mind, for I never see any amusing sights or read any amusing books that it would be a pleasure or a relief to you to talk about, when you are tired."

"Well, no more do I. I am as bad as you in that respect; and I am a Mule too, which you're not. If father was determined to make me either a Prig or a Mule, and I am not a Prig, why, it stands to reason, I must be a Mule. And so I am," said Tom, desperately.

"It's a great pity," said Louisa, after another pause, and speaking thoughtfully out of her dark corner, "it's a great pity, Tom. It's very unfortunate for both of us."

"Oh! You," said Tom; "you are a girl, Loo, and a girl comes out of it better than a boy does. I don't miss anything in you. You are the only pleasure I have—you can brighten even this place—and you can always lead me as you like."

"You are a dear brother, Tom; and while you think I can do

such things, I don't so much mind knowing better. Though I do know better, Tom, and am very sorry for it." She came and kissed him, and went back into her corner again.

"I wish I could collect all the Facts we hear so much about," said Tom, spitefully setting his teeth, "and all the Figures, and all the people who found them out: and I wish I could put a thousand barrels of gunpowder under them, and blow them all up together! However, when I go to live with old Bounderby, I'll have my revenge."

"Your revenge, Tom?"

"I mean, I'll enjoy myself a little, and go about and see something, and hear something. I'll recompense myself for the way in which I have been brought up."

"But don't disappoint yourself beforehand, Tom. Mr. Bounderby thinks as father thinks, and is a great deal rougher, and not half so kind."

"Oh!" said Tom, laughing; "I don't mind that. I shall very well know how to manage and smooth old Bounderby!"

Their shadows were defined upon the wall, but those of the high presses in the room were all blended together on the wall and on the ceiling, as if the brother and sister were overhung by a dark cavern. Or, a fanciful imagination—if such treason could have been there—might have made it out to be the shadow of their subject, and of its lowering association with their future.

"What is your great mode of smoothing and managing, Tom? Is it a secret?"

Unmanageable thoughts "Oh!" said Tom, "if it is a secret, it's not far off. It's you. You are his little pet, you are his favourite; he'll do anything for you. When he says to me what I don't like, I shall say to him, 'My sister Loo will be hurt and disappointed, Mr. Bounderby. She always used to tell me she was sure you would be easier with me than this.' That'll bring him about, or nothing will."

After waiting for some answering remark, and getting none, Tom wearily relapsed into the present time, and twined himself yawning round and about the rails of his chair, and rumpled his head more and more, until he suddenly looked up, and asked:

"Have you gone to sleep, Loo?"

"No, Tom. I am looking at the fire."

"You seem to find more to look at in it than ever I could find," said Tom. "Another of the advantages, I suppose, of being a girl."

"Tom," inquired his sister, slowly, and in a curious tone, as if she were reading what she asked in the fire, and it were not quite plainly written there, "do you look forward with any satisfaction to this change to Mr. Bounderby's?"

"Why, there's one thing to be said of it," returned Tom, pushing his chair from him, and standing up; "it will be getting away from home."

"There is one thing to be said of it," Louisa repeated in her former curious tone; "it will be getting away from home. Yes."

"Not but what I shall be very unwilling, both to leave you, Loo, and to leave you here. But I must go, you know, whether I like it or not; and I had better go where I can take with me some advantage of your influence, than where I should lose it altogether. Don't you see?"

"Yes, Tom."

The answer was so long in coming, though there was no indecision in it, that Tom went and leaned on the back of her chair, to contemplate the fire which so engrossed her, from her point of view, and see what he could make of it.

"Except that it is a fire," said Tom, "it looks to me as stupid and blank as everything else looks. What do you see in it? Not a circus?"

"I don't see anything in it, Tom, particularly. But since I have been looking at it, I have been wondering about you and me, grown up."

"Wondering again!" said Tom.

"I have such unmanageable thoughts," returned his sister, "that they *will* wonder."

"Then I beg of you, Louisa," said Mrs. Gradgrind, who had opened the door without being heard, "to do nothing of that description, for goodness' sake, you inconsiderate girl, or I shall never hear the last of it from your father. And, Thomas, it is really shameful, with my poor head continually wearing me out, that a boy brought up as you have been, and whose education has cost what yours has, should be found encouraging his sister to wonder, when he knows his father has expressly said that she is not to do it."

Louisa denied Tom's participation in the offence; but her mother stopped her with the conclusive answer, "Louisa, don't tell me, in my state of health; for unless you had been encouraged, it is morally and physically impossible that you could have done it."

"I was encouraged by nothing, mother, but by looking at the red sparks dropping out of the fire, and whitening and dying. It made me think, after all, how short my life would be, and how little I could hope to do in it."

"Nonsense!" said Mrs. Gradgrind, rendered almost energetic. "Nonsense! Don't stand there and tell me such stuff, Louisa, to my face, when you know very well that if it was ever to reach your father's ears I should never hear the last of it. After all the trouble that has been taken with you! After the lectures you have attended, and the experiments you have seen! After I have heard you myself, when the whole of my right side has been benumbed, going on with your master about combustion, and calcination, and calorification, and I may say every kind of ation that could drive a poor invalid distracted, to hear you talking in this absurd way about sparks and ashes! I wish," whimpered Mrs. Gradgrind, taking a chair, and discharging her strongest point before succumbing under these mere shadows of facts, "yes, I really *do* wish that I had never had a family, and then you would have known what it was to do without me!"

CHAPTER NINE

SISSY'S PROGRESS

SISSY JUPE had not an easy time of it, between Mr. M'Choak-umchild and Mrs. Gradgrind, and was not without strong impulses, in the first months of her probation, to run away. It hailed facts all day long so very hard, and life in general was opened to her as such a closely ruled ciphering-book, that assuredly she would have run away, but for only one restraint.

It is lamentable to think of; but this restraint was the result of no arithmetical process, was self-imposed in defiance of all calculation, and went dead against any table of probabilities that any Actuary would have drawn up from the premises. The girl believed that her father had not deserted her; she lived in the hope that he would come back, and in the faith that he would be made the happier by her remaining where she was.

The wretched ignorance with which Jupe clung to this consolation, rejecting the superior comfort of knowing, on a sound arithmetical basis, that her father was an unnatural vagabond, filled Mr. Gradgrind with pity. Yet, what was to be done? M'Choakumchild reported that she had a very dense head for figures; that, once possessed with a general idea of the globe, she took the smallest conceivable interest in its exact measurements; that she was extremely slow in the acquisition of dates, unless some pitiful incident happened to be connected therewith; that she would burst into tears on being required (by the mental process) immediately to name the cost of two hundred and forty-seven muslin caps at fourteen-pence half-penny; that she was as low down, in the school, as low could be; that after eight weeks of induction into the elements of Political Economy, she had only yesterday been set right by a prattler three feet high, for returning to the question, "What is the first principle of this science?" the absurd answer, "To do unto others as I would that they should do unto me."

Mr. Gradgrind observed, shaking his head, that all this was very bad; that it showed the necessity of infinite grinding at the mill of knowledge, as per system, schedule, blue book, report, and tabular statements A to Z; and that Jupe "must be kept to it." So Jupe was kept to it, and became low-spirited, but no wiser.

"It would be a fine thing to be you, Miss Louisa!" she said, one night, when Louisa had endeavoured to make her perplexities for next day something clearer to her.

"Do you think so?"

'I should know so much, Miss Louisa. All that is difficult to me now, would be so easy then."

'You might not be the better for it, Sissy."

Sissy submitted, after a little hesitation, "I should not be the worse, Miss Louisa." To which Miss Louisa answered, "I don't know that."

There had been so little communication between these two —both because life at Stone Lodge went monotonously round like a piece of machinery which discouraged human interference, and because of the prohibition relative to Sissy's past career—that they were still almost strangers. Sissy, with her dark eyes wonderingly directed to Louisa's face, was uncertain whether to say more or to remain silent.

"You are more useful to my mother, and more pleasant with her than I can ever be," Louisa resumed. "You are pleasanter to yourself, than *I* am to *my*self."

"But, if you please, Miss Louisa," Sissy pleaded, "I am—O so stupid!"

Louisa, with a brighter laugh than usual, told her she would be wiser by-and-by.

"You don't know," said Sissy, half crying, "what a stupid girl I am. All through school hours I make mistakes. Mr. and Mrs. M'Choakumchild call me up, over and over again, regularly to make mistakes. I can't help them. They seem to come natural to me."

"Mr. and Mrs. M'Choakumchild never make any mistakes themselves, I suppose, Sissy?"

"O no!" she eagerly returned. "They know everything."

"Tell me some of your mistakes."

"I am almost ashamed," said Sissy, with reluctance. "But to-day, for instance, Mr. M'Choakumchild was explaining to us about Natural Prosperity."

"National, I think it must have been," observed Louisa.

"Yes, it was.—But isn't it the same?" she timidly asked.

"You had better say, National, as he said so," returned Louisa, with her dry reserve.

"National Prosperity. And he said, Now, this schoolroom is a Nation. And in this nation, there are fifty millions of money. Isn't this a prosperous nation? Girl number twenty, isn't this a prosperous nation, and a'n't you in a thriving state?"

"What did you say?" asked Louisa.

"Miss Louisa, I said I didn't know. I thought I couldn't know whether it was a prosperous nation or not, and whether I was in a thriving state or not, unless I knew who had got the money, and whether any of it was mine. But that had nothing to do with it. It was not in the figures at all," said Sissy, wiping her eyes.

"That was a great mistake of yours," observed Louisa.

"Yes, Miss Louisa, I know it was, now. Then Mr. M'Choakumchild said he would try me again. And he said, This schoolroom is an immense town, and in it there are a million of inhabitants, and only five-and-twenty are starved to death in the streets, in the course of a year. What is your remark on that proportion? And my remark was—for I couldn't think of a better one—that I thought it must be just as hard upon those who were starved, whether the others were a million, or a million million. And that was wrong, too."

"Of course it was."

"Then Mr. M'Choakumchild said he would try me once more. And he said, Here are the stutterings——"

"Statistics," said Louisa.

"Yes, Miss Louisa—they always remind me of *Statistics* stutterings, and that's another of my mistakes— of accidents upon the sea. And I find (Mr. M'Choakumchild said) that in a given time a hundred thousand persons went to sea on long voyages, and only five hundred of them were drowned or burnt to death. What is the percentage? And I said, Miss;" here Sissy fairly sobbed as confessing with extreme contrition to her greatest error; "I said it was nothing."

"Nothing, Sissy?"

"Nothing, Miss—to the relations and friends of the people who were killed. I shall never learn," said Sissy. "And the worst of all is, that although my poor father wished me so much to learn, and although I am so anxious to learn, because he wished me to, I am afraid I don't like it."

Louisa stood looking at the pretty modest head, as it drooped abashed before her, until it was raised again to glance at her face. Then she asked:

"Did your father know so much himself, that he wished you to be well taught too, Sissy?"

Sissy hesitated before replying, and so plainly showed her sense that they were entering on forbidden ground, that Louisa added.

"No one hears us; and if any one did, I am sure no harm could be found in such an innocent question."

"No, Miss Louisa," answered Sissy, upon this encouragement. shaking her head; "father knows very little indeed. It's as much as he can do to write; and it's more than people in general can do to read his writing. Though it's plain to *me*."

"Your mother!"

"Father says she was quite a scholar. She died when I was born. She was," Sissy made the terrible communication nervously, "she was a dancer."

"Did your father love her?" Louisa asked these questions with a strong, wild, wandering interest peculiar to her; an interest gone astray like a banished creature, and hiding in solitary places.

"O yes! As dearly as he loves me. Father loved me, first, for her sake. He carried me about with him when I was quite a baby. We have never been asunder from that time."

"Yet he leaves you now, Sissy?"

"Only for my good. Nobody understands him as I do; nobody knows him as I do. When he left me for my good—he never would have left me for his own—I know he was almost broken-hearted with the trial. He will not be happy for a single minute, till he comes back."

"Tell me more about him," said Louisa, "I will never ask you again. Where did you live?"

"We travelled about the country, and had no fixed place to live in. Father's a," Sissy whispered the awful word, "a clown."

"To make the people laugh?" said Louisa, with a nod of intelligence.

"Yes. But they wouldn't laugh sometimes, and then father cried. Lately, they very often wouldn't laugh, and he used to come home despairing. Father's not like most. Those who didn't know him as well as I do, and didn't love him as dearly as I do, might believe he was not quite right. Sometimes they played tricks upon him; but they never knew how he felt them, and shrunk up, when he was alone with me. He was far, far timider than they thought!"

"And you were his comfort through everything?"

She nodded, with the tears rolling down her face. "I hope so, and father said I was. It was because he grew so scared and trembling, and because he felt himself to be a poor, weak, ignorant, helpless man (those used to be his words), that he wanted me so much to know a great deal, and be different from him. I used to read to him to cheer his courage, and he was very fond of that. They were wrong books—I am never to speak of them here—but we didn't know there was any harm in them."

"And he liked them?" said Louisa, with a searching gaze on Sissy all this time.

"O very much! They kept him, many times, from what did him real harm. And often and often of a night, he used to forget all his troubles in wondering whether the Sultan would let the lady go on with the story, or would have her head cut off before it was finished."

"And your father was always kind? To the last?" asked Louisa; contravening the great principle, and wondering very much.

"Always, always!" returned Sissy, clasping her hands. "Kinder and kinder than I can tell. He *Sissy's story* was angry only one night, and that was not to me, but Merrylegs. Merrylegs," she whispered the awful fact, "is his performing dog."

"Why was he angry with the dog?" Louisa demanded.

"Father, soon after they came home from performing, told Merrylegs to jump up on the backs of the two chairs and stand across them—which is one of his tricks. He looked at father and didn't do it at once. Everything of father's had gone wrong that night, and he hadn't pleased the public at all. He cried out that the very dog knew he was failing, and had no compassion on him. Then he beat the dog, and I was frightened, and said, 'Father, father! Pray don't hurt the creature who is so fond of you! O Heaven forgive you, father, stop!' And he stopped, and the dog was bloody, and father lay down crying on the floor with the dog in his arms, and the dog licked his face."

Louisa saw that she was sobbing; and going to her, kissed her, took her hand, and sat down beside her.

"Finish by telling me how your father left you, Sissy. Now that I have asked you so much, tell me the end. The blame, if there is any blame, is mine, not yours."

"Dear Miss Louisa," said Sissy, covering her eyes, and sobbing yet; "I came home from the school that afternoon, and found poor father just come home too, from the booth. And he sat rocking himself over the fire, as if he was in pain. And I said, 'Have you hurt yourself, father?' (as he did sometimes, like they all did), and he said, 'A little, my darling.' And when I came to stoop down and look up at his face, I saw that he was crying. The more I spoke to him, the more he hid his face; and at first he shook all over, and said nothing but 'My darling;' and 'My love!'"

Here Tom came lounging in, and stared at the two with a coolness not particularly savouring of interest in anything but himself, and not much of that at present.

"I am asking Sissy a few questions, Tom," observed his sister. "You have no occasion to go away; but don't interrupt us for a moment, Tom dear."

"Oh! very well!" returned Tom. "Only father has brought old Bounderby home, and I want you to come into the drawing-room Because if you come, there's a good chance of old Bounderby's asking me to dinner; and if you don't, there's none."

"I'll come directly."

"I'll wait for you," said Tom, "to make sure."

Sissy resumed in a lower voice. "At last poor father said that he had given no satisfaction again, and never did give any satisfaction now, and that he was a shame and disgrace, and I should have done better without him all along. I said all the affectionate things to him that came into my heart, and presently he was quiet and I sat down by him, and told him all about the school and everything that had been said and done there. When I had no more left to tell, he put his arms round my neck, and kissed me a great many times. Then he asked me to fetch some of the stuff he used, for the little hurt he had had, and to get it at the best place, which was at the other end of the town from there; and then, after kissing me again, he let me go. When I had gone down-stairs, I turned back that I might be a little bit more company to him yet, and looked in at the door, and said, 'Father dear, shall I take Merrylegs?' Father shook his head and said, 'No, Sissy, no; take nothing that's known to be mine, my darling;' and I left him sitting by the fire. Then the thought must have come upon him, poor, poor father! of going away to try something for my sake: for when I came back, he was gone."

"I say! Look sharp for old Bounderby, Loo!" Tom remonstrated.

"There's no more to tell, Miss Louisa. I keep the nine oils ready for him, and I know he will come back. Every letter that I see in Mr. Gradgrind's hand takes my breath away and blinds my eyes, for I think it comes from father, or from Mr. Sleary about father. Mr. Sleary promised to write as soon as ever father should be heard of, and I trust to him to keep his word."

"Do look sharp for old Bounderby, Loo!" said Tom, with an impatient whistle. "He'll be off if you don't look sharp!"

After this, whenever Sissy dropped a curtsy to Mr. Gradgrind in the presence of his family, and said in a faltering way, "I beg your pardon, sir, for being troublesome—but—have you had any letter yet about me?" Louisa would suspend the occupation of the moment, whatever it was, and look for the reply as earnestly as Sissy did. And when Mr. Gradgrind regularly answered, "No, Jupe, nothing of the sort," the trembling of Sissy's lip would be repeated in Louisa's face, and her eyes would follow Sissy with compassion to the door. Mr. Gradgrind usually improved these occasions by remarking, when she was gone, that if Jupe had been properly trained from an early age she would have remonstrated to herself on sound principles the baselessness of these fantastic hopes. Yet it did seem (though not to him, for he saw nothing of it) as if fantastic hope could take as strong a hold as Fact.

This observation must be limited exclusively to his daughter. As to Tom, he was becoming that not unprecedented triumph of calculation which is usually at work on number one. As to Mrs. Gradgrind, if she said anything on the subject, she would come a little way out of her wrappers, like a feminine dormouse, and say:

"Good gracious bless me, how my poor head is vexed and worried by that girl Jupe's so perseveringly asking, over and over again, about her tiresome letters! Upon my word and honour I seem to be fated, and destined, and ordained, to live in the midst of things that I am never to hear the last of. It really is a most extraordinary circumstance that it appears as if I never was to hear the last of anything!"

At about this point, Mr. Gradgrind's eye would fall upon her; and under the influence of that wintry piece of fact, she would become torpid again.

CHAPTER TEN

STEPHEN BLACKPOOL

I ENTERTAIN a weak idea that the English people are as hard-worked as any people upon whom the sun shines. I acknowledge to this ridiculous idiosyncrasy, as a reason why I would give them a little more play.

In the hardest working part of Coketown; in the innermost fortifications of that ugly citadel, where Nature was as strongly bricked out as killing airs and gases were bricked in; at the heart of the labyrinth of narrow courts upon courts, and close streets upon streets, which had come into existence piecemeal, every piece in a violent hurry for some one man's purpose, and the whole an unnatural family, shouldering, and trampling, and pressing one another to death; in the last close nook of this great exhausted receiver, where the chimneys, for want of air to make a draught, were built in an immense variety of stunted and crooked shapes, as though every house put out a sign of the kind of people who might be expected to be born in it; among the multitude of Coketown, generically called "the Hands,"—a race who would have found more favour with some people, if Providence had seen fit to make them only hands, or, like the lower creatures of the seashore, only hands and stomachs—lived a certain Stephen Blackpool, forty years of age.

Stephen looked older, but he had had a hard life. It is said that every life has its roses and thorns; there seemed, however, to *Stephen Blackpool* have been a misadventure or mistake in Stephen's case, whereby somebody else had become possessed of his roses, and he had become possessed of the same somebodyelse's thorns in addition to his own. He had known, to use his words, a peck of trouble. He was usually called Old Stephen, in a kind of rough homage to the fact.

A rather stooping man, with a knitted brow, a pondering expression of face, and a hard-looking head sufficiently capacious, on which his iron-grey hair lay long and thin, Old Stephen might have passed for a particularly intelligent man in his condition. Yet he was not. He took no place among those remarkable "Hands," who, piecing together their broken intervals of leisure through many years, had mastered difficult sciences, and acquired a knowledge of most unlikely things. He held no station among the Hands who could make speeches and carry on debates. Thousands of his compeers could talk much better than he, at any time. He was a good power-loom weaver, and a man of perfect integrity. What more he was, or what else he had in him, if anything, let him show for himself.

The lights in the great factories, which looked, when they were illuminated, like Fairy palaces—or the travellers by express-train said so—were all extinguished; and the bells had rung for knocking off for the night, and had ceased again; and the Hands, men and women, boy and girl, were clattering home. Old Stephen was standing in the street, with the old sensation upon him which the stoppage of the machinery always produced—the sensation of its having worked and stopped in his own head.

"Yet I don't see Rachael, still!" said he.

It was a wet night, and many groups of young women passed him, with their shawls drawn over their bare heads and held close under their chins to keep the rain out. He knew Rachael well, for a glance at any of these groups was sufficient to show him that she was not there. At last, there were no more to come; and then he turned away, saying in a tone of disappointment, "Why, then, I ha' missed her?"

But, he had not gone the length of three streets, when he saw another of the shawled figures in advance of him, at which he looked so keenly that perhaps its mere shadow indistinctly reflected on the wet pavement—if he could have seen it without the figure itself moving along from lamp to lamp, brightening and fading as it went—would have been enough to tell him who was there. Making his pace at once much quicker and much softer, he darted on until he was very near this figure, then fell into his former walk, and called "Rachael!"

She turned, being then in the brightness of a lamp; and raising her hood a little, showed a quiet oval face, dark and rather delicate, irradiated by a pair of very gentle eyes, and further set off by the perfect order of her shining black hair. It was not a face in its first bloom; she was a woman five and thirty years of age.

"Ah, lad! 'Tis thou?" When she had said this, with a smile which would have been quite expressed, though nothing of her had been seen but her pleasant eyes, she replaced her hood again, and they went on together.

"I thought thou wast ahind me, Rachael?"

"No."

"Early t' night, lass?"

" 'Times I'm a little early, Stephen! 'times a little late. I'm never to be counted on, going home."

"Nor going t'other way, neither, 't seems to me, Rachael?"

"No, Stephen."

He looked at her with some disappointment in his face, but with a respectful and patient conviction that she must be right in whatever she did. The expression was not lost upon her; she laid her hand lightly on his arm a moment as if to thank him for it.

"We are such true friends, lad, and such old friends, and getting to be such old folk, now."

"No, Rachael, thou 'rt as young as ever thou wast."

"One of us would be puzzled how to get old, Stephen, without t'other getting so too, both being alive," she answered, laughing; "but, anyways, we're such old friends, that t' hide a word of honest truth fro' one another would be a sin and a pity. 'Tis better not to walk too much together. 'Times, yes! 'Twould be hard, indeed, if 'twas not to be at all," she said, with a cheerfulness she sought to communicate to him.

" 'Tis hard, anyways, Rachael."

"Try to think not; and 'twill seem better."

"I've tried a long time, and 'ta'nt got better. But thou 'rt right; 't might mak fok talk, even of thee. Thou hast been that to me, Rachael, through so many year: thou hast done me so much good, and heartened of me in that cheering way, that thy word is a law to me. Ah lass, and a bright good law! Better than some real ones."

"Never fret about them, Stephen," she answered quickly, and not without an anxious glance at his face. "Let the laws be."

"Yes," he said, with a slow nod or two. "Let 'em be. Let everything be. Let all sorts alone. 'Tis a muddle, and that's aw."

"Always a muddle?" said Rachael, with another gentle touch upon his arm, as if to recall him out of the thoughtfulness, in which he was biting the long ends of his loose neckerchief as he walked along. The touch had its instantaneous effect. He let them fall, turned a smiling face upon her, and said, as he broke into a good-humoured laugh, "Ay, Rachael, lass, awlus a muddle. That's where I stick. I come to the muddle many times and agen, and I never get beyond it."

They had walked some distance, and were near their own homes. The woman's was the first reached. It was in one of the many small streets for which the favourite undertaker (who turned a handsome sum out of the one poor ghastly pomp of the neighbourhood) kept a black ladder, in order that those who had done their daily groping up and down the narrow stairs might slide out of this working world by the windows. She stopped at the corner, and putting her hand in his, wished him good night.

"Good night, dear lass; good night!"

She went, with her neat figure and her sober womanly step, down the dark street, and he stood looking after her until she turned into one of the small houses. There was not a flutter of her coarse shawl, perhaps, but had its interest in this man's eyes; not a tone of her voice but had its echo in his innermost heart.

When she was lost to his view, he pursued his homeward way, glancing up sometimes at the sky, where the clouds were sailing fast and wildly. But, they were broken now, and the rain had ceased, and the moon shone,—looking down the high chimneys of Coketown on the deep furnaces below, and casting Titanic shadows of the steam-engines at rest, upon the walls where they were lodged. The man seemed to have brightened with the night, as he went on.

His home, in such another street as the first, saving that it was narrower, was over a little shop. How it came to pass that any people found it worth their while to sell or buy the wretched little toys, mixed up in its window with cheap newspapers and pork (there was a leg to be raffled for to-morrow night), matters not here. He took his end of candle from a shelf, lighted it at another end of candle on the counter, without disturbing the mistress of the shop who was asleep in her little room, and went up-stairs into his lodging.

It was a room, not unacquainted with the black ladder under various tenants; but as neat, at present, as such a room could be. A few books and writings were on an old bureau in a corner, the furniture was decent and sufficient, and, though the atmosphere was tainted, the room was clean.

Going to the hearth to set the candle down upon a round three-legged table standing there, he stumbled against something. As he recoiled, looking down at it, it raised itself up into the form of a woman in a sitting attitude.

"Heaven's mercy, woman!" he cried, falling *"Back again!"*　farther off from the figure. "Hast thou come back agen?"

Such a woman! A disabled, drunken creature, barely able to preserve her sitting posture by steadying herself with one be-grimed hand on the floor, while the other was so purposeless in trying to push away her tangled hair from her face, that it only blinded her the more with the dirt upon it. A creature so foul to look at, in her tatters, stains and splashes, but so much fouler than that in her moral infamy, that it was a shameful thing even to see her.

After an impatient oath or two, and some stupid clawing of herself with the hand not necessary to her support, she got her hair away from her eyes sufficiently to obtain a sight of him. Then she sat swaying her body to and fro, and making gestures with her unnerved arm, which seemed intended as the accompaniment to a fit of laughter, though her face was stolid and drowsy.

"Eigh, lad? What, yo 'r there?" Some hoarse sounds meant for this, came mockingly out of her at last; and her head dropped forward on her breast.

"Back agen?" she screeched, after some minutes, as if he had that moment said it. "Yes! And back agen. Back agen ever and ever so often. Back? Yes, back. Why not?"

Roused by the unmeaning violence with which she cried it out, she scrambled up, and stood supporting herself with her shoulders against the wall; dangling in one hand by the string, a dunghill-fragment of a bonnet, and trying to look scornfully at him.

"I'll sell thee off agen, and I'll sell thee off agen, and I'll sell thee off a score of times!" she cried, with something between a furious menace and an effort at a defiant dance. "Come awa' from th' bed!" He was sitting on the side of it, with his face hidden in his hands. "Come awa' from 't. 'Tis mine, and I've a right to 't!"

As she staggered to it, he avoided her with a shudder, and passed—his face still hidden—to the opposite end of the room. She threw herself upon the bed heavily, and soon was snoring hard. He sunk into a chair, and moved but once all that night. It was to throw a covering over her; as if his hands were not enough to hide her, even in the darkness.

CHAPTER ELEVEN

NO WAY OUT

THE Fairy palaces burst into illumination, before pale morning showed the monstrous serpents of smoke trailing themselves over Coketown. A clattering of clogs upon the pavement; a rapid ringing of bells; and all the melancholy mad elephants, polished and oiled up for the day's monotony, were at their heavy exercise again.

Stephen bent over his loom, quiet, watchful, and steady. A special contrast, as every man was in the forest of looms where Stephen worked, to the crashing, smashing, tearing piece of mechanism at which he laboured. Never fear, good people of an anxious turn of mind, that Art will consign Nature to oblivion. Set anywhere, side by side, the work of God and the work of man; and the former, even though it be a troop of Hands of very small account, will gain in dignity from the comparison.

So many hundred Hands in this Mill; so many hundred horse Steam Power. It is known, to the force of a single pound weight, what the engine will do; but, not all the calculators of the National Debt can tell me the capacity for good or evil, for love or hatred, for patriotism or discontent, for the decomposition of virtue into vice, or the reverse, at any single moment in the soul of one of these its quiet servants, with the composed faces and the regulated actions. There is no mystery in it; there is an unfathomable mystery in the meanest of them, for ever.—Supposing we were to reserve our arithmetic for material objects, and to govern these awful unknown quantities by other means!

The day grew strong, and showed itself outside, even against the flaming lights within. The lights were turned out, and the work went on. The rain fell, and the Smoke-serpents, submissive to the curse of all that tribe, trailed themselves upon the earth. In the waste-yard outside, the steam from the escape pipe, the litter of barrels and old iron, the shining heaps of coals, the ashes everywhere, were shrouded in a veil of mist and rain.

The work went on, until the noon-bell rang. More clattering upon the pavements. The looms, and wheels, and Hands all out of gear for an hour.

Stephen came out of the hot mill into the damp wind and cold wet streets, haggard and worn. He turned from his own class and his own quarter, taking nothing but a little bread as he walked along, towards the hill on which his principal employer lived, in a red house with black outside shutters, green inside blinds, a black street door, up two white steps, BOUNDERBY (in letters very like himself) upon a brazen plate, and a round brazen door-handle underneath it, like a brazen full-stop.

Mr. Bounderby was at his lunch. So Stephen had expected. Would his servant say that one of the Hands begged leave to speak to him? Message in return, requiring name of such Hand. Stephen Blackpool. There was nothing troublesome against Stephen Blackpool; yes, he might come in.

Stephen Blackpool in the parlour. Mr. Bounderby (whom he just knew by sight), at lunch on chop and sherry. Mrs. Sparsit netting at the fireside, in a side-saddle attitude, with one foot in a cotton stirrup. It was a part, at once of Mrs. Sparsit's dignity and service, not to lunch. She supervised the meal officially, but implied that in her own stately person she considered lunch a weakness.

"Now, Stephen," said Mr. Bounderby, "what's the matter with *you?*"

Stephen made a bow. Not a servile one—these Hands will never do that! Lord bless you, sir, you'll never catch them at that, if they have been with you twenty years!—and, as a complimentary toilet for Mrs. Sparsit, tucked his neckerchief ends into his waistcoat.

"Now, you know," said Mr. Bounderby, taking some sherry, "we have never had any difficulty with you, and you have never been one of the unreasonable ones. You don't expect to be set up in a coach and six, and to be fed on turtle soup and venison, with a gold spoon, as a good many of 'em do!" Mr. Bounderby always represented this to be the sole, immediate, and direct object of any Hand who was not entirely satisfied; "and therefore I know already that you have not come here to make a complaint. Now, you know, I am certain of that, beforehand."

"No, sir, sure I ha' not coom for nowt o' th' kind."

Mr. Bounderby seemed agreeably surprised, notwithstanding his previous strong conviction. "Very well," he returned. "You're a steady Hand, and I was not mistaken. Now, let me hear what it's all about. As it's not that, let me hear what it is. What have you got to say? Out with it, lad!"

Stephen happened to glance towards Mrs. Sparsit. "I can go, Mr. Bounderby, if you wish it," said that self-sacrificing lady, making a feint of taking her foot out of the stirrup.

Mr. Bounderby stayed her, by holding a mouthful of chop in suspension before swallowing it, and putting out his left hand. Then, withdrawing his hand and swallowing his mouthful of chop, he said to Stephen:

"Now you know, this good lady is a born lady, a high lady. You are not to suppose because she keeps my house for me, that she hasn't been very high up the tree—ah, up at the top of the tree! Now, if you have got anything to say that can't be said before a born lady, this lady will leave the room. If what you have got to say *can* be said before a born lady, this lady will stay where she is."

"Sir, I hope I never had nowt to say, not fitten for a born lady to year, sin I were born myseln," was the reply, accompanied with a slight flush.

"Very well," said Mr. Bounderby, pushing away his plate, and leaning back. "Fire away!"

"I ha' coom," Stephen began, raising his eyes *Stephen's cross* from the floor, after a moment's consideration, "to ask yo yor advice. I need 't overmuch. I were married on Eas'r Monday nineteen year sin, long and dree. She were a young lass—pretty enow—wi' good accounts of herseln. Well! She went bad—soon. Not along of me. Gonnows I were not a unkind husband to her."

"I have heard all this before," said Mr. Bounderby. "She took to drinking, left off working, sold the furniture, pawned the clothes, and played old Gooseberry."

"I were patient wi' her."

("The more fool you, I think," said Mr. Bounderby, in confidence to his wine-glass.)

"I were very patient wi' her. I tried to wean her fra 't ower and ower agen. I tried this, I tried that, I tried t'other. I ha' gone home, many's the time, and found all vanished as I had in the world, and her without a sense left to bless herseln lying on bare ground. I ha' dun 't not once, not twice—twenty time!"

Every line in his face deepened as he said it, and put in its affecting evidence of the suffering he had undergone.

"From bad to worse, from worse to worsen. She left me. She disgraced herseln everyways, bitter and bad. She coom back, she coom back, she coom back. What could I do t' hinder her? I ha' walked the streets nights long, ere ever I'd go home. I ha' gone t' th' brigg, minded to fling myseln ower, and ha' no more on 't. I ha' bore that much, that I were owd when I were young."

Mrs. Sparsit, easily ambling along with her netting-needles, raised the Coriolanian eyebrows and shook her head, as much as to say, "The great know trouble as well as the small. Please to turn your humble eye in My direction."

"I ha' paid her to keep awa' fra' me. These five year I ha' paid her. I ha' gotten decent fewtrils about me agen. I ha' lived hard and sad, but not ashamed and fearfo' a' the minnits o' my life. Last night, I went home. There she lay upon my har-stone! There she is!"

In the strength of his misfortune, and the energy of his distress, he fired for the moment like a proud man. In another moment, he stood as he had stood all the time—his usual stoop upon him; his pondering face addressed to Mr. Bounderby, with a curious expression on it, half shrewd, half perplexed, as if his mind were set upon unravelling something very difficult; his hat held tight in his left hand, which rested on his hip; his right arm, with a rugged propriety and force of action, very earnestly emphasising what he said: not least so when it always paused, a little bent, but not withdrawn, as he paused.

"I was acquainted with all this, you know," said Mr. Bounderby, "except the last clause, long ago. It's a bad job; that's what it is. You had better have been satisfied as you were, and not have got married. However, it's too late to say that."

"Was it an unequal marriage, sir, in point of years?" asked Mrs. Sparsit.

"You hear what this lady asks. Was it an unequal marriage in point of years, this unlucky job of yours?" said Mr. Bounderby.

"Not e'en so. I were one and twenty myseln; she were twenty nighbut."

"Indeed, sir?" said Mrs. Sparsit to her Chief, with great placidity. "I inferred, from its being so miserable a marriage, that it was probably an unequal one in point of years."

Mr. Bounderby looked very hard at the good lady in a sidelong way that had an odd sheepishness about it. He fortified himself with a little more sherry.

"Well? Why don't you go on?" he then asked, turning rather irritably on Stephen Blackpool.

"I ha' coom to ask yo, sir, how I am to be ridded o' this woman." Stephen infused a yet deeper gravity into the mixed expression of his attentive face. Mrs. Sparsit uttered a gentle ejaculation, as having received a moral shock.

"What do you mean?" said Bounderby, getting up to lean his back against the chimney-piece. "What are you talking about? You took her for better for worse."

"I mun be ridden o' her. I cannot bear 't nommore. I ha' lived under 't so long, for that I ha' had'n the pity and comforting words o' th' best lass living or dead. Haply, but for her, I should ha' gone hottering mad."

"He wishes to be free, to marry the female of whom he speaks, I fear, sir," observed Mrs. Sparsit in an undertone, and much dejected by the immorality of the people.

"I do. The lady says what's right. I do. I were a coming to 't. I ha' read i' th' papers that great fok (fair faw 'em a' ! I wishes 'em no hurt!) are not bonded together for better for worst so fast, but that they can be set free fro' *their* misfortnet marriages, an marry ower agen. When they dunnot agree, for that their tempers is ill-sorted, they has rooms o' one kind an another in their houses, above a bit, and they can live asunders. We fok ha' only one room, and we can't. When that won't do, they ha' gowd an other cash, an they can say 'This for yo' and that for me,' an they can go their separate ways. We can't. Spite o' all that, they can be set free for smaller wrongs than mine. So, I mun be ridden o' this woman, and I want t' know how?"

"No how," returned Mr. Bounderby.

"If I do her any hurt, sir, there's a law to punish me?"

"Of course there is."

"If I flee from her, there's a law to punish me?"

"Of course there is."

"If I marry t'oother dear lass, there's a law to punish me?"

"Of course there is."

"If I was to live wi' her an not marry her—saying such a thing could be, which it never could or would, an her so good—there's a law to punish me, in every innocent child belonging to me?"

"Of course there is."

"Now, a' God's name," said Stephen Blackpool, "show me the law to help me!"

"Hem! There's a sanctity in this relation of life," said Mr. Bounderby, "and—and—it must be kept up."

"No no, dunnot say that, sir. 'Tan't kep' up that way. Not that way. 'Tis kep' down that way. I'm a weaver, I were in a fact'ry when a chilt, but I ha' gotten een to see wi' and eern to year wi'. I read in th' papers every 'Sizes, every Sessions—and you read too—I know it!—with dismay—how th' supposed unpossibility o' ever getting unchained from one another, at any price, on any terms, brings blood upon this land, and brings many common married fok to battle, murder, and sudden death. Let us ha' this, right understood. Mine's a grievous case, an I want—if yo will be so good—t' know the law that helps me."

"Now, I tell you what!" said Mr. Bounderby, putting his hands in his pockets. "There *is* such a law." *The only way out*

Stephen, subsiding into his quiet manner, and never wandering in his attention, gave a nod.

"But it's not for you at all. It costs money. It costs a mint of money."

"How much might that be?" Stephen calmly asked.

"Why, you'd have to go to Doctors' Commons with a suit, and you'd have to go to a court of Common Law with a suit, and you'd have to go to the House of Lords with a suit, and you'd have to get an Act of Parliament to enable you to marry again, and it would cost you (if it was a case of very plain sailing), I suppose from a thousand to fifteen hundred pound," said Mr. Bounderby. "Perhaps twice the money."

"There's no other law?"

"Certainly not."

"Why then, sir," said Stephen, turning white, and motioning with that right hand of his, as if he gave everything to the four winds, " *'tis* a muddle. 'Tis just a muddle a'toogether, an the sooner I am dead, the better."

(Mrs. Sparsit again dejected by the impiety of the people.)

"Pooh, pooh! Don't you talk nonsense, my good fellow," said Mr. Bounderby, "about things you don't understand; and don't you call the institutions of your country a muddle, or you'll get yourself into a real muddle one of these fine mornings. The institutions of your country are not your piece-work, and the only thing you have got to do, is, to mind your piece-work. You didn't take your wife for fast and for loose; but for better for worse. If she has turned out worse—why, all we have got to say is, she might have turned out better."

" 'Tis a muddle," said Stephen, shaking his head as he moved to the door. " 'Tis a' a muddle!"

"Now, I'll tell you what!" Mr. Bounderby resumed, as a valedictory address. "With what I shall call your unhallowed opinions, you have been quite shocking this lady: who, as I have already told you, is a born lady, and who, as I have not already told you, has had her own marriage misfortunes to the tune of tens of thousands of pounds—tens of Thousands of Pounds!" (he repeated it with great relish). "Now, you have always been a steady Hand hitherto; but my opinion is, and so I tell you plainly, that you are turning into the wrong road. You have been listening to some mischievous stranger or other—they're always about—and the best thing you can do is, to come out of that. Now you know," here his countenance expressed marvellous acuteness, "I can see as far into a grindstone as another man; farther than a good many, perhaps, because I had my nose well kept to it when I was young. I see traces of the turtle soup, and venison, and gold spoon in this. Yes, I do!" cried Mr. Bounderby, shaking his head with obstinate cunning. "By the Lord Harry, I do!"

With a very different shake of the head and deep sigh, Stephen said, "Thank you, sir, I wish you good day." So he left Mr. Bounderby swelling at his own portrait on the wall, as if he were going to explode himself into it; and Mrs. Sparsit still ambling on with her foot in her stirrup, looking quite cast down by the popular vices.

CHAPTER TWELVE

THE OLD WOMAN

OLD STEPHEN descended the two white steps, shutting the black door with the brazen door-plate, by the aid of the brazen full-stop, to which he gave a parting polish with the sleeve of his coat, observing that his hot hand clouded it. He crossed the street with his eyes bent upon the ground, and thus was walking sorrowfully away, when he felt a touch upon his arm.

It was not the touch he needed most at such a moment—the

touch that could calm the wild waters of his soul, as the uplifted hand of the sublimest love and patience could abate the raging of the sea—yet it was a woman's hand too. It was an old woman, tall and shapely still, though withered by time, on whom his eyes fell when he stopped and turned. She was very cleanly and plainly dressed, had country mud upon her shoes, and was newly come from a journey. The flutter of her manner, in the unwonted noise of the streets; the spare shawl, carried unfolded on her arm; the heavy umbrella, and little basket; the loose long-fingered gloves, to which her hands were unused; all bespoke an old woman from the country, in her plain holiday clothes, come into Coketown on an expedition of rare occurrence. Remarking this at a glance, with the quick observation of his class, Stephen Blackpool bent his attentive face—his face, which, like the faces of many of his order, by dint of long working with eyes and hands in the midst of a prodigious noise, had acquired the concentrated look with which we are familiar in the countenances of the deaf—the better to hear what she asked him.

"Pray, sir," said the old woman, "didn't I see you come out of that gentleman's house?" pointing back to Mr. Bounderby's. "I believe it was you, unless I have had the bad luck to mistake the person in following?"

"Yes, missus," returned Stephen, "it were me."

"Have you—you'll excuse an old woman's curiosity—have you seen the gentleman?"

"Yes, missus."

"And how did he look, sir? Was he portly, bold, outspoken, and hearty?" As she straightened her own figure, and held up her head in adapting her action to her words, the idea crossed Stephen that he had seen this old woman before, and had not quite liked her.

"O yes," he returned, observing her more attentively, "he were all that."

"And healthy," said the old woman, "as the fresh wind?"

"Yes," returned Stephen. "He were ett'n and drinking—as large and as loud as a Hummobee."

"Thank you!" said the old woman, with infinite content. "Thank you!"

He certainly never had seen this old woman before. Yet there

was a vague remembrance in his mind, as if he had more than
once dreamed of some old woman like her.

She walked along at his side, and, gently accommodating himself to her humour, he said Coketown was a busy place, was it not?

The old   To which she answered "Eigh sure! Dreadful
woman on   busy!" Then he said, she came from the country,
her pilgrimage   he saw? To which she answered in the affirmative.
"By Parliamentary, this morning. I came forty
mile by Parliamentary this morning, and I'm going back the same
forty mile this afternoon. I walked nine mile to the station this
morning, and if I find nobody on the road to give me a lift, I shall
walk the nine mile back to-night. That's pretty well, sir, at my
age!" said the chatty old woman, her eye brightening with
exultation.

" 'Deed 'tis. Don't do't too often, missus."

"No, no. Once a year," she answered, shaking her head. "I
spend my savings so, once every year. I come regular, to tramp
about the streets, and see the gentlemen."

"Only to see 'em?" returned Stephen.

"That's enough for me," she replied, with great earnestness and
interest of manner. "I ask no more! I have been standing about,
on this side of the way, to see that gentleman," turning her head
back towards Mr. Bounderby's again, "come out. But, he's late
this year, and I have not seen him. You came out instead. Now,
if I am obliged to go back without a glimpse of him—I only want
a glimpse—well! I have seen you, and you have seen him, and
I must make that do." Saying this, she looked at Stephen as if to
fix his features in her mind, and her eye was not so bright as it
had been.

With a large allowance for difference of tastes, and with all
submission to the patricians of Coketown, this seemed so extraordinary a source of interest to take so much trouble about, that
it perplexed him. But they were passing the church now, and as
his eye caught the clock, he quickened his pace.

He was going to his work? the old woman said, quickening hers,
too, quite easily. Yes, time was nearly out. On his telling her where
he worked, the old woman became a more singular old woman than
before.

"An't you happy?" she asked him.

"Why—there's awmost nobbody but has their troubles, missus." He answered evasively, because the old woman appeared to take it for granted that he would be very happy indeed, and he had not the heart to disappoint her. He knew that there was trouble enough in the world; and if the old woman had lived so long, and could count upon his having so little, why so much the better for her, and none the worse for him.

"Ay, ay! You have your troubles at home, you mean?" she said.

"Times. Just now and then," he answered, slightly.

"But, working under such a gentleman, they don't follow you to the Factory?"

No, no; they didn't follow him there, said Stephen. All correct there. Everything accordant there. (He did not go so far as to say, for her pleasure, that there was a sort of Divine Right there; but, I have heard claims almost as magnificent of late years.)

They were now in the black by-road near the place, and the Hands were crowding in. The bell was ringing, and the Serpent was a Serpent of many coils, and the Elephant was getting ready. The strange old woman was delighted with the very bell. It was the beautifullest bell she had ever heard, she said, and sounded grand!

She asked him, when he stopped good-naturedly to shake hands with her before going in, how long he had worked there?

"A dozen year," he told her.

"I must kiss the hand," said she, "that has worked in this fine factory for a dozen year!" And she lifted it, though he would have prevented her, and put it to her lips. What harmony, besides her age and her simplicity, surrounded her, he did not know, but even in this fantastic action there was a something neither out of time nor place: a something which it seemed as if nobody else could have made as serious, or done with such a natural and touching air.

He had been at his loom full half an hour, thinking about this old woman, when, having occasion to move round the loom for its adjustment, he glanced through a window which was in his corner, and saw her still looking up at the pile of building, lost in admiration. Heedless of the smoke and mud and wet, and of her two long journeys, she was gazing at it, as if the heavy thrum that issued from its many stories were proud music to her.

She was gone by and by, and the day went after her, and the lights sprung up again, and the Express whirled in full sight of the Fairy Palace over the arches near: little felt amid the jarring of the machinery, and scarcely heard above its crash and rattle. Long before then his thoughts had gone back to the dreary room above the little shop, and to the shameful figure heavy on the bed, but heavier on his heart.

Machinery slackened; throbbing feebly like a fainting pulse; stopped. The bell again; the glare of light and heat dispelled; the factories, looming heavy in the black wet night—their tall chimneys rising up into the air like competing Towers of Babel.

He had spoken to Rachael only last night, it was true, and had walked with her a little way; but he had his new misfortune on him, in which no one else could give a moment's relief, and, for the sake of it, and because he knew himself to want that softening of his anger which no voice but hers could effect, he felt he might so far disregard what she had said as to wait for her again. He waited, but she had eluded him. She was gone. On no other night in the year could he so ill have spared her patient face.

O! Better to have no home in which to lay his head, than to have a home and dread to go to it, through such a cause. He ate and drank, for he was exhausted—but he little knew or cared what; and he wandered about in the chill rain, thinking and thinking, and brooding and brooding.

No word of a new marriage had ever passed between them; but Rachael had taken great pity on him years ago, and to her alone he had opened his closed heart all this time, on the subject of his miseries; and he knew very well that if he were free to ask her, she would take him. He thought of the home he might at that moment have been seeking with pleasure and pride; of the different man he might have been that night; of the lightness then in his now heavy-laden breast; of the then restored honour, self-respect, and tranquillity all torn to pieces. He thought of the waste of the best part of his life, of the change it made in his character for the worse every day, of the dreadful nature of his existence, bound hand and foot, to a dead woman, and tormented by a demon in her shape. He thought of Rachael, how young when they were first brought together in these circumstances, how mature now, how soon to grow old. He thought of the number of girls and women she had seen marry, how many homes with children in them she had seen grow up around her, how she had contentedly pursued her own lone quiet path—for him—and how he had sometimes seen a shade of melancholy on her blessed face, that smote him with remorse and despair. He set the picture of her up, beside the infamous image of last night; and thought, Could it be, that the whole earthly course of one so gentle, good, and self-denying, was subjugate to such a wretch as that!

Filled with these thoughts—so filled that he had an unwholesome sense of growing larger, of being placed in some new and diseased relation *Going home* towards the objects among which he passed, of seeing the iris round every misty light turn red—he went home for shelter.

CHAPTER THIRTEEN

RACHAEL

A CANDLE faintly burned in the window, to which the black ladder had often been raised for the sliding away of all that was most precious in this world to a striving wife and a brood of hungry babies; and Stephen added to his other thoughts the stern reflection, that of all the casualties of this existence upon earth, not one was dealt out with so unequal a hand as Death. The inequality of Birth was nothing to it. For, say that the child of a King and the child of a Weaver were born to-night in the same moment, what was that disparity, to the death of any human creature who was serviceable to, or beloved by, another, while this abandoned woman lived on!

From the outside of his home he gloomily passed to the inside, with suspended breath and with a slow footstep. He went up to his door, opened it, and so into the room.

Quiet and peace were there. Rachael was there, sitting by the bed.

She turned her head, and the light of her face shone in upon the midnight of his mind. She sat by the bed, watching and tending his wife. That is to say, he saw that some one lay there, and he knew too well it must be she; but Rachael's hands had put a curtain up, so that she was screened from his eyes. Her disgraceful garments were removed, and some of Rachael's were in the room. Everything was in its place and order as he had always kept it, the little fire was newly trimmed, and the hearth was freshly swept. It appeared to him that he saw all this in Rachael's face, and looked at nothing besides. While looking at it, it was shut out from his view by the softened tears that filled his eyes; but not before he had seen how earnestly she looked at him, and how her own eyes were filled too.

She turned again towards the bed, and satisfying herself that all was quiet there, spoke in a low, calm, cheerful voice.

"I am glad you have come at last, Stephen. You are very late."

"I ha' been walking up an down."

"I thought so. But 'tis too bad a night for that. The rain falls very heavy, and the wind has risen."

The wind? True. It was blowing hard. Hark to the thundering in the chimney, and the surging noise! To have been out in such a wind, and not to have known it was blowing!

"I have been here once before, to-day, Stephen. Landlady came round for me at dinner-time. There was some one here that needed looking to, she said. And 'deed she was right. All wandering and lost, Stephen. Wounded too, and bruised."

He slowly moved to a chair and sat down, drooping his head before her.

"I came to do what little I could, Stephen; first, for that she worked with me when we were girls both, and for that you courted her and married her when I was her friend——"

He laid his furrowed forehead on his hand, with a low groan.

"And next, for that I know your heart, and am right sure and certain that 'tis far too merciful to let her die, or even so much as suffer, for want of aid. Thou knowest who said, 'Let him who is without sin among you cast the first stone at her!' There have been plenty to do that. Thou art not the man to cast the last stone, Stephen, when she is brought so low."

"O Rachael, Rachael!"

"Thou hast been a cruel sufferer, Heaven reward thee!" she said, in compassionate accents. "I am thy poor friend, with all my heart and mind."

The wounds of which she had spoken, seemed to be about the neck of the self-made outcast. She dressed them now, still without showing her. She steeped a piece of linen in a basin, into which she poured some liquid from a bottle, and laid it with a gentle hand upon the sore. The three-legged table had been drawn close to the bedside, and on it there were two bottles. This was one.

It was not so far off, but that Stephen, following her hands with his eyes, could read what was printed on it in large letters. He turned of a deadly hue, and a sudden horror seemed to fall upon him.

"I will stay here, Stephen," said Rachael, quietly resuming her seat, "till the bells go Three. 'Tis to be done again at three, and then she may be left till morning."

"But thy rest agen to-morrow's work, my dear."

"I slept sound last night. I can wake many nights, when I am put to it. 'Tis thou who art in need of rest—so white and tired. Try to sleep in the chair there, while I watch. Thou hadst no sleep last night, I can well believe. Tomorrow's work is far harder for thee than for me."

He heard the thundering and surging out of doors, and it seemed to him as if his late angry mood were going about trying to get at him. She had cast it out; she would keep it out; he trusted to her to defend him from himself.

"She don't know me, Stephen; she just drowsily mutters and stares. I have spoken to her times and again, but she don't notice! 'Tis as well so. When she comes to her right mind once more, I shall have done what I can, and she never the wiser."

"How long, Rachael, is 't looked for, that she'll be so?"

"Doctor said she would haply come to her mind tomorrow."

His eyes fell again on the bottle, and a tremble passed over him, causing him to shiver in every limb. She thought he was chilled with the wet. "No," he said, "it was not that. He had had a fright."

"A fright?"

"Ay, ay! coming in. When I were walking. When I were think-ing. When I—" It seized him again; and he stood up, holding by the mantel-shelf, as he pressed his dank cold hair down with a hand that shook as if it were palsied.

"Stephen!"

She was coming to him, but he stretched out his arm to stop her.

"No! Don't, please; don't. Let me see thee setten by the bed. Let me see thee, a' so good, and so forgiving. Let me see thee as I see thee when I coom in. I can never see thee better than so. Never, never, never!"

He had a violent fit of trembling, and then sunk into his chair. After a time he controlled himself, and, resting with an elbow on one knee, and his head upon that hand, could look towards Rachael. Seen across the dim candle with his moistened eyes, she looked as if she had a glory shining round her head. He could have believed she had. He did believe it, as the noise without shook the window, rattled at the door below, and went about the house clamouring and lamenting.

"When she gets better, Stephen, 'tis to be hoped she'll leave thee to thyself again, and do thee no more hurt. Anyways we will hope so now. And now I shall keep silence, for I want thee to sleep."

He closed his eyes, more to please her than to rest his weary head; but, by slow degrees as he listened to the *Stephen's dream* great noise of the wind, he ceased to hear it, or it changed into the working of his loom, or even into the voices of the day (his own included) saying what had been really said. Even this imperfect consciousness faded away at last, and he dreamed a long, troubled dream.

He thought that he, and some one on whom his heart had long been set—but she was not Rachael, and that surprised him, even in the midst of his imaginary happiness—stood in the church being married. While the ceremony was performing, and while he recog-nized among the witnesses some whom he knew to be living, and many whom he knew to be dead, darkness came on, succeeded by the shining of a tremendous light. It broke from one line in the table of commandments at the altar, and illuminated the building with the words. They were sounded through the church, too, as if there were voices in the fiery letters. Upon this, the whole appearance before him and around him changed, and nothing was left as it had been, but himself and the clergyman. They stood in the daylight before a crowd so vast, that if all the people in the world could have been brought together into one space, they could not have looked, he thought, more numerous; and they all abhorred him, and there was not one pitying or friendly eye among the millions that were fastened on his face. He stood on a raised stage, under his own loom; and, looking up at the shape the loom took, and hearing the burial service distinctly read, he knew that he was there to suffer death. In an instant what he stood on fell below him, and he was gone.

Out of what mystery he came back to his usual life, and to places that he knew, he was unable to consider; but he was back in those places by some means, and with this condemnation upon him, that he was never, in this world or the next, through all the unimaginable ages of eternity, to look on Rachael's face or hear her voice. Wandering to and fro, unceasingly, without hope, and in search of he knew not what (he only knew that he was doomed to seek it), he was the subject of a nameless, horrible dread, a mortal fear of one particular shape which everything took. Whatsoever he looked at, grew into that form sooner or later. The object of his miserable existence was to prevent its recognition by any one among the various people encountered. Hopeless labour! If he led them out of rooms where it was, if he shut up drawers and closets where it stood, if he drew the curious from places where he knew it to be secreted, and got them out into the streets, the very chimneys of the mills assumed that shape, and round them was the printed word.

The wind was blowing again, the rain was beating on the house-tops, and the larger spaces through which he had strayed contracted to the four walls of his room. Saving that the fire had died out, it was as his eyes had closed upon it. Rachael seemed to have fallen into a doze, in the chair by the bed. She sat wrapped in her shawl, perfectly still. The table stood in the same place, close by the bedside, and on it, in its real proportions and appearance, was the shape so often repeated.

He thought he saw the curtain move. He looked again, and he was sure it moved. He saw a hand come forth and grope about a little. Then the curtain moved more perceptibly, and the woman in the bed put it back, and sat up.

With her woful eyes, so haggard and wild, so heavy and large, she looked all round the room, and passed the corner where he slept in his chair. Her eyes turned to that corner, and she put her hand over them as a shade, while she looked into it. Again they went all round the room, scarcely heeding Rachael if at all, and returned to that corner. He thought, as she once more shaded them —not so much looking at him, as looking for him with a brutish instinct that he was there—that no single trace was left in those debauched features, or in the mind that went along with them, of the woman he had married eighteen years before. But that he had seen her come to this by inches, he never could have believed her to be the same.

All this time, as if a spell were on him, he was motionless and powerless, except to watch her.

Stupidly dozing, or communing with her incapable self about nothing, she sat for a little while with her hands at her ears, and her head resting on them. Presently, she resumed her staring round the room. And now, for the first time, her eyes stopped at the table with the bottles on it.

Straightway she turned her eyes back to his corner, with the defiance of last night, and moving very cautiously and softly, stretched out her greedy hand. She drew a mug into the bed, and sat for a while considering which of the two bottles she should choose. Finally, she laid her insensate grasp upon the bottle that had swift and certain death in it, and, before his eyes, pulled out the cork with her teeth.

Dream or reality, he had no voice, nor had he power to stir. If this be real, and her allotted time be not yet come, wake, Rachael, wake!

She thought of that, too. She looked at Rachael, and very slowly, very cautiously, poured out the contents. The draught was at her lips. A moment and she would be past all help, let the whole world wake and come about her with its utmost power. But in that moment Rachael started up with a suppressed cry. The creature struggled, struck her, seized her by the hair; but Rachael had the cup.

Stephen broke out of his chair. "Rachael, am I wakin' or dreamin' this dreadfo' night?"

" 'Tis all well, Stephen. I have been asleep, myself. 'Tis near three. Hush! I hear the bells."

The wind brought the sounds of the church clock to the window. They listened, and it struck three. Stephen looked at her, saw how pale she was, noted the disorder of her hair, and the red marks of fingers on her forehead, and felt assured that his senses of sight and hearing had been awake. She held the cup in her hand even now.

"I thought it must be near three," she said, calmly pouring from the cup into the basin, and steeping the linen as before. "I am thankful I stayed! 'Tis done now, when I have put this on. There! And now she's quiet again. The few drops in the basin I'll pour away, for 'tis bad stuff to leave about, though ever so little of it." As she spoke, she drained the basin into the ashes of the fire, and broke the bottle on the hearth.

She had nothing to do, then, but to cover herself with her shawl before going out into the wind and rain.

"Thou 'lt let me walk wi' thee at this hour, Rachael?"

"No, Stephen. 'Tis but a minute, and I'm home."

"Thou 'rt not fearfo';" he said it in a low voice, as they went out at the door; "to leave me alone wi' her!"

As she looked at him, saying, "Stephen?" he went down on his knee before her, on the poor mean stairs, and put an end of her shawl to his lips.

"Thou art an Angel. Bless thee, bless thee!"

"I am, as I have told thee, Stephen, thy poor friend. Angels are not like me. Between them, and a working woman fu' of faults, there is a deep gulf set. My little sister is among them, but she is changed."

She raised her eyes for a moment as she said the words; and then they fell again, in all their gentleness and mildness, on his face.

"Thou changest me from bad to good. Thou mak'st me humbly

wishfo' to be more like thee, and fearfo' to lose thee when this life is ower, and a' the muddle cleared awa'. Thou 'rt an Angel; it may be, thou hast saved my soul alive!"

She looked at him, on his knee at her feet, with her shawl still in his hand, and the reproof on her lips died away when she saw the working of his face.

"I coom home desp'rate. I coom home wi'out a hope and mad wi' thinking that when I said a word o' complaint I was reckoned a onreasonable Hand. I told thee I had had a fright. It were the Poison-bottle on table. I never hurt a livin' creetur; but happenin' so suddenly upon 't, I thowt, 'How can *I* say what I might ha' done to myseln, or her, or both!' "

She put her two hands on his mouth, with a face of terror, to stop him from saying more. He caught them in his unoccupied hand, and holding them, and still clasping the border of her shawl, said hurriedly:

"But I see thee, Rachael, setten by the bed. I *Looking beyond* ha' seen thee, aw this night. In my troublous sleep *the gulf* I ha' known thee still to be there. Evermore I will see thee there. I nevermore will see her or think o' her, but thou shalt be beside her. I nevermore will see or think o' anything that angers me, but thou, so much better than me, shalt be by th' side on 't. And so I will try t' look t' th' time, and so I will try t' trust t' th' time, when thou and me at last shall walk together far awa', beyond the deep gulf, in th' country where thy little sister is."

He kissed the border of her shawl again, and let her go. She bade him good night in a broken voice, and went out into the street.

The wind blew from the quarter where the day would soon appear, and still blew strongly. It had cleared the sky before it, and the rain had spent itself or travelled elsewhere, and the stars were bright. He stood bare-headed in the road, watching her quick disappearance. As the shining stars were to the heavy candle in the window, so was Rachael, in the rugged fancy of this man, to the common experiences of his life.

CHAPTER FOURTEEN

THE GREAT MANUFACTURER

TIME went on in Coketown like its own machinery: so much material wrought up, so much fuel consumed, so many powers worn out, so much money made. But, less inexorable than iron, steel, and brass, it brought its varying seasons even into that wilderness of smoke and brick, and made the only stand that ever *was* made in the place against its direful uniformity.

"Louisa is becoming," said Mr. Gradgrind, "almost a young woman."

Time, with his innumerable horse-power, worked away, not minding what anybody said, and presently turned out young Thomas a foot taller than when his father had last taken particular notice of him.

"Thomas is becoming," said Mr. Gradgrind, "almost a young man."

Time passed Thomas on in the mill, while his father was thinking about it, and there he stood in a long-tailed coat and a stiff shirt-collar.

"Really," said Mr. Gradgrind, "the period has arrived when Thomas ought to go to Bounderby."

Time, sticking to him, passed him on into Bounderby's Bank, made him an inmate of Bounderby's house, necessitated the purchase of his first razor, and exercised him diligently in his calculations relative to number one.

The same great manufacturer, always with an immense variety of work on hand, in every stage of development, passed Sissy onward in his mill, and worked her up into a very pretty article indeed.

"I fear, Jupe," said Mr. Gradgrind, "that your continuance at the school any longer would be useless."

"I am afraid it would, sir," Sissy answered with a curtsey.

"I cannot disguise from you, Jupe," said Mr. Gradgrind, knitting his brow, "that the result of your probation there has disappointed me; has greatly disappointed me. You have not acquired, under Mr. and Mrs. M'Choakumchild, anything like that amount of exact knowledge which I looked for. You are extremely deficient in your facts. Your acquaintance with figures is very limited. You are altogether backward, and below the mark."

"I am sorry, sir," she returned; "but I know it is quite true. Yet I have tried hard, sir."

"Yes," said Mr. Gradgrind, "yes, I believe you have tried hard; I have observed you, and I can find no fault in that respect."

"Thank you, sir. I have thought sometimes," Sissy very timid here, "that perhaps I tried to learn too much, and that if I had asked to be allowed to try a little less, I might have———"

"No, Jupe, no," said Mr. Gradgrind, shaking his head in his profoundest and most eminently practical way. "No. The course you pursued, you pursued according to the system—the system—and there is no more to be said about it. I can only suppose that the circumstances of your early life were too unfavourable to the development of your reasoning powers, and that we began too late. Still, as I have said already, I am disappointed."

"I wish I could have made a better acknowledgment, sir, of your kindness to a poor forlorn girl who had no claim upon you, and of your protection of her."

"Don't shed tears," said Mr. Gradgrind. "Don't shed tears. I don't complain of you. You are an affectionate, earnest, good young woman—and—and we must make that do."

"Thank you, sir, very much," said Sissy, with a grateful curtsey.

"You are useful to Mrs. Gradgrind, and (in a generally pervading way) you are serviceable in the family also; so I understand from Miss Louisa, and, indeed, so I have observed myself. I therefore hope," said Mr. Gradgrind, "that you can make yourself happy in those relations."

"I should have nothing to wish, sir, if———"

"I understand you," said Mr. Gradgrind; "you still refer to your father. I have heard from Miss Louisa that you still preserve that bottle. Well! If your training in the science of arriving at exact results had been more successful, you would have been wiser on these points. I will say no more."

He really liked Sissy too well to have a contempt for her; otherwise he held her calculating powers in such very slight estimation that he must have fallen upon that conclusion. Somehow or other, he had become possessed by an idea that there was something in this girl which could hardly be set forth in a tabular form. Her capacity of definition might be easily stated at a very low figure, her mathematical knowledge at nothing; yet he was not sure that if he had been required, for example, to tick her off into columns in a parliamentary return, he would have quite known how to divide her.

In some stages of his manufacture of the human fabric, the processes of Time are very rapid. Young Thomas and Sissy being both at such a stage of their working up, these changes were effected in a year or two; while Mr. Gradgrind himself seemed stationary in his course, and underwent no alteration.

Except one, which was apart from his necessary progress through the mill. Time hustled him into a little noisy and rather dirty machinery, in a by-corner, and made him Member of Parliament for Coketown: one of the respected members for ounce weights and measures, one of the representatives of the multiplication table, one of the deaf honourable gentlemen, dumb honourable gentlemen, blind honourable gentlemen, lame honourable gentlemen, dead honourable gentlemen, to every other consideration. Else wherefore live we in a Christian land, eighteen hundred and odd years after our Master?

All this while, Louisa had been passing on, so quiet and reserved, and so much given to watching the bright ashes at twilight as they fell into the grate and became extinct, that from the period when her father had said she was almost a young woman—which seemed but yesterday—she had scarcely attracted his notice again, when he found her quite a young woman.

"Quite a young woman," said Mr. Gradgrind, musing. "Dear me!"

Soon after this discovery, he became more thoughtful than usual for several days, and seemed much engrossed by one subject. On a certain night, when he was going out, and Louisa came to bid him good-bye before his departure—as he was not to be home until late and she would not see him again until the morning—he held her in his arms, looking at her in his kindest manner, and said:

"My dear Louisa, you are a woman!"

She answered with the old, quick, searching look of the night when she was found at the Circus; then cast down her eyes. "Yes, father."

"My dear," said Mr. Gradgrind, "I must speak with you alone and seriously. Come to me in my room after breakfast to-morrow, will you?"

"Yes, father."

"Your hands are rather cold, Louisa. Are you not well?"

"Quite well, father."

"And cheerful?"

She looked at him again, and smiled in her peculiar manner. "I am as cheerful, father, as I usually am, or usually have been."

"That's well," said Mr. Gradgrind. So, he kissed her and went away; and Louisa returned to the serene apartment of the hair-cutting character, and leaning her elbow on her hand, looked again at the short-lived sparks that so soon subsided into ashes.

"Are you there, Loo?" said her brother, looking in at the door. He was quite a young gentleman of pleasure now, and not quite a prepossessing one.

"Dear Tom," she answered, rising and embracing him, "how long is it since you have been to see me?"

"Why, I have been otherwise engaged, Loo, in the evenings; and in the daytime old Bounderby has been keeping me at it rather. But I touch him up with you when he comes it too strong, and so we preserve an understanding. I say! Has father said anything particular to you to-day or yesterday, Loo?"

"No, Tom. But he told me to-night that he wished to do so in the morning."

"Ah! That's what I mean," said Tom. "Do *Broad hints* you know where he is to-night?"—with a very deep expression.

"No."

"Then I'll tell you. He's with old Bounderby. They are having a regular confab together up at the Bank. Why at the Bank, do you think? Well, I'll tell you again. To keep Mrs. Sparsit's ears as far off as possible, I expect."

With her hand upon her brother's shoulder, Louisa still stood looking at the fire. Her brother glanced at her face with greater interest than usual, and, encircling her waist with his arm, drew her coaxingly to him.

"You are very fond of me, an't you, Loo?"

"Indeed I am, Tom, though you do let such long intervals go by without coming to see me."

"Well, sister of mine," said Tom, "when you say that, you are near my thoughts. We might be so much oftener together— mightn't we? Always together, almost—mightn't we? It would do me a great deal of good if you were to make up your mind to know what, Loo. It would be a splendid thing for me. It would be uncommonly jolly!"

Her thoughtfulness baffled his cunning scrutiny. He could make nothing of her face. He pressed her in his arm, and kissed her cheek. She returned the kiss, but still looked at the fire.

"I say, Loo! I thought I'd come, and just hint to you what was going on: though I supposed you'd most likely guess, even if you didn't know. I can't stay, because I'm engaged to some fellows to-night. You won't forget how fond you are of me?"

"No, dear Tom, I won't forget."

"That's a capital girl," said Tom. "Good-bye, Loo."

She gave him an affectionate good-night, and went out with him to the door, whence the fires of Coketown could be seen, making the distance lurid. She stood there, looking steadfastly towards them, and listening to his departing steps. They retreated quickly, as glad to get away from Stone Lodge; and she stood there yet, when he was gone and all was quiet. It seemed as if, first in her own fire within the house, and then in the fiery haze without, she tried to discover what kind of woof Old Time, that greatest and longest-established Spinner of all, would weave from the threads he had already spun into a woman. But his factory is a secret place, his work is noiseless, and his Hands are mutes.

CHAPTER FIFTEEN

FATHER AND DAUGHTER

ALTHOUGH Mr. Gradgrind did not take after Blue Beard, his room was quite a blue chamber in its abundance of blue books. Whatever they could prove (which is usually anything you like), they proved there, in an army constantly strengthening by the arrival of new recruits. In that charmed apartment, the most complicated social questions were cast up, got into exact totals, and finally settled—if those concerned could only have been brought to know it. As if an astronomical observatory should be made without any windows, and the astronomer within should arrange the starry universe solely by pen, ink, and paper, so Mr. Gradgrind, in *his* Observatory (and there are many like it), had no need to cast an eye upon the teeming myriads of human beings around him, but could settle all their destinies on a slate, and wipe out all their tears with one dirty little bit of sponge.

To this Observatory, then: a stern room, with a deadly statistical clock in it, which measured every second with a beat like a rap upon a coffin-lid; Louisa repaired on the appointed morning. A window looked towards Coketown; and when she sat down near her father's table, she saw the high chimneys and the long tracts of smoke looming in the heavy distance gloomily.

"My dear Louisa," said her father, "I prepared you last night to give me your serious attention in the conversation we are now going to have together. You have been so well trained, and you do, I am happy to say, so much justice to the education you have received, that I have perfect confidence in your good sense. You are not impulsive, you are not romantic, you are accustomed to view everything from the strong dispassionate ground of reason and calculation. From that ground alone, I know you will view and consider what I am going to communicate."

He waited, as if he would have been glad that she said something. But she said never a word.

"Louisa, my dear, you are the subject of a proposal of marriage that has been made to me."

Again he waited, and again she answered not one word. This so far surprised him, as to induce him gently to repeat, "a proposal of marriage, my dear." To which she returned, without any visible emotion whatever:

"I hear you, father. I am attending, I assure you."

"Well!" said Mr. Gradgrind, breaking into a smile, after being for the moment at a loss, "you are even more dispassionate than I expected, Louisa. Or, perhaps, you are not unprepared for the announcement I have it in charge to make?"

"I cannot say that, father, until I hear it. Prepared or unprepared, I wish to hear it all from you. I wish to hear you state it to me, father."

Strange to relate, Mr. Gradgrind was not so collected at this moment as his daughter was. He took a paper-knife in his hand, turned it over, laid it down, took it up again, and even then had to look along the blade of it, considering how to go on.

"What you say, my dear Louisa, is perfectly reasonable. I have undertaken then to let you know that——in short, that Mr. Bounderby has informed me that he has long watched your progress with particular interest and pleasure, and has long hoped that the time might ultimately arrive when he should offer you his hand in marriage. That time, to which he has so long, and certainly with great constancy, looked forward, is now come. Mr. Bounderby has made his proposal of marriage to me, and has entreated me to make it known to you, and to express his hope that you will take it into your favourable consideration."

Silence between them. The deadly statistical clock very hollow. The distant smoke very black and heavy.

"Father," said Louisa, "do you think I love Mr. Bounderby?"

Mr. Gradgrind was extremely discomfited by this unexpected question. "Well, my child," he returned, "I—really—cannot take upon myself to say."

"Father," pursued Louisa in exactly the same voice as before, "do you ask me to love Mr. Bounderby?"

"My dear Louisa, no. No. I ask nothing."

"Father," she still pursued, "does Mr. Bounderby ask me to love him?"

"Really, my dear," said Mr. Gradgrind, "it is difficult to answer your question——"

"Difficult to answer it, Yes or No, father?"

"Certainly, my dear. Because," here was something to demonstrate, and it set him up again, "because the reply depends so materially, Louisa, on the sense in which we use the expression. Now, Mr. Bounderby does not do you the injustice, and does not do himself the injustice, of pretending to anything fanciful, fantastic, or (I am using synonymous terms) sentimental. Mr. Bounderby would have seen you grow up under his eyes, to very little purpose, if he could so far forget what is due to your good sense, not to say to his, as to address you from any such ground. Therefore, perhaps the expression itself—I merely suggest this to you, my dear—may be a little misplaced?"

"What would you advise me to use in its stead, father?"

"Why, my dear Louisa," said Mr. Gradgrind, completely recovered by this time, "I would advise you *Important facts* (since you ask me) to consider this question, as you have been accustomed to consider every other question, simply as one of tangible Fact. The ignorant and the giddy may embarrass such subjects with irrelevant fancies, and other absurdities that have no existence, properly viewed—really no existence—but it is no compliment to you to say, that you know better. Now, what are the Facts of this case? You are, we will say in round numbers, twenty years of age; Mr. Bounderby is, we will say in round numbers, fifty. There is some disparity in your respective years, but in your means and positions there is none; on the contrary, there is a great suitability. Then the question arises, Is this one disparity sufficient to operate as a bar to such a marriage? In considering this question, it is not unimportant to take into account the statistics of marriage, so far as they have yet been obtained, in England and Wales. I find, on reference to the figures, that a large proportion of these marriages are contracted between parties of very unequal ages, and that the elder of these contracting parties is, in rather more than three-fourths of these instances, the bridegroom. It is remarkable as showing the wide prevalence of this law, that among the natives of the British possessions in India, also in a considerable part of China, and among the Calmucks of Tartary, the best means of computation yet furnished us by travellers, yield similar results. The disparity I have mentioned, therefore, almost ceases to be disparity, and (virtually) all but disappears."

"What do you recommend, father," asked Louisa, her reserved composure not in the least affected by these gratifying results, "that I should substitute for the term I used just now? For the misplaced expression?"

"Louisa," returned her father, "it appears to me that nothing can be plainer. Confining yourself rigidly to Fact, the question of Fact you state to yourself is: Does Mr. Bounderby ask me to marry him? Yes, he does. The sole remaining question then is: Shall I marry him? I think nothing can be plainer than that?"

"Shall I marry him?" repeated Louisa, with great deliberation.

"Precisely. And it is satisfactory to me, as your father, my dear Louisa, to know that you do not come to the consideration of that question with the previous habits of mind, and habits of life, that belong to many young women."

"No, father," she returned, "I do not."

"I now leave you to judge for yourself," said Mr. Gradgrind. "I have stated the case, as such cases are usually stated among practical minds; I have stated it, as the case of your mother and myself was stated in its time. The rest, my dear Louisa, is for you to decide."

From the beginning, she had sat looking at him fixedly. As he now leaned back in his chair, and bent his deep-set eyes upon her in his turn, perhaps he might have seen one wavering moment in her, when she was impelled to throw herself upon his breast, and give him the pent-up confidences of her heart. But, to see it, he must have overleaped at a bound the artificial barriers he had for many years been erecting, between himself and all those subtle essences of humanity which will elude the utmost cunning of algebra until the last trumpet ever to be sounded shall blow even algebra to wreck. The barriers were too many and too high for such a leap. With his unbending, utilitarian, matter-of-fact face, he hardened her again; and the moment shot away into the plumbless depths of the past, to mingle with all the lost opportunities that are drowned there.

Removing her eyes from him, she sat so long looking silently towards the town, that he said, at length; "Are you consulting the chimneys of the Coketown works, Louisa?"

"There seems to be nothing there but languid and monotonous smoke. Yet when the night comes, Fire bursts out, father!" she answered, turning quickly.

"Of course I know that, Louisa. I do not see the application of the remark." To do him justice he did not, at all.

She passed it away with a slight motion of her hand, and concentrating her attention upon him again, said, "Father, I have often thought that life is very short."—This was so distinctly one of his subjects that he interposed.

"It is short, no doubt, my dear. Still, the average duration of human life is proved to have increased of late years. The calculations of various life assurance and annuity offices, among other figures which cannot go wrong, have established the fact."

"I speak of my own life, father."

"O indeed? Still," said Mr. Gradgrind, "I need not point out to you, Louisa, that it is governed by the laws which govern lives in the aggregate."

"While it lasts, I would wish to do the little I can, and the little I am fit for. What does it matter?"

Mr. Gradgrind seemed rather at a loss to understand the last four words; replying, "How, matter? What matter, my dear?"

"Mr. Bounderby," she went on in a steady, straight way, without regarding this, "asks me to marry him. The question I have to ask myself is, shall I marry him? That is so, father, is it not? You have told me so, father. Have you not?"

"Certainly, my dear."

"Let it be so. Since Mr. Bounderby likes to *Louisa conveys* take me thus, I am satisfied to accept his pro- *her decision* posal. Tell him, father, as soon as you please, that this was my answer. Repeat it, word for word, if you can, because I should wish him to know what I said."

"It is quite right, my dear," retorted her father approvingly, "to be exact. I will observe your very proper request. Have you any wish in reference to the period of your marriage, my child?"

"None, father. What does it matter?"

Mr. Gradgrind had drawn his chair a little nearer to her, and taken her hand. But, her repetition of these words seemed to strike with some little discord on his ear. He paused to look at her, and, still holding her hand, said:

"Louisa, I have not considered it essential to ask you one question, because the possibility implied in it appeared to me to be too remote. But perhaps I ought to do so. You have never entertained in secret any other proposal?"

"Father," she returned, almost scornfully, "what other proposal can have been made to *me?* Whom have I seen? Where have I been? What are my heart's experiences?"

"My dear Louisa," returned Mr. Gradgrind, reassured and satisfied. "You correct me justly. I merely wished to discharge my duty."

"What do *I* know, father," said Louisa in her quiet manner, "of tastes and fancies; of aspirations and affections; of all that part of my nature in which such light things might have been nourished? What escape have I had from problems that could be demonstrated, and realities that could be grasped?" As she said it, she unconsciously closed her hand, as if upon a solid object, and slowly opened it as though she were releasing dust or ash.

"My dear," assented her eminently practical parent, "quite true, quite true."

"Why father," she pursued, "what a strange question to ask *me!* The baby-preference that even I have heard of as common among children, has never had its innocent resting-place in my breast. You have been so careful of me, that I never had a child's heart. You have trained me so well, that I never dreamed a child's dream. You have dealt so wisely with me, father, from my cradle to this hour, that I never had a child's belief or a child's fear."

Mr. Gradgrind was quite moved by his success, and by this testimony to it.

"My dear Louisa," said he, "you abundantly repay my care. Kiss me, my dear girl."

So, his daughter kissed him. Detaining her in his embrace, he said, "I may assure you now, my favourite child, that I am made happy by the sound decision at which you have arrived. Mr.

Bounderby is a very remarkable man; and what little disparity can be said to exist between you—if any—is more than counterbalanced by the tone your mind has acquired. It has always been my object so to educate you, as that you might, while still in your early youth, be (if I may so express myself) almost any age. Kiss me once more, Louisa. Now, let us go and find your mother."

Accordingly, they went down to the drawing-room, where the esteemed lady with no nonsense about her, was recumbent as usual, while Sissy worked beside her. She gave some feeble signs of returning animation when they entered, and presently the faint transparency was presented in a sitting attitude.

"Mrs. Gradgrind," said her husband, who had waited for the achievement of this feat with some impatience, "allow me to present to you Mrs. Bounderby."

"Oh!" said Mrs. Gradgrind, "so you have settled it! Well, I'm sure I hope your health may be good, Louisa; for if your head begins to split as soon as you are married, which was the case with mine, I cannot consider that you are to be envied, though I have no doubt you think you are, as all girls do. However, I give you joy, my dear—and I hope you may now turn all your ological studies to good account, I am sure I do! I must give you a kiss of congratulation, Louisa; but don't touch my right shoulder, for there's something running down it all day long. And now you see," whimpered Mrs. Gradgrind, adjusting her shawls after the affectionate ceremony, "I shall be worrying myself, morning, noon, and night, to know what I am to call him!"

"Mrs. Gradgrind," said her husband, solemnly, "what do you mean?"

"Whatever I am to call him, Mr. Gradgrind, when he is married to Louisa! I must call him something. It's impossible," said Mrs. Gradgrind, with a mingled sense of politeness and injury, "to be constantly addressing him and never giving him a name. I cannot call him Josiah, for the name is insupportable to me. You yourself wouldn't hear of Joe, you very well know. Am I to call my own son-in-law, Mister? Not, I believe, unless the time has arrived when, as an invalid, I am to be trampled upon by my relations. Then, what am I to call him!"

Nobody present having any suggestion to offer in the remarkable emergency, Mrs. Gradgrind departed this life for the time being, after delivering the following codicil to her remarks already executed:

"As to the wedding, all I ask, Louisa, is,—and I ask it with a fluttering in my chest, which actually extends to the soles of my feet,—that it may take place soon. Otherwise, I know it is one of those subjects I shall never hear the last of."

When Mr. Gradgrind had presented Mrs. Bounderby, Sissy had suddenly turned her head, and looked, in wonder, in pity, in sorrow, in doubt, in a multitude of emotions, towards Louisa. Louisa had known it, and seen it, without looking at her. From that moment she was impassive, proud and cold—held Sissy at a distance—changed to her altogether.

CHAPTER SIXTEEN

HUSBAND AND WIFE

MR. BOUNDERBY's first disquietude on hearing of his happiness, was occasioned by the necessity of imparting it to Mrs. Sparsit. He could not make up his mind how to do that, or what the consequences of the step might be. Whether she *Approaching the first difficulty* would instantly depart, bag and baggage, to Lady Scadgers, or would positively refuse to budge from the premises; whether she would be plaintive or abusive, tearful or tearing; whether she would break her heart, or break the looking-glass; Mr. Bounderby could not at all foresee. However, as it must be done, he had no choice but to do it; so, after attempting several letters, and failing in them all, he resolved to do it by word of mouth.

On his way home, on the evening he set aside for this momentous purpose, he took the precaution of stepping into a chemist's shop and buying a bottle of the very strongest smelling-salts. "By George!" said Mr. Bounderby, "if she takes it in the fainting way, I'll have the skin off her nose, at all events!" But, in spite of being thus forearmed, he entered his own house with anything but a courageous air; and appeared before the object of his misgivings, like a dog who was conscious of coming direct from the pantry.

"Good evening, Mr. Bounderby!"

"Good evening, ma'am, good evening." He drew up his chair, and Mrs. Sparsit drew back hers, as who should say, "Your fireside, sir. I freely admit it. It is for you to occupy it all, if you think proper."

"Don't go to the North Pole, ma'am!" said Mr. Bounderby.

"Thank you, sir," said Mrs. Sparsit, and returned, though short of her former position.

Mr. Bounderby sat looking at her, as, with the points of a stiff, sharp pair of scissors she picked out holes for some inscrutable ornamental purpose, in a piece of cambric. An operation which, taken in connexion with the bushy eyebrows and the Roman nose, suggested with some liveliness the idea of a hawk engaged upon the eyes of a tough little bird. She was so steadfastly occupied, that many minutes elapsed before she looked up from her work; when she did so Mr. Bounderby bespoke her attention with a hitch of his head.

"Mrs. Sparsit ma'am," said Mr. Bounderby, putting his hands in his pockets, and assuring himself with his right hand that the cork of the little bottle was ready for use. "I have on occasion to say to you, that you are not only a lady born and bred, but a devilish sensible woman."

"Sir," returned the lady, "this is indeed not the first time that you have honoured me with similar expressions of your good opinion."

"Mrs. Sparsit ma'am," said Mr. Bounderby, "I am going to astonish you."

"Yes, sir?" returned Mrs. Sparsit, interrogatively, and in the most tranquil manner possible. She generally wore mittens, and she now laid down her work, and smoothed those mittens.

"I am going, ma'am," said Bounderby, "to marry Tom Grad-grind's daughter."

"Yes, sir," returned Mrs. Sparsit. "I hope you may be happy,

Mr. Bounderby. Oh, indeed I hope you may be happy, sir!" And she said it with such great condescension as well as with such great compassion for him, that Bounderby,—far more disconcerted than if she had thrown her work-box at the mirror, or swooned on the hearthrug,—corked up the smelling-salts tight in his pocket, and thought, "Now confound this woman, who could have ever guessed that she would take it in this way?"

"I wish with all my heart, sir," said Mrs. Sparsit, in a highly superior manner; somehow she seemed, in a moment, to have established a right to pity him ever afterwards; "that you may be in all respects very happy."

"Well, ma'am," returned Bounderby, with some resentment in his tone: which was clearly lowered, though in spite of himself, "I am obliged to you. I hope I shall be."

"*Do* you, sir?" said Mrs. Sparsit, with great affability. "But naturally you do; of course you do."

A very awkward pause on Mr. Bounderby's part, succeeded. Mrs. Sparsit sedately resumed her work and occasionally gave a small cough, which sounded like the cough of conscious strength and forbearance.

"Well, ma'am," resumed Bounderby, "under these circumstances, I imagine it would not be agreeable to a character like yours to remain here, though you would be very welcome here."

"Oh, dear no, sir, I could on no account think of that!" Mrs. Sparsit shook her head, still in her highly superior manner, and a little changed the small cough—coughing now, as if the spirit of prophecy rose within her, but had better be coughed down.

"However, ma'am," said Bounderby, "there are apartments at the Bank, where a born and bred lady, as keeper of the place, would be rather a catch than otherwise; and if the same terms——"

"I beg your pardon, sir. You were so good as to promise that you would always substitute the phrase, annual compliment."

"Well, ma'am, annual compliment. If the same annual compliment would be acceptable there, why, I see nothing to part us, unless you do."

"Sir," returned Mrs. Sparsit. "The proposal is like yourself, and if the position I shall assume at the Bank is one that I could occupy without descending lower in the social scale——"

"Why, of course it is," said Bounderby. "If it was not, ma'am, you don't suppose that I should offer it to a lady who has moved in the society you have moved in. Not that *I* care for such society, you know! But *you* do."

"Mr. Bounderby, you are very considerate."

"You'll have your own private apartments, and you'll have your coals and your candles, and all the rest of it, and you'll have your maid to attend upon you, and you'll have your light porter to protect you, and you'll be what I take the liberty of considering precious comfortable," said Bounderby.

"Sir," rejoined Mrs. Sparsit, "say no more. In yielding up my trust here, I shall not be freed from the necessity of eating the bread of dependence;" she might have said the sweetbread, for that delicate article in a savoury brown sauce was her favourite supper: "and I would rather receive it from your hand, than from any other. Therefore, sir, I accept your offer gratefully, and with many sincere acknowledgments for past favours. And I hope, sir," said Mrs. Sparsit, concluding in an impressively compassionate manner, "I fondly hope that Miss Gradgrind may be all you desire, and deserve!"

Nothing moved Mrs. Sparsit from that position any more. It was in vain for Bounderby to bluster or to assert himself in any of his explosive ways; Mrs. Sparsit was resolved to have compassion on him, as a Victim. She was polite, obliging, cheerful, hopeful; but, the more polite, the more obliging, the more cheerful, the more hopeful, the more exemplary altogether, she; the forlorner Sacrifice and Victim, he. She had that tenderness for his melancholy fate, that his great red countenance used to break out into cold perspirations when she looked at him.

Meanwhile the marriage was appointed to be solemnized in eight weeks' time, and Mr. Bounderby went every evening to Stone Lodge as an accepted wooer. Love was made on these occasions in the form of bracelets; and, on all occasions during the period of betrothal, took a manufacturing aspect. Dresses were made, jewellery was made, cakes and gloves were made, settlements were made, and an extensive assortment of Facts did appropriate honour to the contract. The business was all Fact, from first to last. The Hours did not go through any of those rosy performances, which foolish poets have ascribed to them at such times; neither did the clocks go any faster, or any slower, than at other seasons. The deadly statistical recorder in the Gradgrind observatory knocked every second on the head as it was born, and buried it with his accustomed regularity.

So the day came, as all other days come to people who will only stick to reason; and when it came, there were married in the church of the florid wooden legs—that popular order of architecture—Josiah Bounderby Esquire of Coketown, to Louisa eldest daughter of Thomas Gradgrind Esquire of Stone Lodge, M.P. for that borough. And when they were united in holy matrimony, they went home to breakfast at Stone Lodge aforesaid.

There was an improving party assembled on the auspicious occasion, who knew what everything they had to eat and drink was made of, and how it was imported or exported, and in what quantities, and in what bottoms, whether native or foreign, and all about it. The bridesmaids, down to little Jane Gradgrind, were, in an intellectual point of view, fit helpmates for the calculating boy; and there was no nonsense about any of the company.

After breakfast, the bridegroom addressed them in the following terms:

"Ladies and gentlemen, I am Josiah Bounderby of Coketown. Since you have done my wife and myself the honour of drinking our healths and happiness, I suppose I must acknowledge the same; though, as you all know me, and know what I am, and what my extraction was, you won't expect a speech from a man who, when he sees a Post, says 'that's a Post,' and when he sees a Pump, says 'that's a Pump,' *Mr. Bounderby's* and is not to be got to call a Post a Pump, or a *marriage* Pump a Post, or either of them a Toothpick. *oration* If you want a speech this morning, my friend and father-in-law, Tom Gradgrind, is a Member of Parliament, and you know where to get it. I am not your man. However, if I feel a little independent when I look around this table to-day, and reflect how little I thought of marrying Tom Gradgrind's daughter when I was a ragged street-boy, who never washed his face unless it was at a pump, and that not oftener than once a fortnight, I hope I may be excused. So, I hope you like my feeling independent; if you don't, I can't help it. I *do* feel independent. Now I have mentioned, and you have mentioned, that I am this day married to Tom Gradgrind's daughter. I am very glad to be so. It has long been my wish to be so. I have watched her bringing-up, and I believe she is worthy of me. At the same time—not to deceive you—I believe I am worthy of her. So, I thank you, on both our parts, for the good-will you have shown towards us; and the best wish I can give the unmarried part of the present company, is this: I hope every bachelor may find as good a wife as I have found. And I hope every spinster may find as good as husband as my wife has found."

Shortly after which oration, as they were going on a nuptial trip to Lyons, in order that Mr. Bounderby might take the opportunity of seeing how the Hands got on in those parts, and whether they, too, required to be fed with gold spoons; the happy pair departed for the railroad. The bride, in passing downstairs, dressed for her journey, found Tom waiting for her—flushed, either with his feelings or the vinous part of the breakfast.

"What a game girl you are, to be such a first-rate sister, Loo!" whispered Tom.

She clung to him as she should have clung to some far better nature that day, and was a little shaken in her reserved composure for the first time.

"Old Bounderby's quite ready," said Tom. "Time's up. Goodbye! I shall be on the look-out for you, when you come back. I say, my dear Loo! An'T it uncommonly jolly now!"

END OF THE FIRST BOOK

BOOK THE SECOND

REAPING

CHAPTER ONE

EFFECTS IN THE BANK

A SUNNY midsummer day. There was such a thing sometimes, even in Coketown.

Seen from a distance in such weather, Coketown lay shrouded in a haze of its own, which appeared impervious to the sun's rays. You only knew the town was there, because you knew there could have been no such sulky blotch upon the prospect without a town. A blur of soot and smoke, now confusedly tending this way, now that way, now aspiring to the vault of Heaven, now murkily creeping along the earth, as the wind rose and fell, or changed its quarter: a dense formless jumble, with sheets of cross light in it, that showed nothing but masses of darkness:—Coketown in the distance was suggestive of itself, though not a brick of it could be seen.

The wonder was, it was there at all. It had been ruined so often, that it was amazing how it had borne so many shocks. Surely there never was such fragile china-ware as that of which the millers of Coketown were made. Handle them never so lightly, and they fell to pieces with such ease that you might suspect them of having been flawed before. They were ruined, when they were required to send labouring children to school; they were ruined when inspectors were appointed to look into their works; they were ruined, when such inspectors considered it doubtful whether they were quite justified in chopping people up with their machinery; they were utterly undone, when it was hinted that perhaps they need not always make quite so much smoke. Besides Mr. Bounderby's gold spoon which was generally received in Coketown, another prevalent fiction was very popular there. It took the form of a threat. Whenever a Coketowner felt he was ill-used—that is to say, whenever he was not left entirely alone, and it was proposed to hold him accountable for the consequences of any of his acts—he was sure to come out with the awful menace, that he would "sooner pitch his property into the Atlantic." This had terrified the Home Secretary within an inch of his life, on several occasions.

However, the Coketowners were so patriotic after all, that they never had pitched their property into the Atlantic yet, but, on the contrary, had been kind enough to take mighty good care of it. So there it was, in the haze yonder; and it increased and multiplied.

The streets were hot and dusty on the summer day, and the sun was so bright that it even shone through the heavy vapour drooping over Coketown, and could not be looked at steadily. Stokers emerged from low underground doorways into factory yards, and sat on steps, and posts, and palings, wiping their swarthy visages, and contemplating coals. The whole town seemed to be frying in oil. There was a stifling smell of hot oil everywhere. The steam-engines shone with it, the dresses of the Hands were soiled with it, the mills throughout their many stories oozed and trickled it. The atmosphere of those Fairy palaces was like the breath of the simoom: and their inhabitants, wasting with heat, toiled languidly in the desert. But no temperature made the melancholy mad elephants more mad or more sane. Their wearisome heads went up and down at the same rate, in hot weather and cold, wet weather and dry, fair weather and foul. The measured motion of their shadows on the walls, was the substitute Coketown had to show for the shadows of rustling woods; while, for the summer hum of insects, it could offer, all the year round, from the dawn of Monday to the night of Saturday, the whirr of shafts and wheels.

Drowsily they whirred all through this sunny day, making the passenger more sleepy and more hot as he passed the humming walls of the mills. Sun-blinds, and sprinklings of water, a little cooled the main streets and the shops; but the mills and the courts and alleys, baked at a fierce heat. Down upon the river that was black and thick with dye, some Coketown boys who were at large—a rare sight there—rowed a crazy boat, which made a spumous track upon the water as it jogged along, while every dip of an oar stirred up vile smells. But the sun itself, however beneficent, generally, was less kind to Coketown than hard frost, and rarely looked intently into any of its closer regions without engendering more death than life. So does the eye of Heaven itself become an evil eye, when incapable or sordid hands are interposed between it and the things it looks upon to bless.

Mrs. Sparsit sat in her afternoon apartment at the Bank, on the shadier side of the frying street. Office-hours were over: and at that period of the day, in warm weather, she usually embellished with her genteel presence, a managerial board-room over the public office. Her own private sitting-room was a story higher, at the window of which post of observation she was ready, every morning, to greet Mr. Bounderby, as he came across the road, with the sympathizing recognition appropriate to a Victim. He had been married now a year; and Mrs. Sparsit had never released him from her determined pity a moment.

The Bank offered no violence to the wholesome monotony of the town. It was another red brick house, with black outside shutters, green inside blinds, a black street-door up two white steps, a brazen door-plate, and a brazen door-handle full stop. It was a size larger than Mr. Bounderby's house, as other houses were from a size to half-a-dozen sizes smaller; in all other particulars, it was strictly according to pattern.

Mrs. Sparsit was conscious that by coming in the eveningtide among the desks and writing implements, she shed a feminine, not to say also aristocratic, grace upon the office. Seated, with her needlework or netting apparatus, at the window, she had a self-laudatory sense of correcting, by her ladylike deportment, the rude business aspect of the place. With this impression of her interesting character upon her, Mrs. Sparsit considered herself, in some sort, the Bank Fairy. The townspeople who, in their passing and repassing, saw her there, regarded her as the Bank Dragon keeping watch over the treasures of the mine.

What those treasures were, Mrs. Sparsit knew as little as they did. Gold and silver coin, precious paper, secrets that if divulged would bring vague destruction upon vague persons (generally, however, people whom she disliked), were the chief items in her ideal catalogue thereof. For the rest, she knew that after office-hours, she reigned supreme over all the office furniture, and over a locked-up iron room with three locks, against the door of which strong chamber the light porter laid his head every night, on a truckle bed, that disappeared at cockcrow. Further, she was lady paramount over certain vaults in the basement, sharply spiked off from communication with the predatory world; and over the relics of the current day's work, consisting of blots of ink, worn-out pens, fragments of wafers, and scraps of paper torn so small, that nothing interesting could ever be deciphered on them when Mrs. Sparsit tried. Lastly, she was guardian over a little armoury of cutlasses and carbines, arrayed in vengeful order above one of the official chimney-pieces; and over that respectable tradition never to be separated from a place of business claiming to be wealthy—a row of fire-buckets—vessels calculated to be of no physical utility on any occasion, but observed to exercise a fine moral influence, almost equal to bullion, on most beholders.

A deaf serving-woman and the light porter completed Mrs. Sparsit's empire. The deaf serving-woman was rumoured to be wealthy; and a saying had for years gone about among the lower orders of Coketown, that she would be murdered some night when the Bank was shut, for the sake of her money. It was generally considered, indeed, that she had been due some time, and ought to have fallen long ago; but she had kept her life, and her situation, with an ill-conditioned tenacity that occasioned much offence and disappointment.

Mrs. Sparsit's tea was just set for her on a pert little table, with its tripod of legs in an attitude, which she insinuated after office-hours, into the company of the stern leathern-topped, long board-table that bestrode the middle of the room. The light porter placed the tea-tray on it, knuckling his forehead as a form of homage.

"Thank you, Bitzer," said Mrs. Sparsit.

"Thank *you,* ma'am," returned the light porter. He was a very light porter indeed; as light as in the days when he blinkingly defined a horse, for girl number twenty.

"All is shut up, Bitzer?" said Mrs. Sparsit.

"All is shut up, ma'am."

"And what," said Mrs. Sparsit, pouring out her tea, "is the news of the day? Anything?"

"Well, ma'am, I can't say that I have heard anything particular. Our people are a bad lot, ma'am; but that is no news, unfortunately."

"What are the restless wretches doing now?" asked Mrs. Sparsit.

"Merely going on in the old way, ma'am. Uniting, and leaguing, and engaging to stand by one another."

"It is much to be regretted," said Mrs. Sparsit, making her nose more Roman and her eyebrows more Coriolanian in the strength of her severity, "that the united masters allow of any such classcombinations." *Mrs. Sparsit on the people*

"Yes, ma'am," said Bitzer.

"Being united themselves, they ought one and all to set their faces against employing any man who is united with any other man," said Mrs. Sparsit.

"They have done that, ma'am," returned Bitzer; "but it rather fell through, ma'am."

"I do not pretend to understand these things," said Mrs. Sparsit, with dignity, "my lot having been signally cast in a widely different sphere; and Mr. Sparsit, as a Powler, being also quite out of the pale of any such dissensions. I only know that these people must be conquered, and that it's high time it was done, once for all."

"Yes, ma'am," returned Bitzer, with a demonstration of great respect for Mrs. Sparsit's oracular authority. "You couldn't put it clearer, I am sure, ma'am."

As this was his usual hour for having a little confidential chat with Mrs. Sparsit, and as he had already caught her eye and seen that she was going to ask him something, he made a pretence of arranging the rulers, inkstands, and so forth, while that lady went on with her tea, glancing through the open window, down into the street.

"Has it been a busy day, Bitzer?" asked Mrs. Sparsit.

"Not a very busy day, my lady. About an average day." He now and then slided into my lady, instead of ma'am, as an involuntary acknowledgment of Mrs. Sparsit's personal dignity and claims to reverence.

"The clerks," said Mrs. Sparsit, carefully brushing an imperceptible crumb of bread and butter from her left-hand mitten, "are trustworthy, punctual, and industrious, of course?"

"Yes, ma'am, pretty fair, ma'am. With the usual exception."

He held the respectable office of general spy and informer in the establishment, for which volunteer service he received a present at Christmas, over and above his weekly wage. He had grown into an extremely clear-headed, cautious, prudent young man, who was safe to rise in the world. His mind was so exactly regulated, that he had no affections or passions. All his proceedings were the result of the nicest and coldest calculation; and it was not without cause that Mrs. Sparsit habitually observed of him, that he was a young man of the steadiest principle she had ever known. Having satisfied himself, on his father's death, that his mother had a right of settlement in Coketown, this excellent young economist had asserted that right for her with such a steadfast adherence to the principle of the case, that she had been shut up in the workhouse ever since. It must be admitted that he allowed her half a pound of tea a year, which was weak in him: first, because all gifts have an inevitable tendency to pauperise the recipient, and secondly, because his only reasonable transaction in that commodity would have been to buy it for as little as he could possibly give, and sell it for as much as he could possibly get; it having been clearly ascertained by philosophers that in this is comprised the whole duty of man—not a part of man's duty, but the whole.

"Pretty fair, ma'am. With the usual exception, ma'am," repeated Bitzer.

"Ah—h!" said Mrs. Sparsit, shaking her head over her tea-cup, and taking a long gulp.

"Mr. Thomas, ma'am, I doubt Mr. Thomas very much, ma'am, I don't like his ways at all."

"Bitzer," said Mrs. Sparsit, in a very impressive manner, "do you recollect my having said anything to you respecting names?"

"I beg your pardon, ma'am. It's quite true that you did object to names being used, and they're always best avoided."

"Please to remember that I have a charge here," said Mrs. Sparsit, with her air of state. "I hold a trust here, Bitzer, under Mr. Bounderby. However improbable both Mr. Bounderby and myself might have deemed it years ago, that he would ever become my patron, making me an annual compliment, I cannot but regard him in that light. From Mr. Bounderby I have received every acknowledgment of my social station, and every recognition of my family descent, that I could possibly expect. More, far more. Therefore, to my patron I will be scrupulously true. And I do not consider, I will not consider, I cannot consider," said Mrs. Sparsit, with a most extensive stock on hand of honour and morality, "that I *should* be scrupulously true, if I allowed names to be mentioned under this roof, that are unfortunately—most unfortunately—no doubt of that—connected with his."

Bitzer knuckled his forehead again, and again begged pardon.

"No, Bitzer," continued Mrs. Sparsit, "say an individual, and I will hear you; say Mr. Thomas, and you must excuse me."

"With the usual exception, ma'am," said Bitzer, trying back, "of an individual."

"Ah—h!" Mrs. Sparsit repeated the ejaculation, the shake of the head over her tea-cup, and the long gulp, as taking up the conversation again at the point where it had been interrupted.

"An individual, ma'am," said Bitzer, "has never been what he ought to have been, since he first came into the place. He is a dissipated, extravagant idler. He is not worth his salt, ma'am. He wouldn't get it either, if he hadn't a friend and relation at court, ma'am!"

"Ah—h!" said Mrs. Sparsit, with another melancholy shake of her head.

"I only hope, ma'am," pursued Bitzer, "that his friend and relation may not supply him with the means of carrying on. Otherwise, ma'am, we know out of whose pocket *that* money comes."

"Ah—h!" sighed Mrs. Sparsit again, with another melancholy shake of her head.

"He is to be pitied, ma'am. The last party I have alluded to, is to be pitied, ma'am," said Bitzer.

"Yes Bitzer," said Mrs. Sparsit. "I have always pitied the delusion, always."

"As to an individual, ma'am," said Bitzer, dropping his voice and drawing nearer, "he is as improvident as any of the people in this town. And you know what *their* improvidence is, ma'am. No one could wish to know it better than a lady of your eminence does."

"They would do well," returned Mrs. Sparsit, "to take example by you, Bitzer."

Bitzer takes a moral view of himself

"Thank you, ma'am. But, since you do refer to me, now look at me, ma'am. I have put by a little, ma'am, already. That gratuity which I receive at Christmas, ma'am: I never touch it. I don't even go the length of my wages, though they're not high, ma'am. Why can't they do as I have done, ma'am? What one person can do, another can do."

This, again, was among the fictions of Coketown. Any capitalist there, who had made sixty thousand pounds out of sixpence, always professed to wonder why the sixty thousand nearest Hands didn't each make sixty thousand pounds out of sixpence, and more or less reproached them every one for not accomplishing the little feat. What I did you can do. Why don't you go and do it?

"As to their wanting recreations, ma'am," said Bitzer, "it's stuff and nonsense. *I* don't want recreations. I never did, and I never shall; I don't like 'em. As to their combining together; there are many of them, I have no doubt, that by watching and informing upon one another could earn a trifle now and then, whether in money or good will, and improve their livelihood. Then, why don't they improve it, ma'am? It's the first consideration of a rational creature, and it's what they pretend to want."

"Pretend indeed!" said Mrs. Sparsit.

"I am sure we are constantly hearing, ma'am, till it becomes quite nauseous, concerning their wives and families," said Bitzer. "Why look at me, ma'am! *I* don't want a wife and family. Why should they?"

"Because they are improvident," said Mrs. Sparsit.

"Yes, ma'am," returned Bitzer, "that's where it is. If they were more provident and less perverse, ma'am, what would they do? They would say, 'While my hat covers my family,' or 'while my bonnet covers my family,'—as the case might be, ma'am—'I have only one to feed, and that's the person I most like to feed.'"

"To be sure," assented Mrs. Sparsit, eating muffin.

"Thank you, ma'am," said Bitzer, knuckling his forehead again, in return for the favour of Mrs. Sparsit's improving conversation. "Would you wish a little more hot water, ma'am, or is there anything else that I could fetch you?"

"Nothing just now, Bitzer."

"Thank you, ma'am. I shouldn't wish to disturb you at your meals, ma'am, particularly tea, knowing your partiality for it," said Bitzer, craning a little to look over into the street from where he stood; "but there's a gentleman been looking up here for a minute or so, ma'am, and he has come across as if he was going to knock. That *is* his knock, ma'am, no doubt."

He stepped to the window; and looking out, and drawing in his head again, confirmed himself with, "Yes, ma'am. Would you wish the gentleman to be shown in, ma'am?"

"I don't know who it can be," said Mrs. Sparsit, wiping her mouth and arranging her mittens.

"A stranger, ma'am, evidently."

"What a stranger can want at the Bank at this time of the evening, unless he comes upon business for which he is too late, I don't know," said Mrs. Sparsit, "but I hold a charge in this establishment from Mr. Bounderby, and I will never shrink from it. If to see him is any part of the duty I have accepted, I will see him. Use your own discretion, Bitzer."

Here the visitor, all unconscious of Mrs. Sparsit's magnanimous words, repeated his knock so loudly that the light porter hastened down to open the door; while Mrs. Sparsit took the precaution of concealing her little table, with all its appliances upon it, in a cupboard, and then decamped up-stairs, that she might appear, if needful, with the greater dignity.

A visitor at the Bank

"If you please, ma'am, the gentleman would wish to see you," said Bitzer, with his light eye at Mrs. Sparsit's keyhole. So, Mrs.

Sparsit, who had improved the interval by touching up her cap, took her classical features down-stairs again, and entered the boardroom in the manner of a Roman matron going outside the city walls to treat with an invading general.

The visitor having strolled to the window, and being then engaged in looking carelessly out, was as unmoved by this impressive entry as man could possibly be. He stood whistling to himself with all imaginable coolness, with his hat still on, and a certain air of exhaustion upon him, in part arising from excessive summer, and in part from excessive gentility. For it was to be seen with half an eye that he was a thorough gentleman, made to the model of the time; weary of everything, and putting no more faith in anything than Lucifer.

"I believe, sir," quoth Mrs. Sparsit, "you wished to see me."

"I beg your pardon," he said, turning and removing his hat; "pray excuse me."

"Humph!" thought Mrs. Sparsit, as she made a stately bend. "Five and thirty, good-looking, good figure, good teeth, good voice, good breeding, well-dressed, dark hair, bold eyes." All which Mrs. Sparsit observed in her womanly way—like the Sultan who put his head in the pail of water—merely in dipping down and coming up again.

"Please to be seated, sir," said Mrs. Sparsit.

"Thank you. Allow me." He placed a chair for her, but remained himself carelessly lounging against the table. "I left my servant at the railway looking after the luggage—very heavy train and vast quantity of it in the van—and strolled on, looking about me. Exceedingly odd place. Will you allow me to ask you if it's *always* as black as this?"

"In general much blacker," returned Mrs. Sparsit, in her uncompromising way.

"Is it possible! Excuse me: you are not a native, I think?"

"No, sir," returned Mrs. Sparsit. "It was once my good or ill fortune, as it may be—before I became a widow—to move in a very different sphere. My husband was a Powler."

"Beg your pardon, really!" said the stranger. "Was—?"

Mrs. Sparsit repeated, "A Powler."

"Powler Family," said the stranger, after reflecting a few moments. Mrs. Sparsit signified assent. The stranger seemed a little more fatigued than before.

"You must be very much bored here?" was the inference he drew from the communication.

"I am the servant of circumstances, sir," said Mrs. Sparsit, "and I have long adapted myself to the governing power of my life."

"Very philosophical," returned the stranger, "and very exemplary and laudable, and—" It seemed to be scarcely worth his while to finish the sentence, so he played with his watch-chain wearily.

"May I be permitted to ask, sir," said Mrs. Sparsit, "to what I am indebted for the favour of—"

"Assuredly," said the stranger. "Much obliged to you for reminding me. I am the bearer of a letter of introduction to Mr. Bounderby the banker. Walking through this extraordinarily black town, while they were getting dinner ready at the hotel, I asked a fellow whom I met; one of the working people; who appeared to have been taking a shower-bath of something fluffy, which I assume to be the raw material"—

Mrs. Sparsit inclined her head.

"—Raw material—where Mr. Bounderby, the banker, might reside. Upon which, misled no doubt by the word Banker, he directed me to the Bank. Fact being, I presume, that Mr. Bounderby the Banker does *not* reside in the edifice in which I have the honour of offering this explanation?"

"No, sir," returned Mrs. Sparsit, "he does not."

"Thank you. I had no intention of delivering my letter at the present moment, nor have I. But strolling on to the Bank to kill time, and having the good fortune to observe at the window," towards which he languidly waved his hand, then slightly bowed, "a lady of a very superior and agreeable appearance, I considered that I could not do better than take the liberty of asking that lady where Mr. Bounderby the Banker *does* live. Which I accordingly venture, with all suitable apologies, to do."

The inattention and indolence of his manner were sufficiently relieved, to Mrs. Sparsit's thinking, by a certain gallantry at ease, which offered her homage too. Here he was, for instance, at this moment, all but sitting on the table, and yet lazily bending over her, as if he acknowledged an attraction in her that made her charming—in her way.

"Banks, I know, are always suspicious, and officially must be," said the stranger, whose lightness and smoothness of speech were pleasant likewise; suggesting matter far more sensible and humorous than it ever contained—which was perhaps a shrewd device of the founder of this numerous sect, whosoever may have been that great man: "therefore I may observe that my letter—here it is—is from the member for this place—Gradgrind—whom I have had the pleasure of knowing in London."

Mrs. Sparsit recognized the hand, intimated that such confirmation was quite unnecessary, and gave Mr. Bounderby's address, with all needful clues and directions in aid.

"Thousand thanks," said the stranger. "Of course you know the Banker well?"

"Yes, sir," rejoined Mrs. Sparsit. "In my dependent relation towards him, I have known him ten years."

"Quite an eternity! I think he married Gradgrind's daughter?"

"Yes," said Mrs. Sparsit, suddenly compressing her mouth, "he had that—honour."

"The lady is quite a philosopher, I am told?"

"Indeed, sir," said Mrs. Sparsit. "*Is* she?"

"Excuse my impertinent curiosity," pursued the stranger, fluttering over Mrs. Sparsit's eyebrows, with a propitiatory air, "but you know the family, and know the world. I am about to know the family, and may have much to do with them. Is the lady so very alarming? Her father gives her such a portentously hardheaded reputation, that I have a burning desire to know. Is she absolutely unapproachable? Repellantly and stunningly clever? I see, by your meaning smile, you think not. You have poured balm into my anxious soul. As to age, now. Forty? Five and thirty?"

Mrs. Sparsit laughed outright. "A chit," said she. "Not twenty when she was married."

"I give you my honour, Mrs. Powler," returned the stranger, detaching himself from the table, "that I never was so astonished in my life!"

It really did seem to impress him, to the utmost extent of his capacity of being impressed. He looked at his informant for full a quarter of a minute, and appeared to have the surprise in his hand all the time. "I assure you, Mrs. Powler," he then said, much exhausted, "that the father's manner prepared me for a grim and stony maturity. I am obliged to you, of all things, for correcting so absurd a mistake. Pray excuse my intrusion. Many thanks. Good day!"

He bowed himself out; and Mrs. Sparsit, hiding in the window curtain, saw him languishing down the street on the shady side of the way, observed of all the town.

"What do you think of the gentleman, Bitzer?" she asked the light porter, when he came to take away.

"Spends a deal of money on his dress, ma'am."

"It must be admitted," said Mrs. Sparsit, "that it's very tasteful."

"Yes, ma'am," returned Bitzer, "if that's worth the money."

"Besides which, ma'am," resumed Bitzer, while he was polishing the table, "he looks to me as if he gamed."

"It's immoral to game," said Mrs. Sparsit.

"It's ridiculous, ma'am," said Bitzer, "because the chances are against the players."

Whether it was that the heat prevented Mrs. Sparsit from working, or whether it was that her hand was out, she did no work that night. She sat at the window, when the sun began to sink behind the smoke; she sat there, when the smoke was burning red, when the colour faded from it, when darkness seemed to rise slowly out of the ground, and creep upward, upwards, up to the house-tops, up the church steeple, up to the summits of the factory chimneys, up to the sky. Without a candle in the room, Mrs. Sparsit sat at the window, with her hands before her, not thinking much of the sounds of evening; the whooping of boys, the barking of dogs, the rumbling of wheels, the steps and voices of passengers, the shrill street cries, the clogs upon the pavement when it was their hour for going by, the shutting-up of shop-shutters. Not until the light porter announced that her nocturnal sweetbread was ready, did Mrs. Sparsit arouse herself from her reverie, and convey her dense black eyebrows—by that time creased with meditation, as if they needed ironing out—up-stairs.

"O, you Fool!" said Mrs. Sparsit, when she was alone at her supper. Whom she meant, she did not say; but she could scarcely have meant the sweetbread.

CHAPTER TWO

MR. JAMES HARTHOUSE

The Gradgrind party wanted assistance in cutting the throats of the Graces. They went about recruiting; and where could they enlist recruits more hopefully, than among the fine gentlemen who, having found out everything to be worth nothing, were equally ready for anything?

Recruiting

Moreover, the healthy spirits who had mounted to this sublime height were attractive to many of the Gradgrind school. They liked fine gentlemen; they pretended that they did not, but they did. They became exhausted in imitation of them; and they yawyawed in their speech like them; and they served out, with an enervated air, the little mouldy rations of political economy, on which they regaled their disciples. There never before was seen on earth such a wonderful hybrid race as was thus produced.

Among the fine gentlemen not regularly belonging to the Gradgrind school, there was one of a good family and a better appearance, with a happy turn of humour which had told immensely with the House of Commons on the occasion of his entertaining it with his (and the Board of Directors') view of a railway accident, in which the most careful officers ever known, employed by the most liberal managers ever heard of, assisted by the finest mechanical contrivances ever devised, the whole in action on the best line ever constructed, had killed five people and wounded thirty-two, by a casualty without which the excellence of the whole system would have been positively incomplete. Among the slain was a cow, and among the scattered articles unowned, a widow's cap. And the honourable member had so tickled the House (which has a delicate sense of humour) by putting the cap on the cow, that it became impatient of any serious reference to the Coroner's Inquest, and brought the railway off with Cheers and Laughter.

Now, this gentleman had a younger brother of still better appearance than himself, who had tried life as a Cornet of Dragoons, and found it a bore; and had afterwards tried it in the train of an English minister abroad, and found it a bore; and had then strolled to Jerusalem, and got bored there; and had then gone yachting about the world, and got bored everywhere. To whom this honourable and jocular member fraternally said one day, "Jem, there's a good opening among the hard Fact fellows, and they want men. I wonder you don't go in for statistics." Jem, rather taken by the novelty of the idea, and very hard up for a change, was as ready to "go in" for statistics as for anything else. So, he went in. He coached himself up with a blue book or two; and his brother put it about among the hard Fact fellows, and said, "If you want to bring in, for any place, a handsome dog who can make you a devilish good speech, look after my brother Jem, for he's your man." After a few dashes in the public meeting way, Mr. Gradgrind and a council of political sages approved of Jem, and it was resolved to send him down to Coketown, to become known there and in the neighbourhood. Hence the letter Jem had last night shown to Mrs. Sparsit, which Mr. Bounderby now held in his hand; superscribed, "Josiah Bounderby, Esquire, Banker, Coketown. Specially to introduce James Harthouse, Esquire. Thomas Gradgrind."

Within an hour of the receipt of this dispatch and Mr. James Harthouse's card, Mr. Bounderby put on his hat and went down to the Hotel. There he found Mr. James Harthouse looking out of window, in a state of mind so disconsolate, that he was already half-disposed to "go in" for something else.

"My name, sir," said the visitor, "is Josiah Bounderby, of Coketown."

Mr. James Harthouse was very happy indeed (though he scarcely looked so), to have a pleasure he had long expected.

"Coketown, sir," said Bounderby, obstinately taking a chair, "is not the kind of place you have been accustomed to. Therefore, if you will allow me—or whether you will or not, for I am a plain man—I'll tell you something about it before we go any further."

Mr. Harthouse would be charmed.

"Don't be too sure of that," said Bounderby. "I don't promise it. First of all, you see our smoke. That's meat and drink to us. It's the healthiest thing in the world in all respects, and particularly for the lungs. If you are one of those who want us to consume it, I differ from you. We are not going to wear the bottoms of our boilers out any faster than we wear 'em out now, for all the humbugging sentiment in Great Britain and Ireland."

By way of "going in" to the fullest extent, Mr. Harthouse rejoined, "Mr. Bounderby, I assure you I am entirely and completely of your way of thinking. On conviction."

"I am glad to hear it," said Bounderby. "Now, you have heard a lot of talk about the work in our mills, no doubt. You have? Very good. I'll state the fact of it to you. It's the pleasantest work there is, and it's the lightest work there is, and it's the best paid work there is. More than that, we couldn't improve the mills themselves, unless we laid down Turkey carpets on the floors. Which we're not a-going to do."

"Mr. Bounderby, perfectly right."

"Lastly," said Bounderby, "as to our Hands. There's not a Hand in this town, sir, man, woman, or child, but has one ultimate object in life. That object is, to be fed on turtle soup and venison with a gold spoon. Now, they're not agoing—none of 'em—ever to be fed on turtle soup and venison with a gold spoon. And now you know the place."

Mr. Harthouse professed himself in the highest degree instructed and refreshed, by this condensed epitome of the whole Coketown question.

"Why, you see," replied Mr. Bounderby, "it suits my disposition to have a full understanding with a man, particularly with a public man, when I make his acquaintance. I have only one thing more to say to you, Mr. Harthouse, before assuring you of the pleasure with which I shall respond, to the utmost of my poor ability, to my friend Tom Gradgrind's letter of introduction. You are a man of family. Don't you deceive yourself by supposing for a moment that I am a man of family. I am a bit of dirty riff-raff, and a genuine scrap of tag, rag, and bobtail."

If anything could have exalted Jem's interest in Mr. Bounderby, it would have been this very circumstance. Or, so he told him.

"So now," said Bounderby, "we may shake hands on equal terms. I say, equal terms, because although I know what I am, and the exact depth of the gutter I have lifted myself out of, better than any man does, I am as proud as you are. I am just as proud as you are. Having now asserted my independence in a proper manner, I may come to how do you find yourself, and I hope you're pretty well."

The better, Mr. Harthouse gave him to understand as they shook hands, for the salubrious air of Coketown. Mr. Bounderby received the answer with favour.

"Perhaps you know," said he, "or perhaps you don't know, I married Tom Gradgrind's daughter. If you have nothing better to do than to walk up town with me, I shall be glad to introduce you to Tom Gradgrind's daughter."

"Mr. Bounderby," said Jem, "you anticipate my dearest wishes."

They went out without further discourse; and Mr. Bounderby piloted the new acquaintance who so strongly contrasted with him, to the private red brick dwelling, with the black outside shutters, the green inside blinds, and the black street door up the two white steps. In the drawing-room of which mansion, there presently entered to them the most remarkable girl Mr. James Harthouse had ever seen. She was so constrained, and yet so careless; so reserved, and yet so watchful; so cold and proud, and yet so sensitively ashamed of her husband's braggart humility—from which she shrunk as if every example of it were a cut or a blow; that it was quite a new sensation to observe her. In face she was no less remarkable than in manner. Her features were handsome; but their natural play was so locked up, that it seemed impossible to guess at their genuine expression. Utterly indifferent, perfectly self-reliant, never at a loss, and yet never at her ease, with her figure in company with them there, and her mind apparently quite alone—it was of no use "going in" yet awhile to comprehend this girl, for she baffled all penetration.

From the mistress of the house, the visitor glanced to the house itself. There was no mute sign of a woman in the room. No graceful little adornment, no fanciful little device, however trivial, anywhere expressed her influence. Cheerless and comfortless, boastfully and doggedly rich, there the room stared at its present occupants, unsoftened and unrelieved by the least trace of any womanly occupation. As Mr. Bounderby stood in the midst of his household gods, so those unrelenting divinities occupied their places around Mr. Bounderby, and they were worthy of one another, and well matched.

"This, sir," said Bounderby, "is my wife, Mrs. Bounderby: Tom Gradgrind's eldest daughter. Loo, Mr. James *"Loo, Mr.* Harthouse. Mr. Harthouse has joined your *James Harthouse"* father's muster-roll. If he is not Tom Gradgrind's colleague before long, I believe we shall at last hear of him in connexion with one of our neighbouring towns. You observe, Mr. Harthouse, that my wife is my junior. I don't know what she saw in me to marry me, but she saw something in me, I suppose, or she wouldn't have married me. She has lots of expensive knowledge, sir, political and otherwise. If you want to cram for anything, I should be troubled to recommend you to a better adviser than Loo Bounderby."

To a more agreeable adviser, or one from whom he would be more likely to learn, Mr. Harthouse could never be recommended.

"Come!" said his host. "If you're in the complimentary line, you'll get on here, for you'll meet with no competition. I have never been in the way of learning compliments myself, and I don't profess to understand the art of paying 'em. In fact, despise 'em. But, your bringing-up was different from mine; mine was a real thing, by George! You're a gentleman, and I don't pretend to be one. I am Josiah Bounderby of Coketown, and that's enough for me. However, though I am not influenced by manners and station, Loo Bounderby may be. She hadn't my advantages—disadvantages you would call 'em, but I call 'em advantages—so you'll not waste your power, I dare say."

"Mr. Bounderby," said Jem, turning with a smile to Louisa, "is a noble animal in a comparatively natural state, quite free from the harness in which a conventional hack like myself works."

"You respect Mr. Bounderby very much," she quietly returned. "It is natural that you should."

He was disgracefully thrown out, for a gentleman who had seen so much of the world, and thought, "Now, how am I to take this?"

"You are going to devote yourself, as I gather from what Mr. Bounderby has said, to the service of your country. You have made up your mind," said Louisa, still standing before him where she had first stopped—in all the singular contrariety of her self-possession, and her being obviously very ill at ease—"to show the nation the way out of all its difficulties."

"Mrs. Bounderby," he returned, laughing, "upon my honour, no. I will make no such pretence to you. I have seen a little, here and there, up and down; I have found it all to be very worthless, as everybody has, and as some confess they have, and some do not; and I am going in for your respected father's opinions—really because I have no choice of opinions, and may as well back them as anything else."

"Have you none of your own?" asked Louisa.

"I have not so much as the slightest predilection left. I assure you I attach not the least importance to any opinions. The result of the varieties of boredom I have undergone, is a conviction (unless conviction is too industrious a word for the lazy sentiment I entertain on the subject), that any set of ideas will do just as much good as any other set, and just as much harm as any other set. There's an English family with a charming Italian motto. What will be, will be. It's the only truth going!"

This vicious assumption of honesty and dishonesty—a vice so dangerous, so deadly, and so common—seemed, he observed, a little to impress her in his favour. He followed up the advantage, by saying in his pleasantest manner; a manner to which she might attach as much or as little meaning as she pleased: "The side that can prove anything in a line of units, tens, hundreds, and thousands, Mrs. Bounderby, seems to me to afford the most fun, and to give a man the best chance. I am quite as much attached to it as if I believed it. I am quite ready to go in for it, to the same extent as if I believed it. And what more could I possibly do, if I did believe it!"

"You are a singular politician," said Louisa.

"Pardon me; I have not even that merit. We are the largest party in the state, I assure you, Mrs. Bounderby, if we all fell out of our adopted ranks and were reviewed together."

Mr. Bounderby, who had been in danger of bursting in silence, interposed here with a project for postponing the family dinner till half-past six, and taking Mr. James Harthouse in the meantime on a round of visits to the voting and interesting notabilities of Coketown and its vicinity. The round of visits was made; and Mr. James Harthouse, with a discreet use of his blue coaching, came off triumphantly, though with a considerable accession of boredom.

In the evening, he found the dinner-table laid for four, but they sat down only three. It was an appropriate occasion for Mr. Bounderby to discuss the flavour of the hap'orth of stewed eels he had purchased in the streets at eight years old; and also of the inferior water, specially used for laying the dust, with which he had washed down that repast. He likewise entertained his guest over the soup and fish, with the calculation that he (Bounderby) had eaten in his youth at least three horses under the guise of polonies and saveloys. These recitals, Jem, in a languid manner, received with "charming!" every now and then; and they probably would have decided him to "go in" for Jerusalem again to-morrow morning, had he been less curious respecting Louisa.

"Is there nothing," he thought, glancing at her as she sat at the head of the table, where her youthful figure, small and slight, but very graceful, looked as pretty as it looked misplaced; "is there nothing that will move that face?"

Yes! By Jupiter, there was something, and here it was, in an unexpected shape. Tom appeared. She changed as the door opened, and broke into a beaming smile.

A beautiful smile. Mr. James Harthouse might not have thought so much of it, but that he had wondered so long at her impassive face. She put out her hand—a pretty little soft hand; and her fingers closed upon her brother's, as if she would have carried them to her lips.

"Ay, ay?" thought the visitor. "This whelp is the only creature she cares for. So, so!"

The whelp was presented, and took his chair. The appellation was not flattering, but not unmerited.

The whelp   "When I was your age, young Tom," said Bounderby, "I was punctual, or I got no dinner!"

"When you were my age," returned Tom, "you hadn't a wrong balance to get right, and hadn't to dress afterwards."

"Never mind that now," said Bounderby.

"Well, then," grumbled Tom. "Don't begin with me."

"Mrs. Bounderby," said Harthouse, perfectly hearing this under-strain as it went on; "your brother's face is quite familiar to me. Can I have seen him abroad? Or at some public school, perhaps?"

"No," she returned, quite interested, "he has never been abroad yet, and was educated here, at home. Tom, love, I am telling Mr. Harthouse that he never saw you abroad."

"No such luck, sir," said Tom.

There was little enough in him to brighten her face, for he was a sullen young fellow, and ungracious in his manner even to her. So much the greater must have been the solitude of her heart, and her need of some one on whom to bestow it. "So much the more is this whelp the only creature she has ever cared for," thought Mr. James Harthouse, turning it over and over. "So much the more. So much the more."

Both in his sister's presence, and after she had left the room, the whelp took no pains to hide his contempt for Mr. Bounderby, whenever he could indulge it without the observation of that independent man, by making wry faces, or shutting one eye. Without responding to these telegraphic communications, Mr. Harthouse encouraged him much in the course of the evening, and showed an unusual liking for him. At last, when he rose to return to his hotel, and was a little doubtful whether he knew the way by night, the whelp immediately proffered his services as guide, and turned out with him to escort him thither.

CHAPTER THREE

THE WHELP

I<small>T</small> was very remarkable that a young gentleman who had been brought up under one continuous system of unnatural restraint, should be a hypocrite; but it was certainly the case with Tom. It was very strange that a young gentleman who had never been left to his own guidance for five consecutive minutes, should be incapable at last of governing himself; but so it was with Tom. It was altogether unaccountable that a young gentleman whose imagination had been strangled in his cradle, should be still inconvenienced by its ghost in the form of grovelling sensualities; but such a monster, beyond all doubt, was Tom.

"Do you smoke?" asked Mr. James Harthouse, when they came to the hotel.

"I believe you!" said Tom.

He could do no less than ask Tom up; and Tom could do no less than go up. What with a cooling drink adapted to the weather, but not so weak as cool; and what with a rarer tobacco than was to be bought in those parts; Tom was soon in a highly free and easy state at his end of the sofa, and more than ever disposed to admire his new friend at the other end.

Tom blew his smoke aside, after he had been smoking a little while, and took an observation of his friend. "He don't seem to care about his dress," thought Tom, "and yet how capitally he does it. What an easy swell he is!"

Mr. James Harthouse, happening to catch Tom's eye, remarked that he drank nothing, and filled his glass with his own negligent hand.

"Thank'ee," said Tom. "Thank'ee. Well, Mr. Harthouse, I hope you have had about a dose of old Bounderby to-night." Tom said this with one eye shut up again, and looking over his glass knowingly at his entertainer.

"A very good fellow indeed!" returned Mr. James Harthouse.

"You think so, don't you?" said Tom. And shut up his eye again.

Mr. James Harthouse smiled; and rising from his end of the sofa, and lounging with his back against the chimney-piece, so that he stood before the empty fire-grate as he smoked, in front of Tom and looking down at him, observed:

"What a comical brother-in-law you are!"

"What a comical brother-in-law old Bounderby is, I think you mean," said Tom.

"You are a piece of caustic, Tom," retorted Mr. James Harthouse.

There was something so very agreeable in being so intimate with such a waistcoat; in being called Tom, in such an intimate way, by such a voice; in being on such off-hand terms so soon, with such a pair of whiskers; that Tom was uncommonly pleased with himself.

"Oh! I don't care for old Bounderby," said he, "if you mean that. I have always called old Bounderby by the same name when I have talked about him, and I have always thought of him in the same way. I am not going to begin to be polite now, about old Bounderby. It would be rather late in the day."

"Don't mind me," returned James; "but take care when his wife is by, you know."

"His wife?" said Tom. "My sister Loo? O yes!" And he laughed, and took a little more of the cooling drink.

James Harthouse continued to lounge in the same place and attitude, smoking his cigar in his own easy way, and looking pleasantly at the whelp, as if he knew himself to be a kind of agreeable demon who had only to hover over him, and he must give up his whole soul if required. It certainly did seem that the whelp yielded to this influence. He looked at his companion sneakingly, he looked at him admiringly, he looked at him boldly, and put up one leg on the sofa.

"My sister Loo?" said Tom. "*She* never cared for old Bounderby."

"That's the past tense, Tom," returned Mr. James Harthouse, striking the ash from his cigar with his little finger. "We are in the present tense, now."

"Verb neuter, not to care. Indicative mood, present tense. First person singular, I do not care; second person singular, thou dost not care; third person singular, she does not care," returned Tom.

"Good! Very quaint!" said his friend. "Though you don't mean it."

"But I *do* mean it," cried Tom. "Upon my honour! Why, you won't tell me, Mr. Harthouse, that you really suppose my sister Loo does care for old Bounderby."

"My dear fellow," returned the other, "what am I bound to suppose, when I find two married people living in harmony and happiness?"

Tom had by this time got both his legs on the sofa. If his second leg had not been already there when he was called a dear fellow, he would have put it up at that great stage of the conversation. Feeling it necessary to do something then, he stretched himself out at greater length, and, reclining with the back of his head on the end of the sofa, and smoking with an infinite assumption of negligence, turned his common face, and not too sober eyes, towards the face looking down upon him so carelessly yet so potently.

The whelp under a spell

"You know our governor, Mr. Harthouse," said Tom, "and therefore, you needn't be surprised that Loo married old Bounderby. She never had a lover, and the governor proposed old Bounderby, and she took him."

"Very dutiful in your interesting sister," said Mr. James Harthouse.

"Yes, but she wouldn't have been as dutiful, and it would not have come off as easily," returned the whelp, "if it hadn't been for me."

The tempter merely lifted his eyebrows; but the whelp was obliged to go on.

"*I* persuaded her," he said, with an edifying air of superiority. "I was stuck into old Bounderby's bank (where I never wanted to be), and I knew I should get into scrapes there, if she put old Bounderby's pipe out; so I told her my wishes, and she came into them. She would do anything for me. It was very game of her, wasn't it?"

"It was charming, Tom!"

"Not that it was altogether so important to her as it was to me," continued Tom coolly, "because my liberty and comfort, and perhaps my getting on, depended on it; and she had no other lover, and staying at home was like staying in jail—especially when I was gone. It wasn't as if she gave up another lover for old Bounderby; but still it was a good thing in her."

"Perfectly delightful. And she gets on so placidly."

"Oh," returned Tom, with contemptuous patronage, "she's a regular girl. A girl can get on anywhere. She has settled down to the life, and *she* don't mind. It does just as well as another. Besides, though Loo is a girl, she's not a common sort of girl. She can shut herself up within herself, and think—as I have often known her sit and watch the fire—for an hour at a stretch."

"Ay, ay? Has resources of her own," said Harthouse, smoking quietly.

"Not so much of that as you may suppose," returned Tom; "for our governor had her crammed with all sorts of dry bones and sawdust. It's his system."

"Formed his daughter on his own model?" suggested Harthouse.

"His daughter? Ah! and everybody else. Why he formed Me that way?" said Tom.

"Impossible!"

"He did, though," said Tom, shaking his head. "I mean to say, Mr. Harthouse, that when I first left home and went to old Bounderby's, I was as flat as a warming-pan, and knew no more about life, than any oyster does."

"Come, Tom! I can hardly believe that. A joke's a joke."

"Upon my soul!" said the whelp. "I am serious; I am indeed!" He smoked with great gravity and dignity for a little while, and then added, in a highly complacent tone, "Oh! I have picked up a little since. I don't deny that. But I have done it myself; no thanks to the governor."

"And your intelligent sister?"

"My intelligent sister is about where she was. She used to complain to me that she had nothing to fall back upon, that girls usually fall back upon; and I don't see how she is to have got over that since. But *she* don't mind," he sagaciously added, puffing at his cigar again. "Girls can always get on, somehow."

"Calling at the Bank yesterday evening, for Mr. Bounderby's address, I found an ancient lady there, who seems to entertain great admiration for your sister," observed Mr. James Harthouse, throwing away the last small remnant of the cigar he had now smoked out.

"Mother Sparsit!" said Tom. "What! you have seen her already, have you?"

His friend nodded. Tom took his cigar out of his mouth, to shut up his eye (which had grown rather unmanageable) with the greater expression, and to tap his nose several times with his finger.

"Mother Sparsit's feeling for Loo is more than admiration, I should think," said Tom. "Say affection and devotion. Mother

Sparsit never set her cap at Bounderby when he was a bachelor. Oh no!"

These were the last words spoken by the whelp, before a giddy drowsiness came upon him, followed by complete oblivion. He was roused from the latter state by an uneasy dream of being stirred up with a boot, and also of a voice saying: "Come, it's late. Be off!"

"Well!" he said, scrambling from the sofa. "I must take my leave of you though. I say. Yours is very good tobacco. But it's too mild."

"Yes, it's too mild," returned his entertainer.

"It's—it's ridiculously mild," said Tom. "Where's the door? Good night!"

He had another odd dream of being taken by a waiter through a mist, which, after giving him some trouble and difficulty, resolved itself into the main street, in which he stood alone. He then walked home pretty easily, though not yet free from an impression of the presence and influence of his new friend—as if he were lounging somewhere in the air, in the same negligent attitude, regarding him with the same look.

The whelp went home, and went to bed. If he had had any sense of what he had done that night, and had been less of a whelp and more of a brother, he might have turned short on the road, might have gone down to the ill-smelling river that was dyed black, might have gone to bed in it for good and all, and have curtained his head for ever with its filthy waters.

CHAPTER FOUR

MEN AND BROTHERS

"OH my friends, the down-trodden operatives of Coketown! Oh my friends and fellow-countrymen, the slaves of an iron-handed and a grinding despotism! Oh my friends and fellow-sufferers, and fellow-workmen, and fellow-men! I tell you that the hour is come, when we must rally round one another as One united power, and crumble into dust the oppressors that too long have battened upon the plunder of our families, upon the sweat of our brows, upon the labour of our hands, upon the strength of our sinews, upon the God-created glorious rights of Humanity, and upon the holy and eternal privileges of Brotherhood!"

"Good!" "Hear, hear, hear!" "Hurrah!" and other cries, arose in many voices from various parts of the densely crowded and suffocatingly close Hall, in which the orator, perched on a stage, delivered himself of this and what other froth and fume he had in him. He had declaimed himself into a violent heat, and was as hoarse as he was hot. By dint of roaring at the top of his voice under a flaring gas-light, clenching his fists, knitting his brows, setting his teeth, and pounding with his arms, he had taken so much out of himself by this time, that he was brought to a stop, and called for a glass of water.

As he stood there, trying to quench his fiery face with his drink of water, the comparison between the orator and the crowd of attentive faces turned towards him, was extremely to his disadvantage. Judging him by Nature's evidence, he was above the mass in very little but the stage on which he stood. In many great respects he was essentially below them. He was not so honest, he was not so manly, he was not so good-humoured; he substituted cunning for their simplicity, and passion for their safe solid sense. An ill-made, high-shouldered man, with lowering brows, and his features crushed into an habitually sour expression, he contrasted most unfavourably, even in his mongrel dress, with the great body of his hearers in their plain working clothes. Strange as it always is to consider any assembly in the act of submissively resigning itself to the dreariness of some complacent person, lord or commoner, whom three-fourths of it could, by no human means, raise out of the slough of inanity to their own intellectual level, it was particularly strange, and it was even particularly affecting, to see this crowd of earnest faces, whose honesty in the main no competent observer free from bias could doubt, so agitated by such a leader.

Good! Hear, hear! Hurrah! The eagerness both of attention and intention, exhibited in all the countenances, made them a most impressive sight. There was no carelessness, no languor, no idle curiosity; none of the many shades of indifference to be seen in all other assemblies, visible for one moment there. That every man felt his condition to be, somehow or other, worse than it might be; that every man considered it incumbent on him to join the rest, towards the making of it better; that every man felt his only hope to be in his allying himself to the comrades by whom he was surrounded; and that in this belief, right or wrong (unhappily wrong then), the whole of that crowd were gravely, deeply, faithfully in earnest; must have been as plain to any one who chose to see what was there, as the bare beams of the roof and the whitened brick walls. Nor could any such spectator fail to know in his own breast, that these men, through their very delusions, showed great qualities, susceptible of being turned to the happiest and best account; and that to pretend (on the strength of sweeping axioms, howsoever cut and dried) that they went astray wholly without cause, and of their own irrational wills, was to pretend that there could be smoke without fire, death without birth, harvest without seed, anything or everything produced from nothing.

The orator having refreshed himself, wiped his corrugated forehead from left to right several times with his handkerchief folded into a pad, and concentrated all his revived forces, in a sneer of great disdain and bitterness.

A *professional* leader

"But, oh my friends and brothers! Oh men and Englishmen, the down-trodden operatives of Coketown! What shall we say of that man—that working-man, that I should find it necessary so to libel the glorious name—who, being practically and well acquainted with the grievances and wrongs of you, the injured pith and marrow of this land, and having heard you, with a noble and majestic unanimity that will make Tyrants tremble, resolve for to subscribe to the funds of the United Aggregate Tribunal, and to abide by the injunctions issued by that body for your benefit, whatever they may be—what, I ask you, will you say of that working-man, since such I must acknowledge him to be, who, at such a time, deserts his post, and sells his flag; who, at such a time, turns a traitor and a craven and a recreant; who, at such a time, is not ashamed to make to you the dastardly and humiliating avowal that he will hold himself aloof, and will *not* be one of those associated in the gallant stand for Freedom and for Right?"

The assembly was divided at this point. There were some groans and hisses, but the general sense of honour was much too strong for the condemnation of a man unheard. "Be sure you're right, Slackbridge!" "Put him up!" "Let's hear him!" Such things were said on many sides. Finally, one strong voice called out, "Is the man heer? If the man's heer, Slackbridge, let's hear the man himseln, 'stead o' yo." Which was received with a round of applause.

Slackbridge, the orator, looked about him with a withering smile; and, holding out his right hand at arm's length (as the manner of all Slackbridges is), to still the thundering sea, waited until there was a profound silence.

"Oh my friends and fellow-men!" said Slackbridge then, shaking his head with violent scorn, "I do not wonder that you, the prostrate sons of labour, are incredulous of the existence of such a man. But he who sold his birthright for a mess of pottage existed, and Judas Iscariot existed, and Castlereagh existed, and this man exists!"

Here, a brief press and confusion near the stage, ended in the man himself standing at the orator's side before the concourse. He was pale and a little moved in the face—his lips especially showed it; but he stood quiet, with his left hand at his chin, waiting to be heard. There was a chairman to regulate the proceedings, and this functionary now took the case into his own hands.

"My friends," said he, "by virtue o' my office as your president, I ashes o' our friend Slackbridge, who may be a little over hetter in this business, to take his seat, whiles this man Stephen Blackpool is heern. You all know this man Stephen Blackpool. You know him awlung o' his misfort'ns, and his good name."

With that, the chairman shook him frankly by the hand, and sat down again. Slackbridge likewise sat down, wiping his hot forehead—always from left to right, and never the reverse way.

"My friends," Stephen began, in the midst of a dead calm; "I ha' hed what's been spok'n o' me, and 'tis lickly that I shan't mend it. But I'd liefer you'd hearn the truth concernin' myseln, fro my lips than fro onny other man's, though I never cud'n speak afore so monny, wi'out being moydert and muddled."

Slackbridge shook his head as if he would shake it off, in his bitterness.

"I'm th' one single Hand in Bounderby's mill, o' a' the men theer, as don't coom in wi' th' proposed reg'lations. I canna' coom in wi' 'em. My friends, I doubt their doin' yo onny good. Licker they'll do yo hurt."

Slackbridge laughed, folded his arms, and frowned sarcastically.

"But 't an't sommuch for that as I stands out. If that were aw, I'd coom in wi' th' rest. But I ha' my reasons—mine, yo see—for being hindered; not on'y now, but awlus—awlus—life long!"

Slackbridge jumped up and stood beside him, gnashing and tearing. "Oh my friends, what but this did I tell you? Oh my fellow-countrymen, what warning but this did I give you? And how shows this recreant conduct in a man on whom unequal laws are known to have fallen heavy? Oh you Englishmen, I ask you how does this subornation show in one of yourselves, who is thus consenting to his own undoing and to yours, and to your children's and your children's children's?"

There was some applause, and some crying of Shame upon the man; but the greater part of the audience were quiet. They looked at Stephen's worn face, rendered more pathetic by the homely emotions it evinced; and, in the kindness of their nature, they were more sorry than indignant.

" 'Tis this Delegate's trade for t' speak," said Stephen, "an he's paid for 't, an he knows his work. Let him keep to 't. Let him give no heed to what I ha' had'n to bear. That's not for him. That's not for nobbody but me."

There was a propriety, not to say a dignity in these words, that made the hearers yet more quiet and attentive. The same strong voice called out, "Slackbridge, let the man be heern, and howd thee tongue!" Then the place was wonderfully still.

"My brothers," said Stephen, whose low voice was distinctly heard, "and my fellow-workmen—for that yo are to me, though not, as I knows on, to this delegate here—I ha' but a word to sen, and I could sen nommore if I was to speak till Strike o' day. I know weel, aw what's afore me. I know weel that yo aw resolve to ha' nommore ado wi' a man who is not wi' yo in this matther. I know weel that if I was a lyin parisht i' th' road, yo'd feel it right to pass me by, as a forrenner and stranger. What I ha' getn, I mun mak th' best on."

"Stephen Blackpool," said the chairman, rising, "think on 't agen. Think on 't once agen, lad, afore thou'rt shunned by aw owd friends." *Stephen cast out*

There was an universal murmur to the same effect, though no man articulated a word. Every eye was fixed on Stephen's face. To repent of his determination, would be to take a load from all their minds. He looked around him, and knew that it was so. Not a grain of anger with them was in his heart; he knew them, far below their surface weaknesses and misconceptions, as no one but their fellow-labourer could.

"I ha' thowt on 't, above a bit, sir. I simply canna coom in. I mun go th' way as lays afore me. I mun tak my leave o' aw heer."

He made a sort of reverence to them by holding up his arms, and stood for the moment in that attitude: not speaking until they slowly dropped at his sides.

"Monny's the pleasant word as soom heer has spok'n wi' me; monny's the face I see heer, as I first seen when I were young and lighter heart'n than now. I ha' never had no fratch afore, sin ever I were born, wi' any o' my like; Gonnows I ha' none now that's o' my makin'. You'll ca' me traitor and that—yo I mean t' say," addressing Slackbridge, 'but 'tis easier to ca' than mak' out. So let be."

He had moved away a pace or two to come down from the platform, when he remembered something he had not said, and returned again.

"Haply," he said, turning his furrowed face slowly about, that he might as it were individually address the whole audience, those both near and distant; "haply, when this question has been tak'n up and discoosed, there'll be a threat to turn out if I'm let to work among yo. I hope I shall die ere ever such a time cooms, and I shall work solitary among yo unless it cooms—truly, I mun do 't, my friends; not to brave you, but to live. I ha' nobbut work to live by; and wheerever can I go, I who ha' worked sin I were no heighth at aw, in Coketown heer? I mak' no complaints o' bein' turned to the wa', o' being outcasten and overlooken fro this time forrard, but hope I shall be let to work. If there is any right for me at aw, my friends, I think 'tis that."

Not a word was spoken. Not a sound was audible in the building, but the slight rustle of men moving a little apart, all along the centre of the room, to open a means of passing out, to the man with whom they had all bound themselves to renounce companionship. Looking at no one, and going his way with a lowly steadiness upon him that asserted nothing and sought nothing, Old Stephen, with all his troubles on his head, left the scene.

Then Slackbridge, who had kept his oratorical arm extended during the going out, as if he were repressing with infinite solicitude and by a wonderful moral power the vehement passions of the multitude, applied himself to raising their spirits. Had not the Roman Brutus, oh my British countrymen, condemned his son to death; and had not the Spartan mothers, oh my soon to be victorious friends, driven their flying children on the points of their enemies' swords? Then was it not the sacred duty of the men of Coketown, with forefathers before them, an admiring world in company with them, and a posterity to come after them, to hurl out traitors from the tents they had pitched in a sacred and a Godlike cause? The winds of heaven answered Yes; and bore Yes, east, west, north, and south. And consequently three cheers for the United Aggregate Tribunal!

Slackbridge acted as fugleman, and gave the time. The multitude of doubtful faces (a little conscience-stricken) brightened at the sound, and took it up. Private feeling must yield to the common cause. Hurrah! The roof yet vibrated with the cheering, when the assembly dispersed.

Thus easily did Stephen Blackpool fall into the loneliest of lives, the life of solitude among a familiar crowd. The stranger in the land who looks into ten thousand faces for some answering look and never finds it, is in cheering society as compared with him who passes ten averted faces daily, that were once the countenances of friends. Such experience was to be Stephen's now, in every waking moment of his life; at his work, on his way to it and from it, at his door, at his window, everywhere. By general consent, they even avoided that side of the street on which he habitually walked; and left it, of all the working men, to him only.

He had been for many years, a quiet silent man, associating but little with other men, and used to companionship with his own thoughts. He had never known before the strength of the want in his heart for the frequent recognition of a nod, a look, a word; or the immense amount of relief that had been poured into it by drops through such small means. It was even harder than he could have believed possible, to separate in his own conscience his abandonment by all his fellows from a baseless sense of shame and disgrace.

The first four days of his endurance were days so long and heavy, that he began to be appalled by the prospect before him. Not only did he see no Rachael all the time, but he avoided every chance of seeing her; for, although he knew that the prohibition did not yet formally extend to the women working in the factories, he found that some of them with whom he was acquainted were changed to him, and he feared to try others, and dreaded that Rachael might be even singled out from the rest if she were seen in his company. So, he had been quite alone during the four days, and had spoken to no one, when, as he was leaving his work at night, a young man of a very light complexion accosted him in the street.

"Your name's Blackpool, ain't it?" said the young man.

Stephen coloured to find himself with his hat in his hand, in his gratitude for being spoken to, or in the suddenness of it, or both. He made a feint of adjusting the lining, and said, "Yes."

"You are the Hand they have sent to Coventry, I mean?" said Bitzer, the very light young man in question.

Stephen answered "Yes," again.

"I supposed so, from their all appearing to keep away from you. Mr. Bounderby wants to speak to you. You know his house, don't you?"

Stephen said "Yes," again.

"Then go straight up there, will you?" said Bitzer. "You're expected, and have only to tell the servant it's you. I belong to the Bank; so, if you go straight up without me (I was sent to fetch you), you'll save me a walk."

Stephen, whose way had been in the contrary direction, turned

about, and betook himself as in duty bound, to the red brick castle
of the giant Bounderby.

CHAPTER FIVE

MEN AND MASTERS

"WELL, Stephen," said Bounderby, in his windy manner, "what's
this I hear? What have these pests of the earth been doing to *you?*
Come in, and speak up."

It was into the drawing-room that he was thus bidden. A tea-
table was set out; and Mr. Bounderby's young wife, and her
brother, and a great gentleman from London, were present. To
whom Stephen made his obeisance, closing the door and standing
near it, with his hat in his hand.

"This is the man I was telling you about, Harthouse," said
Mr. Bounderby. The gentleman he addressed, who was talking to
Mrs. Bounderby on the sofa, got up, saying in an indolent way,
"Oh really?" and dawdled to the hearthrug where Mr. Bounderby
stood.

"Now," said Bounderby, "speak up!"

After the four days he had passed, this address fell rudely and
discordantly on Stephen's ear. Besides being a rough handling of
his wounded mind, it seemed to assume that he really was the
self-interested deserter he had been called.

"What were it, sir," said Stephen, "as yo were pleased to want
wi' me?"

"Why, I have told you," returned Bounderby. "Speak up like
a man, since you are a man, and tell us about yourself and this
Combination."

"Wi' your pardon, sir," said Stephen Blackpool, "I ha' nowt to
sen about it."

Mr. Bounderby, who was always more or less like a Wind, finding something in his way here began to blow at it directly.

"Now, look here, Harthouse," said he, "here's a specimen of 'em. When this man was here once *The wind rises* before, I warned this man against the mischievous strangers who are always about—and who ought to be hanged wherever they are found—and I told this man that he was going in the wrong direction. Now, would you believe it, that although they have put this mark upon him, he is such a slave to them still, that he's afraid to open his lips about them?"

"I sed as I had nowt to sen, sir; not as I was fearfo' o' openin' my lips."

"You said. Ah! *I* know what you said; more than that, I know what you mean, you see. Not always the same thing, by the Lord Harry! Quite different things. You had better tell us at once, that that fellow Slackbridge is not in the town, stirring up the people to mutiny; and that he is not a regular qualified leader of the people: that is, a most confounded scoundrel. You had better tell us so at once; you can't deceive me. You want to tell us so. Why don't you?"

"I'm as sooary as yo, sir, when the people's leaders is bad," said Stephen, shaking his head. "They taks such as offers. Haply 'tis na' the sma'est o' their misfortuns when they can get no better."

The wind began to get boisterous.

"Now, you'll think this pretty well, Harthouse," said Mr. Bounderby. "You'll think this tolerably strong. You'll say, upon my soul this is a tidy specimen of what my friends have to deal with; but this is nothing, sir! You shall hear me ask this man a question. Pray, Mr. Blackpool"—wind springing up very fast—"may I take the liberty of asking you how it happens that you refused to be in this Combination?"

"How 't happens?"

"Ah!" said Mr. Bounderby, with his thumbs in the arms of his coat, and jerking his head and shutting his eyes in confidence with the opposite wall: "how it happens."

"I'd leefer not coom to 't, sir; but sin you put th' question —an not want'n t' be ill-manner'n—I'll answer. I ha' passed a promess."

"Not to me, you know," said Bounderby. (Gusty weather with deceitful calms. One now prevailing.)

"O no, sir. Not to yo."

"As for me, any consideration for me has had just nothing at all to do with it," said Bounderby, still in confidence with the wall. "If only Josiah Bounderby of Coketown had been in question, you would have joined and made no bones about it?"

"Why yes, sir. 'Tis true."

"Though he knows," said Mr. Bounderby, now blowing a gale, "that there are a set of rascals and rebels whom transportation is too good for! Now, Mr. Harthouse, you have been knocking about in the world some time. Did you ever meet with anything like that man out of this blessed country?" And Mr. Bounderby pointed him out for inspection, with an angry finger.

"Nay, ma'am," said Stephen Blackpool, staunchly protesting against the words that had been used, and instinctively addressing himself to Louisa, after glancing at her face. "Not rebels, nor yet rascals. Nowt o' th' kind, ma'am, nowt o' th' kind. They've not doon me a kindness, ma'am, as I know and feel. But there's not a dozen men amoong 'em, ma'am—a dozen? Not six—but what believes as he has doon his duty by the rest and by himseln. God forbid as I, that ha' known, and had'n experience o' these men aw my life—I, that ha' ett'n an' droonken wi' 'em, an' seet'n wi' 'em, and toil'n wi' 'em, and lov'n 'em, should fail fur to stan by 'em wi' the truth, let 'em ha' doon to me what they may!"

He spoke with the rugged earnestness of his place and character —deepened perhaps by a proud consciousness that he was faithful to his class under all their mistrust; but he fully remembered where he was, and did not even raise his voice.

"No, ma'am, no. They're true to one another, faithfo' to one another, fectionate to one another, e'en to death. Be poor amoong 'em, be sick amoong 'em, grieve amoong 'em for onny o' th' monny causes that carries grief to the poor man's door, an they'll be tender wi' yo, gentle wi' yo, comfortable wi' yo, Chrisen wi' yo. Be sure o' that, ma'am. They'd be riven to bits, ere ever they'd be different."

"In short," said Mr. Bounderby, "it's because they are so full of virtues that they have turned you adrift. Go through with it while you are about it. Out with it."

"How 'tis, ma'am," resumed Stephen, appearing still to find his natural refuge in Louisa's face, "that what is best in us fok, seems to turn us most to trouble an misfort'n an mistake, I dunno. But 'tis so. I know 'tis, as I know the heavens is over me ahint the smoke. We're patient too, an wants in general to do right. An I canna think the fawt is aw wi' us."

"Now, my friend," said Mr. Bounderby, whom he could not have exasperated more, quite unconscious of it though he was, than by seeming to appeal to any one else, "if you will favour me with your attention for half a minute, I should like to have a word or two with you. You said just now, that you had nothing to tell us about this business. You are quite sure of that before we go any further."

"Sir, I am sure on 't."

"Here's a gentleman from London present," Mr. Bounderby made a backhanded point at Mr. James Harthouse with his thumb, "a Parliament gentleman. I should like him to hear a short bit of dialogue between you and me, instead of taking the substance of it—for I know precious well, beforehand, what it will be; nobody knows better than I do, take notice!—instead of receiving it on trust from my mouth."

Stephen bent his head to the gentleman from London, and showed a rather more troubled mind than usual. He turned his eyes involuntarily to his former refuge, but at a look from that quarter (expressive though instantaneous) he settled them on Mr. Bounderby's face.

"Now, what do you complain of?" asked Mr. Bounderby.

"I ha' not coom here, sir," Stephen reminded him, "to complain. I coom for that I were sent for."

"What," repeated Mr. Bounderby, folding his arms, "do you people, in a general way, complain of?"

Stephen looked at him with some little irresolution for a moment, and then seemed to make up his mind.

"Sir, I were never good at showin' o 't, though I ha' had'n my share in feeling o 't. 'Deed we are in a muddle, sir. Look round town—so rich as 'tis—and see   *All a muddle* the numbers o' people as has been broughten into bein' heer, fur to weave, an to card, an to piece out a livin', aw the same one way, somehows, 'twixt their cradles and their graves.

Look how we live, an wheer we live, an in what numbers, an by what chances, and wi' what sameness; and look how the mills is awlus a goin', and how they never works us no nigher to onny dis'ant object—'ceptin' awlus, Death. Look how you considers of us, and writes of us, and talks of us, and goes up wi' yor deputations to Secretaries o' State 'bout us, and how yo are awlus right, and how we are awlus wrong, and never had'n no reason in us sin ever we were born. Look how this ha' growen an growen, sir, bigger an bigger, broader an broader, harder an harder, fro year to year, fro generation unto generation. Who can look on 't, sir, and fairly tell a man 'tis not a muddle?"

"Of course," said Mr. Bounderby. "Now perhaps you'll let the gentleman know, how you would set this muddle (as you're so fond of calling it) to rights."

"I dunno, sir. I canna be expecten to 't. 'Tis not me as should be looken to for that, sir. 'Tis them as is put ower me, and ower aw the rest of us. What do they tak upon themseln, sir, if not to do 't?"

"I'll tell you something towards it, at any rate," returned Mr. Bounderby. "We will make an example of half a dozen Slackbridges. We'll indict the blackguards for felony, and get 'em shipped off to penal settlements."

Stephen gravely shook his head.

"Don't tell me we won't, man," said Mr. Bounderby, by this time blowing a hurricane, "because we will, I tell you!"

"Sir," returned Stephen, with the quiet confidence of absolute certainty, "if yo was t' tak a hundred Slackbridges—aw as there is, and aw the number ten times towd—an was t' sew 'em up in separate sacks, an sink 'em in the deepest ocean as were made ere ever dry land coom to be, yo'd leave the muddle just wheer 'tis. Mischeevous strangers!" said Stephen, with an anxious smile; "when ha' we not heern, I am sure, sin ever we can call to mind, o' th' mischeevous strangers! 'Tis not by *them* the trouble's made, sir. 'Tis not wi' *them* 't commences. I ha' no favour for 'em—I ha' no reason to favour 'em—but 'tis hopeless and useless to dream o' takin' them fro their trade, 'stead o' takin' their trade fro them! Aw that's now about me in this room were heer afore I coom, an will be heer when I am gone. Put that clock aboard a ship an pack it off to Norfolk Island, an the time will go on just the same. So 'tis wi' Slackbridge every bit."

Reverting for a moment to his former refuge, he observed a cautionary movement of her eyes towards the door. Stepping back, he put his hand upon the lock. But he had not spoken out of his own will and desire; and he felt it in his heart a noble return for his late injurious treatment to be faithful to the last to those who had repudiated him. He stayed to finish what was in his mind.

"Sir, I canna, wi' my little learning an my common way, tell the genelman what will better aw this—though some working men o' this town could, above my powers—but I can tell him what I know will never do 't. The strong hand will never do 't. Vict'ry and triumph will never do 't. Agreeing fur to mak one side unnat'rally awlus and for ever right, and toother side unnat'rally awlus and for ever wrong, will never, never do 't. Nor yet lettin' alone will never do 't. Let thousands upon thousands alone, aw leading the like lives and aw faw'en into the like muddle, and they will be as one, and yo will be as anoother, wi' a black unpassable world betwixt yo, just as long or short a time as sitch-like misery can last. Not drawin' nigh to fok, wi' kindness and patience an cheery ways, that so draws nigh to one another in their monny troubles, and so cherishes one another in their distresses wi' what they need themseln—like, I humbly believe, as no people the genelman ha' seen in aw his travels can beat—will never do 't till th' Sun turns t' ice. Most o' aw, rating 'em as so much Power, and reg'latin' 'em as if they was figures in a soom, or machines: wi'out loves and likens, wi'out memories and inclinations, wi'out souls to weary and souls to hope—when aw goes quiet, draggin' on wi' 'em as if they'd nowt o' th' kind, and when aw goes onquiet, reproachin' 'em for their want o' sitch humanly feelins in their dealins wi' yo—this will never do 't, sir, till God's work is onmade."

Stephen stood with the open door in his hand, waiting to know if anything more were expected of him.

"Just stop a moment," said Mr. Bounderby, excessively red in the face. "I told you, the last time you were here with a grievance, that you had better turn about and come out of that. And I also told you, if you remember, that I was up to the gold spoon look-out."

"I were not up to 't myseln, sir; I do assure yo."

"Now it's clear to me," said Mr. Bounderby, "that you are one of those chaps who have always got a grievance. And you go about, sowing it and raising crops. That's the business of *your* life, my friend."

Stephen shook his head, mutely protesting that indeed he had other business to do for his life.

"You are such a waspish, raspish, ill-conditioned chap, you see," said Mr. Bounderby, "that even your own Union, the men who know you best, will have nothing to do with you. I never thought those fellows could be right in anything; but I tell you what! I so far go along with them for a novelty, that *I*'ll have nothing to do with you either."

Stephen raised his eyes quickly to his face.

"You can finish off what you're at," said Mr. Bounderby, with a meaning nod, "and then go elsewhere."

"Sir, yo know weel," said Stephen expressively, "that if I canna get work wi' yo, I canna get it elsewheer."

The reply was, "What I know, I know; and what you know, you know. I have no more to say about it."

Stephen glanced at Louisa again, but her eyes were raised to his no more; therefore, with a sigh, and saying, barely above his breath, "Heaven help us aw in this world!" he departed.

CHAPTER SIX

FADING AWAY

The old
woman again

IT was falling dark when Stephen came out of Mr. Bounderby's house. The shadows of night had gathered so fast, that he did not look about him when he closed the door, but plodded straight along the street. Nothing was further from his thoughts than the curious old woman he had encountered on his previous visit to the same house, when he heard a step behind him that he knew, and turning, saw her in Rachael's company.

He saw Rachael first, as he had heard her only.

"Ah, Rachael, my dear! Missus, thou wi' her!"

"Well, and now you are surprised to be sure, and with reason I must say," the old woman returned. "Here I am again, you see."

"But how wi' Rachael?" said Stephen, falling into their step, walking between them, and looking from the one to the other.

"Why, I come to be with this good lass pretty much as I came to be with you," said the old woman, cheerfully, taking the reply upon herself. "My visiting time is later this year than usual, for I have been rather troubled with shortness of breath, and so put it off till the weather was fine and warm. For the same reason I don't make all my journey in one day, but divide it into two days, and get a bed to-night at the Travellers' Coffee House down by the railroad (a nice clean house), and go back Parliamentary, at six in the morning. Well, but what has this to do with this good lass, says you? I'm going to tell you. I have heard of Mr. Bounderby being married. I read it in the paper, where it looked grand—oh, it looked fine!" the old woman dwelt on it with strange enthusiasm: "and I want to see his wife. I have never seen her yet. Now, if you'll believe me, she hasn't come out of that house since noon to-day. So not to give her up too easily, I was waiting about, a little last bit more, when I passed close to this good lass two or three times; and her face being so friendly I spoke to her, and she spoke to me. There!" said the old woman to Stephen, "you can make all the rest out for yourself now, a deal shorter than I can I dare say!"

Once again, Stephen had to conquer an instinctive propensity to dislike this old woman, though her manner was as honest and simple as a manner possibly could be. With a gentleness that was as natural to him as he knew it to be to Rachael, he pursued the subject that interested her in her old age.

"Well, missus," said he, "I ha' seen the lady, and she were young and hansom. Wi' fine dark thinkin' eyes, and a still way, Rachael, as I ha' never seen the like on."

"Young and handsome. Yes!" cried the old woman, quite delighted. "As bonny as a rose! And what a happy wife!"

"Aye, missus, I suppose she be," said Stephen. But with a doubtful glance at Rachael.

"Suppose she be? She must be. She's your master's wife," returned the old woman.

Stephen nodded assent. "Though as to master," said he, glancing again at Rachael, "not master onny more. That's aw enden 'twixt him and me."

"Have you left his work, Stephen?" asked Rachael, anxiously and quickly.

"Why, Rachael," he replied, "whether I ha' lef'n his work, or whether his work ha' lef'n me, cooms t' th' same. His work and me are parted. 'Tis as weel so—better, I were thinkin' when yo coom up wi' me. It would ha' brought'n trouble upon trouble if I had stayed theer. Haply 'tis a kindness to monny that I go; haply 'tis a kindness to myseln; anyways it mun be done. I mun turn my face fro Coketown fur th' time, and seek a fort'n dear, by beginnin' fresh."

"Where will you go, Stephen?"

"I dunno t' night," said he, lifting off his hat, and smoothing his thin hair with the flat of his hand. "But I'm not goin t' night, Rachael, nor yet t' morrow. 'Tan't easy overmuch t' know wheer t' turn, but a good heart will coom to me."

Herein, too, the sense of even thinking unselfishly aided him. Before he had so much as closed Mr. Bounderby's door, he had reflected that at least his being obliged to go away was good for her, as it would save her from the chance of being brought into question for not withdrawing from him. Though it would cost him a hard pang to leave her, and though he could think of no similar place in which his condemnation would not pursue him, perhaps it was almost a relief to be forced away from the endurance of the last four days, even to unknown difficulties and distresses.

So he said, with truth, "I'm more leetsome, Rachael, under 't, than I could'n ha' believed." It was not her part to make his burden heavier. She answered with her comforting smile, and the three walked on together.

Age, especially when it strives to be self-reliant and cheerful, finds much consideration among the poor. The old woman was so decent and contented, and made so light of her infirmities, though they had increased upon her since her former interview with Stephen, that they both took an interest in her. She was too sprightly to allow of their walking at a slow pace on her account, but she was very grateful to be talked to, and very willing to talk to any extent: so, when they came to their part of the town, she was more brisk and vivacious than ever.

"Coom to my poor place, missus," said Stephen, "and tak a coop o' tea. Rachael will coom then; and arterwards I'll see thee safe t' thy Travellers' lodgin'. 'T may be long, Rachael, ere ever I ha' th' chance o' thy coompany agen."

They complied, and the three went on to the house where he lodged. When they turned into a narrow street, Stephen glanced at his window with a dread that always haunted his desolate home; but it was open, as he had left it, and no one was there. The evil spirit of his life had flitted away again, months ago, and he had heard no more of her since. The only evidence of her last return now, were the scantier movables in his room, and the greyer hair upon his head.

He lighted a candle, set out his little tea-board, got hot water from below, and brought in small portions of tea and sugar, a loaf, and some butter from the nearest shop. The bread was new and crusty, the butter fresh, and the sugar lump, of course—in fulfilment of the standard testimony of the Coketown magnates, that these people lived like princes, sir. Rachael made the tea (so large a party necessitated the borrowing of a cup), and the visitor enjoyed it mightily. It was the first glimpse of socialty the host had had for many days. He too, with the world a wide heath before him, enjoyed the meal—again in corroboration of the magnates, as exemplifying the utter want of calculation on the part of these people, sir.

"I ha' never thowt yet, missus," said Stephen, "o' askin' thy name."

The old lady announced herself as "Mrs. Pegler."

"A widder, I think?" said Stephen.

"Oh, many long years!" Mrs. Pegler's husband (one of the best on record) was already dead, by Mrs. Pegler's calculation, when Stephen was born.

" 'Twere a bad job, too, to lose so good a one," said Stephen. "Onny children?"

Mrs. Pegler's cup, rattling against her saucer as she held it, denoted some nervousness on her part. "No," she said. "Not now, not now."

"Dead, Stephen," Rachael softly hinted.

"I'm sooary I ha' spok'n on 't," said Stephen, "I ought t' hadn in my mind as I might touch a sore place. I—I blame myseln."

While he excused himself, the old lady's cup rattled more and more. "I had a son," she said, curiously distressed, and not by any of the usual appearances of sorrow; "and he did well, wonderfully well. But he is not to be spoken of if you please. He is—" Putting down her cup, she moved her hands as if she would have added, by her action, "dead!" Then she said aloud, "I have lost him."

Stephen had not yet got the better of his having given the old lady pain, when his landlady came stumbling up the narrow stairs, and calling him to the door, whispered in his ear. Mrs. Pegler was by no means deaf, for she caught a word as it was uttered.

"Bounderby!" she cried, in a suppressed voice, starting up from the table. "Oh hide me! Don't let me be seen for the world. Don't let him come up till I've got away. Pray, pray!" She trembled, and was excessively agitated; getting behind Rachael, when Rachael tried to reassure her; and not seeming to know what she was about.

"But hearken, missus, hearken," said Stephen, astonished. " 'Tisn't Mr. Bounderby; 'tis his wife. Yor not fearfo' o' her. Yo was hey-go-mad about her, but an hour sin."

"But are you sure it's the lady, and not the gentleman?" she asked, still trembling.

"Certain sure!"

"Well then, pray don't speak to me, nor yet take any notice of me," said the old woman. "Let me be quite to myself in this corner."

Stephen nodded; looking to Rachael for an explanation, which she was quite unable to give him; took the candle, went downstairs, and in a few moments returned, lighting Louisa into the room. She was followed by the whelp.

Rachael had risen, and stood apart with her shawl and bonnet in her hand, when Stephen, himself profoundly astonished by this visit, put the candle on the table. Then he too stood, with his doubled hand upon the table near it, waiting to be addressed.

For the first time in her life Louisa had come into one of the dwellings of the Coketown Hands; for the first time in her life she was face to face with anything like individuality in connexion with them. She knew of their existence by hundreds and by thousands. She knew what results in work a given number of them would produce in a given space of time. She knew them in crowds passing to and from their nests, like ants or beetles. But she knew from her reading infinitely more of the ways of toiling insects than of these toiling men and women.

Something to be worked so much and paid so much, and there ended; something to be infallibly settled by laws of supply and demand; something that blundered against those laws, and floundered into difficulty; something that was a little pinched when wheat was dear, and over-ate itself when wheat was cheap; something that increased at such a rate of percentage, and yielded such another percentage of crime, and such another percentage of pauperism; something wholesale, of which vast fortunes were made; something that occasionally rose like a sea, and did some harm and waste (chiefly to itself), and fell again; this she knew the Coketown Hands to be. But, she had scarcely thought more of separating them into units, than of separating the sea itself into its component drops.

She stood for some moments looking round the room. From the few chairs, the few books, the common prints, and the bed, she glanced to the two women, and to Stephen.

"I have come to speak to you, in consequence of what passed just now. I should like to be serviceable to you, if you will let me. Is this your wife?"

Rachael raised her eyes, and they sufficiently answered no, and dropped again.

"I remember," said Louisa, reddening at her mistake; "I recollect, now, to have heard your domestic misfortunes spoken of, though I was not attending to the particulars at the time. It was not my meaning to ask a question that would give pain to any one here. If I should ask any other question that may happen to have that result, give me credit, if you please, for being in ignorance how to speak to you as I ought."

As Stephen had but a little while ago instinctively addressed himself to her, so she now instinctively addressed herself to Rachael. Her manner was short and abrupt, yet faltering and timid.

"He has told you what has passed between himself and my husband? You would be his first resource, I think."

"I have heard the end of it, young lady," said Rachael.

"Did I understand, that, being rejected by one employer, he would probably be rejected by all? I thought he said as much?"

"The chances are very small, young lady—next to nothing—for a man who gets a bad name among them."

"What shall I understand that you mean by a bad name?"

"The name of being troublesome."

"Then, by the prejudices of his own class, and by the prejudices of the other, he is sacrificed alike? Are the two so deeply separated in this town, that there is no place whatever for an honest workman between them?"

Rachael shook her head in silence.

"He fell into suspicion," said Louisa, "with his fellow-weavers, because he had made a promise not to be one of them. I think it must have been to you that he made that promise. Might I ask you why he made it?"

Rachael burst into tears. "I didn't seek it of him, poor lad. I prayed him to avoid trouble for his own good, little thinking he'd come to it through me. But I know he'd die a hundred deaths, ere ever he'd break his word. I know that of him well."

Stephen had remained quietly attentive in his usual thoughtful attitude, with his hand at his chin. He now spoke in a voice rather less steady than usual.

"No one, excepting myseln, can ever know what honour an what love, an respect, I bear to Rachael, or wi' what cause. When I passed that promess, I towd her true, she were th' Angel o' my life. 'Twere a solemn promess. 'Tis gone fro' me, for ever."

Louisa turned her head to him, and bent it with a deference that was new in her. She looked from him to Rachael. and her features softened. "What will you do?" she asked him. And her voice had softened too.

"Weel, ma'am," said Stephen, making the best of it, with a smile; "when I ha' finished off, I mun quit this part, and try another. Fortnet or misfortnet, a man can but try; there's nowt to be done wi'out tryin'—cept laying down and dying."

"How will you travel?"

"Afoot, my kind ledy, afoot."

Louisa coloured, and a purse appeared in her hand. The rustling of a bank-note was audible, as she unfolded one and laid it on the table.

"Rachael, will you tell him—for you know how, without offence —that this is freely his, to help him on his way? Will you entreat him to take it?"

"I canna do that, young lady," she answered, turning her head aside. "Bless you for thinking o' the poor lad wi' such tenderness. But 'tis for him to know his heart, and what is right according to it."

Louisa looked, in part incredulous, in part frightened, in part overcome with quick sympathy, when this man of so much self-command, who had been so plain and steady through the late interview, lost his composure in a moment, and now stood with his hand before his face. She stretched out hers, as if she would have touched him; then checked herself and remained still.

"Not e'en Rachael," said Stephen, when he stood again with his face uncovered, "could mak sitch a kind offerin', by onny words, kinder. T' show that I'm not a man wi'out reason and gratitude, I'll tak two pound. I'll borrow 't for t' pay 't back. 'Twill be the sweetest work as ever I ha' done, that puts it in my power t' acknowledge once more my lastin' thankfulness for this present action."

She was fain to take up the note again, and to substitute the much smaller sum he had named. He was neither courtly, nor handsome, nor picturesque, in any respect; and yet his manner of accepting it, and of expressing his thanks without more words, had a grace in it that Lord Chesterfield could not have taught his son in a century.

Tom had sat upon the bed, swinging one leg and sucking his

walking-stick with sufficient unconcern, until the visit had attained this stage. Seeing his sister ready to depart, he got up, rather hurriedly, and put in a word.

Tom thinks of something   "Just wait a moment, Loo! Before we go, I should like to speak to him a moment. Something comes into my head. If you'll step out on the stairs, Blackpool, I'll mention it. Never mind a light, man!" Tom was remarkably impatient of his moving towards the cupboard, to get one. "It don't want a light."

Stephen followed him out, and Tom closed the room door, and held the lock in his hand.

"I say!" he whispered. "I think I can do you a good turn. Don't ask me what it is, because it may not come to anything. But there's no harm in my trying."

His breath fell like a flame of fire on Stephen's ear, it was so hot.

"That was our light porter at the Bank," said Tom, "who brought you the message to-night. I call him our light porter, because I belong to the Bank too."

Stephen thought, "What a hurry he is in!" He spoke so confusedly.

"Well," said Tom. "Now look here! When are you off?"

"T' day's Monday," replied Stephen, considering. "Why, sir, Friday or Saturday, nigh 'bout."

"Friday or Saturday," said Tom. "Now look here! I am not sure that I can do you the good turn I want to do you—that's my sister, you know, in your room—but I may be able to, and if I should not be able to, there's no harm done. So I tell you what. You'll know our light porter again?"

"Yes sure," said Stephen.

"Very well," returned Tom. "When you leave work of a night, between this and your going away, just hang about the Bank an hour or so, will you? Don't take on, as if you meant anything, if he should see you hanging about there; because I shan't put him up to speak to you, unless I find I can do you the service I want to do you. In that case he'll have a note or a message for you, but not else. Now look here! You are sure to understand."

He had wormed a finger, in the darkness, through a buttonhole of Stephen's coat, and was screwing that corner of the garment tight up round and round, in an extraordinary manner.

"I understand, sir," said Stephen.

"Now look here!" repeated Tom. "Be sure you don't make any mistake then, and don't forget. I shall tell my sister as we go home, what I have in view, and she'll approve, I know. Now look here! You're all right, are you? You understand all about it? Very well then. Come along, Loo!"

He pushed the door open as he called to her, but did not return into the room, or wait to be lighted down the narrow stairs. He was at the bottom when she began to descend, and was in the street before she could take his arm.

Mrs. Pegler remained in her corner until the brother and sister were gone, and until Stephen came back with the candle in his hand. She was in a state of inexpressible admiration of Mrs. Bounderby, and, like an unaccountable old woman, wept, "because she was such a pretty dear." Yet Mrs. Pegler was so flurried lest the object of her admiration should return by chance, or anybody else should come, that her cheerfulness was ended for that night. It was late too, to people who rose early and worked hard; therefore the party broke up; and Stephen and Rachael escorted their mysterious acquaintance to the door of the Travellers' Coffee House, where they parted from her.

They walked back together to the corner of the street where Rachael lived, and as they drew nearer and nearer to it, silence crept upon them. When they came to the dark corner where their unfrequent meetings always ended, they stopped, still silent, as if both were afraid to speak.

"I shall strive t' see thee agen, Rachael, afore I go, but if not——"

"Thou wilt not, Stephen, I know. 'Tis better that we make up our minds to be open wi' one another."

"Thou 'rt awlus right. 'Tis bolder and better. I ha' been thinkin' then, Rachael, that as 'tis but a day or two that remains, 'twere better for thee, my dear, not t' be seen wi' me. 'T might bring thee into trouble, fur no good."

" 'Tis not for that, Stephen, that I mind. But thou know'st our old agreement. 'Tis for that."

"Well, well," said he. " 'Tis better, onnyways."

"Thou 'lt write to me, and tell me all that happens, Stephen?"

"Yes. What can I say now, but Heaven be wi' thee, Heaven bless thee, Heaven thank thee and reward thee!"

"May it bless thee, Stephen, too, in all thy wanderings, and send thee peace and rest at last!"

"I towd thee, my dear," said Stephen Blackpool—"that night— that I would never see or think o' onnything that angered me, but thou, so much better than me, should'st be beside it. Thou 'rt beside it now. Thou mak'st me see it wi' a better eye. Bless thee. Good night. Good-bye!"

It was but a hurried parting in a common street, yet it was a sacred remembrance to these two common people. Utilitarian economists, skeletons of schoolmasters, Commissioners of Fact, genteel and used-up infidels, gabblers of many little dog's-eared creeds, the poor you will have always with you. Cultivate in them, while there is yet time, the utmost graces of the fancies and affections, to adorn their lives so much in need of ornament; or, in the day of your triumph, when romance is utterly driven out of their souls, and they and a bare existence stand face to face, Reality will take a wolfish turn, and make an end of you.

Stephen worked the next day, and the next, uncheered by a word from any one, and shunned in all his comings and goings as before. At the end of the second day, he saw land; at the end of the third, his loom stood empty.

He had overstayed his hour in the street outside the Bank, on each of the two first evenings; and nothing had happened there, good or bad. That he might not be remiss in his part of the engagement, he resolved to wait full two hours, on this third and last night.

There was the lady who had once kept Mr. Bounderby's house, sitting at the first floor window as he had seen her before; and there was the light porter, sometimes talking with her there, and sometimes looking over the blind below which had BANK upon it, and sometimes coming to the door and standing on the steps for a breath of air. When he first came out, Stephen thought he might be looking for him, and passed near; but the light porter only cast his winking eyes upon him slightly, and said nothing.

Two hours were a long stretch of lounging about, after a long day's labour. Stephen sat upon the step of a door, leaned against a wall under an archway, strolled up and down, listened for the church clock, stopped and watched children playing in the street. Some purpose or other is so natural to every one, that a mere loiterer always looks and feels remarkable. When the first hour was out, Stephen even began to have an uncomfortable sensation upon him of being for the time a disreputable character.

Then came the lamplighter, and two lengthening lines of light all down the long perspective of the street, until they were blended and lost in the distance. Mrs. Sparsit closed the first floor window, drew down the blind, and went up-stairs. Presently, a light went up-stairs after her, passing first the fanlight of the door, and afterwards the two staircase windows, on its way up. By-and-by, one corner of the second floor blind was disturbed, as if Mrs. Sparsit's eye were there; also the other corner, as if the light porter's eye were on that side. Still, no communication was made to Stephen. Much relieved when the two hours were at last accomplished, he went away at a quick pace, as a recompense for so much loitering.

He had only to take leave of his landlady, and lie down on his temporary bed upon the floor; for his bundle was made up for to-morrow, and all was arranged for his departure. He meant to be clear of the town very early; before the Hands were in the streets.

It was barely daybreak, when, with a parting look round his room, mournfully wondering whether he should ever see it again, he went out. *Stephen's departure* The town was as entirely deserted as if the inhabitants had abandoned it, rather than hold communication with him. Everything looked wan at that hour. Even the coming sun made but a pale waste in the sky, like a sad sea.

By the place where Rachael lived, though it was not in his way; by the red brick streets; by the great silent factories, not trembling yet; by the railway, where the danger-lights were waning in the strengthening day; by the railway's crazy neighbourhood, half pulled down and half built up; by scattered red brick villas, where the besmoked evergreens were sprinkled with a dirty powder, like untidy snuff-takers; by coal-dust paths and many varieties of ugliness; Stephen got to the top of the hill, and looked back.

Day was shining radiantly upon the town then, and the bells were going for the morning work. Domestic fires were not yet lighted, and the high chimneys had the sky to themselves. Puffing out their poisonous volumes, they would not be long in hiding it; but, for half an hour, some of the many windows were golden, which showed the Coketown people a sun eternally in eclipse, through a medium of smoked glass.

So strange to turn from the chimneys to the birds. So strange to have the road-dust on his feet instead of the coal-grit. So strange to have lived to his time of life, and yet to be beginning like a boy this summer morning! With these musings in his mind, and his bundle under his arm, Stephen took his attentive face along the high road. And the trees arched over him, whispering that he left a true and loving heart behind.

CHAPTER SEVEN

GUNPOWDER

MR. JAMES Harthouse, "going in" for his adopted party, soon began to score. With the aid of a little more coaching for the political sages, a little more genteel listlessness for the general society, and a tolerable management of the assumed honesty in dishonesty, most effective and most patronized of the polite deadly sins, he speedily came to be considered of much promise. The not being troubled with earnestness was a grand point in his favour, enabling him to take to the hard Fact fellows with as good a grace as if he had been born one of the tribe, and to throw all other tribes overboard, as conscious hypocrites.

"Whom none of us believe, my dear Mrs. Bounderby, and who do not believe themselves. The only difference between us and the professors of virtue or benevolence, or philanthropy—never mind the name—is, that we know it is all meaningless, and say so; while they know it equally and will never say so."

Why should she be shocked or warned by this reiteration? It was not so unlike her father's principles, and her early training, that it need startle her. Where was the great difference between the two schools, when each chained her down to material realities, and inspired her with no faith in anything else? What was there in her soul for James Harthouse to destroy, which Thomas Grad-grind had nurtured there in its state of innocence!

It was even the worse for her at this pass, that in her mind—implanted there before her eminently practical father began to form it—a struggling disposition to believe in a wider and nobler humanity than she had ever heard of, constantly strove with doubts and resentments. With doubts, because the aspiration had been so laid waste in her youth. With resentments, because of the wrong that had been done her, if it were indeed a whisper of the truth. Upon a nature long accustomed to self-suppression, thus torn and divided, the Harthouse philosophy came as a relief and justification. Everything being hollow and worthless, she had missed nothing and sacrificed nothing. What did it matter, she had said to her father, when he proposed her husband. What did it matter, she said still. With a scornful self-reliance, she asked herself, What did anything matter—and went on.

Towards what? Step by step, onward and downward, towards some end, yet so gradually, that she believed herself to remain motionless. As to Mr. Harthouse, whither *he* tended, he neither considered nor cared. He had no particular design or plan before him: no energetic wickedness ruffled his lassitude. He was as much amused and interested, at present, as it became so fine a gentleman to be; perhaps even more than it would have been consistent with his reputation to confess. Soon after his arrival he languidly wrote to his brother, the honourable and jocular member, that the Bounderbys were "great fun;" and further, that the female Bounderby, instead of being the Gorgon he had expected, was young, and remarkably pretty. After that, he wrote no more about them, and devoted his leisure chiefly to their house. He was very often in their house, in his flittings and visitings about the Coketown district; and was much encouraged by Mr. Bounderby. It was quite in Mr. Bounderby's gusty way to boast to all his world that *he* didn't care about your highly connected people, but that if his wife Tom Gradgrind's daughter did, she was welcome to their company.

Mr. James Harthouse began to think it would be a new sensation, if the face which changed so beautifully for the whelp, would change for him.

He was quick enough to observe; he had a good memory, and did not forget a word of the brother's revelations. He interwove them with everything he saw of the sister, and he began to understand her. To be sure, the better and profounder part of her character was not within his scope of perception; for in natures, as in seas, depth answers unto depth; but he soon began to read the rest with a student's eye.

Mr. *Bounderby's* retreat
Mr. Bounderby had taken possession of a house and grounds, about fifteen miles from the town, and accessible within a mile or two, by a railway striding on many arches over a wild country, undermined by deserted coal-shafts, and spotted at night by fires and black shapes of stationary engines at pits' mouths. This country, gradually softening towards the neighbourhood of Mr. Bounderby's retreat, there mellowed into a rustic landscape, golden with heath, and snowy with hawthorn in the spring of the year, and tremulous with leaves and their shadows all the summer time. The bank had foreclosed a mortgage effected on the property thus pleasantly situated, by one of the Coketown magnates, who, in his determination to make a shorter cut than usual to an enormous fortune, overspeculated himself by about two hundred thousand pounds. These accidents did sometimes happen in the best regulated families of Coketown, but the bankrupts had no connexion whatever with the improvident classes.

It afforded Mr. Bounderby supreme satisfaction to install himself in this snug little estate, and with demonstrative humility to grow cabbages in the flower-garden. He delighted to live, barrack-fashion, among the elegant furniture, and he bullied the very pictures with his origin. "Why, sir," he would say to a visitor, "I am told that Nickits," the late owner, "gave seven hundred pound for that Seabeach. Now, to be plain with you, if I ever, in the whole course of my life, take seven looks at it, at a hundred pound a look, it will be as much as I shall do. No, by George! I don't forget that I am Josiah Bounderby of Coketown. For years upon years, the only pictures in my possession, or that I could have got into my possession, by any means, unless I stole 'em, were the engravings of a man shaving himself in a boot, on the blacking bottles that I was overjoyed to use in cleaning boots with, and that I sold when they were empty for a farthing a-piece, and glad to get it!"

Then he would address Mr. Harthouse in the same style.

"Harthouse, you have a couple of horses down here. Bring half a dozen more if you like, and we'll find room for 'em. There's stabling in this place for a dozen horses; and unless Nickits is belied, he kept the full number. A round dozen of 'em, sir. When that man was a boy, he went to Westminster School. Went to Westminster School as a King's Scholar, when I was principally living on garbage, and sleeping in market baskets. Why, if I wanted to keep a dozen horses—which I don't, for one's enough for me—I couldn't bear to see 'em in their stalls here, and think what my own lodging used to be. I couldn't look at 'em, sir, and not order 'em out. Yet so things come round. You see this place; you know what sort of a place it is; you are aware that there's not a completer place of its size in this kingdom or elsewhere—I don't care where—and here, got into the middle of it, like a maggot into a nut, is Josiah Bounderby. While Nickits (as a man came into my office, and told me yesterday), Nickits, who used to act in Latin, in the Westminster School plays, with the chief-justices and nobility of this country applauding him till they were black in the face, is drivelling at this minute—drivelling, sir! —in a fifth floor, up a narrow dark back street in Antwerp."

It was among the leafy shadows of this retirement, in the long sultry summer days, that Mr. Harthouse began to prove the face which had set him wondering when he first saw it, and to try if it would change for him.

"Mrs. Bounderby, I esteem it a most fortunate accident that I find you alone here. I have for some time had a particular wish to speak to you."

It was not by any wonderful accident that he found her, the time of day being that at which she was always alone, and the place being her favourite resort. It was an opening in a dark wood, where some felled trees lay, and where she would sit watching the fallen leaves of last year, as she had watched the falling ashes at home.

He sat down beside her, with a glance at her face.

"Your brother. My young friend Tom——"

Her colour brightened, and she turned to him with a look of interest. "I never in my life," he thought, saw anything so remarkable and so captivating as the lighting of those features!" His face betrayed his thoughts—perhaps without betraying him, for it might have been according to its instructions so to do.

"Pardon me. The expression of your sisterly interest is so beautiful—Tom should be so proud of it—I know this is inexcusable, but I am so compelled to admire."

"Being so impulsive," she said composedly.

"Mrs. Bounderby, no: you know I make no pretence with you. You know I am a sordid piece of human nature, ready to sell myself at any time for any reasonable sum, and altogether incapable of any Arcadian proceeding whatever."

"I am waiting," she returned, "for your further reference to my brother."

"You are rigid with me, and I deserve it. I am as worthless a dog as you will find, except that I am not false—not false. But you surprised and started me from my subject, which was your brother. I have an interest in him."

"Have you an interest in anything, Mr. Harthouse?" she asked, half incredulously and half gratefully.

"If you had asked me when I first came here, I should have said no. I must say now—even at the hazard of appearing to make a pretence, and of justly awakening your incredulity—yes."

She made a slight movement, as if she were trying to speak, but could not find voice; at length she said, "Mr. Harthouse, I give you credit for being interested in my brother."

"Thank you. I claim to deserve it. You know how little I do claim, but I will go that length. You have done so much for him, you are so fond of him; your whole life, Mrs. Bounderby, expresses such charming self-forgetfulness on his account—pardon me again—I am running wide of the subject. I am interested in him for his own sake."

She had made the slightest action possible, as if she would

have risen in a hurry and gone away. He had turned the course of what he said at that instant, and she remained.

"Mrs. Bounderby," he resumed, in a lighter manner, and yet with a show of effort in assuming it, which was even more expressive than the manner he dismissed; "it is no irrevocable offence in a young fellow of your brother's years, if he is heedless, inconsiderate, and expensive—a little dissipated, in the common phrase. Is he?"

"Yes?"

"Allow me to be frank. Do you think he games at all?"

"I think he makes bets." Mr. Harthouse waiting, as if that were not her whole answer, she added, "I know he does."

"Of course he loses?"

"Yes."

"Everybody does lose who bets. May I hint at the probability of your sometimes supplying him with money for these purposes?"

She sat, looking down; but, at this question, raised her eyes searchingly and a little resentfully.

"Acquit me of impertinent curiosity, my dear Mrs. Bounderby. I think Tom may be gradually falling into trouble, and I wish to stretch out a helping hand to him from the depths of my wicked experience.—Shall I say again, for his sake? Is that necessary?"

She seemed to try to answer, but nothing came of it. *James Harthouse in confidence*

"Candidly to confess everything that has occurred to me," said James Harthouse, again gliding with the same appearance of effort into his more airy manner; "I will confide to you my doubt whether he has had many advantages. Whether—forgive my plainness—whether any great amount of confidence is likely to have been established between himself and his most worthy father."

"I do not," said Louisa, flushing with her own great remembrance in that wise, "think it likely."

"Or, between himself, and—I may trust to your perfect understanding of my meaning, I am sure—and his highly esteemed brother-in-law."

She flushed deeper and deeper, and was burning red when she replied in a fainter voice, "I do not think that likely, either."

"Mrs. Bounderby," said Harthouse, after a short silence, "may there be a better confidence between yourself and me? Tom has borrowed a considerable sum of you?"

"You will understand, Mr. Harthouse," she returned, after some indecision: she had been more or less uncertain, and troubled throughout the conversation, and yet had in the main preserved her self-contained manner; "you will understand that if I tell you what you press to know, it is not by way of complaint or regret. I would never complain of anything, and what I have done I do not in the least regret."

"So spirited, too!" thought James Harthouse.

"When I married, I found that my brother was even at that time heavily in debt. Heavily for him, I mean. Heavily enough to oblige me to sell some trinkets. They were no sacrifice. I sold them very willingly. I attached no value to them. They were quite worthless to me."

Either she saw in his face that he knew, or she only feared in her conscience that he knew, that she spoke of some of her husband's gifts. She stopped, and reddened again. If he had not known it before, he would have known it then, though he had been a much duller man than he was.

"Since then, I have given my brother, at various times, what money I could spare: in short, what money I have had. Confiding in you at all, on the faith of the interest you profess for him, I will not do so by halves. Since you have been in the habit of visiting here, he has wanted in one sum as much as a hundred pounds. I have not been able to give it to him. I have felt uneasy for the consequences of his being so involved, but I have kept these secrets until now, when I trust them to your honour. I have held no confidence with any one, because—you anticipated my reason just now." She abruptly broke off.

He was a ready man, and he saw, and seized, an opportunity here of presenting her own image to her, slightly disguised as her brother.

"Mrs. Bounderby, though a graceless person, of the world worldly, I feel the utmost interest, I assure you, in what you tell me. I cannot possibly be hard upon your brother. I understand and share the wise consideration with which you regard his errors. With all possible respect both for Mr. Gradgrind and for Mr. Bounderby, I think I perceive that he has not been fortunate in his training.

Bred at a disadvantage towards the society in which he has his part to play, he rushes into these extremes for himself, from opposite extremes that have long been forced—with the very best intentions we have no doubt—upon him. Mr. Bounderby's fine bluff English independence, though a most charming characteristic, does not—as we have agreed— invite confidence. If I might venture to remark that it is the least in the world deficient in that delicacy to which a youth mistaken, a character misconceived, and abilities misdirected, would turn for relief and guidance, I should express what it presents to my own view."

As she sat looking straight before her, across the changing lights upon the grass into the darkness of the wood beyond, he saw in her face her application of his very distinctly uttered words.

"All allowance," he continued, "must be made. I have one great fault to find with Tom, however, which I cannot forgive, and for which I take him heavily to account."

Louisa turned her eyes to his face, and asked him what fault was that?

"Perhaps," he returned, "I have said enough. Perhaps it would have been better, on the whole, if no allusion to it had escaped me."

"You alarm me, Mr. Harthouse. Pray let me know it."

"To relieve you from needless apprehension—and as this confidence regarding your brother, which I prize I am sure above all possible things, has been established between us—I obey. I cannot forgive him for not being more sensible in every word, look, and act of his life, of the affection of his best friend; of the devotion of his best friend; of her unselfishness; of her sacrifice. The return he makes her, within my observation, is a very poor one. What she has done for him demands his constant love and gratitude, not his ill-humour and caprice. Careless fellow as I am, I am not so indifferent, Mrs. Bounderby, as to be regardless of this vice in your brother, or inclined to consider it a venial offence."

The wood floated before her, for her eyes were suffused with tears. They rose from a deep well, long concealed, and her heart was filled with acute pain that found no relief in them.

"In a word, it is to correct your brother in this, Mrs. Bounderby, that I must aspire. My better knowledge of his circumstances, and my direction and advice in extricating them—rather valuable, I hope, as coming from a scapegrace on a much larger scale—will give me some influence over him, and all I gain I shall certainly use towards this end. I have said enough, and more than enough. I seem to be protesting that I am a sort of good fellow, when, upon my honour, I have not the least intention to make any protestation to that effect, and openly announce that I am nothing of the sort. Yonder, among the trees," he added, having lifted up his eyes and looked about; for he had watched her closely until now; "is your brother himself; no doubt, just come down. As he seems to be loitering in this direction, it may be as well, perhaps, to walk towards him, and throw ourselves in his way. He has been very silent and doleful of late. Perhaps, his brotherly conscience is touched—if there are such things as consciences. Though, upon my honour, I hear of them much too often to believe in them."

He assisted her to rise, and she took his arm, and they advanced to meet the whelp. He was idly beating the branches as he lounged along: or he stooped viciously to rip the moss from the trees with his stick. He was startled when they came upon him while he was engaged in this latter pastime, and his colour changed.

"Halloa!" he stammered; "I didn't know you were here."

"Whose name, Tom," said Mr. Harthouse, putting his hand upon his shoulder and turning him, so that they all three walked towards the house together, "have you been carving on the trees?"

"Whose name?" returned Tom. "Oh! You mean what girl's name?"

"You have suspicious appearance of inscribing some fair creature's on the bark, Tom."

"Not much of that, Mr. Harthouse, unless some fair creature with a slashing fortune at her own disposal would take a fancy to me. Or she might be as ugly as she was rich, without any fear of losing me. I'd carve her name as often as she liked."

"I am afraid you are mercenary, Tom."

"Mercenary," repeated Tom. "Who is not mercenary? Ask my sister."

"Have you so proved it to be a failing of mine, Tom?" said Louisa, showing no other sense of his discontent and ill-nature.

"You know whether the cap fits you, Loo," returned her brother sulkily. "If it does, you can wear it."

"Tom is misanthropical to-day, as all bored people are now and then," said Mr. Harthouse. "Don't believe him, Mrs. Bounderby. He knows much better. I shall disclose some of his opinions of you, privately expressed to me, unless he relents a little."

"At all events, Mr. Harthouse," said Tom, softening in his admiration of his patron, but shaking his head sullenly too, "you can't tell her that I ever praised her for being mercenary. I may have praised her for being the contrary, and I should do it again, if I had as good reason. However, never mind this now; it's not very interesting to you, and I am sick of the subject."

They walked on to the house, where Louisa quitted her visitor's arm and went in. He stood looking after her, as she ascended the steps, and passed into the shadow of the door; then put his hand upon her brother's shoulder again, and invited him with a confidential nod to a walk in the garden.

"Tom, my fine fellow, I want to have a word with you."

They had stopped among a disorder of roses—it was part of Mr. Bounderby's humility to keep Nickits's roses on a reduced scale—and Tom sat down on a terrace-parapet, plucking buds and picking them to pieces; while his powerful Familiar stood over him, with a foot upon the parapet, and his figure easily resting on the arm supported by that knee. They were just visible from her window. Perhaps she saw them.

"Tom, what's the matter?"

"Oh! Mr. Harthouse," said Tom with a groan, "I am hard up, and bothered out of my life."

"My good fellow, so am I."

"You!" returned Tom. "You are the picture of independence. Mr. Harthouse, I am in a horrible mess. You have no idea what a state I have got myself into—what a state my sister might have got me out of, if she would only have done it."

He took to biting the rose-buds now, and tearing them away from his teeth with a hand that trembled like an infirm old man's. After one exceedingly observant look at him, his companion relapsed into his lightest air.

"Tom, you are inconsiderate: you expect too much of your sister. You have had money of her, you dog, you know you have."

"Well, Mr. Harthouse, I know I have. How else was I to get it? Here's old Bounderby always boasting that at my age he lived upon twopence a month, or something of that sort. Here's

my father drawing what he calls a line, and tying me down
to it from a baby, neck and heels. Here's my mother who
never had anything of her own, except her complaints. What *is*
a fellow to do for money, and where *am* I to look for it, if not to
my sister?"

He was almost crying and scattered the buds about by dozens.
Mr. Harthouse took him persuasively by the coat.

"But, my dear Tom, if your sister has not got it——"

Unnatural
conduct "Not got it, Mr. Harthouse? I don't say she
has got it. I may have wanted more than she was
likely to have got. But then she ought to get it.
She could get it. It's of no use pretending to make
a secret of matters now, after what I have told you already; you
know she didn't marry old Bounderby for her own sake, or for his
sake, but for my sake. Then why doesn't she get what I want, out
of him, for my sake? She is not obliged to say what she is going
to do with it; she is sharp enough; she could manage to coax it
out of him, if she chose. Then why doesn't she choose, when I
tell her of what consequence it is? But no. There she sits in his
company like a stone, instead of making herself agreeable and
getting it easily. I don't know what you may call this, but *I* call
it unnatural conduct."

There was a piece of ornamental water immediately below the
parapet, on the other side, into which Mr. James Harthouse had
a very strong inclination to pitch Mr. Thomas Gradgrind Junior,
as the injured men of Coketown threatened to pitch their property
into the Atlantic. But he preserved his easy attitude; and nothing
more solid went over the stone balustrades than the accumulated
rosebuds now floating about, a little surface-island.

"My dear Tom," said Harthouse, "let me try to be your banker."

"For God's sake," replied Tom, suddenly, "don't talk about
bankers!" And very white he looked, in contrast with the roses.
Very white.

Mr. Harthouse, as a thoroughly well bred man, accustomed to
the best society, was not to be surprised—he could as soon have
been affected—but he raised his eyelids a little more, as if they
were lifted by a feeble touch of wonder. Albeit it was as much
against the precepts of his school to wonder, as it was against the
doctrines of the Gradgrind College.

"What is the present need, Tom? Three figures? Out with them. Say what they are."

"Mr. Harthouse," returned Tom, now actually crying; and his tears were better than his injuries, however pitiful a figure he made; "it's too late; the money is of no use to me at present. I should have had it before to be of use to me. But I am very much obliged to you; you're a true friend."

A true friend! "Whelp, whelp!" thought Mr. Harthouse, lazily; "what an Ass you are!"

"And I take your offer as a great kindness," said Tom, grasping his hand. "As a great kindness, Mr. Harthouse."

"Well," returned the other, "it may be of more use by and by. And, my good fellow, if you will open your bedevilments to me when they come thick upon you, I may show you better ways out of them than you can find for yourself."

"Thank you," said Tom, shaking his head dismally, and chewing rosebuds. "I wish I had known you sooner, Mr. Harthouse."

"Now, you see, Tom," said Mr. Harthouse in conclusion, himself tossing over a rose or two, as a contribution to the island, which was always drifting to the wall as if it wanted to become a part of the mainland: "every man is selfish in everything he does, and I am exactly like the rest of my fellow-creatures. I am desperately intent;" the languor of his desperation being quite tropical; "on your softening towards your sister—which you ought to do; and on your being a more loving and agreeable sort of brother—which you ought to be."

"I will be, Mr. Harthouse."

"No time like the present, Tom. Begin at once."

"Certainly I will. And my sister Loo shall say so."

"Having made which bargain, Tom," said Harthouse, clapping him on the shoulder again, with an air which left him at liberty to infer—as he did, poor fool—that this condition was imposed upon him in mere careless good nature to lessen his sense of obligation, "we will tear ourselves asunder until dinner-time."

When Tom appeared before dinner, though his mind seemed heavy enough, his body was on the alert; and he appeared before Mr. Bounderby came in. "I didn't mean to be cross, Loo," he said, giving her his hand, and kissing her. "I know you are fond of me, and you know I am fond of you."

After this, there was a smile upon Louisa's face that day, for some one else. Alas, for some one else!

"So much the less is the whelp the only creature that she cares for," thought James Harthouse, reversing the reflection of his first day's knowledge of her pretty face. "So much the less, so much the less."

CHAPTER EIGHT

EXPLOSION

The next morning was too bright a morning for sleep, and James Harthouse rose early, and sat in the pleasant bay window of his dressing-room, smoking the rare tobacco that had had so wholesome an influence on his young friend. Reposing in the sunlight, with the fragrance of his eastern pipe about him, and the dreamy smoke vanishing into the air, so rich and soft with summer odours, he reckoned up his advantages as an idle winner might count his gains. He was not at all bored for the time, and could give his mind to it.

He had established a confidence with her, from which her husband was excluded. He had established a confidence with her, that absolutely turned upon her indifference towards her husband, and the absence, now and at all times, of any congeniality between them. He had artfully, but plainly, assured her that he knew her heart in its last most delicate recesses; he had come so near to her through its tenderest sentiment; he had associated himself with that feeling; and the barrier behind which she lived had melted away. All very odd, and very satisfactory!

And yet he had not, even now, any earnest wickedness of purpose in him. Publicly and privately, it were much better for the age in which he lived, that he and the legion of whom he was one were designedly bad, than indifferent and purposeless. It is the drifting icebergs setting with any current anywhere, that wreck the ships.

When the Devil goeth about like a roaring lion, he goeth about in a shape by which few but savages and hunters are attracted. But, when he is trimmed, smoothed, and varnished, according to the mode: when he is aweary of vice, and aweary of virtue, used up as to brimstone, and used up as to bliss; then, whether he take to the serving out of red tape, or to the kindling of red fire, he is the very Devil.

So, James Harthouse reclined in the window, indolently smoking, and reckoning up the steps he had taken on the road by which he happened to be travelling. The end to which it led was before him, pretty plainly; but he troubled himself with no calculations about it. What will be, will be.

As he had rather a long ride to take that day—for there was a public occasion "to do" at some distance, which afforded a tolerable opportunity of going in for the Gradgrind men—he dressed early, and went down to breakfast. He was anxious to see if she had relapsed since the previous evening. No. He resumed where he had left off. There was a look of interest for him again.

He got through the day as much (or as little) to his own satisfaction, as was to be expected under the fatiguing circumstances; and came riding back at six o'clock. There was a sweep of some half mile between the lodge and the house, and he was riding along at a foot pace over the smooth gravel, once Nickits's, when Mr. Bounderby burst out of the shrubbery, with such violence as to make his horse shy across the road.

"Harthouse!" cried Mr. Bounderby. "Have you heard?"

Mr. Bounderby's burst

"Heard what?" said Harthouse, soothing his horse, and inwardly favouring Mr. Bounderby with no good wishes.

"Then you *haven't* heard!"

"I have heard you, and so has this brute. I have heard nothing else."

Mr. Bounderby, red and hot, planted himself in the centre of the path before the horse's head, to explode his bombshell with more effect.

"The Bank's robbed!"

"You don't mean it!"

"Robbed last night, sir. Robbed in an extraordinary manner. Robbed with a false key."

"Of much?"

Mr. Bounderby, in his desire to make the most of it, really seemed mortified by being obliged to reply, "Why, no; not of very much. But it might have been."

"Of how much?"

"Oh! as a sum—if you stick to a sum—of not more than a hundred and fifty pound," said Bounderby, with impatience. "But it's not the sum; it's the fact. It's the fact of the Bank being robbed, that's the important circumstance. I am surprised you don't see it."

"My dear Bounderby," said James, dismounting, and giving his bridle to his servant, "I *do* see it; and am as overcome as you can possibly desire me to be, by the spectacle afforded to my mental view. Nevertheless, I may be allowed, I hope, to congratulate you—which I do with all my soul, I assure you—on your not having sustained a greater loss."

"Thank'ee," replied Bounderby, in a short, ungracious manner. "But I tell you what. It might have been twenty thousand pound."

"I suppose it might."

"Suppose it might! By the Lord, you *may* suppose so. By George!" said Mr. Bounderby, with sundry menacing nods and shakes of his head. "It might have been twice twenty. There's no knowing what it would have been, or wouldn't have been, as it was, but for the fellows being disturbed."

Louisa had come up now, and Mrs. Sparsit, and Bitzer.

"Here's Tom Gradgrind's daughter knows pretty well what it might have been, if you don't," blustered Bounderby. "Dropped, sir, as if she was shot when I told her! Never knew her do such a thing before. Does her credit, under the circumstances, in my opinion!"

She still looked faint and pale. James Harthouse begged her to take his arm; and as they moved on very slowly, asked her how the robbery had been committed.

"Why, I am going to tell you," said Bounderby, irritably giving his arm to Mrs. Sparsit. "If you hadn't been so mighty particular

about the sum, I should have begun to tell you before. You know
this lady (for she *is* a lady), Mrs. Sparsit?"

"I have already had the honour——"

"Very well. And this young man, Bitzer, you saw him too on
the same occasion?" Mr. Harthouse inclined his head in assent,
and Bitzer knuckled his forehead.

"Very well. They live at the Bank. You know they live at the
Bank, perhaps? Very well. Yesterday afternoon, at the close of
business hours, everything was put away as usual. In the iron
room that this young fellow sleeps outside of, there was never
mind how much. In the little safe in young Tom's closet, the safe
used for petty purposes, there was a hundred and fifty odd pound."

"A hundred and fifty-four, seven, one," said Bitzer.

"Come!" retorted Bounderby, stopping to wheel round upon
him, "let's have none of *your* interruptions. It's enough to be
robbed while you're snoring because you're too comfortable,
without being put right with *your* four seven ones. I didn't snore,
myself, when I was your age, let me tell you. I hadn't victuals
enough to snore. And I didn't four seven one. Not if I knew it."

Bitzer knuckled his forehead again, in a sneaking manner, and
seemed at once particularly impressed and depressed by the
instance last given of Mr. Bounderby's moral abstinence.

"A hundred and fifty odd pound," resumed Mr. Bounderby.
"That sum of money, young Tom locked in his safe, not a very
strong safe, but that's no matter now. Everything was left, all right.
Some time in the night, while this young fellow snored—Mrs.
Sparsit, ma'am, you say you have heard him snore?"

"Sir," returned Mrs. Sparsit, "I cannot say that I have heard
him precisely snore, and therefore must not make that statement.
But on winter evenings, when he has fallen asleep at his table,
I have heard him, what I should prefer to describe as partially
choke. I have heard him on such occasions produce sounds of a
nature similar to what may be sometimes heard in Dutch clocks.
Not," said Mrs. Sparsit, with a lofty sense of giving strict evidence, "that I would convey any imputation on his moral character.
Far from it. I have always considered Bitzer a young man of the
most upright principle; and to that I beg to bear my testimony."

"Well!" said the exasperated Bounderby, "while he was snoring, *or* choking, *or* Dutch-clocking, *or* something or other—being asleep—some fellows, somehow, whether previously concealed in the house or not remains to be seen, got to young Tom's safe, forced it, and abstracted the contents. Being then disturbed, they made off; letting themselves out at the main door, and double-locking it again (it was double-locked, and the key under Mrs. Sparsit's pillow) with a false key, which was picked up in the street near the Bank, about twelve o'clock to-day. No alarm takes place, till this chap, Bitzer, turns out this morning, and begins to open and prepare the offices for business. Then, looking at Tom's safe, he sees the door ajar, and finds the lock forced, and the money gone."

"Where is Tom, by the by?" asked Harthouse, glancing round.

"He has been helping the police," said Bounderby, "and stays behind at the Bank. I wish these fellows had tried to rob me when I was at his time of life. They would have been out of pocket if they had invested eighteenpence in the job; I can tell 'em that."

"Is anybody suspected?"

"Suspected? I thould think there was somebody suspected. Egod!" said Bounderby, relinquishing Mrs. Sparsit's arm to wipe his heated head. "Josiah Bounderby of Coketown is not to be plundered and nobody suspected. No, thank you!"

Might Mr. Harthouse inquire Who was sus-
Who did it? pected?

"Well," said Bounderby, stopping and facing about to confront them all, "I'll tell you. It's not to be mentioned everywhere; it's not to be mentioned anywhere; in order that the scoundrels concerned (there's a gang of 'em) may be thrown off their guard. So take this in confidence. Now wait a bit." Mr. Bounderby wiped his head again. "What should you say to," here he violently exploded, "to a Hand being in it?"

"I hope," said Harthouse, lazily, "not our friend Blackpot?"

"Say Pool instead of Pot, sir," returned Bounderby, "and that's the man."

Louisa faintly uttered some word of incredulity and surprise.

"O yes! I know!" said Bounderby, immediately catching at the sound. "I know! I am used to that. I know all about it. They are the finest people in the world, these fellows are. They have got the gift of the gab, they have. They only want to have their rights explained to them, they do. But I tell you what. Show me a dissatisfied Hand, and I'll show you a man that's fit for anything bad, I don't care what it is."

Another of the popular fictions of Coketown, which some pains had been taken to disseminate—and which some people really believed.

"But I am acquainted with these chaps," said Bounderby. "I can read 'em off, like books. Mrs. Sparsit, ma'am, I appeal to you. What warning did I give that fellow, the first time he set foot in the house, when the express object of his visit was to know how he could knock Religion over, and floor the Established Church? Mrs. Sparsit, in point of high connexions, you are on a level with the aristocracy—did I say, or did I not say, to that fellow, 'you can't hide the truth from me: you are not the kind of fellow I like; you'll come to no good'?"

"Assuredly, sir," returned Mrs. Sparsit, "you did, in a highly impressive manner, give him such an admonition."

"When he shocked you, ma'am," said Bounderby; "when he shocked your feelings?"

"Yes, sir," returned Mrs. Sparsit, with a meek shake of her head, "he certainly did so. Though I do not mean to say but that my feelings may be weaker on such points—more foolish if the term is preferred—than they might have been, if I had always occupied my present position."

Mr. Bounderby stared with a bursting pride at Mr. Harthouse, as much as to say, "I am the proprietor of this female, and she's worth your attention, I think." Then, resumed his discourse.

"You can recall for yourself, Harthouse, what I said to him when you saw him. I didn't mince the matter with him. I am never mealy with 'em. I KNOW 'em. Very well, sir. Three days after that, he bolted. Went off, nobody knows where: as my mother did in my infancy—only with this difference, that he is a worse subject than my mother, if possible. What did he do before he went? What do you say," Mr. Bounderby, with his hat in his hand, gave a beat upon the crown at every little division of his sentences, as if it were a tambourine, "to his being seen—night after night —watching the Bank?—to his lurking about there—after dark?— To its striking Mrs. Sparsit—that he could be lurking for no good—To her calling Bitzer's attention to him, and their both taking notice of him—And to its appearing on inquiry to-day—that he was also noticed by the neighbours?" Having come to the climax, Mr. Bounderby, like an oriental dancer, put his tambourine on his head.

"Suspicious," said James Harthouse, "certainly."

"I think so, sir," said Bounderby, with a defiant nod. "I think so. But there are more of 'em in it. There's an old woman. One never hears of these things till the mischief's done; all sorts of defects are found out in the stable door after the horse is stolen; there's an old woman turns up now. An old woman who seems to have been flying into town on a broomstick, every now and then. *She* watches the place a whole day before this fellow begins, and on the night when you saw him, she steals away with him and holds a council with him—I suppose, to make her report on going off duty, and be damned to her."

There was such a person in the room that night, and she shrunk from observation, thought Louisa.

"This is not all of 'em, even as we already know 'em," said Bounderby, with many nods of hidden meaning. "But I have said enough for the present. You'll have the goodness to keep it quiet, and mention it to no one. It may take time, but we shall have 'em. It's policy to give 'em line enough, and there's no objection to that."

"Of course, they will be punished with the utmost rigour of the law, as notice-boards observe," replied James Harthouse, "and serve them right. Fellows who go in for Banks must take the consequences. If there were no consequences, we should all go in for Banks." He had gently taken Louisa's parasol from her hand, and had put it up for her; and she walked under its shade, though the sun did not shine there.

"For the present, Loo Bounderby," said her husband, "here's Mrs. Sparsit to look after. Mrs. Sparsit's nerves have been acted upon by this business, and she'll stay here a day or two. So, make her comfortable."

"Thank you very much, sir," that discreet lady observed, "but pray do not let My comfort be a consideration. Anything will do for Me."

It soon appeared that if Mrs. Sparsit had a failing in her

association with that domestic establishment, it was that she was
so excessively regardless of herself and regardful of others, as to
be a nuisance. On being shown her chamber, she was so dreadfully
sensible of its comforts as to suggest the inference that she would
have preferred to pass the night on the mangle in the laundry.
True, the Powlers and the Scadgerses were accustomed to splendour, "but it is my duty to remember," Mrs. Sparsit was fond of
observing with a lofty grace: particularly when any of the
domestics were present, "that what I was, I am no longer. Indeed,"
said she, "if I could altogether cancel the remembrance that Mr.
Sparsit was a Powler, or that I myself am related to the Scadgers
family; or if I could even revoke the fact, and make myself a
person of common descent and ordinary connexions; I would
gladly do so. I should think it, under existing circumstances, right
to do so." The same Hermitical state of mind led to her renunciation of made dishes and wines at dinner, until fairly commanded
by Mr. Bounderby to take them; when she said, "Indeed you are
very good, sir;" and departed from a resolution of which she
had made rather formal and public announcement, to "wait for
the simple mutton." She was likewise, deeply apologetic for wanting
the salt; and, feeling amiably bound to bear out Mr. Bounderby
to the fullest extent in the testimony he had borne to her nerves,
occasionally sat back in her chair and silently wept; at which
periods a tear of large dimensions, like a crystal ear-ring, might be
observed (or rather, must be, for it insisted on public notice)
sliding down her Roman nose.

But Mrs. Sparsit's greatest point, first and
last, was her determination to pity Mr. Boun- *So natural*
derby. There were occasions when in looking at *to say*
him she was involuntarily moved to shake her *Miss Gradgrind!*
head, as who would say, "Alas poor Yorick!"
After allowing herself to be betrayed into these evidences of
emotion, she would force a lambent brightness, and would be
fitfully cheerful, and would say, "You have still good spirits, sir,
I am thankful to find;" and would appear to hail it as a blessed
dispensation that Mr. Bounderby bore up as he did. One idiosyncrasy for which she often apologized, she found it excessively
difficult to conquer. She had a curious propensity to call Mrs.

Bounderby "Miss Gradgrind," and yielded to it some three or four score times in the course of the evening. Her repetition of this mistake covered Mrs. Sparsit with modest confusion; but indeed, she said, it seemed so natural to say Miss Gradgrind: whereas, to persuade herself that the young lady whom she had had the happiness of knowing from a child could be really and truly Mrs. Bounderby, she found almost impossible. It was a further singularity of this remarkable case, that the more she thought about it, the more impossible it appeared; "the differences," she observed, "being such."

In the drawing-room after dinner, Mr. Bounderby tried the case of the robbery, examined the witnesses, made notes of the evidence, found the suspected persons guilty, and sentenced them to the extreme punishment of the law. That done, Bitzer was dismissed to town with instructions to recommend Tom to come home by the mail-train.

When candles were brought, Mrs. Sparsit murmured, "Don't be low, sir. Pray let me see you cheerful, sir, as I used to do." Mr. Bounderby, upon whom these consolations had begun to produce the effect of making him, in a bull-headed blundering way, sentimental, sighed like some large sea-animal. "I cannot bear to see you so, sir," said Mrs. Sparsit. "Try a hand at backgammon, sir, as you used to do when I had the honour of living under your roof." "I haven't played backgammon, ma'am," said Mr. Bounderby, "since that time." "No, sir," said Mrs. Sparsit, soothingly, "I am aware that you have not. I remember that Miss Gradgrind takes no interest in the game. But I shall be happy, sir, if you will condescend."

They played near a window, opening on the garden. It was a fine night: not moonlight, but sultry and fragrant. Louisa and Mr. Harthouse strolled out into the garden, where their voices could be heard in the stillness, though not what they said. Mrs. Sparsit, from her place at the backgammon board, was constantly straining her eyes to pierce the shadows without. "What's the matter, ma'am?" said Mr. Bounderby; "you don't see a Fire, do you?" "Oh dear no, sir," returned Mrs. Sparsit, "I was thinking of the dew." "What have you got to do with the dew, ma'am?" said Mr. Bounderby. "It's not myself, sir," returned Mrs. Sparsit, "I am fearful of Miss Gradgrind's taking cold." "She never takes cold," said Mr. Bounderby. "Really, sir?" said Mrs. Sparsit. And was affected with a cough in her throat.

When the time drew near for retiring, Mr. Bounderby took a glass of water. "Oh, sir?" said Mrs. Sparsit. "Not your sherry warm, with lemon-peel and nutmeg?" "Why I have got out of the habit of taking it now, ma'am," said Mr. Bounderby. "The more's the pity, sir," returned Mrs. Sparsit; "you are losing all your good old habits. Cheer up, sir! If Miss Gradgrind will permit me, I will offer to make it for you, as I have often done."

Miss Gradgrind readily permitting Mrs. Sparsit to do anything she pleased, that considerate lady made the beverage, and handed it to Mr. Bounderby. "It will do you good, sir. It will warm your heart. It is the sort of thing you want, and ought to take, sir." And when Mr. Bounderby said, "Your health, ma'am!" she answered with great feeling, "Thank you, sir. The same to you, and happiness also." Finally, she wished him good night, with great pathos; and Mr. Bounderby went to bed, with a maudlin persuasion that he had been crossed in something tender, though he could not, for his life, have mentioned what it was.

Long after Louisa had undressed and lain down, she watched and waited for her brother's coming home. That could hardly be, she knew, until an hour past midnight; but in the country silence, which did anything but calm the trouble of her thoughts, time lagged wearily. At last, when the darkness and stillness had seemed for hours to thicken one another, she heard the bell at the gate. She felt as though she would have been glad that it rang on until day-light; but it ceased, and the circles of its last sound spread out fainter and wider in the air, and all was dead again.

She waited yet some quarter of an hour, as she judged. Then she arose, put on a loose robe, and went out of her room in the dark, and up the staircase to her brother's room. His door being shut, she softly opened it and spoke to him, approaching his bed with a noiseless step.

She kneeled down beside it, passed her arm over his neck, and drew his face to hers. She knew that he only feigned to be asleep, but she said nothing to him.

He started by and by, as if he were just then awakened, and asked who it was, and what was the matter?

"Tom, have you anything to tell me? If ever you loved me in your life, and have anything concealed from every one besides, tell it to me."

"I don't know what you mean, Loo. You have been dreaming."

Tom has nothing to tell

"My dear brother," she laid her head down on his pillow, and her hair flowed over him as if she would hide him from every one but herself, "is there nothing that you have to tell me? Is there nothing you can tell me if you will? You can tell me nothing that will change me. O Tom, tell me the truth!"

"I don't know what you mean, Loo!"

"As you lie here alone, my dear, in the melancholy night, so you must lie somewhere one night, when even I, if I am living then, shall have left you. As I am here beside you, barefoot, unclothed, undistinguishable in darkness, so must I lie through all the night of my decay, until I am dust. In the name of that time, Tom, tell me the truth now!"

"What is it you want to know?"

"You may be certain," in the energy of her love she took him to her bosom as if he were a child, "that I will not reproach you. You may be certain that I will be compassionate and true to you. You may be certain that I will save you at whatever cost. O Tom, have you nothing to tell me? Whisper very softly. Say only 'yes,' and I shall understand you!"

She turned her ear to his lips, but he remained doggedly silent.

"Not a word, Tom?"

"How can I say Yes, or how can I say No, when I don't know what you mean? Loo, you are a brave, kind girl, worthy I begin to think of a better brother than I am. But I have nothing more to say. Go to bed, go to bed."

"You are tired," she whispered presently, more in her usual way.

"Yes, I am quite tired out."

"You have been so hurried and disturbed to-day. Have any fresh discoveries been made?"

"Only those you have heard of, from—him."

"Tom, have you said to any one that we made a visit to those people, and that we saw those three together?"

"No. Didn't you yourself particularly ask me to keep it quiet when you asked me to go there with you?"

"Yes. But I did not know then what was going to happen."

"Nor I neither. How could I?"

He was very quick upon her with this retort.

"Ought I to say, after what has happened," said his sister, standing by the bed—she had gradually withdrawn herself and risen, "that I made that visit? Should I say so? Must I say so?"

"Good Heavens, Loo," returned her brother, "you are not in the habit of asking my advice. Say what you like. If you keep it to yourself, I shall keep it to *my*self. If you disclose it, there's an end of it."

It was too dark for either to see the other's face; but each seemed very attentive, and to consider before speaking.

"Tom, do you believe the man I gave the money to, is really implicated in this crime?"

"I don't know. I don't see why he shouldn't be."

"He seemed to me an honest man."

"Another person may seem to you dishonest, and yet not be so."

There was a pause, for he had hesitated and stopped.

"In short," resumed Tom, as if he had made up his mind, "if you come to that, perhaps I was so far from being altogether in his favour, that I took him outside the door to tell him quietly, that I thought he might consider himself very well off to get such a windfall as he had got from my sister, and that I hoped he would make good use of it. You remember whether I took him out or not. I say nothing against the man; he may be a very good fellow, for anything I know; I hope he is."

"Was he offended by what you said?"

"No, he took it pretty well; he was civil enough. Where are you, Loo?" He sat up in bed and kissed her. "Good night, my dear, good night."

"You have nothing more to tell me?"

"No. What should I have? You wouldn't have me tell you a lie!"

"I wouldn't have you do that to-night, Tom, of all the nights in your life; many and much happier as I hope they will be."

"Thank you, my dear Loo. I am so tired, that I am sure I wonder I don't say anything to get to sleep. Go to bed, go to bed."

Kissing her again, he turned round, drew the coverlet over his head, and lay as still as if that time had come by which she had adjured him. She stood for some time at the bedside before she slowly moved away. She stopped at the door, looked back when she had opened it, and asked him if he had called her? But he lay still, and she softly closed the door and returned to her room.

Then the wretched boy looked cautiously up and found her gone, crept out of bed, fastened his door, and threw himself upon his pillow again: tearing his hair, morosely crying, grudgingly loving her, hatefully but impenitently spurning himself, and no less hatefully and unprofitably spurning all the good in the world.

CHAPTER NINE

HEARING THE LAST OF IT

MRS. SPARSIT, lying by to recover the tone of her nerves in Mr. Bounderby's retreat, kept such a sharp look-out, night and day, under her Coriolanian eyebrows, that her eyes, like a couple of lighthouses on an iron-bound coast, might have warned all prudent mariners from that bold rock her Roman nose and the dark and craggy region in its neighbourhood, but for the placidity of her manner. Although it was hard to believe that her retiring for the night could be anything but a form, so severely wide awake were those classical eyes of hers, and so impossible did it seem that her rigid nose could yield to any relaxing influence, yet her manner of sitting, smoothing her uncomfortable, not to say, gritty mittens (they were constructed of a cool fabric like a meat-safe), or of ambling to unknown places of destination with her foot in her cotton stirrup, was so perfectly serene, that most observers would have been constrained to suppose her a dove, embodied by some freak of nature, in the earthly tabernacle of a bird of the hook-beaked order.

She was a most wonderful woman for prowling about the house. How she got from story to story was a mystery beyond solution. A lady so decorous in herself, and so highly connected, was not to be suspected of dropping over the banisters or sliding down them, yet her extraordinary facility of locomotion suggested the wild idea. Another noticeable circumstance in Mrs. Sparsit was, that she was never hurried. She would shoot with consummate velocity from the roof to the hall, yet would be in full possession of her breath and dignity on the moment of her arrival there. Neither was she ever seen by human vision to go at a great pace.

She took very kindly to Mr. Harthouse, and had some pleasant conversation with him soon after her arrival. She made him her stately curtsey in the garden, one morning before breakfast.

"It appears but yesterday, sir," said Mrs. Sparsit, "that I had the honour of receiving you at the Bank, when you were so good as to wish to be made acquainted with Mr. Bounderby's address."

"An occasion, I am sure, not to be forgotten by myself in the course of Ages," said Mr. Harthouse, inclining his head to Mrs. Sparsit with the most indolent of all possible airs.

"We live in a singular world, sir," said Mrs. Sparsit.

"I have had the honour, by a coincidence of which I am proud, to have made a remark, similar in effect, though not so epigrammatically expressed."

"A singular world, I would say, sir," pursued Mrs. Sparsit; after acknowledging the compliment with a drooping of her dark eyebrows, not altogether so mild in its expression as her voice was in its dulcet tones; "as regards the intimacies we form at one time, with individuals, we were quite ignorant of, at another. I recall, sir, that on that occasion you went so far as to say you were actually apprehensive of Miss Gradgrind."

"Your memory does me more honour than my insignificance deserves. I availed myself of your obliging hints to correct my timidity, and it is unnecessary to add that they were perfectly accurate. Mrs. Sparsit's talent for—in fact for anything requiring accuracy—with a combination of strength of mind—and Family —is too habitually developed to admit of any question." He was almost falling asleep over this compliment; it took him so long to get through, and his mind wandered so much in the course of its execution.

"You found Miss Gradgrind—I really cannot call her Mrs. Bounderby; it's very absurd of me—as youthful as I described her?" asked Mrs. Sparsit, sweetly.

"You drew her portrait perfectly," said Mr. Harthouse. "Presented her dead image."

"Very engaging, sir," said Mrs. Sparsit, causing her mittens slowly to revolve over one another.

"Highly so."

"It used to be considered," said Mrs. Sparsit,
Mrs. Sparsit "that Miss Gradgrind was wanting in animation,
more superior but I confess she appears to me considerably
than ever and strikingly improved in that respect. Ay, and
indeed here *is* Mr. Bounderby!" cried Mrs.
Sparsit, nodding her head a great many times, as if she had been talking and thinking of no one else. "How do you find yourself this morning, sir? Pray let us see you cheerful, sir."

Now, these persistent assuagements of his misery, and lightenings of his load, had by this time begun to have the effect of making Mr. Bounderby softer than usual towards Mrs. Sparsit, and harder than usual to most other people from his wife downward. So, when Mrs. Sparsit said with forced lightness of heart, "You want your breakfast, sir, but I dare say Miss Gradgrind will soon be here to preside at the table," Mr. Bounderby replied, "If I waited to be taken care of by my wife, ma'am, I believe you know pretty well I should wait till Doomsday, so I'll trouble *you* to take charge of the teapot." Mrs. Sparsit complied, and assumed her old position at table.

This again made the excellent woman vastly sentimental. She was so humble withal, that when Louisa appeared, she rose, protesting she never could think of sitting in that place under existing circumstances, often as she had had the honour of making Mr. Bounderby's breakfast, before Mrs. Gradgrind—she begged pardon, she meant to say Miss Bounderby—she hoped to be excused, but she really could not get it right yet, though she trusted to become familiar with it by and by—had assumed her present position. It was only (she observed) because Miss Gradgrind happened to be a little late, and Mr. Bounderby's time was so very precious, and she knew it of old to be so essential that he should breakfast to the moment, that she had taken the liberty of complying with his request; long as his will had been a law to her.

"There! Stop where you are, ma'am," said Mr. Bounderby, "stop where you are! Mrs. Bounderby will be very glad to be relieved of the trouble, I believe."

"Don't say that, sir," returned Mrs. Sparsit, almost with severity, "because that is very unkind to Mrs. Bounderby. And to be unkind is not to be you, sir."

"You may set your mind at rest, ma'am.—You can take it very quietly, can't you, Loo?" said Mr. Bounderby, in a blustering way to his wife.

"Of course. It is of no moment. Why should it be of any importance to me?"

"Why should it be of any importance to any one, Mrs. Sparsit, ma'am?" said Mr. Bounderby, swelling with a sense of slight. "You attach too much importance to these things, ma'am. By George, you'll be corrupted in some of your notions here. You are old-fashioned, ma'am. You are behind Tom Gradgrind's children's time."

"What is the matter with you?" asked Louisa, coldly surprised. "What has given you offence?"

"Offence!" repeated Bounderby. "Do you suppose if there was any offence given me, I shouldn't name it, and request to have it corrected? I am a straightforward man, I believe. I don't go beating about for side-winds."

"I suppose no one ever had occasion to think you too diffident, or too delicate," Louisa answered him composedly: "I have never made that objection to you, either as a child or as a woman. I don't understand what you would have."

"Have?" returned Mr. Bounderby. "Nothing. Otherwise, don't you, Loo Bounderby, know thoroughly well that I, Josiah Bounderby of Coketown, would have it?"

She looked at him, as he struck the table and made the teacups ring, with a proud colour in her face that was a new change, Mr. Harthouse thought. "You are incomprehensible this morning," said Louisa. "Pray take no further trouble to explain yourself. I am not curious to know your meaning. What does it matter?"

Nothing more was said on this theme, and Mr. Harthouse was soon idly gay on indifferent subjects. But from this day, the Sparsit action upon Mr. Bounderby threw Louisa and James

Harthouse more together, and strengthened the dangerous aliena-
tion from her husband and confidence against him with another,
into which she had fallen by degrees so fine that she could not
retrace them if she tried. But whether she ever tried or no, lay
hidden in her own closed heart.

Mrs. Sparsit was so much affected on this particular occasion,
that, assisting Mr. Bounderby to his hat after breakfast, and
being then alone with him in the hall, she imprinted a chaste kiss
upon his hand, murmured "My benefactor!" and retired, overwhelmed with grief. Yet it is an indubitable fact, within the
cognisance of this history, that five minutes after he had left the
house in the self-same hat, the same descendant of the Scadgerses
and connexion by matrimony of the Powlers, shook her right-hand
mitten at his portrait, made a contemptuous grimace at that work
of art, and said "Serve you right, you Noodle, and I am glad of it."

Mr. Bounderby had not been long gone, when Bitzer appeared.
Bitzer had come down by train, shrieking and rattling over the
long line of arches that bestrode the wild country of past and
present coalpits, with an express from Stone Lodge. It was a hasty
note to inform Louisa that Mrs. Gradgrind lay very ill. She had
never been well within her daughter's knowledge; but, she had
declined within the last few days, had continued sinking all
through the night, and was now as nearly dead, as her limited
capacity of being in any state that implied the ghost of an intention to get out of it, allowed.

Accompanied by the lightest of porters, fit colourless servitor
at Death's door when Mrs. Gradgrind knocked, Louisa rumbled to
Coketown, over the coalpits past and present, and was whirled into
its smoky jaws. She dismissed the messenger to his own devices,
and rode away to her old home.

She had seldom been there since her marriage. Her father was
usually sifting and sifting at his parliamentary cinderheap in
London (without being observed to turn up many precious articles
among the rubbish), and was still hard at it in the national dust-
yard. Her mother had taken it rather as a disturbance than otherwise, to be visited, as she reclined upon her sofa; young people,
Louisa felt herself all unfit for; Sissy she had never softened to
again, since the night when the stroller's child had raised her eyes

to look at Mr. Bounderby's intended wife. She had no inducements to go back, and had rarely gone.

Neither, as she approached her old home now, did any of the best influences of old home descend upon her. The dreams of childhood—its airy fables; its graceful, beautiful, humane, impossible adornments of the world beyond: so good to be believed in once, so good to be remembered when outgrown, for then the least among them rises to the stature of a great Charity in the heart, suffering little children to come into the midst of it, and to keep with their pure hands a garden in the stony ways of this world, wherein it were better for all the children of Adam that they should oftener sun themselves, simple and trustful, and not worldly-wise—what had she to do with these? Remembrances of how she had journeyed to the little that she knew, by the enchanted roads of what she and millions of innocent creatures had hoped and imagined; of how, first coming upon Reason through the tender light of Fancy, she had seen it a beneficent god, deferring to gods as great as itself: not a grim Idol, cruel and cold, with its victims bound hand to foot, and its big dumb shape set up with a sightless stare, never to be moved by anything but so many calculated tons of leverage—what had she to do with these? Her remembrances of home and childhood were remembrances of the drying up of every spring and fountain in her young heart as it gushed out. The golden waters were not there. They were flowing for the fertilisation of the land where grapes are gathered from thorns, and figs from thistles.

She went, with a heavy, hardened kind of sorrow upon her, into the house and into her mother's room. Since the time of her leaving home, Sissy had lived with the rest of the family on equal terms. Sissy was at her mother's side; *Mrs. Gradgrind's sick chamber* and Jane, her sister, now ten or twelve years old, was in the room.

There was great trouble before it could be made known to Mrs. Gradgrind that her eldest child was there. She reclined, propped up, from mere habit, on a couch: as nearly in her old usual attitude, as anything so helpless could be kept in. She had positively refused to take to her bed; on the ground that if she did, she would never hear the last of it.

Her feeble voice sounded so far away in her bundle of shawls, and the sound of another voice addressing her seemed to take such a long time in getting down to her ears, that she might have been lying at the bottom of a well. The poor lady was nearer Truth than she ever had been: which had much to do with it.

On being told that Mrs. Bounderby was there, she replied, at cross-purposes, that she had never called him by that name since he married Louisa; that pending her choice of an unobjectionable name, she had called him J; and that she could not at present depart from that regulation, not being yet provided with a permanent substitute. Louisa had sat by her for some minutes, and had spoken to her often, before she arrived at a clear understanding who it was. She then seemed to come to it all at once.

"Well, my dear," said Mrs. Gradgrind, "and I hope you are going on satisfactorily to yourself. It was all your father's doing. He set his heart upon it. And he ought to know."

"I want to hear of you, mother; not of myself."

"You want to hear of me, my dear? That's something new, I am sure, when anybody wants to hear of me. Not at all well, Louisa. Very faint and giddy."

"Are you in pain, dear mother?"

"I think there's a pain somewhere in the room," said Mrs. Gradgrind, "but I couldn't positively say that I have got it."

After this strange speech, she lay silent for some time. Louisa, holding her hand, could feel no pulse; but kissing it, could see a slight thin thread of life in fluttering motion.

"You very seldom see your sister," said Mrs. Gradgrind. "She grows like you. I wish you would look at her. Sissy, bring her here."

She was brought, and stood with her hand in her sister's. Louisa had observed her with her arm round Sissy's neck, and she felt the difference of this approach.

"Do you see the likeness, Louisa?"

"Yes, mother. I should think her like me. But——"

"Eh! Yes, I always say so," Mrs. Gradgrind cried, with unexpected quickness. "And that reminds me. I—I want to speak to you, my dear. Sissy, my good girl, leave us alone a minute."

Louisa had relinquished the hand: had thought that her sister's was a better and brighter face than hers had ever been: had seen in it, not without a rising feeling of resentment, even in that place and at that time, something of the gentleness of the other face in the room; the sweet face with the trusting eyes, made paler than watching and sympathy made it, by the rich dark hair.

Left alone with her mother, Louisa saw her lying with an awful lull upon her face, like one who was floating away upon some great water, all resistance over, content to be carried down the stream. She put the shadow of a hand to her lips again, and recalled her.

"You were going to speak to me, mother."

"Eh? Yes, to be sure, my dear. You know your father is almost always away now, and therefore I must write to him about it."

"About what, mother? Don't be troubled. About what?"

"You must remember, my dear, that whenever I have said anything, on any subject, I have never heard the last of it: and consequently, that I have long left off saying anything."

"I can hear you, mother." But, it was only by dint of bending down to her ear, and at the same time attentively watching the lips as they moved, that she could link such faint and broken sounds into any chain of connexion.

"You learnt a great deal, Louisa, and so did your brother. Ologies of all kinds from morning to night. If there is any Ology left, of any description, that has not been worn to rags in this house, all I can say is, I hope I shall never hear its name."

"I can hear you, mother, when you have strength to go on." This, to keep her from floating away.

"But there is something—not an Ology at all—that your father has missed, or forgotten, Louisa. I don't know what it is. I have often sat with Sissy near me, and thought about it. I shall never get its name now. But your father may. It makes me restless. I want to write to him, to find out for God's sake, what it is. Give me a pen, give me a pen."

Even the power of restlessness was gone, except from the poor head, which could just turn from side to side.

She fancied, however, that her request had been complied with, and that the pen she could not have held was in her hand. It matters little what figures of wonderful no-meaning she began to trace upon her wrappers. The hand soon stopped in the midst of them; the light that had always been feeble and dim behind the weak transparency, went out; and even Mrs. Gradgrind, emerged from the shadow in which man walketh and disquieteth himself in vain, took upon her the dread solemnity of the sages and patriarchs.

CHAPTER TEN

MRS. SPARSIT'S STAIRCASE

Mrs. Sparsit's nerves being slow to recover their tone, the worthy woman made a stay of some weeks in duration at Mr. Bounderby's retreat, where, notwithstanding her anchorite turn of mind based upon her becoming consciousness of her altered station, she resigned herself with noble fortitude to lodging, as one may say, in clover, and feeding on the fat of the land. During the whole term of this recess from the guardianship of the Bank, Mrs. Sparsit was a pattern of consistency; continuing to take such pity on Mr. Bounderby to his face, as is rarely taken on man, and to call his portrait a Noodle to *its* face, with the greatest acrimony and contempt.

Mr. Bounderby, having got it into his explosive composition that Mrs. Sparsit was a highly superior woman to perceive that he had that general cross upon him in his deserts (for he had not yet settled what it was), and further that Louisa would have objected to her as a frequent visitor if it had comported with his greatness that she should object to anything he chose to do, resolved not to lose sight of Mrs. Sparsit easily. So when her nerves were strung up to the pitch of again consuming sweetbreads in solitude, he said to her at the dinner-table, on the day before her departure, "I tell you what, ma'am; you shall come down here of a Saturday, while the fine weather lasts, and stay till Monday." To which Mrs. Sparsit returned, in effect, though not of the Mahomedan persuasion: "To hear is to obey."

Now, Mrs. Sparsit was not a poetical woman; but she took an idea in the nature of an allegorical fancy, into her head. Much watching of Louisa, and much consequent observation of her impenetrable demeanour, which keenly whetted and sharpened Mrs. Sparsit's edge, must have given her as it were a lift, in the way of inspiration. She erected in her mind a mighty Staircase, with a dark pit of shame and ruin at the bottom; and down those stairs, from day to day and hour to hour, she saw Louisa coming.

It became the business of Mrs. Sparsit's life, to look up at her staircase, and to watch Louisa coming down. Sometimes slowly, sometimes quickly, sometimes several steps at one bout, sometimes stopping, never turning back. If she had once turned back, it might have been the death of Mrs. Sparsit in spleen and grief.

She had been descending steadily, to the day, and on the day, when Mr. Bounderby issued the weekly invitation recorded above. Mrs. Sparsit was in good spirits, and inclined to be conversational.

"And pray, sir," said she, "if I may venture to ask a question appertaining to any subject on which you show reserve—which is indeed hardly in me, for I well know you have a reason for everything you do—have you received intelligence respecting the robbery?"

"Why, ma'am, no; not yet. Under the circumstances, I didn't expect it yet. Rome wasn't built in a day, ma'am."

Mr. Bounderby can wait

"Very true, sir," said Mrs. Sparsit, shaking her head.

"Nor yet in a week, ma'am."

"No, indeed, sir," returned Mrs. Sparsit, with a gentle melancholy upon her.

"In a similar manner, ma'am," said Bounderby, "I can wait, you know. If Romulus and Remus could wait, Josiah Bounderby can wait. They were better off in their youth than I was, however. They had a she-wolf for a nurse; *I* had only a she-wolf for a grandmother. She didn't give any milk, ma'am; she gave bruises. She was a regular Alderney at that."

"Ah!" Mrs. Sparsit sighed and shuddered.

"No, ma'am," continued Bounderby, "I have not heard anything more about it. It's in hand, though; and young Tom, who rather sticks to business at present—something new for him;

he hadn't the schooling *I* had—is helping. My injunction is, Keep it quiet, and let it seem to blow over. Do what you like under the rose, but don't give a sign of what you're about; or half a hundred of 'em will combine together and get this fellow who has bolted out of reach for good. Keep it quiet, and the thieves will grow in confidence by little and little, and we shall have 'em."

"Very sagacious indeed, sir," said Mrs. Sparsit. "Very interesting. The old woman you mentioned, sir——"

"The old woman I mentioned, ma'am," said Bounderby, cutting the matter short, as it was nothing to boast about, "is not laid hold of; but, she may take her oath she will be, if that is any satisfaction to her villainous old mind. In the meantime, ma'am, I am of opinion, if you ask me my opinion, that the less she is talked about, the better."

That same evening, Mrs. Sparsit in her chamber window, resting from her packing operations, looked towards her great staircase and saw Louisa still descending.

She sat by Mr. Harthouse, in an alcove in the garden, talking very low, he stood leaning over her, as they whispered together, and his face almost touched her hair. "If not quite!" said Mrs. Sparsit, straining her hawk's eyes to the utmost. Mrs. Sparsit was too distant to hear a word of their discourse, or even to know that they were speaking softly, otherwise than from the expression of their figures; but what they said was this:

"You recollect the man, Mr. Harthouse?"

"Oh, perfectly."

"His face, and his manner, and what he said?"

"Perfectly. And an infinitely dreary person he appeared to me to be. Lengthy and prosy in the extreme. It was knowing to hold forth, in the humble-virtue school of eloquence; but, I assure you I thought at the time, 'My good fellow, you are over-doing this!' "

"It has been very difficult to me to think ill of that man."

"My dear Louisa—as Tom says." Which he never did say. "You know no good of the fellow?"

"No, certainly."

"Nor of any other such person?"

"How can I," she returned, with more of her first manner on her than he had lately seen, "when I know nothing of them, men or women?"

"My dear Louisa, then consent to receive the submissive representation of your devoted friend, who knows something of several varieties of his excellent fellow-creatures—for excellent they are, I am quite ready to believe, in spite of such little foibles as always helping themselves to what they can get hold of. This fellow talks. Well; every fellow talks. He professes morality. Well; all sorts of humbugs profess morality. From the House of Commons to the House of Correction, there is a general profession of morality, except among our people; it really is that exception which makes our people quite reviving. You saw and heard the case. Here was one of the fluffy classes pulled up extremely short by my esteemed friend Mr. Bounderby—who, as we know, is not possessed of that delicacy which would soften so tight a hand. The member of the fluffy classes was injured, exasperated, left the house grumbling, met somebody who proposed to him to go in for some share in this Bank business, went in, put something in his pocket which had nothing in it before, and relieved his mind extremely. Really he would have been an uncommon, instead of a common, fellow, if he had not availed himself of such an opportunity. Or he may have originated it altogether, if he had the cleverness."

"I almost feel as though it must be bad in me," returned Louisa, after sitting thoughtful awhile, "to be so ready to agree with you, and to be so lightened in my heart by what you say."

"I only say what is reasonable; nothing worse. I have talked it over with my friend Tom more than once—of course I remain on terms of perfect confidence with Tom—and he is quite of my opinion, and I am quite of his. Will you walk?"

They strolled away, among the lanes beginning to be indistinct in the twilight—she leaning on his arm—and she little thought how she was going down, down, down, Mrs. Sparsit's staircase.

Coming down the staircase

Night and day, Mrs. Sparsit kept it standing. When Louisa had arrived at the bottom and disappeared in the gulf, it might fall in upon her if it would; but, until then, there it was to be, a Building, before Mrs. Sparsit's eyes. And there Louisa always was, upon it. And always gliding down, down, down!

Mrs. Sparsit saw James Harthouse come and go; she heard of him here and there; she saw the changes of the face he had studied; she, too, remarked to a nicety how and when it clouded, how and when it cleared; she kept her black eyes wide open, with no touch of pity, with no touch of compunction, all absorbed in interest. In the interest of seeing her, ever drawing, with no hand to stay her, nearer and nearer to the bottom of this new Giant's Staircase.

With all her deference for Mr. Bounderby as contradistinguished from his portrait, Mrs. Sparsit had not the smallest intention of interrupting the descent. Eager to see it accomplished, and yet patient, she waited for the last fall, as for the ripeness and fulness of the harvest of her hopes. Hushed in expectancy, she kept her wary gaze upon the stairs; and seldom so much as darkly shook her right mitten (with her fist in it), at the figure coming down.

CHAPTER ELEVEN

LOWER AND LOWER

THE figure descended the great stairs, steadily, steadily; always verging, like a weight in deep water, to the black gulf at the bottom.

Mr. Gradgrind, apprised of his wife's decease, made an expedition from London, and buried her in a business-like manner. He then returned with promptitude to the national cinder-heap, and resumed his sifting for the odds and ends he wanted, and his throwing of the dust about into the eyes of other people who wanted other odds and ends—in fact resumed his parliamentary duties.

In the meantime, Mrs. Sparsit kept unwinking watch and ward. Separated from her staircase, all the week, by the length of iron road dividing Coketown from the country-house, she yet maintained her cat-like observation of Louisa, through her husband, through her brother, through James Harthouse, through the outsides of letters and packets, through everything animate and inanimate that at any time went near the stairs. "Your foot on the last step, my lady," said Mrs. Sparsit, apostrophising the descending figure, with the aid of her threatening mitten, "and all your art shall never blind me."

Art or nature though, the original stock of Louisa's character or the graft of circumstances upon it,—her curious reserve did baffle, while it stimulated, one as sagacious as Mrs. Sparsit. There were times when Mr. James Harthouse was not sure of her. There were times when he could not read the face he had studied so long; and when this lonely girl was a greater mystery to him, than any woman of the world with a ring of satellites to help her.

So the time went on; until it happened that Mr. Bounderby was called away from home by business which required his presence elsewhere, for three or four days. It was on a Friday that he intimated this to Mrs. Sparsit at the Bank, adding: "But you'll go down to-morrow, ma'am, all the same. You'll go down just as if I was there. It will make no difference to you."

"Pray, sir," returned Mrs. Sparsit, reproachfully, "let me beg you not to say that. Your absence will make a vast difference to me, sir, as I think you very well know."

"Well, ma'am, then you must get on in my absence as well as you can," said Mr. Bounderby, not displeased.

"Mr. Bounderby," retorted Mrs. Sparsit, "your will is to me a law, sir; otherwise, it might be my inclination to dispute your kind commands, not feeling sure that it will be quite so agreeable to Miss Gradgrind to receive me, as it ever is to your own munificent hospitality. But you shall say no more, sir. I will go, upon your invitation."

"Why, when I invite you to my house, ma'am," said Bounderby, opening his eyes, "I should hope you want no other invitation."

"No, indeed, sir," returned Mrs. Sparsit, "I should hope not. Say no more, sir. I would, sir, I could see you gay again."

"What do you mean, ma'am?" blustered Bounderby.

"Sir," rejoined Mrs. Sparsit, "there was wont to be an elasticity in you which I sadly miss. Be buoyant, sir!"

Mr. Bounderby, under the influence of this difficult adjuration, backed up by her compassionate eye, could only scratch his head in a feeble and ridiculous manner, and afterwards assert himself at a distance, by being heard to bully the small fry of business all the morning.

"Bitzer," said Mrs. Sparsit that afternoon, when her patron was gone on his journey, and the Bank was closing, "present my compliments to young Mr. Thomas, and ask him if he would step up and partake of a lamb chop and walnut ketchup, with a glass of India ale?" Young Mr. Thomas being usually ready for anything in that way, returned a gracious answer, and followed on its heels. "Mr. Thomas," said Mrs. Sparsit, "these plain viands being on table, I thought you might be tempted."

"Thank'ee, Mrs. Sparsit," said the whelp. And gloomily fell to.

"How is Mr. Harthouse, Mr. Tom?" asked Mrs. Sparsit.

"Oh, he's all right," said Tom.

"Where may he be at present?" Mrs. Sparsit asked in a light conversational manner, after mentally devoting the whelp to the Furies for being so uncommunicative.

"He is shooting in Yorkshire," said Tom. "Sent Loo a basket half as big as a church, yesterday."

"The kind of gentleman, now," said Mrs. Sparsit, sweetly, "whom one might wager to be a good shot!"

"Crack," said Tom.

He had long been a down-looking young fellow, but this characteristic had so increased of late, that he never raised his eyes to any face for three seconds together. Mrs. Sparsit consequently had ample means of watching his looks, if she were so inclined.

"Mr. Harthouse is a great favourite of mine," said Mrs. Sparsit, "as indeed he is of most people. May we expect to see him again shortly, Mr. Tom?"

"Why, *I* expect to see him to-morrow," returned the whelp.

"Good news!" cried Mrs. Sparsit, blandly.

"I have got an appointment with him to meet him in the evening at the station here," said Tom, "and I am going to dine with him afterwards, I believe. He is not coming down to the country house for a week or so, being due somewhere else. At least, he says so; but I shouldn't wonder if he was to stop here over Sunday, and stray that way."

"Which reminds me!" said Mrs. Sparsit. "Would you remember a message to your sister, Mr. Tom, if I was to charge you with one?"

"Well? I'll try," returned the reluctant whelp, "if it isn't a long un."

"It is merely my respectful compliments," said Mrs. Sparsit, "and I fear I may not trouble her with my society this week; being still a little nervous, and better perhaps by my poor self."

"Oh! If that's all," observed Tom, "it wouldn't much matter, even if I was to forget it, for Loo's not likely to think of you unless she sees you."

Having paid for his entertainment with this agreeable compliment, he relapsed into a hangdog silence until there was no more India ale left, when he said, "Well, Mrs. Sparsit, I must be off!" and went off.

Next day, Saturday, Mrs. Sparsit sat at her window all day long looking at the customers coming in and out, watching the postmen, keeping an eye on the general traffic of the street, revolving many things in her mind, but, above all, keeping her attention on her staircase. The evening come, she put on her bonnet and shawl, and went quietly out: having her reasons for hovering in a furtive way about the station by which a passenger would arrive from Yorkshire, and for preferring to peep into it round pillars and corners, and out of ladies' waiting-room windows, to appearing in its precincts openly.

Mrs. Sparsit's journey

Tom was in attendance, and loitered about until the expected train came in. It brought no Mr. Harthouse. Tom waited until the crowd had dispersed, and the bustle was over; and then referred to a posted list of trains, and took counsel with porters. That done, he strolled away idly, stopping in the street and looking up it and down it, and lifting his hat off and putting it on again, and yawning and stretching himself, and exhibiting all the symptoms of mortal weariness to be expected in one who had still to wait until the next train should come in, an hour and forty minutes hence.

"This is a device to keep him out of the way," said Mrs. Sparsit, starting from the dull office window whence she had watched him last. "Harthouse is with his sister now!"

It was the conception of an inspired moment, and she shot off with her utmost swiftness to work it out. The station for the country house was at the opposite end of the town, the time was short, the road not easy; but she was so quick in pouncing on a disengaged coach, so quick in darting out of it, producing her money, seizing her ticket, and diving into the train, that she was borne along the arches spanning the land of coal-pits past and present, as if she had been caught up in a cloud and whirled away.

All the journey, immovable in the air though never left behind; plain to the dark eyes of her mind, as the electric wires which ruled a colossal strip of music-paper out of the evening sky, were plain to the dark eyes of her body; Mrs. Sparsit saw her staircase, with the figure coming down. Very near the bottom now. Upon the brink of the abyss.

An overcast September evening, just at nightfall, saw beneath its drooping eyelid Mrs. Sparsit glide out of her carriage, pass down the wooden steps of the little station into a stony road, cross it into a green lane, and become hidden in a summer-growth of leaves and branches. One or two late birds sleepily chirping in their nests, and a bat heavily crossing and recrossing her, and the reek of her own tread in the thick dust that felt like velvet, were all Mrs. Sparsit heard or saw until she very softly closed a gate.

She went up to the house, keeping within the shrubbery, and went round it, peeping between the leaves at the lower windows. Most of them were open, as they usually were in such warm weather, but there were no lights yet, and all was silent. She tried the garden with no better effect. She thought of the wood, and stole towards it, heedless of long grass and briers: of worms, snails, and slugs, and all the creeping things that be. With her dark eyes and her hook nose warily in advance of her, Mrs. Sparsit softly crushed her way through the thick undergrowth, so intent upon her object that she probably would have done no less, if the wood had been a wood of adders.

Hark!

The smaller birds might have tumbled out of their nests, fascinated by the glittering of Mrs. Sparsit's eye in the gloom, as she stopped and listened.

Low voices close at hand. His voice and hers. The appointment *was* a device to keep the brother away! There they were yonder, by the felled tree.

Bending low among the dewy grass, Mrs. Sparsit advanced closer to them. She drew herself up, and stood behind a tree, like Robinson Crusoe in his ambuscade against the savages; so near to them that at a spring, and that no great one, she could have touched them both. He was there secretly, and had not shown himself at the house. He had come on horseback, and must have passed through the neighbouring fields; for his horse was tied to the meadow side of the fence, within a few paces.

"My dearest love," said he, "what could I do? Knowing you were alone, was it possible that I could stay away?"

"You may hang your head, to make yourself the more attractive; *I* don't know what they see in you when you hold it up," thought Mrs. Sparsit; "but you little think, my dearest love, whose eyes are on you!"

That she hung her head, was certain. She urged him to go away, she commanded him to go away; but she neither turned her face to him, nor raised it. Yet it was remarkable that she sat as still as ever the amiable woman in ambuscade had seen her sit, at any period in her life. Her hands rested in one another, like the hands of a statue; and even her manner of speaking was not hurried.

"My dear child," said Harthouse; Mrs. Sparsit saw with delight that his arm embraced her; "will you not bear with my society for a little while?"

"Not here."

"Where, Louisa?"

"Not here."

"But we have so little time to make so much of, and I have come so far, and am altogether so devoted, and distracted. There never was a slave at once so devoted and ill-used by his mistress. To look for your sunny welcome that has warmed me into life, and to be received in your frozen manner, is heart-rending."

"Am I to say again, that I must be left to myself here?"

"But we must meet, my dear Louisa. Where shall we meet?"

They both started. The listener started, guiltily, too; for she thought there was another listener among the trees. It was only rain, beginning to fall fast, in heavy drops.

"Shall I ride up to the house a few minutes hence, innocently supposing that its master is at home and will be charmed to receive me?"

"No!"

"Your cruel commands are implicitly to be obeyed; though I am the most unfortunate fellow in the world, I believe, to have been insensible to all other women, and to have fallen prostrate at last under the foot of the most beautiful, and the most engaging, and the most imperious. My dearest Louisa, I cannot go myself, or let you go, in this hard abuse of your power."

Mrs. Sparsit's triumph

Mrs. Sparsit saw him detain her with his encircling arm, and heard him then and there, within her (Mrs. Sparsit's) greedy hearing, tell her how he loved her, and how she was the stake for which he ardently desired to play away all that he had in life. The objects he had lately pursued, turned worthless beside her; such success as was almost in his grasp, he flung away from him like the dirt it was, compared with her. Its pursuit, nevertheless, if it kept him near her, or its renunciation if it took him from her, or flight if she shared it, or secrecy if she commanded it, or any fate, or every fate, all was alike to him, so that she was true to him,—the man who had seen how cast away she was, whom she had inspired at their first meeting with an admiration, an interest, of which he had thought himself incapable, whom she had received into her confidence, who was devoted to her and adored her. All this, and more, in his hurry, and in hers, in the whirl of her own gratified malice, in the dread of being discovered, in the rapidly increasing noise of heavy rain among the leaves, and a thunderstorm rolling up—Mrs. Sparsit received into her mind, set off with such an unavoidable halo of confusion and indistinctness, that when at length he climbed the fence and led his horse away, she was not sure where they were to meet, or when, except that they had said it was to be that night.

But one of them yet remained in the darkness before her; and while she tracked that one she must be right. "Oh, my dearest love," thought Mrs. Sparsit, "you little think how well attended you are!"

Mrs. Sparsit saw her out of the wood, and saw her enter the house. What to do next? It rained now, in a sheet of water. Mrs. Sparsit's white stockings were of many colours, green predominating; prickly things were in her shoes; caterpillars slung themselves, in hammocks of their own making, from various parts of her dress; rills ran from her bonnet, and her Roman nose. In such condition, Mrs. Sparsit stood hidden in the density of the shrubbery, considering what next.

Lo, Louisa coming out of the house! Hastily cloaked and muffled, and stealing away. She elopes! She falls from the lowermost stair, and is swallowed up in the gulf.

Indifferent to the rain, and moving with a quick determined step, she struck into a side-path parallel with the ride. Mrs. Sparsit followed in the shadow of the trees, at but a short distance; for it was not easy to keep a figure in view going quickly through the umbrageous darkness.

When she stopped to close the side-gate without noise, Mrs. Sparsit stopped. When she went on, Mrs. Sparsit went on. She went by the way Mrs. Sparsit had come, emerged from the green lane, crossed the stony road, and ascended the wooden steps to the railroad. A train for Coketown would come through presently, Mrs. Sparsit knew; so she understood Coketown to be her first place of destination.

In Mrs. Sparsit's limp and streaming state, no extensive precautions were necessary to change her usual appearance; but, she stopped under the lee of the station wall, tumbled her shawl into a new shape, and put it on over her bonnet. So disguised she had no fear of being recognized when she followed up the railroad steps, and paid her money in the small office. Louisa sat waiting in a corner. Mrs. Sparsit sat waiting in another corner. Both listened to the thunder, which was loud, and to the rain, as it washed off the roof, and pattered on the parapets of the arches. Two or three lamps were rained out and blown out; so, both saw the lightning to advantage as it quivered and zigzagged on the iron tracks.

The seizure of the station with a fit of trembling, gradually deepening to a complaint of the heart, announced the train. Fire and steam, and smoke, and red light; a hiss, a crash, a bell, and a shriek; Louisa put into one carriage, Mrs. Sparsit put into another: the little station a desert speck in the thunderstorm.

Though her teeth chattered in her head from wet and cold, Mrs. Sparsit exulted hugely. The figure had plunged down the precipice, and she felt herself, as it were, attending on the body. Could she, who had been so active in the getting up of the funeral triumph, do less than exult? "She will be at Coketown long before him," thought Mrs. Sparsit, "though his horse is never so good. Where will she wait for him? And where will they go together? Patience. We shall see."

The tremendous rain occasioned infinite confusion, when the train stopped at its destination. Gutters and pipes had burst, drains had overflowed, streets were under water. In the first instant of alighting, Mrs. Sparsit turned her distracted eyes towards the waiting coaches, which were in great request. "She will get into one," she considered, "and will be away before I can follow in another. At all risks of being run over, I must see the number, and hear the order given to the coachman."

But, Mrs. Sparsit was wrong in her calculation. Louisa got into no coach, and was already gone. The black eyes kept upon the railroad-carriage in which she had travelled, settled upon it a moment too late. The door not being opened after several minutes, Mrs. Sparsit passed it and repassed it, saw nothing, looked in, and found it empty. Wet through and through: with her feet squelching and squashing in her shoes whenever she moved; with a rash of rain upon her classical visage; with a bonnet like an over-ripe fig; with all her clothes spoiled; with damp impressions of every button, string, and hook-and-eye she wore, printed off upon her highly connected back; with a stagnant verdure on her general exterior, such as accumulates on an old park fence in a mouldy lane; Mrs. Sparsit had no resource but to burst into tears of bitterness and say, "I have lost her!"

CHAPTER TWELVE

DOWN

THE national dustmen, after entertaining one another with a great many noisy little fights among themselves, had dispersed for the present, and Mr. Gradgrind was at home for the vacation.

He sat writing in the room with the deadly statistical clock, proving something no doubt—probably, in the main, that the Good Samaritan was a Bad Economist. The noise of the rain did not disturb him much; but it attracted his attention sufficiently to make him raise his head sometimes, as if he were rather remonstrating with the elements. When it thundered very loudly, he glanced towards Coketown, having it in his mind that some of the tall chimneys might be struck by lightning.

The thunder was rolling into distance, and the rain was pouring down like a deluge, when the door of his room opened. He looked round the lamp upon his table, and saw, with amazement, his eldest daughter.

"Louisa!"

"Father, I want to speak to you."

"What is the matter? How strange you look! And good Heaven," said Mr. Gradgrind, wondering more and more, "have you come here exposed to this storm?"

She put her hands to her dress, as if she hardly knew. "Yes." Then she uncovered her head, and letting her cloak and hood fall where they might, stood looking at him: so colourless, so dishevelled, so defiant and despairing, that he was afraid of her.

"What is it? I conjure you, Louisa, tell me what is the matter."

She dropped into a chair before him, and put her cold hand on his arm.

"Father, you have trained me from my cradle?"

"Yes, Louisa."

"I curse the hour in which I was born to such a destiny."

He looked at her in doubt and dread, vacantly repeating: "Curse the hour? Curse the hour?"

Great failure of the House of Gradgrind

"How could you give me life, and take from me all the inappreciable things that raise it from the state of conscious death? Where are the graces of my soul? Where are the sentiments of my heart? What have you done, O father, what have you done, with the garden that should have bloomed once, in this great wilderness here?"

She struck herself with both her hands upon her bosom.

"If it had ever been here, its ashes alone would save me from the void in which my whole life sinks. I did not mean to say this; but, father, you remember the last time we conversed in this room?"

He had been so wholly unprepared for what he heard now, that it was with difficulty he answered, "Yes, Louisa."

"What has risen to my lips now, would have risen to my lips then, if you had given me a moment's help. I don't reproach you, father. What you have never nurtured in me, you have never nurtured in yourself; but O! if you had only done so long ago, or if you had only neglected me, what a much better and much happier creature I should have been this day!"

On hearing this, after all his care, he bowed his head upon his hand and groaned aloud.

"Father, if you had known, when we were last together here, what even I feared while I strove against it—as it has been my task from infancy to strive against every natural prompting that has arisen in my heart; if you had known that there lingered in my breast, sensibilities, affections, weaknesses capable of being cherished into strength, defying all the calculations ever made by man, and no more known to his arithmetic than his Creator is,— would you have given me to the husband whom I am now sure that I hate?"

He said, "No. No, my poor child."

"Would you have doomed me, at any time, to the frost and blight that have hardened and spoiled me? Would you have robbed me—for no one's enrichment—only for the greater desolation of this world—of the immaterial part of my life, the spring and summer of my belief, my refuge from what is sordid and bad in the real things around me, my school in which I should have learned to be more humble and more trusting with them, and to hope in my little sphere to make them better?"

"O no, no. No, Louisa."

"Yet, father, if I had been stone blind; if I had groped my way by my sense of touch, and had been free, while I knew the shapes and surfaces of things, to exercise my fancy somewhat, in regard to them; I should have been a million times wiser, happier, more loving, more contented, more innocent and human in all good respects, than I am with the eyes I have. Now, hear what I have come to say."

He moved, to support her with his arm. She rising as he did so, they stood close together: she, with a hand upon his shoulder, looking fixedly in his face.

"With a hunger and thirst upon me, father, which have never been for a moment appeased; with an ardent impulse towards some region where rules, and figures, and definitions were not quite absolute; I have grown up, battling every inch of my way."

"I never knew you were unhappy, my child."

"Father, I always knew it. In this strife I have almost repulsed and crushed my better angel into a demon. What I have learned has left me doubting, misbelieving, despising, regretting, what I have not learned; and my dismal resource has been to think that life would soon go by, and that nothing in it could be worth the pain and trouble of a contest."

"And you so young, Louisa!" he said with pity.

"And I so young. In this condition, father—for I show you now, without fear or favour, the ordinary deadened state of my mind as I know it—you proposed my husband to me. I took him. I never made a pretence to him or you that I loved him. I knew, and, father, you knew, and he knew, that I never did. I was not wholly indifferent, for I had a hope of being pleasant and useful to Tom. I made that wild escape into something visionary, and have slowly found out how wild it was. But Tom had been the subject of all the little tenderness of my life; perhaps he became so because I knew so well how to pity him. It matters little now, except as it may dispose you to think more leniently of his errors."

As her father held her in his arms, she put her other hand upon his other shoulder, and still looking fixedly in his face, went on.

"When I was irrevocably married, there rose up into rebellion against the tie, the old strife, made fiercer by all those causes of disparity which arise out of our two individual natures, and which no general laws shall ever rule or state for me, father, until they shall be able to direct the anatomist where to strike his knife into the secrets of my soul."

"Louisa!" he said, and said imploringly; for he well remembered what had passed between them in their former interview.

"I do not reproach you, father, I make no complaint. I am here with another object."

"What can I do, child? Ask me what you will."

"I am coming to it. Father, chance then threw into my way a new acquaintance; a man such as I had had no experience of; used to the world; light, polished, easy; making no pretences; avowing the low estimate of everything, that I was half afraid to form in secret; conveying to me almost immediately, though I don't know how or by what degrees, that he understood me, and read my thoughts. I could not find that he was worse than I. There seemed to be a near affinity between us. I only wondered it should be worth his while, who cared for nothing else, to care so much for me."

"For you, Louisa!"

Her father might instinctively have loosened his hold, but that he felt her strength departing from her, and saw a wild dilating fire in the eyes steadfastly regarding him.

"I say nothing of his plea for claiming my confidence. It matters very little how he gained it. Father, he did gain it. What you know of the story of my marriage, he soon knew, just as well."

Her father's face was ashy white, and he held her in both his arms.

"I have done no worse, I have not disgraced you. But if you ask me whether I have loved him, or do love him, I tell you plainly, father, that it may be so. I don't know."

She took her hands suddenly from his shoulders, and pressed

them both upon her side; while in her face, not like itself—and in her figure, drawn up, resolute to finish by a last effort what she had to say—the feelings long suppressed broke loose.

"This night, my husband being away, he has been with me, declaring himself my lover. This minute he expects me, for I could release myself of his presence by no other means. I do not know that I am sorry, I do not know that I am ashamed, I do not know that I am degraded in my own esteem. All that I know is, your philosophy and your teaching will not save me. Now, father, you have brought me to this. Save me by some other means!"

He tightened his hold in time to prevent her sinking on the floor, but she cried out in a terrible voice, "I shall die if you hold me! Let me *Shipwrecked* fall upon the ground!" And he laid her down there, and saw the pride of his heart and the triumph of his system, lying, an insensible heap, at his feet.

END OF THE SECOND BOOK

BOOK THE THIRD

GARNERING

CHAPTER ONE

ANOTHER THING NEEDFUL

LOUISA awoke from a torpor, and her eyes languidly opened on her old bed at home, and her old room. It seemed, at first, as if all that had happened since the days when these objects were familiar to her were the shadows of a dream; but gradually, as the objects became more real to her sight, the events became more real to her mind.

She could scarcely move her head for pain and heaviness, her eyes were strained and sore, and she was very weak. A curious passive inattention had such possession of her, that the presence of her little sister in the room did not attract her notice for some time. Even when their eyes had met, and her sister had approached the bed, Louisa lay for minutes looking at her in silence, and suffering her timidly to hold her passive hand, before she asked:

"When was I brought to this room?"

"Last night, Louisa."

"Who brought me here?"

"Sissy, I believe."

"Why do you believe so?"

"Because I found her here this morning. She didn't come to my bedside to wake me, as she always does; and I went to look for her. She was not in her own room either; and I went looking for her all over the house, until I found her here taking care of you and cooling your head. Will you see father? Sissy said I was to tell him when you woke."

"What a beaming face you have, Jane!" said Louisa, as her young sister—timidly still—bent down to kiss her.

"Have I? I am very glad you think so. I am sure it must be Sissy's doing."

The arm Louisa had begun to twine around her neck, unbent itself. "You can tell father if you will." Then, staying her for a moment, she said, "It was you who made my room so cheerful, and gave it this look of welcome?"

"Oh no, Louisa, it was done before I came. It was——" Louisa turned upon her pillow, and heard no more. When her sister had withdrawn, she turned her head back again, and lay with her face towards the door, until it opened and her father entered.

He had a jaded anxious look upon him, and his hand, usually steady, trembled in hers. He sat down at the side of the bed, tenderly asking how she was, and dwelling on the necessity of her keeping very quiet after her agitation and exposure to the weather last night. He spoke in a subdued and troubled voice, very different from his usual dictatorial manner; and was often at a loss for words.

"My dear Louisa. My poor daughter." He was so much at a loss at that place, that he stopped altogether. He tried again.

"My unfortunate child." The place was so difficult to get over, that he tried again.

"It would be hopeless for me, Louisa, to endeavour to tell you how overwhelmed I have been, and still am, by what broke upon me last night. The ground on which I stand has ceased to be solid under my feet. The only support on which I leaned, and the strength of which it seemed, and still does seem, impossible to question, has given way in an instant. I am stunned by these discoveries. I have no selfish meaning in what I say; but I find the shock of what broke upon me last night, to be very heavy indeed."

A lesson in humility

She could give him no comfort herein. She had suffered the wreck of her whole life upon the rock.

"I will not say, Louisa, that if you had by any happy chance undeceived me some time ago, it would have been better for us both; better for your peace, and better for mine. For I am sensible that it may not have been a part of my system to invite any confidence of that kind. I had proved my—my system to myself, and I have rigidly administered it; and I must bear the responsibility of its failures. I only entreat you to believe, my favourite child, that I have meant to do right."

He said it earnestly, and to do him justice he had. In gauging fathomless deeps with his little mean excise-rod, and in staggering over the universe with his rusty stiff-legged compasses, he had meant to do great things. Within the limits of his short tether he had tumbled about, annihilating the flowers of existence with greater singleness of purpose than many of the blatant personages whose company he kept.

"I am well assured of what you say, father. I know I have been your favourite child. I know you have intended to make me happy. I have never blamed you, and I never shall."

He took her outstretched hand, and retained it in his.

"My dear, I have remained all night at my table, pondering again and again on what has so painfully passed between us. When I consider your character; when I consider that what has been known to me for hours, has been concealed by you for years; when I consider under what immediate pressure it has been forced from you at last; I come to the conclusion that I cannot but mistrust myself."

He might have added more than all, when he saw the face now looking at him. He did add it in effect, perhaps, as he softly moved her scattered hair from her forehead with his hand. Such little actions, slight in another man, were very noticeable in him; and his daughter received them as if they had been words of contrition.

"But," said Mr. Gradgrind, slowly, and with hesitation, as well as with a wretched sense of helplessness, "if I see reason to mistrust myself for the past, Louisa, I should also mistrust myself for the present and the future. To speak unreservedly to you, I do. I am far from feeling convinced now, however differently I might have felt only this time yesterday, that I am fit for the trust you repose in me; that I know how to respond to the appeal you have come home to make to me; that I have the right instinct —supposing it for the moment to be some quality of that nature —how to help you, and to set you right, my child."

She had turned upon her pillow, and lay with her face upon her arm, so that he could not see it. All her wildness and passion had subsided; but, though softened, she was not in tears. Her father was changed in nothing so much as in the respect that he would have been glad to see her in tears.

"Some persons hold," he pursued, still hesitating, "that there is a wisdom of the Head, and that there is a wisdom of the Heart. I have not supposed so; but, as I have said, I mistrust myself now. I have supposed the head to be all-sufficient. It may not be all-sufficient; how can I venture this morning to say it is! If that other kind of wisdom should be what I have neglected, and should be the instinct that is wanted, Louisa——"

He suggested it very doubtfully, as if he were half unwilling to admit it even now. She made him no answer, lying before him on her bed, still half-dressed, much as he had seen her lying on the floor of his room last night.

"Louisa," and his hand rested on her hair again, "I have been absent from here, my dear, a good deal of late; and though your sister's training has been pursued according to—the system," he appeared to come to that word with great reluctance always, "it has necessarily been modified by daily associations begun, in her case, at an early age. I ask you—ignorantly and humbly, my daughter—for the better, do you think?"

"Father," she replied, without stirring, "if any harmony has been awakened in her young breast that was mute in mine until it turned to discord, let her thank Heaven for it, and go upon her happier way, taking it as her greatest blessing that she has avoided my way."

"O my child, my child!" he said, in a forlorn manner, "I am an unhappy man to see you thus! What avails it to me that you do not reproach me, if I so bitterly reproach myself!" He bent his head, and spoke low to her. "Louisa, I have a misgiving that some change may have been slowly working about me in this house, by mere love and gratitude: that what the Head had left undone and could not do, the Heart may have been doing silently. Can it be so?"

She made him no reply.

"I am not too proud to believe it, Louisa. How could I be arrogant, and you before me! Can it be so? Is it so, my dear?"

He looked upon her once more, lying cast away there; and without another word went out of the room. He had not been long gone, when she heard a light tread near the door, and knew that some one stood beside her.

She did not raise her head. A dull anger that she should be seen in her distress, and that the involuntary look she had so resented should come to this fulfilment, smouldered within her like an unwholesome fire. All closely imprisoned forces rend and destroy. The air that would be healthful to the earth, the water that would enrich it, the heat that would ripen it, tear it when caged up. So in her bosom even now; the strongest qualities she possessed, long turned upon themselves, became a heap of obduracy, that rose against a friend.

It was well that soft touch came upon her neck, and that she understood herself to be supposed to have fallen asleep. The sympathetic hand did not claim her resentment. Let it lie there, let it lie.

It lay there, warming into life a crowd of gentler thoughts; and she rested. As she softened with the quiet, and the consciousness of being so watched, some tears made their way into her eyes. The face touched hers, and she knew that there were tears upon it too, and she the cause of them.

As Louisa feigned to rouse herself, and sat up, Sissy retired, so that she stood placidly near the bedside.

"I hope I have not disturbed you. I have come to ask if you would let me stay with you?"

"Why should you stay with me? My sister will miss you. You are everything to her."

"Am I?" returned Sissy, shaking her head. "I would be something to you, if I might."

"What?" said Louisa, almost sternly.

"Whatever you want most, if I could be that. At all events, I

would like to try to be as near it as I can. And however far off
that may be, I will never tire of trying. Will you let me?"

"My father sent you to ask me."

"No indeed," replied Sissy. "He told me that I might come in
now, but he sent me away from the room this morning—or at
least—" She hesitated and stopped.

"At least, what?" said Louisa, with her searching eyes upon her.

"I thought it best myself that I should be sent away, for I felt
very uncertain whether you would like to find me here."

"Have I always hated you so much?"

"I hope not, for I have always loved you, and have always
wished that you should know it. But you changed to me a little,
shortly before you left home. Not that I wondered at it. You
knew so much, and I knew so little, and it was so natural in many
ways, going as you were among other friends, that I had nothing
to complain of, and was not at all hurt."

Her colour rose as she said it modestly and hurriedly. Louisa
understood the loving pretence, and her heart smote her.

"May I try?" said Sissy, emboldened to raise
her hand to the neck that was insensibly droop-   *May Sissy try?*
ing towards her.

Louisa, taking down the hand that would have embraced her
in another moment, held it in one of hers, and answered:

"First, Sissy, do you know what I am? I am so proud and so
hardened, so confused and troubled, so resentful and unjust to
every one and to myself, that everything is stormy, dark, and
wicked to me. Does not that repel you?"

"No!"

"I am so unhappy, and all that should have made me otherwise
is so laid waste, that if I had been bereft of sense to this hour,
and instead of being as learned as you think me, had to begin to
acquire the simplest truths, I could not want a guide to peace,
contentment, honour, all the good of which I am quite devoid,
more abjectly than I do. Does not that repel you?"

"No!"

In the innocence of her brave affection, and the brimming up
of her old devoted spirit, the once deserted girl shone like a beautiful light upon the darkness of the other.

Louisa raised the hand that it might clasp her neck and join its fellow there. She fell upon her knees, and clinging to this stroller's child looked up at her almost with veneration.

"Forgive me, pity me, help me! Have compassion on my great need, and let me lay this head of mine upon a loving heart!"

"O lay it here!" cried Sissy. "Lay it here, my dear."

CHAPTER TWO

VERY RIDICULOUS

MR. JAMES HARTHOUSE passed a whole night and day in a state of so much hurry, that the World, with its best glass in its eye, would scarcely have recognized him during that insane interval, as the brother Jem of the honourable and jocular member. He was positively agitated. He several times spoke with an emphasis, similar to the vulgar manner. He went in and went out in an unaccountable way, like a man without an object. He rode like a highwayman. In a word, he was so horribly bored by existing circumstances, that he forgot to go in for boredom in the manner prescribed by the authorities.

After putting his horse at Coketown through the storm, as if it were a leap, he waited up all night; from time to time ringing his bell with the greatest fury, charging the porter who kept watch with delinquency in withholding letters or messages that could not fail to have been entrusted to him, and demanding restitution on the spot. The dawn coming, the morning coming, and the day coming, and neither message nor letter coming with either, he went down to the country-house. There, the report was, Mr. Bounderby away, and Mrs. Bounderby in town. Left for town suddenly last evening. Not even known to be gone until receipt of message, importing that her return was not to be expected for the present.

In these circumstances he had nothing for it but to follow her to town. He went to the house in town. Mrs. Bounderby not there.

He looked in at the Bank. Bounderby away and Mrs. Sparsit away. Mrs. Sparsit away? Who could have been reduced to sudden extremity for the company of that griffin!

"Well! I don't know," said Tom, who had his own reasons for being uneasy about it. "She was off somewhere at daybreak this morning. She's always full of mystery; I hate her. So I do that white chap; he's always got his blinking eyes upon a fellow."

"Where were you last night, Tom?"

"Where was I last night!" said Tom. "Come! I like that. I was waiting for you, Mr. Harthouse, till it came down as *I* never saw it come down before. Where was I too! Where were you, you mean."

"I was prevented from coming—detained."

"Detained!" murmured Tom. "Two of us were detained. I was detained looking for you, till I lost every train but the mail. It would have been a pleasant job to go down by that on such a night, and have to walk home through a pond. I was obliged to sleep in town after all."

"Where?"

"Where? Why, in my own bed at Bounderby's."

"Did you see your sister?"

"How the deuce," returned Tom, staring, "could I see my sister when she was fifteen miles off?"

Cursing these quick retorts of the young gentleman to whom he was so true a friend, Mr. Harthouse disembarrassed himself of that interview with the smallest conceivable amount of ceremony, and debated for the hundredth time what all this could mean? He made only one thing clear. It was, that whether she was in town or out of town, whether he had been premature with her who was so hard to comprehend, or she had lost courage, or they were discovered, or some mischance or mistake, at present incomprehensible, had occurred, he must remain to confront his fortune, whatever it was. The hotel where he was known to live when condemned to that region of blackness, was the stake to which he was tied. As to all the rest—What will be, will be.

"So, whether I am waiting for a hostile message, or an assignation, or a penitent remonstrance, or an impromptu wrestle with my friend Bounderby in the Lancashire manner—which would seem as likely as anything else in the present state of affairs—I'll dine," said Mr. James Harthouse. "Bounderby has the advantage in point of weight; and if anything of a British nature is to come off between us, it may be as well to be in training."

Therefore he rang the bell, and tossing himself negligently on a sofa, ordered "Some dinner at six—with a beefsteak in it," and got through the intervening time as well as he could. That was not particularly well; for he remained in the greatest perplexity, and, as the hours went on, and no kind of explanation offered itself, his perplexity augmented at compound interest.

However, he took affairs as coolly as it was in human nature to do, and entertained himself with the facetious idea of the training more than once. "It wouldn't be bad," he yawned at one time, "to give the waiter five shillings, and throw him." At another time it occurred to him, "Or a fellow of about thirteen or fourteen stone might be hired by the hour." But these jests did not tell materially on the afternoon, or his suspense; and, sooth to say, they both lagged fearfully.

It was impossible, even before dinner, to avoid often walking about in the pattern of the carpet, looking out of the window, listening at the door for footsteps, and occasionally becoming rather hot when any steps approached that room. But, after dinner, when the day turned to twilight, and the twilight turned to night, and still no communication was made to him, it began to be as he expressed it, "like the Holy Office and slow torture." However, still true to his conviction that indifference was the genuine high-breeding (the only conviction he had), he seized this crisis as the opportunity for ordering candles and a newspaper.

He had been trying in vain, for half an hour, to read this newspaper, when the waiter appeared and said, at once mysteriously and apologetically:

"Beg your pardon, sir. You're wanted, sir, if you please."

Mr. Harthouse is wanted

A general recollection that this was the kind of thing the Police said to the swell mob, caused Mr. Harthouse to ask the waiter in return, with bristling indignation, what the Devil he meant by "wanted"?

"Beg your pardon, sir. Young lady outside, sir, wishes to see you."

"Outside? Where?"

"Outside this door, sir."

Giving the waiter to the personage before mentioned, as a blockhead duly qualified for that consignment, Mr. Harthouse hurried into the gallery. A young woman whom he had never seen stood there. Plainly dressed, very quiet, very pretty. As he conducted her into the room and placed a chair for her, he observed, by the light of the candles, that she was even prettier than he had at first believed. Her face was innocent and youthful, and its expression remarkably pleasant. She was not afraid of him, or in any way disconcerted; she seemed to have her mind entirely preoccupied with the occasion of her visit, and to have substituted that consideration for herself.

"I speak to Mr. Harthouse?" she said, when they were alone.

"To Mr. Harthouse." He added in his mind, "And you speak to him with the most confiding eyes I ever saw, and the most earnest voice (though so quiet) I ever heard."

"If I do not understand—and I do not, sir"—said Sissy, "what your honour as a gentleman binds you to, in other matters," the blood really rose in his face as she began in these words, "I am sure I may rely upon it to keep my visit secret, and to keep secret what I am going to say. I will rely upon it, if you will tell me I may so far trust——"

"You may, I assure you."

"I am young, as you see; I am alone, as you see. In coming to you, sir, I have no advice or encouragement beyond my own hope."

He thought, "But that is very strong," as he followed the momentary upward glance of her eyes. He thought besides, "This is a very odd beginning. I don't see where we are going."

"I think," said Sissy, "you have already guessed whom I left just now!"

"I have been in the greatest concern and uneasiness during the last four-and-twenty hours (which have appeared as many years)," he returned, "on a lady's account. The hopes I have been encouraged to form that you come from that lady, do not deceive me, I trust."

"I left her within an hour."

"At——?"

"At her father's."

Mr. Harthouse's face lengthened in spite of his coolness, and his perplexity increased. "Then I certainly," he thought, "do *not* see where we are going."

"She hurried there last night. She arrived there in great agitation, and was insensible all through the night. I live at her father's and was with her. You may be sure, sir, you will never see her again as long as you live."

Mr. Harthouse drew a long breath; and, if ever man found himself in the position of not knowing what to say, made the discovery beyond all question that he was so circumstanced. The child-like ingenuousness with which his visitor spoke, her modest fearlessness, her truthfulness which put all artifice aside, her entire forgetfulness of herself in her earnest quiet holding to the object with which she had come; all this, together with her reliance on his easily given promise—which in itself shamed him—presented something in which he was so inexperienced, and against which he knew any of his usual weapons would fall so powerless; that not a word could he rally to his relief.

At last he said:

"So startling an announcement, so confidently made, and by such lips, is really disconcerting in the last degree. May I be permitted to inquire, if you are charged to convey that information to me in those hopeless words, by the lady of whom we speak?"

"I have no charge from her."

"The drowning man catches at the straw. With no disrespect for your judgment, and with no doubt of your sincerity, excuse my saying that I cling to the belief that there is yet hope that I am not condemned to perpetual exile from that lady's presence."

"There is not the least hope. The first object of my coming here, sir, is to assure you that you must believe that there is no more hope of your ever speaking with her again, than there would be if she had died when she came home last night."

"Must believe? But if I can't—or if I should, by infirmity of nature, be obstinate—and won't——"

"It is still true. There is no hope."

James Harthouse looked at her with an incredulous smile upon his lips; but her mind looked over and beyond him, and the smile was quite thrown away.

He bit his lip, and took a little time for consideration.

"Well! If it should unhappily appear," he said, "after due pains and duty on my part, that I am brought to a position so desolate as this banishment, I shall not become the lady's persecutor. But you said you had no commission from her?"

"I have only the commission of my love for her, and her love for me. I have no other trust, than that I have been with her since she came home, and that she has given me her confidence. I have no further trust, than that I know something of her character and her marriage. O Mr. Harthouse, I think you had that trust too!"

He was touched in the cavity where his heart should have been —in that nest of addled eggs, where the birds of heaven would have lived if they had not been whistled away—by the fervour of this reproach.

"I am not a moral sort of fellow," he said, "and I never make any pretensions to the character of a moral sort of fellow. I am as immoral as need be. At the same time, in bringing any distress upon the lady who is the subject of the present conversation, or in unfortunately compromising her in any way, or in committing myself by any expression of sentiments towards her, not perfectly reconcilable with—in fact with—the domestic hearth; or in taking any advantage of her father's being a machine, or of her brother's being a whelp, or of her husband's being a bear; I beg to be allowed to assure you that I have had no particularly evil intentions, but have glided on from one step to another with a smoothness so perfectly diabolical, that I had not the slightest idea the catalogue was half so long until I began to turn it over. Whereas I find," said Mr. James Harthouse, in conclusion, "that it is really in several volumes."

Though he said all this in his frivolous way, the way seemed, for that once, a conscious polishing of but an ugly surface. He was silent for a moment; and then proceeded with a more self-possessed air, though with traces of vexation and disappointment that would not be polished out.

"After what has been just now represented to me, in a manner I find it impossible to doubt—I know of hardly any other source from which I could have accepted it so readily—I feel bound to say to you, in whom the confidence you have mentioned has been reposed, that I cannot refuse to contemplate the possibility (however unexpected) of my seeing the lady no more. I am solely to blame for the thing having come to this—and—and, I cannot say," he added, rather hard up for a general peroration, "that I have any sanguine expectation of ever becoming a moral sort of fellow, or that I have any belief in any moral sort of fellow whatever."

Sissy's face sufficiently showed that her appeal to him was not finished.

"You spoke," he resumed, as she raised her eyes to him again, "of your first object. I may assume that there is a second to be mentioned?"

"Yes."

"Will you oblige me by confiding it?"

"Mr. Harthouse," returned Sissy, with a blending of gentleness and steadiness that quite defeated him, and with a simple confidence in his being bound to do what she required, that held him at a singular disadvantage, "the only reparation that remains with you, is to leave here immediately and finally. I am quite sure that you can mitigate in no other way the wrong and harm you have done. I am quite sure that it is the only compensation you have left it in your power to make. I do not say that it is much, or that it is enough; but it is something, and it is necessary. Therefore, though without any other authority than I have given you, and even without the knowledge of any other person than yourself and myself, I ask you to depart from this place to-night, under an obligation never to return to it."

Sissy's appeal

If she had asserted any influence over him beyond her plain faith in the truth and right of what she said; if she had concealed the least doubt of irresolution, or had harboured for the best purpose any reserve or pretence; if she had shown, or felt, the lightest trace of any sensitiveness to his ridicule or his astonishment, or any remonstrance he might offer; he would have carried it against her at this point. But he could as easily have changed a clear sky by looking at it in surprise, as affect her.

"But do you know," he asked, quite at a loss, "the extent of what you ask? You probably are not aware that I am here on a public kind of business, preposterous enough in itself, but which

I have gone in for, and sworn by, and am supposed to be devoted to in quite a desperate manner? You probably are not aware of that, but I assure you it's the fact."

It had no effect on Sissy, fact or no fact.

"Besides which," said Mr. Harthouse, taking a turn or two across the room, dubiously, "it's so alarmingly absurd. It would make a man so ridiculous, after going in for those fellows, to back out in such an incomprehensible way."

"I am quite sure," repeated Sissy, "that it is the only reparation in your power, sir. I am quite sure, or I would not have come here."

He glanced at her face, and walked about again. "Upon my soul, I don't know what to say. So immensely absurd!"

It fell to his lot, now, to stipulate for secrecy.

"If I were to do such a very ridiculous thing," he said, stopping again presently, and leaning against the chimney-piece, "it could only be in the most inviolable confidence."

"I will trust to you, sir," returned Sissy, "and you will trust to me."

His leaning against the chimney-piece reminded him of the night with the whelp. It was the self-same chimney-piece, and somehow he felt as if *he* were the whelp to-night. He could make no way at all.

"I suppose a man never was placed in a more ridiculous position," he said, after looking down, and looking up, and laughing, and frowning, and walking off, and walking back again. "But I see no way out of it. What will be, will be. *This* will be, I suppose. I must take off myself, I imagine—in short, I engage to do it."

Sissy rose. She was not surprised by the result, but she was happy in it, and her face beamed brightly.

"You will permit me to say," continued Mr. James Harthouse, "that I doubt if any other ambassador, or ambassadress, could have addressed me with the same success. I must not only regard myself as being in a very ridiculous position, but as being vanquished at all points. Will you allow me the privilege of remembering my enemy's name?"

"*My* name?" said the ambassadress.

"The only name I could possibly care to know, to-night."

"Sissy Jupe."

"Pardon my curiosity at parting. Related to the family?"

"I am only a poor girl," returned Sissy. "I was separated from my father—he was only a stroller—and taken pity on by Mr. Gradgrind. I have lived in the house ever since."

She was gone.

"It wanted this to complete the defeat," said Mr. James Harthouse, sinking, with a resigned air, on the sofa, after standing transfixed a little while. "The defeat may now be considered perfectly accomplished. Only a poor girl—only a stroller—only James Harthouse made nothing of—only James Harthouse a Great Pyramid of failure."

The Great Pyramid put it into his head to go up the Nile. He took a pen upon the instant, and wrote the following note (in appropriate hieroglyphics) to his brother:

Dear Jack,—All up at Coketown. Bored out of the place, and going in for camels.   *Affectionately,*

                                        JEM.

He rang the bell.

"Send my fellow here."

"Gone to bed, sir."

"Tell him to get up, and pack up."

He wrote two more notes. One, to Mr. Bounderby, announcing his retirement from that part of the country, and showing where he would be found for the next fortnight. The other, similar in effect, to Mr. Gradgrind. Almost as soon as the ink was dry upon their superscriptions he had left the tall chimneys of Coketown behind, and was in a railway carriage, tearing and glaring over the dark landscape.

The moral sort of fellows might suppose that Mr. James Harthouse derived some comfortable reflections afterwards, from this prompt retreat, as one of his few actions that made any amends for anything, and as a token to himself that he had escaped the climax of a very bad business. But it was not so, at all. A secret sense of having failed and been ridiculous—a dread of what other fellows who went in for similar sorts of things, would say at his expense if they knew it—so oppressed him, that what was about the very best passage in his life was the one of all others he would not have owned to on any account, and the only one that made him ashamed of himself.

CHAPTER THREE

VERY DECIDED

THE indefatigable Mrs. Sparsit, with a violent cold upon her, her voice reduced to a whisper, and her stately frame so racked by continual sneezes that it seemed in danger of dismemberment, gave chase to her patron until she found him in the metropolis; and there, majestically sweeping in upon him at his hotel in St. James's Street, exploded the combustibles with which she was charged, and blew up. Having executed her mission with infinite relish, this high-minded woman then fainted away on Mr. Bounderby's coat-collar.

Mr. Bounderby's first procedure was to shake Mrs. Sparsit off, and leave her to progress as she might through various stages of suffering on the floor. He next had recourse to the administration of potent restoratives, such as screwing the patient's thumbs, smiting her hands, abundantly watering her face, and inserting salt in her mouth. When these attentions had recovered her (which they speedily did), he hustled her into a fast train without offering any other refreshment, and carried her back to Coketown more dead than alive.

Regarded as a classical ruin, Mrs. Sparsit was an interesting spectacle on her arrival at her *A classical ruin* journey's end; but considered in any other light, the amount of damage she had by that time sustained was excessive, and impaired her claims to admiration. Utterly heedless of the wear and tear of her clothes and constitution, and adamant to her pathetic sneezes, Mr. Bounderby immediately crammed her into a coach, and bore her off to Stone Lodge.

"Now, Tom Gradgrind," said Bounderby, bursting into his father-in-law's room late at night; "here's a lady here—Mrs.

Sparsit—you know Mrs. Sparsit—who has something to say to you that will strike you dumb."

"You have missed my letter!" exclaimed Mr. Gradgrind, surprised by the apparition.

"Missed your letter, sir!" bawled Bounderby. "The present time is no time for letters. No man shall talk to Josiah Bounderby of Coketown about letters, with his mind in the state it's in now."

"Bounderby," said Mr. Gradgrind, in a tone of temperate remonstrance, "I speak of a very special letter I have written to you in reference to Louisa."

"Tom Gradgrind," replied Bounderby, knocking the flat of his hand several times with great vehemence on the table, "I speak of a very special messenger that has come to me, in reference to Louisa. Mrs. Sparsit, ma'am, stand forward!"

That unfortunate lady hereupon essaying to offer testimony, without any voice and with painful gestures expressive of an inflamed throat, became so aggravating and underwent so many facial contortions, that Mr. Bounderby, unable to bear it, seized her by the arm and shook her.

"If you can't get it out, ma'am," said Bounderby, "leave *me* to get it out. This is not a time for a lady, however highly connected, to be totally inaudible, and seemingly swallowing marbles. Tom Gradgrind, Mrs. Sparsit latterly found herself, by accident, in a situation to overhear a conversation out of doors between your daughter and your precious gentleman friend, Mr. James Harthouse."

"Indeed!" said Mr. Gradgrind.

"Ah! Indeed!" cried Bounderby. "And in that conversation——"

"It is not necessary to repeat its tenor, Bounderby. I know what passed."

"You do? Perhaps," said Bounderby, staring with all his might at his so quiet and assuasive father-in-law, "you know where your daughter is at the present time?"

"Undoubtedly. She is here."

"Here?"

"My dear Bounderby, let me beg you to restrain these loud outbreaks, on all accounts. Louisa is here. The moment she could detach herself from that interview with the person of whom you speak, and whom I deeply regret to have been the means of introducing to you, Louisa hurried here, for protection. I myself had not been at home many hours, when I received her—here, in this room. She hurried by the train to town, she ran from town to this house through a raging storm, and presented herself before me in a state of distraction. Of course, she has remained here ever since. Let me entreat you, for your own sake and for hers, to be more quiet."

Mr. Bounderby silently gazed about him for some moments in every direction except Mrs. Sparsit's direction; and then, abruptly turning upon the niece of Lady Scadgers, said to that wretched woman:

"Now, ma'am! We shall be happy to hear any little apology you may think proper to offer, for going about the country at express pace, with no other luggage than a Cock-and-a-Bull, ma'am!"

"Sir," whispered Mrs. Sparsit, "my nerves are at present too much shaken, and my health is at present too much impaired, in your service, to admit of my doing more than taking refuge in tears."

(Which she did).

"Well, ma'am," said Bounderby, "without making any observation to you that may not be made with propriety to a woman of good family, what I have got to add to that, is that there is something else in which it appears to me you may take refuge, namely, a coach. And the coach in which we came here being at the door, you'll allow me to hand you down to it, and pack you home to the Bank: where the best course for you to pursue, will be to put your feet into the hottest water you can bear, and take a glass of scalding rum and butter after you get into bed." With these words, Mr. Bounderby extended his right hand to the weeping lady, and escorted her to the conveyance in question, shedding many plaintive sneezes by the way. He soon returned alone.

"Now, as you showed me in your face, Tom Gradgrind, that you wanted to speak to me," he resumed, "here I am. But, I am not in a very agreeable state, I tell you plainly: not relishing this business, even as it is, and not considering that I am at any time as dutifully and submissively treated by your daughter, as Josiah Bounderby of Coketown ought to be treated by his wife. You have your opinion, I dare say; and I have mine, I know. If you mean to say anything to-night, that goes against this candid remark, you had better let it alone."

Mr. Gradgrind, it will be observed, being much softened, Mr. Bounderby took particular pains to harden himself at all points. It was his amiable nature.

"My dear Bounderby," Mr. Gradgrind began in reply.

"Now, you'll excuse me," said Bounderby, "but I don't want to be too dear. That, to start with. When I begin to be dear to a man, I generally find that his intention is to come over me. I am not speaking to you politely; but, as you are aware, I am *not* polite. If you like politeness, you know where to get it. You have your gentleman-friends, you know, and they'll serve you with as much of the article as you want. I don't keep it myself."

"Bounderby," urged Mr. Gradgrind, "we are all liable to mistakes——"

"I thought you couldn't make 'em," interrupted Bounderby.

"Perhaps I thought so. But, I say we are all liable to mistakes; and I should feel sensible of your delicacy, and grateful for it, if you would spare me these references to Harthouse. I shall not associate him in our conversation with your intimacy and encouragement; pray do not persist in connecting him with mine."

"I never mentioned his name!" said Bounderby.

"Well, well!" returned Mr. Gradgrind, with a patient, even a submissive, air. And he sat for a little while pondering. "Bounderby, I see reason to doubt whether we have ever quite understood Louisa."

"Who do you mean by We?"

"Let me say I, then," he returned, in answer to the coarsely blurted question; "I doubt whether I have understood Louisa. I doubt whether I have been quite right in the manner of her education."

"There you hit it," returned Bounderby. "There I agree with you. You have found it out at last, have you? Education! I'll tell you what education is—To be tumbled out of *Mr. Gradgrind* doors, neck and crop, and put upon the shortest *hits it* allowance of everything except blows. That's what *I* call education."

"I think your good sense will perceive," Mr. Gradgrind remonstrated in all humility, "that whatever the merits of such a system may be, it would be difficult of general application to girls."

"I don't see it at all, sir," returned the obstinate Bounderby.

"Well," sighed Mr. Gradgrind, "we will not enter into the question. I assure you I have no desire to be controversial. I seek to repair what is amiss, if I possibly can; and I hope you will assist me in a good spirit, Bounderby, for I have been very much distressed."

"I don't understand you, yet," said Bounderby, with determined obstinacy, "and therefore I won't make any promises."

"In the course of a few hours, my dear Bounderby," Mr. Gradgrind proceeded, in the same depressed and propitiatory manner, "I appear to myself to have become better informed as to Louisa's character, than in previous years. The enlightenment has been painfully forced upon me, and the discovery is not mine. I think there are—Bounderby, you will be surprised to hear me say this—I think there are qualities in Louisa, which—which have been harshly neglected, and—and a little perverted. And—and I would suggest to you, that—that if you would kindly meet me in a timely endeavour to leave her to her better nature for a while—and to encourage it to develop itself by tenderness and consideration—it—it would be the better for the happiness of all of us. Louisa," said Mr. Gradgrind, shading his face with his hand, "has always been my favourite child."

The blustrous Bounderby crimsoned and swelled to such an extent on hearing these words, that he seemed to be, and probably was, on the brink of a fit. With his very ears a bright purple shot with crimson, he pent up his indignation, however, and said:

"You'd like to keep her here for a time?"

"I—I had intended to recommend, my dear Bounderby, that you should allow Louisa to remain here on a visit, and be attended by Sissy (I mean of course Cecilia Jupe), who understands her, and in whom she trusts."

"I gather from all this, Tom Gradgrind," said Bounderby, standing up with his hands in his pockets, "that you are of opinion that there's what people call some incompatibility between Loo Bounderby and myself." *Mr. Bounderby on incompatibility*

"I fear there is at present a general incompatibility between Louisa, and—and—and almost all the relations in which I have placed her," was her father's sorrowful reply.

"Now, look you here, Tom Gradgrind," said Bounderby the flushed, confronting him with his legs wide apart, his hands deeper in his pockets, and his hair like a hayfield wherein his windy anger was boisterous. "You have said your say; I am going to say mine. I am a Coketown man. I am Josiah Bounderby of Coketown. I know the bricks of this town, and I know the works of this town, and I know the chimneys of this town, and I know the smoke of this town, and I know the Hands of this town. I know 'em all pretty well. They're real. When a man tells me anything about imaginative qualities, I always tell that man, whoever he is, that I know what he means. He means turtle soup and venison, with a gold spoon, and that he wants to be set up with a coach and six. That's what your daughter wants. Since you are of opinion that she ought to have what she wants, I recommend you to provide it for her. Because, Tom Gradgrind, she will never have it from me."

"Bounderby," said Mr. Gradgrind, "I hoped, after my entreaty, you would have taken a different tone."

"Just wait a bit," retorted Bounderby, "you have said your say, I believe. I heard you out; hear me out, if you please. Don't make yourself a spectacle of unfairness as well as inconsistency, because, although I am sorry to see Tom Gradgrind reduced to his present position, I should be doubly sorry to see him brought so low as that. Now, there's an incompatibility of some sort or another, I am given to understand by you, between your daughter and me. I'll give *you* to understand, in reply to that, that there unquestionably is an incompatibility of the first magnitude—to be summed up in this—that your daughter don't properly know her husband's merits, and is not impressed with such a sense as would become her, by George! of the honour of his alliance. That's plain speaking, I hope."

"Bounderby," urged Mr. Gradgrind, "this is unreasonable."

"Is it?" said Bounderby. "I am glad to hear you say so. Because when Tom Gradgrind, with his new lights, tells me that what I say is unreasonable, I am convinced at once it must be devilish sensible. With your permission I am going on. You know my origin; and you know that for a good many years of my life I didn't want a shoeing-horn, in consequence of not having a shoe. Yet you may believe or not, as you think proper, that there are ladies—born ladies—belonging to families—Families!—who next to worship the ground I walk on."

He discharged this like a Rocket, at his father-in-law's head.

"Whereas your daughter," proceeded Bounderby, "is far from being a born lady. That you know, yourself. Not that I care a pinch of candle-snuff about such things, for you are very well aware I don't; but that such is the fact, and you, Tom Gradgrind, can't change it. Why do I say this?"

"Not, I fear," observed Mr. Gradgrind, in a low voice, "to spare me."

"Hear me out," said Bounderby, "and refrain from cutting in till your turn comes round. I say this, because highly connected females have been astonished to see the way in which your daughter has conducted herself, and to witness her insensibility. They have wondered how I have suffered it. And I wonder myself, now, and I won't suffer it."

"Bounderby," returned Mr. Gradgrind, rising, "the less we say to-night the better, I think."

"On the contrary, Tom Gradgrind, the more we say to-night, the better, I think. That is," the consideration checked him, "till I have said all I mean to say, and then I don't care how soon we stop. I come to a question that may shorten the business. What do you mean by the proposal you made just now?"

"What do I mean, Bounderby?"

"By your visiting proposition," said Bounderby, with an inflexible jerk of the hayfield.

"I mean that I hope you may be induced to arrange in a friendly manner, for allowing Louisa a period of repose and reflection here, which may tend to a gradual alteration for the better in many respects."

"To a softening down of your ideas of the incompatibility?" said Bounderby.

"If you put it in those terms."

"What made you think of this?" said Bounderby.

"I have already said, I fear Louisa has not been understood. Is it asking too much, Bounderby, that you, so far her elder, should aid in trying to set her right? You have accepted a great charge of her; for better for worse, for——"

Mr. Bounderby may have been annoyed by the repetition of his own words to Stephen Blackpool, but he cut the quotation short with an angry start.

"Come!" said he, "I don't want to be told about that. I know what I took her for, as well as you do. Never you mind what I took her for; that's my look out."

"I was merely going on to remark, Bounderby, that we may all be more or less in the wrong, not even excepting you; and that some yielding on your part, remembering the trust you have accepted, may not only be an act of true kindness, but perhaps a debt incurred towards Louisa."

"I think differently," blustered Bounderby. "I am going to finish this business according to my own opinions. Now, I don't want to make a quarrel of it with you, Tom Gradgrind. To tell the truth, I don't think it would be worthy of my reputation to quarrel on such a subject. As to your gentleman-friend, he may take himself off, wherever he likes best. If he falls in my way, I shall tell him my mind; if he don't fall in my way, I shan't, for it won't be worth my while to do it. As to your daughter, whom I made Loo Bounderby, and might have done better by leaving Loo Gradgrind, if she don't come home to-morrow, by twelve o'clock at noon, I shall understand that she prefers to stay away, and I shall send her wearing apparel and so forth over here, and you'll take charge of her for the future. What I shall say to people in general, of the incompatibility that led to my so laying down the law, will be this. I am Josiah Bounderby, and I had my bringing-up; she's the daughter of Tom Gradgrind, and she had her bringing-up; and the two horses wouldn't pull together. I am pretty well known to be rather an uncommon man, I believe; and most people will understand fast enough that it must be a woman rather out of the common, also, who, in the long run, would come up to my mark."

"Let me seriously entreat you to reconsider this, Bounderby," urged Mr. Gradgrind, "before you commit yourself to such a decision."

"I always come to a decision," said Bounderby, tossing his hat on: "and whatever I do, I do at once. I should be surprised at Tom Gradgrind's addressing such a remark to Josiah Bounderby of Coketown, knowing what he knows of him, if I could be surprised by anything Tom Gradgrind did, after his making himself a party to sentimental humbug. I have given you my decision, and I have got no more to say. Good night!"

So Mr. Bounderby went home to his town house to bed. At five minutes past twelve o'clock next day, he directed Mrs. Bounderby's property to be carefully packed up and sent to Tom Gradgrind's; advertised his country retreat for sale by private contract; and resumed a bachelor life.

CHAPTER FOUR

LOST

THE robbery at the Bank had not languished before, and did not cease to occupy a front place in the attention of the principal of that establishment now. In boastful proof of this promptitude and activity, as a remarkable man, and a self-made man, and a commercial wonder more admirable than Venus, who had risen out of the mud instead of the sea, he liked to show how little his domestic affairs abated his business ardour. Consequently, in the first few weeks of his resumed bachelorhood, he even advanced upon his usual display of bustle, and every day made such a rout in renewing his investigations into the robbery, that the officers who had it in hand almost wished it had never been committed.

They were at fault too, and off the scent. Although they had been so quiet since the first outbreak of the matter, that most people really did suppose it to have been abandoned as hopeless, nothing new occurred. No implicated man or woman took untimely courage or made a self-betraying step. More remarkable yet, Stephen Blackpool could not be heard of, and the mysterious old woman remained a mystery.

Things having come to this pass, and showing no latent signs of stirring beyond it, the upshot of Mr. Bounderby's investigations was, that he resolved to hazard a bold burst. He drew up a placard, offering Twenty Pounds reward for the apprehension of Stephen Blackpool, suspected of complicity in the robbery of the Coketown Bank on such a night; he described the said Stephen Blackpool by dress, complexion, estimated height, and manner, as minutely as he could; he recited how he had left the town, and in what direction he had been last seen going; he had the whole printed in great black letters on a staring broadsheet; and he caused the walls to be posted with it in the dead of night, so that it should strike upon the sight of the whole population at one blow.

The factory-bells had need to ring their loudest that morning to disperse the groups of workers who stood in the tardy daybreak, collected round the placards, devouring them with eager eyes. Not the least eager of the eyes assembled, were the eyes of those who could not read. These people, as they listened to the friendly voice that read aloud—there was always some such ready to help them—stared at the characters which meant so much with a vague awe and respect that would have been half ludicrous, if any aspect of public ignorance could ever be otherwise than threatening and full of evil. Many ears and eyes were busy with a vision of the matter of these placards, among turning spindles, rattling looms, and whirring wheels, for hours afterwards; and when the Hands cleared out again into the streets, there were still as many readers as before.

Slackbridge, the delegate, had to address his
Slackbridge   audience too that night; and Slackbridge had ob-
improves   tained a clean bill from the printer, and had
an occasion   brought it in his pocket. Oh my friends and
                    fellow-countrymen, the down-trodden operatives
of Coketown, oh my fellow-brothers and fellow-workmen and fel-
low-citizens and fellow-men, what a to-do was there, when Slack-
bridge unfolded what he called "that damning document," and held it up to the gaze, and for the execration of the working-man community! "Oh my fellow-men, behold of what a traitor in the camp of those great spirits who are enrolled upon the holy scroll of Justice and of Union, is appropriately capable! Oh my prostrate friends, with the galling yoke of tyrants on your necks and the iron foot of despotism treading down your fallen forms into the dust of the earth, upon which right glad would your oppressors

be to see you creeping on your bellies all the days of your lives, like the serpent in the garden—oh my brothers, and shall I as a man not add, my sisters too, what do you say, *now,* of Stephen Blackpool, with a slight stoop in his shoulders and about five foot seven in height, as set forth in this degrading and disgusting document, this blighting bill, this pernicious placard, this abominable advertisement; and with what majesty of denouncement will you crush the viper, who would bring this stain and shame upon the God-like race that happily has cast him out for ever! Yes, my compatriots, happily cast him out and sent him forth! For you remember how he stood here before you on this platform; you remember how, face to face and foot to foot, I pursued him through all his intricate windings; you remember how he sneaked and slunk, and sidled, and splitted of straws, until, with not an inch of ground to which to cling, I hurled him out from amongst us: an object for the undying finger of scorn to point at, and for the avenging fire of every free and thinking mind to scorch and sear! And now, my friends—my labouring friends, for I rejoice and triumph in that stigma—my friends whose hard but honest beds are made in toil, and whose scanty but independent pots are boiled in hardship; and now, I say, my friends, what appellation has that dastard craven taken to himself, when, with the mask torn from his features, he stands before us in all his native deformity, a What? A thief! A plunderer! A proscribed fugitive, with a price upon his head; a fester and a wound upon the noble character of the Coketown operative! Therefore, my band of brothers in a sacred bond, to which your children and your children's children yet unborn have set their infant hands and seals, I propose to you on the part of the United Aggregate Tribunal, ever watchful for your welfare, ever zealous for your benefit, that this meeting does Resolve: That Stephen Blackpool, weaver, referred to in this placard, having been already solemnly disowned by the community of Coketown Hands, the same are free from the shame of his misdeeds, and cannot as a class be reproached with his dishonest actions!"

Thus Slackbridge; gnashing and perspiring after a prodigious sort. A few stern voices called out "No!" and a score or two hailed, with assenting cries of "Hear, hear!" the caution from one man, "Slackbridge, y' or over hetter in't; y' or a goen too fast!" But these were pigmies against an army; the general assemblage subscribed to the gospel according to Slackbridge, and gave three cheers for him, as he sat demonstratively panting at them.

These men and women were yet in the streets, passing quietly to their homes, when Sissy, who had been called away from Louisa some minutes before, returned.

"Who is it?" asked Louisa.

"It is Mr. Bounderby," said Sissy, timid of the name, "and your brother Mr. Tom, and a young woman who says her name is Rachael, and that you know her."

"What do they want, Sissy dear?"

"They want to see you. Rachael has been crying, and seems angry."

"Father," said Louisa, for he was present, "I cannot refuse to see them, for a reason that will explain itself. Shall they come in here?"

As he answered in the affirmative, Sissy went away to bring them. She reappeared with them directly. Tom was last; and remained standing in the obscurest part of the room, near the door.

"Mrs. Bounderby," said her husband, entering with a cool nod, "I don't disturb you, I hope. This is an unseasonable hour, but here is a young woman who has been making statements which render my visit necessary. Tom Gradgrind, as your son, young Tom, refuses for some obstinate reason or other to say anything at all about those statements, good or bad, I am obliged to confront her with your daughter."

"You have seen me once before, young lady," said Rachael, standing in front of Louisa.

Tom coughed.

"You have seen me, young lady," repeated Rachael, as she did not answer, "once before."

Tom coughed again.

"I have."

Rachael cast her eyes proudly towards Mr. Bounderby, and said, "Will you make it known, young lady, where, and who was there?"

"I went to the house where Stephen Blackpool lodged, on the night of his discharge from his work, and I saw you there. He was there too; and an old woman who did not speak, and whom I could scarcely see, stood in a dark corner. My brother was with me."

"Why couldn't you say so, young Tom?" demanded Bounderby.

"I promised my sister I wouldn't." Which Louisa hastily confirmed. "And besides," said the whelp bitterly, "she tells her own story so precious well—and so full—that what business had I to take it out of her mouth!"

"Say, young lady, if you please," pursued Rachael, "why in an evil hour, you ever came to Stephen's that night."

"I felt compassion for him," said Louisa, her colour deepening, "and I wished to know what he was going to do, and wished to offer him assistance."

"Thank you, ma'am," said Bounderby. "Much flattered and obliged."

"Did you offer him," asked Rachael, "a bank-note?"

"Yes; but he refused it, and would only take two pounds in gold."

Rachael cast her eyes towards Mr. Bounderby again.

"Oh certainly!" said Bounderby. "If you put the question whether your ridiculous and improbable account was true or not, I am bound to say it's confirmed."

"Young lady," said Rachael, "Stephen Blackpool is now named as a thief in public print all over this town, and where else! There have been a meeting to-night *Rachael asserts* where he have been spoken of in the same shame- *Stephen's* ful way. Stephen! The honestest lad, the truest *innocence* lad, the best!" Her indignation failed her, and she broke off sobbing.

"I am very, very sorry," said Louisa.

"O young lady, young lady," returned Rachael, "I hope you may be, but I don't know! I can't say what you may ha' done! The like of you don't know us, don't care for us, don't belong to us. I am not sure why you may ha' come that night. I can't tell but what you may ha' come wi' some aim of your own, not mindin to what trouble you brought such as the poor lad. I said then, Bless you for coming; and I said it of my heart, you seemed to take so pitifully to him; but I don't know now, I don't know!"

Louisa could not reproach her for her unjust suspicions; she was so faithful to her idea of the man, and so afflicted.

"And when I think," said Rachael through her sobs, "that the poor lad was so grateful, thinking you so good to him—when I mind that he put his hand over his hard-worken face to hide the tears that you brought up there—O, I hope you may be sorry, and ha' no bad cause to be it; but I don't know, I don't know!"

"You're a pretty article," growled the whelp, moving uneasily in his dark corner, "to come here with these precious imputations! You ought to be bundled out for not knowing how to behave yourself, and you would be by rights."

She said nothing in reply; and her low weeping was the only sound that was heard, until Mr. Bounderby spoke.

"Come!" said he, "you know what you have engaged to do. You had better give your mind to that; not this."

" 'Deed, I am loath," returned Rachael, drying her eyes, "that any here should see me like this; but I won't be seen so again. Young lady, when I had read what's put in print of Stephen—and what has just as much truth in it as if it had been put in print of you—I went straight to the Bank to say I knew where Stephen was, and to give a sure and certain promise that he should be here in two days. I couldn't meet wi' Mr. Bounderby then, and your brother sent me away, and I tried to find you, but you was not to be found, and I went back to work. Soon as I come out of the Mill to-night, I hastened to hear what was said of Stephen—for I know wi' pride he will come back to shame it!—and then I went again to seek Mr. Bounderby, and I found him, and I told him every word I knew; and he believed no word I said, and brought me here."

"So far, that's true enough," assented Mr. Bounderby, with his hands in his pockets and his hat on. "But I have known you people before to-day, you'll observe, and I know you never die for want of talking. Now, I recommend you not so much to mind talking just now, as doing. You have undertaken to do something; all I remark upon that at present is, do it!"

"I have written to Stephen by the post that went out this afternoon, as I have written to him once before sin' he went away," said Rachael; "and he will be here, at furthest, in two days."

"Then, I'll tell you something. You are not aware perhaps," retorted Mr. Bounderby, "that you yourself have been looked after now and then, not being considered quite free from suspicion in this business, on account of most people being judged according to the company they keep. The post-office hasn't been forgotten either. What I'll tell you is, that no letter to Stephen Blackpool has ever got into it. Therefore, what has become of yours, I leave you to guess. Perhaps you're mistaken, and never wrote any."

"He hadn't been gone from here, young lady," said Rachael, turning appealingly to Louisa, "as much as a week, when he sent me the only letter I have had from him, saying that he was forced to seek work in another name."

"Oh, by George!" cried Bounderby, shaking his head, with a whistle, "he changes his name, does he! That's rather unlucky, too, for such an immaculate chap. It's considered a little suspicious in Courts of Justice, I believe, when an Innocent happens to have many names."

"What," said Rachael, with the tears in her eyes again, "what, young lady, in the name of Mercy, was left the poor lad to do! The masters against him on one hand, the men against him on the other, he only wantin to work hard in peace, and do what he felt right. Can a man have no soul of his own, no mind of his own? Must he go wrong all through wi' this side, or must he go wrong all through wi' that, or else be hunted like a hare?"

"Indeed, indeed, I pity him from my heart," returned Louisa; "and I hope that he will clear himself."

"You need have no fear of that, young lady. He is sure!"

"All the surer, I suppose," said Mr. Bounderby, "for your refusing to tell me where he is? Eh?"

"He shall not, through any act of mine, come back wi' the unmerited reproach of being brought back. He shall come back of his own accord to clear himself, and put all those that have injured his good character, and he not here for its defence, to shame. I have told him what has been done against him," said Rachael, throwing off all distrust as a rock throws off the sea, "and he will be here, at furthest, in two days."

"Notwithstanding which," added Mr. Bounderby, "if he can be laid hold of any sooner, he shall have an earlier opportunity of clearing himself. As to you, I have nothing against you; what you came and told me turns out to be true, and I have given you the means of proving it to be true, and there's an end of it. I wish you good night all! I must be off to look a little further into this."

Tom came out of his corner when Mr. Bounderby moved, moved with him, kept close to him, and went away with him. The only parting salutation of which he delivered himself was a sulky "Good night, father!" With a brief speech, and a scowl at his sister, he left the house.

Since his sheet-anchor had come home, Mr. Gradgrind had been sparing of speech. He still sat silent, when Louisa mildly said:

"Rachael, you will not distrust me one day, when you know me better."

"It goes against me," Rachael answered, in a gentler manner, "to mistrust any one; but when I am so mistrusted—when we all are—I cannot keep such things quite out of my mind. I ask your pardon for having done you an injury. I don't think what I said now. Yet I might come to think it again, wi' the poor lad so wronged."

"Did you tell him in your letter," inquired Sissy, "that suspicion seemed to have fallen upon him, because he had been seen about the Bank at night? He would then know what he would have to explain on coming back, and would be ready."

"Yes, dear," she returned; "but I can't guess what can have ever taken him there. He never used to go there. It was never in his way. His way was the same as mine, and not near it."

Sissy had already been at her side asking her where she lived, and whether she might come to-morrow night, to inquire if there were news of him.

"I doubt," said Rachael, "if he can be here till next day."

"Then I will come next night too," said Sissy.

When Rachael, assenting to this, was gone, Mr. Gradgrind lifted up his head, and said to his daughter:

"Louisa, my dear, I have never, that I know of, seen this man. Do you believe him to be implicated?"

"I think I have believed it, father, though with great difficulty. I do not believe it now."

"That is to say, you once persuaded yourself to believe it, from knowing him to be suspected. His appearance and manner; are they so honest?"

"Very honest."

"And her confidence not to be shaken! I ask myself," said Mr.

Gradgrind, musing, "does the real culprit know of these accusations? Where is he? Who is he?"

His hair had latterly began to change its colour. As he leaned upon his hand again, looking grey and old, Louisa, with a face of fear and pity, hurriedly went over to him, and sat close at his side. Her eyes by accident met Sissy's at the moment. Sissy flushed and started, and Louisa put her finger on her lip.

Next night, when Sissy returned home and told Louisa that Stephen was not come, she told it in a whisper. Next night again, when she came home with the same account, and added that he had not been heard of, she spoke in the same low frightened tone. From the moment of that interchange of looks, they never uttered his name, or any reference to him, aloud; nor ever pursued the subject of the robbery, when Mr. Gradgrind spoke of it.

The two appointed days ran out, three days and nights ran out, and Stephen Blackpool was not come, and remained unheard of. On the fourth day, Rachael, with unabated confidence, but considering her despatch to have miscarried, went up to the Bank, and showed her letter from him with his address, at a working colony, one of many, not upon the main road, sixty miles away. Messengers were sent to that place, and the whole town looked for Stephen to be brought in next day. *Anxious waiting*

During this whole time the whelp moved about with Mr. Bounderby like his shadow, assisting in all the proceedings. He was greatly excited, horribly fevered, bit his nails down to the quick, spoke in a hard rattling voice, and with lips that were black and burnt up. At the hour when the suspected man was looked for, the whelp was at the station; offering to wager that he had made off before the arrival of those who were sent in quest of him, and that he would not appear.

The whelp was right. The messengers returned alone. Rachael's letter had gone, Rachael's letter had been delivered, Stephen Blackpool had decamped in that same hour; and no soul knew more of him. The only doubt in Coketown was, whether Rachael had written in good faith, believing that he really would come back, or warning him to fly. On this point opinion was divided.

Six days, seven days, far on into another week. The wretched

whelp plucked up a ghastly courage, and began to grow defiant.
"Was the suspected fellow the thief? A pretty question! If not,
where was the man, and why did he not come back?"

Where was the man, and why did he not come back? In the
dead of night the echoes of his own words, which had rolled
Heaven knows how far away in the daytime, came back instead,
and abided by him until morning.

CHAPTER FIVE

FOUND

DAY and night again, day and night again. No Stephen Blackpool. Where was the man, and why did he not come back?

Every night, Sissy went to Rachael's lodging, and sat with her
in her small neat room. All day, Rachael toiled as such people
must toil, whatever their anxieties. The smoke-serpents were indifferent who was lost or found, who turned out bad or good; the
melancholy mad elephants, like the Hard Fact men, abated
nothing of their set routine, whatever happened. Day and night
again, day and night again. The monotony was unbroken. Even
Stephen Blackpool's disappearance was falling into the general
way, and becoming as monotonous a wonder as any piece of
machinery in Coketown.

"I misdoubt," said Rachael, "if there is as many as twenty
left in all this place, who have any trust in the poor lad now."

She said it to Sissy, as they sat in her lodging, lighted only
by the lamp at the street corner. Sissy had come there when
it was already dark, to await her return from work; and they
had since sat at the window where Rachael had found her, wanting no brighter light to shine on their sorrowful talk.

"If it hadn't mercifully brought about, that I was to have you
to speak to," pursued Rachael, "times are, when I think my

mind would not have kept right. But I get hope and strength through you; and you believe that though appearances may rise against him, he will be proved clear?"

"I do believe so," returned Sissy, "with my whole heart. I feel so certain, Rachael, that the confidence you hold in yours against all discouragement, is not like to be wrong, that I have no more doubt of him than if I had known him through as many years of trial as you have."

"And I, my dear," said Rachael, with a tremble in her voice, "have known him through them all, to be, according to his quiet ways, so faithful to everything honest and good, that if he was never to be heard of more, and I was to live to be a hundred years old, I could say with my last breath, God knows my heart, I have never once left trusting Stephen Blackpool!"

"We all believe, up at the Lodge, Rachael, that he will be freed from suspicion, sooner or later."

"The better I know it to be so believed there, my dear," said Rachael, "and the kinder I feel it that you come away from there, purposely to comfort me, and keep me company, and be seen wi' me when I am not yet free from all suspicion myself, the more grieved I am that I should ever have spoken those mistrusting words to the young lady. And yet——"

"You don't mistrust her now, Rachael?"

"Now that you have brought us more together, no. But I can't at all times keep out of my mind——"

Her voice so sunk into a low and slow communing with herself, that Sissy, sitting by her side, was obliged to listen with attention.

"I can't at all times keep out of my mind, mistrustings of some one. I can't think who 'tis, I can't think how or why it may be done, but I mistrust that some one has put Stephen out of the way. I mistrust that by his coming back of his own accord, and showing himself innocent before them all, some one would be confounded, who—to prevent that—has stopped him, and put him out of the way."

"That is a dreadful thought," said Sissy, turning pale.

"It *is* a dreadful thought to think he may be murdered."

Sissy shuddered, and turned paler yet.

"When it makes its way into my mind, dear," said Rachael, "and it will come sometimes, though I do all I can to keep it out, wi' counting on to high numbers as I work, and saying over and over again pieces that I knew when I were a child—I fall into such a wild, hot hurry, that, however tired I am, I want to walk fast, miles and miles. I must get the better of this before bed-time. I'll walk home wi' you."

"He might fall ill upon the journey back," said Sissy, faintly offering a worn-out scrap of hope; "and in such a case there are many places on the road where he might stop."

"But he is in none of them. He has been sought for in all, and he's not there."

"True," was Sissy's reluctant admission.

"He'd walk the journey in two days. If he was footsore and couldn't walk, I sent him, in the letter he got, the money to ride, lest he should have none of his own to spare."

"Let us hope that to-morrow will bring something better, Rachael. Come into the air!"

Her gentle hand adjusted Rachael's shawl upon her shining black hair in the usual manner of her wearing it, and they went out. The night being fine, little knots of Hands were here and there lingering at street-corners; but it was supper-time with the greater part of them, and there were but few people in the streets.

"You're not so hurried now, Rachael, and your hand is cooler."

"I get better, dear, if I can only walk, and breathe a little fresh. 'Times when I can't, I turn weak and confused."

"But you must not begin to fail, Rachael, for you may be wanted at any time to stand by Stephen. To-morrow is Saturday. If no news comes to-morrow, let us walk in the country on Sunday morning and strengthen you for another week. Will you go?"

"Yes, dear."

They were by this time in the street where Mr. Bounderby's house stood. The way to Sissy's destination led them past the door, and they were going straight towards it. Some train had newly arrived in Coketown, which had put a number of vehicles in motion, and scattered a considerable bustle about the town. Several coaches were rattling before them and behind them as they approached Mr. Bounderby's, and one of the latter drew up with such briskness as they were in the act of passing the house, that they looked round involuntarily. The bright gaslight over Mr. Bounderby's steps showed them Mrs. Sparsit in the coach, in an ecstasy of excitement, struggling to open the door; Mrs. Sparsit seeing them at the same moment, called to them to stop.

"It's a coincidence," exclaimed Mrs. Sparsit, as she was released by the coachman. "It's a Providence! Come out, ma'am!" then said Mrs. Sparsit, to some one inside, "come out, or we'll have you dragged out!"

Mrs. Sparsit takes a captive

Hereupon, no other than the mysterious old woman descended. Whom Mrs. Sparsit incontinently collared.

"Leave her alone, everybody!" cried Mrs. Sparsit, with great energy. "Let nobody touch her. She belongs to me. Come in, ma'am!" then said Mrs. Sparsit, reversing her former word of command. "Come in, ma'am, or we'll have you dragged in!"

The spectacle of a matron of classical deportment, seizing an ancient woman by the throat, and hailing her into a dwelling-house, would have been under any circumstances, sufficient temptation to all true English stragglers so blest as to witness it, to force a way into that dwelling-house and see the matter out. But when the phenomenon was enhanced by the notoriety and mystery by this time associated all over the town with the Bank robbery, it would have lured the stragglers in, with an irresistible attraction, though the roof had been expected to fall upon their heads. Accordingly, the chance witnesses on the ground, consisting of the busiest of the neighbours to the number of some five-and-twenty, closed in after Sissy and Rachael, as they closed in after Mrs. Sparsit and her prize; and the whole body made a disorderly irruption into Mr. Bounderby's dining-room, where the people behind lost not a moment's time in mounting on the chairs, to get the better of the people in front.

"Fetch Mr. Bounderby down!" cried Mrs. Sparsit. "Rachael, young woman; you know who this is?"

"It's Mrs. Pegler," said Rachael.

"I should think it is!" cried Mrs. Sparsit, exulting. "Fetch Mr. Bounderby. Stand away, everybody!" Here old Mrs. Pegler, muffling herself up, and shrinking from observation, whispered a word of entreaty. "Don't tell me," said Mrs. Sparsit, aloud. "I have told you twenty times, coming along, that I will *not* leave you till I have handed you over to him myself."

Mr. Bounderby now appeared, accompanied by Mr. Gradgrind

and the whelp, with whom he had been holding conference up-stairs. Mr. Bounderby looked more astonished than hospitable, at sight of this uninvited party in his dining-room.

"Why, what's the matter now!" said he. "Mrs. Sparsit, ma'am?"

"Sir," explained that worthy woman, "I trust it is my good fortune to produce a person you have much desired to find. Stimulated by my wish to relieve your mind, sir, and connecting together such imperfect clues to the part of the country in which that person might be supposed to reside, as have been afforded by the young woman, Rachael, fortunately now present to identify, I have had the happiness to succeed, and to bring that person with me—I need not say most unwillingly on her part. It has not been, sir, without some trouble that I have effected this; but trouble in your service is to me a pleasure, and hunger, thirst, and cold a real gratification."

Here Mrs. Sparsit ceased; for Mr. Bounderby's visage exhibited an extraordinary combination of all possible colours and expressions of discomfiture, as old Mrs. Pegler was disclosed to his view.

"Why, what do you mean by this?" was his highly unexpected demand, in great warmth. "I ask you, what do you mean by this, Mrs. Sparsit, ma'am?"

"Sir!" exclaimed Mrs. Sparsit, faintly.

"Why don't you mind your own business, ma'am?" roared Bounderby. "How dare you go and poke your officious nose into my family affairs?"

This allusion to her favourite feature overpowered Mrs. Sparsit. She sat down stiffly in a chair, as if she were frozen; and with a fixed stare at Mr. Bounderby, slowly grated her mittens against one another, as if they were frozen too.

"My dear Josiah!" cried Mrs. Pegler, trembling. "My darling boy! I am not to blame. It's not my fault, Josiah. I told this lady over and over again, that I knew she was doing what would not be agreeable to you, but she would do it."

"What did you let her bring you for? Couldn't you knock her cap off, or her tooth out, or scratch her, or do something or other to her?" asked Bounderby.

"My own boy! She threatened me that if I resisted her, I should be brought by constables, and it was better to come quietly than make that stir in such a"—Mrs. Pegler glanced timidly but proudly round the walls—"such a fine house as this. Indeed, indeed, it is not my fault! My dear, noble, stately boy! I have always lived quiet and secret, Josiah, my dear. I have never broken the condition once. I have never said I was your mother. I have admired you at a distance; and if I have come to town sometimes, with long times between, to take a proud peep at you, I have done it unbeknown, my love, and gone away again."

Mr. Bounderby, with his hands in his pockets, walked in impatient mortification up and down at the side of the long dining-table, while the spectators greedily took in every syllable of Mrs. Pegler's appeal, and at each succeeding syllable became more and more round-eyed. Mr. Bounderby still walking up and down when Mrs. Pegler had done, Mr. Gradgrind addressed that maligned old lady:

"I am surprised, madam," he observed with severity, "that in your old age you have the face to claim Mr. Bounderby for your son, after your unnatural and inhuman treatment of him."

"*Me* unnatural!" cried poor old Mrs. Pegler. "*Me* inhuman! To my dear boy?"

"Dear!" repeated Mr. Gradgrind. "Yes; dear in his self-made prosperity, madam, I dare say. Not very dear, however, when you deserted him in his infancy, and left him to the brutality of a drunken grandmother."

"*I* deserted my Josiah!" cried Mrs. Pegler, clasping her hands. "Now, Lord forgive you, sir, for your wicked imaginations, and for your scandal against the memory of my poor mother, who died in my arms before Josiah was born. May you repent of it, sir, and live to know better!"

She was so very earnest and injured, that Mr. Gradgrind, shocked by the possibility which dawned upon him, said in a gentler tone:

"Do you deny, then, madam, that you left your son to—to be brought up in the gutter?"

"Josiah in the gutter!" exclaimed Mrs. Pegler. "No such a thing, sir. Never! For shame on you! *Mr. Bounderby's gutter repudiated* My dear boy knows, and will give *you* to know, that though he come of humble parents, he come of parents that loved him as dear as the best could, and never thought it hardship on themselves to pinch a bit that he might write and cipher beautiful, and I've his books at home to show it! Aye, have I!" said Mrs. Pegler, with indignant pride. "And my dear boy knows, and will give *you* to know, sir, that after his beloved father died, when he was eight years old, his mother, too, could pinch a bit, as it was her duty and her pleasure and her pride to do it, to help him out in life, and put him 'prentice. And a steady lad he was, and a kind master he had to lend him a hand, and well he worked his own way forward to be rich and thriving. And *I'll* give you to know, sir—for this my dear boy won't—that though his mother kept but a little village shop, he never forgot her, but pensioned me on thirty pound a year—more than I want, for I put by out of it— only making the condition that I was to keep down in my own part, and make no boasts about him, and not trouble him. And I never have, except with looking at him once a year, when he has never knowed it. And it's right," said poor old Mrs. Pegler, in affectionate championship, "that I *should* keep down in my own part, and I have no doubts that if I was here I should do a many unbefitting things, and I am well contented, and I can keep my pride in my Josiah to myself, and I can love for love's own sake! And I am ashamed of you, sir," said Mrs. Pegler, lastly, "for your slanders and suspicions. And for I never stood here before, nor never wanted to stand here when my dear son said no. And I shouldn't be here now, if it hadn't been for being brought here. And for shame upon you, O for shame, to accuse me of being a bad mother to my son, with my son standing here to tell you so different!"

The bystanders, on and off the dining-room chairs, raised a murmur of sympathy with Mrs. Pegler, and Mr. Gradgrind felt himself innocently placed in a very distressing predicament, when Mr. Bounderby, who had never ceased walking up and down, and had every moment swelled larger and larger, and grown redder and redder, stopped short.

"I don't exactly know," said Mr. Bounderby, "how I come to be favoured with the attendance of the present company, but I don't inquire. When they're quite satisfied, perhaps they'll be so good as to disperse; whether they're satisfied or not, perhaps they'll be so good as to disperse. I'm not bound to deliver a lecture on my family affairs, I have not undertaken to do it, and I'm not a going to do it. Therefore those who expect any explanation whatever upon that branch of the subject, will be disappointed—par-

ticularly Tom Gradgrind, and he can't know it too soon. In
reference to the Bank robbery, there has been a mistake made,
concerning my mother. If there hadn't been over-officiousness it
wouldn't have been made, and I hate over-officiousness at all times,
whether or no. Good evening!"

Although Mr. Bounderby carried it off in these terms, holding
the door open for the company to depart, there was a blustering
sheepishness upon him, at once extremely crestfallen and super-
latively absurd. Detected as the Bully of humility, who had built
his windy reputation upon lies, and in his boastfulness had put
the honest truth as far away from him as if he had advanced the
mean claim (there is no meaner) to tack himself on to a pedigree,
he cut a most ridiculous figure. With the people filing off at the
door he held, who he knew would carry what had passed to the
whole town, to be given to the four winds, he could not have
looked a Bully more shorn and forlorn, if he had had his ears
cropped. Even that unlucky female, Mrs. Sparsit, fallen from her
pinnacle of exultation into the Slough of Despond, was not in so
bad a plight as that remarkable man and self-made Humbug,
Josiah Bounderby of Coketown.

Rachael and Sissy, leaving Mrs. Pegler to occupy a bed at her
son's for that night, walked together to the gate of Stone Lodge
and there parted. Mr. Gradgrind joined them before they had gone
very far, and spoke with much interest of Stephen Blackpool; for
whom he thought this signal failure of the suspicions against Mrs.
Pegler was likely to work well.

As to the whelp; throughout this scene as on all other late occasions, he had stuck close to Bounderby. He seemed to feel that
as long as Bounderby could make no discovery without his knowledge, he was so far safe. He never visited his sister, and had only
seen her once since she went home: that is to say on the night
when he still stuck close to Bounderby, as already related.

There was one dim unformed fear lingering about his sister's
mind, to which she never gave utterance, which surrounded the
graceless and ungrateful boy with a dreadful mystery. The same
dark possibility had presented itself in the same shapeless guise,
this very day, to Sissy, when Rachael spoke of some one who
would be confounded by Stephen's return, having put him out of
the way. Louisa had never spoken of harbouring any suspicion of

her brother in connexion with the robbery, she and Sissy had held no confidence on the subject, save in that one interchange of looks when the unconscious father rested his grey head on his hand; but it was understood between them, and they both knew it. This other fear was so awful, that it hovered about each of them like a ghostly shadow; neither daring to think of its being near her-self, far less of its being near the other.

And still the forced spirit which the whelp had plucked up, throve with him. If Stephen Backpool was not the thief, let him show himself. Why didn't he?

Another night. Another day and night. No Stephen Blackpool. Where was the man, and why did he not come back?

CHAPTER SIX

THE STARLIGHT

THE Sunday was a bright Sunday in autumn, clear and cool, when early in the morning Sissy and Rachael met, to walk in the country.

As Coketown cast ashes not only on its own head but on the neighbourhood's too—after the manner of those pious persons who do penance for their own sins by putting other people into sackcloth—it was customary for those who now and then thirsted for a draught of pure air, which is not absolutely the most wicked among the vanities of life, to get a few miles away by the railroad, and then begin their walk, or their lounge in the fields. Sissy and Rachael helped themselves out of the smoke by the usual means, and were put down at a station about midway between the town and Mr. Bounderby's retreat.

Though the green landscape was blotted here and there with heaps of coal, it was green elsewhere, and there were trees to see, and there were larks singing (though it was Sunday), and there were pleasant scents in the air, and all was over-arched by a bright blue sky. In the distance one way, Coketown showed as a black mist; in another distance hills began to rise; in a third, there was a faint change in the light of the horizon where it shone upon the far-off sea. Under their feet, the grass was fresh; beautiful shadows of branches flickered upon it, and specked it; hedgerows were luxuriant; everything was at peace. Engines at pits' mouths, and lean old horses that had worn the circle of their daily labour into the ground, were alike quiet; wheels had ceased for a short space to turn; and the great wheel of earth seemed to revolve without the shocks and noises of another time.

They walked on across the fields and down the shady lanes, sometimes getting over a fragment of a fence so rotten that it dropped at a touch of the foot, sometimes passing near a wreck of bricks and beams overgrown with grass, marking the site of deserted works. They followed paths and tracks, however slight. Mounds where the grass was rank and high, and where brambles, dock-weed, and such-like vegetation, were confusedly heaped together, they always avoided; for dismal stories were told in that country of the old pits hidden beneath such indications.

The sun was high when they sat down to rest. They had seen no one, near or distant, for a long time; and the solitude remained unbroken. "It is so still here, Rachael, and the way is so untrodden, that I think we must be the first who have been here all the summer."

As Sissy said it, her eyes were attracted by another of those rotten fragments of fence upon the ground. She got up to look at it. "And yet I don't know. This has not been broken very long. The wood is quite fresh where it gave way. Here are footsteps too.—O Rachael!"

She ran back, and caught her round the neck. Rachael had already started up.

"What is the matter?"

"I don't know. There is a hat lying in the grass."

They went forward together. Rachael took it up, shaking from head to foot. She broke into a passion of tears and lamentations: Stephen Blackpool was written in his own hand on the inside.

"O the poor lad, the poor lad! He has been made away with. He is lying murdered here!"

"Is there—has the hat any blood upon it?" Sissy faltered. They were afraid to look; but they did examine it, and found no mark of violence, inside or out. It had been lying there some days, for rain and dew had stained it, and the mark of its shape was on the grass where it had fallen. They looked fearfully about them, without moving, but could see nothing more. "Rachael," Sissy whispered, "I will go on a little by myself."

The old pit   She had unclasped her hand, and was in the act of stepping forward, when Rachael caught her in both arms with a scream that resounded over the wide landscape. Before them, at their very feet, was the brink of a black ragged chasm hidden by the thick grass. They sprang back, and fell upon their knees, each hiding her face upon the other's neck.

"O, my good Lord! He's down there! Down there!" At first this, and her terrific screams, were all that could be got from Rachael, by any tears, by any prayers, by any representations, by any means. It was impossible to hush her; and it was deadly necessary to hold her, or she would have flung herself down the shaft.

"Rachael, dear Rachael, good Rachael, for the love of Heaven, not these dreadful cries! Think of Stephen, think of Stephen, think of Stephen!"

By an earnest repetition of this entreaty, poured out in all the agony of such a moment, Sissy at last brought her to be silent, and to look at her with a tearless face of stone.

"Rachael, Stephen may be living. You wouldn't leave him lying maimed at the bottom of this dreadful place, a moment, if you could bring help to him?"

"No, no, no!"

"Don't stir from here, for his sake! Let me go and listen."

She shuddered to approach the pit; but she crept towards it on her hands and knees, and called to him as loud as she could call. She listened, but no sound replied. She called again and listened; still no answering sound. She did this, twenty, thirty times. She took a little clod of earth from the broken ground where he had stumbled, and threw it in. She could not hear it fall.

The wide prospect, so beautiful in its stillness but a few

minutes ago, almost carried despair to her brave heart, as she rose and looked all round her, seeing no help. "Rachael, we must lose not a moment. We must go in different directions, seeking aid. You shall go by the way we have come, and I will go forward by the path. Tell any one you see, and every one what has happened. Think of Stephen, think of Stephen!"

She knew by Rachael's face that she might trust her now. And after standing for a moment to see her running, wringing her hands as she ran, she turned and went upon her own search; she stopped at the hedge to tie her shawl there as a guide to the place, then threw her bonnet aside, and ran as she had never run before.

Run, Sissy, run, in Heaven's name! Don't stop for breath. Run, run! Quickening herself by carrying such entreaties in her thoughts, she ran from field to field, and lane to lane, and place to place, as she had never run before; until she came to a shed by an engine-house, where two men lay in the shade, asleep on straw.

First to wake them, and next to tell them, all so wild and breathless as she was, what had brought her there, were difficulties; but they no sooner understood her than their spirits were on fire like hers. One of the men was in a drunken slumber, but on his comrade's shouting to him that a man had fallen down the Old Hell Shaft, he started out to a pool of dirty water, put his head in it and came back sober.

With these two men she ran to another half-a-mile further, and with that one to another, while they ran elsewhere. Then a horse was found; and she got another man to ride for life or death to the railroad, and send a message to Louisa, which she wrote and gave him. By this time a whole village was up; and windlasses, ropes, poles, candles, lanterns, all things necessary, were fast collecting and being brought into one place, to be carried to the Old Hell Shaft.

It seemed now hours and hours since she had left the lost man lying in the grave where he had been buried alive. She could not bear to remain away from it any longer—it was like deserting him—and she hurried swiftly back, accompanied by half-a-dozen labourers, including the drunken man whom the news had sobered, and who was the best man of all. When they came to the

Old Hell Shaft, they found it as lonely as she had left it. The men called and listened as she had done, and examined the edge of the chasm, and settled how it had happened, and then sat down to wait until the implements they wanted should come up.

Every sound of insects in the air, every stirring of the leaves, every whisper among these men, made Sissy tremble, for she thought it was a cry at the bottom of the pit. But the wind blew idly over it, and no sound arose to the surface, and they sat upon the grass, waiting and waiting. After they had waited some time, straggling people who had heard of the accident began to arrive. In the midst of this, Rachael returned; and with her party there was a surgeon, who brought some wine and medicines. But, the expectation among the people that the man would be found alive, was very slight indeed.

There being now people enough present to impede the work, the sobered man put himself at the head of the rest, or was put there by the general consent, and made a large ring round the Old Hell Shaft, and appointed men to keep it. Besides such volunteers as were accepted to work, only Sissy and Rachael were at first permitted within this ring; but later in the day, when the message brought an express from Coketown, Mr. Gradgrind and Louisa, and Mr. Bounderby, and the whelp, were also there.

The sun was four hours lower than when Sissy and Rachael had first sat down upon the grass, before a means of enabling two men to descend securely was rigged with poles and ropes. Difficulties had arisen in the construction of this machine, simple as it was; requisites had been found wanting, and messages had had to go and return. It was five o'clock in the afternoon of the bright autumnal Sunday, before a candle was sent down to try the air, while three or four rough faces stood crowded close together, attentively watching it: the men at the windlass lowering as they were told. The candle was brought up again, feebly burning, and then some water was cast in. Then the bucket was hooked on; and the sobered man and another got in with lights, giving the word "Lower away!"

As the rope went out, tight and strained, and the windlass creaked, there was not a breath among the one or two hundred men and women looking on, that came as it was wont to come.

The signal was given and the windlass stopped, with abundant rope to spare. Apparently so long an interval ensued with the men at the windlass standing idle, that some women shrieked that another accident had happened! But the surgeon who held the watch, declared five minutes not to have elapsed yet, and sternly admonished them to keep silence. He had not well done speaking, when the windlass was reversed and worked again. Practised eyes knew that it did not go as heavily as it would if both workmen had been coming up, and that only one was returning.

The rope came in tight and strained; and ring after ring was coiled upon the barrel of the windlass, and all eyes were fastened on the pit. The sobered man was brought up and leaped out briskly on the grass. There was an universal cry of "Alive or dead?" and then a deep, profound hush.

When he said "Alive!" a great shout arose and many eyes had tears in them.   *Alive!*

"But he's hurt very bad," he added, as soon as he could make himself heard again. "Where's doctor? He's hurt so very bad, sir, that we donno how to get him up."

They all consulted together, and looked anxiously at the surgeon, as he asked some questions, and shook his head on receiving the replies. The sun was setting now; and the red light in the evening sky touched every face there, and caused it to be distinctly seen in all its rapt suspense.

The consultation ended in the men returning to the windlass, and the pitman going down again, carrying the wine and some other small matters with him. Then the other man came up. In the meantime, under the surgeon's directions, some men brought a hurdle, on which others made a thick bed of spare clothes covered with loose straw, while he himself contrived some bandages and slings from shawls and handkerchiefs. As these were made, they were hung upon an arm of the pitman who had last come up, with instructions how to use them: and as he stood, shown by the light he carried, leaning his powerful loose hand upon one of the poles, and sometimes glancing down the pit, and sometimes glancing round upon the people, he was not the least conspicuous figure in the scene. It was dark now, and torches were kindled.

It appeared from the little this man said to those about him, which was quickly repeated all over the circle, that the lost man had fallen upon a mass of crumbled rubbish with which the pit was half choked up, and that his fall had been further broken by some jagged earth at the side. He lay upon his back with one arm doubled under him, and according to his own belief had hardly stirred since he fell, except that he had moved his free hand to a side pocket, in which he remembered to have some bread and meat (of which he had swallowed crumbs), and had likewise scooped up a little water in it now and then. He had come straight away from his work, on being written to, and had walked the whole journey; and was on his way to Mr. Bounderby's country house after dark, when he fell. He was crossing that dangerous country at such a dangerous time, because he was innocent of what was laid to his charge, and couldn't rest from coming the nearest way to deliver himself up. The Old Hell Shaft, the pitman said, with a curse upon it, was worthy of its bad name to the last; for though Stephen could speak now, he believed it would soon be found to have mangled the life out of him.

When all was ready, this man, still taking his last hurried charges from his comrades and the surgeon after the windlass had begun to lower him, disappeared into the pit. The rope went out as before, the signal was made as before, and the windlass stopped. No man removed his hand from it now. Every one waited with his grasp set, and his body bent down to the work, ready to reverse and wind in. At length the signal was given, and all the ring leaned forward.

For, now, the rope came in, tightened and strained to its utmost as it appeared, and the men turned heavily, and the windlass complained. It was scarcely endurable to look at the rope, and think of its giving way. But, ring after ring was coiled upon the barrel of the windlass safely, and the connecting chains appeared, and finally the bucket with the two men holding on at the sides—a sight to make the head swim, and oppress the heart —and tenderly supporting between them, slung and tied within, the figure of a poor, crushed, human creature.

A low murmur of pity went round the throng, and the women wept aloud, as this form, almost without form, was moved very slowly from its iron deliverance, and laid upon the bed of straw. At first, none but the surgeon went close to it. He did what he could in its adjustment on the couch, but the best that he could do was to cover it. That gently done, he called to him Rachael and Sissy. And at that time the pale, worn, patient face was seen looking up at the sky, with the broken right hand lying bare on the outside of the covering garments, as if waiting to be taken by another hand.

They gave him drink, moistened his face with water, and administered some drops of cordial and wine. Though he lay quite motionless looking up at the sky, he smiled and said, "Rachael."

She stooped down on the grass at his side, and bent over him until her eyes were between his and the sky, for he could not so much as turn them to look at her.

"Rachael, my dear."

She took his hand. He smiled again and said, "Don't let 't go."

"Thou 'rt in great pain, my own dear Stephen?"

"I ha' been, but not now. I ha' been—dreadful, and dree, and long, my dear—but 'tis ower now. Ah, Rachael, aw a muddle! Fro' first to last, a muddle! Fro' first to last, a muddle!"

The spectre of his old look seemed to pass as he said the word.

"I ha' fell into th' pit, my dear, as have cost wi'in the knowledge o' old fok now livin', hundreds and hundreds o' men's lives—fathers, sons, brothers, dear to thousands an thousands, an keeping 'em fro' want and hunger. I ha' fell into a pit that ha' been wi' th' Fire-damp crueller than battle. I ha' read on 't in the public petition, as onny one may read, fro' the men that works in pits, in which they ha' pray'n and pray'n the lawmakers for Christ's sake not to let their work be murder to 'em, but to spare 'em for th' wives and children that they loves as well as gentlefok loves theirs. When it were in work, it killed wi'out need; when 'tis let alone, it kills wi'out need. See how we die an no need, one way an another—in a muddle—every day!"

He faintly said it, without any anger against any one. Merely as the truth.

"Thy little sister, Rachael, thou hast not forgot her. Thou 'rt not like to forget her now, and me so nigh her. Thou know'st —poor, patient, suff'rin' dear—how thou didst work for her, seet'n all day long in her little chair at thy winder, and how she died, young and misshapen, awlung o' sickly air as had'n no need to be, an awlung o' working people's miserable homes. A muddle! Aw a muddle!"

Louisa approached him; but he could not see her, lying with his face turned up to the night sky.

"If aw th' things that tooches us, my dear, was not so muddled, I should'n ha' had'n need to coom heer. If we was not in a muddle among ourseln, I should'n ha' been, by my own fellow weavers and workin' brothers, so mistook. If Mr. Bounderby had ever know'd me right—if he'd ever know'd me at aw—he would'n ha' took'n offence wi' me. He would'n ha' suspect'n me. But look up yonder, Rachael! Look aboove!"

Following his eyes, she saw that he was gazing at a star.

Stephen's dying prayer

"It ha' shined upon me," he said reverently, "in my pain and trouble down below. It ha' shined into my mind. I ha' look'n at 't and thowt o' thee, Rachael, till the muddle in my mind have cleared awa, above a bit, I hope. If soom ha' been wantin' in unnerstan'in' me better, I, too, ha' been wantin' in unnerstan'in' them better. When I got thy letter, I easily believen that what the yoong ledy sen and done to me, and what her brother sen and done to me, was one, and that there were a wicked plot betwixt 'em. When I fell, I were in anger wi' her, an' hurryin' on t' be as onjust t' her as oothers was t' me. But in our judgments, like as in our doins, we mun bear and forbear. In my pain an trouble, lookin' up yonder,—wi' it shinin' on me— I ha' seen more clear, and ha' made it my dyin' prayer that aw th' world may on'y coom toogether more, and get a better unnerstan'in' o' one another, than when I were in 't my own weak seln."

Louisa hearing what he said, bent over him on the opposite side to Rachael, so that he could see her.

"You ha' heard?" he said, after a few moments' silence. "I ha' not forgot you, ledy."

"Yes, Stephen, I have heard you. And your prayer is mine."

"You ha' a father. Will yo tak' a message to him?"

"He is here," said Louisa, with dread. "Shall I bring him to you?"

"If yo please."

Louisa returned with her father. Standing hand-in-hand, they both looked down upon the solemn countenance.

"Sir, yo will clear me an mak my name good wi' aw men. This I leave to yo."

Mr. Gradgrind was troubled and asked how?

"Sir," was the reply: "yor son will tell yo how. Ask him. I mak no charges: I leave none ahint me: not a single word. I ha' seen an spok'n wi' yor son, one night. I ask no more o' yo than that yo clear me—an I trust to yo to do 't."

The bearers being now ready to carry him away, and the surgeon being anxious for his removal, those who had torches or lanterns, prepared to go in front of the litter. Before it was raised, and while they were arranging how to go, he said to Rachael, looking upward at the star:

"Often as I coom to myseln, and found it shinin' on me down there in my trouble, I thowt it were the star as guided to Our Saviour's home. I awmust think it be the very star!"

They lifted him up, and he was overjoyed to find that they were about to take him in the direction whither the star seemed to him to lead.

"Rachael, beloved lass! Don't let go my hand. We may walk toogether t' night, my dear!"

"I will hold thy hand, and keep beside thee, Stephen, all the way."

"Bless thee! Will soombody be pleased to coover my face!"

They carried him very gently along the fields, and down the lanes, and over the wide landscape; Rachael always holding the hand in hers. Very few whispers broke the mournful silence. It was soon a funeral procession. The star had shown him where to find the God of the poor; and through humility, and sorrow, and forgiveness, he had gone to his Redeemer's rest.

CHAPTER SEVEN

WHELP-HUNTING

BEFORE the ring formed round the Old Hell Shaft was broken, one figure had disappeared from within it. Mr. Bounderby and his shadow had not stood near Louisa, who held her father's arm, but in a retired place by themselves. When Mr. Gradgrind was summoned to the couch, Sissy, attentive to all that happened, slipped behind that wicked shadow—a sight in the horror of his face, if there had been eyes there for any sight but one—and whispered in his ear. Without turning his head, he conferred with her a few moments, and vanished. Thus the whelp had gone out of the circle before the people moved.

When the father reached home, he sent a message to Mr. Bounderby's, desiring his son to come to him directly. The reply was, that Mr. Bounderby having missed him in the crowd, and seeing nothing of him since, had supposed him to be at Stone Lodge.

"I believe, father," said Louisa, "he will not come back to town to-night." Mr. Gradgrind turned away, and said no more.

In the morning, he went down to the Bank himself as soon as it was opened, and seeing his son's place empty (he had not the courage to look in at first) went back along the street to meet Mr. Bounderby on his way there. To whom he said that, for reasons he would soon explain, but entreated not then to be asked for, he had found it necessary to employ his son at a distance for a little while. Also, that he was charged with the duty of vindicating Stephen Blackpool's memory, and declaring the thief. Mr. Bounderby quite confounded, stood stock-still in the street after his father-in-law had left him, swelling like an immense soap-bubble, without its beauty.

Mr. Gradgrind went home, locked himself in his room, and kept it all that day. When Sissy and Louisa tapped at his door, he said, without opening it, "Not now, my dears; in the evening." On their return in the evening, he said, "I am not able yet—to-morrow." He ate nothing all day, and had no candle after dark; and they heard him walking to and fro late at night.

But, in the morning he appeared at breakfast at the usual hour, and took his usual place at the table. Aged and bent he looked, and quite bowed down; and yet he looked a wiser man, and a better man, than in the days when in this life he wanted nothing but Facts. Before he left the room, he appointed a time for them to come to him; and so, with his grey head drooping, went away.

"Dear father," said Louisa, when they kept their appointment, "you have three young children left. They will be different, *I* will be different yet, with Heaven's help."

She gave her hand to Sissy, as if she meant with her help too.

"Your wretched brother," said Mr. Gradgrind. "Do you think he had planned this robbery, when he went with you to the lodging?"

"I fear so, father. I know he had wanted money very much, and had spent a great deal."

"The poor man being about to leave the town, it came into his evil brain to cast suspicion on him?"

"I think it must have flashed upon him while he sat there, father. For, I asked him to go there with me. The visit did not originate with him."

"He had some conversation with the poor man. Did he take him aside?"

"He took him out of the room. I asked him afterwards, why he had done so, and he made a plausible excuse; but since last night, father, and when I remember the circumstances by its light, I am afraid I can imagine too truly what passed between them."

"Let me know," said her father, "if your thoughts present your guilty brother in the same dark view as mine."

"I fear, father," hesitated Louisa, "that he must have made some representation to Stephen Blackpool—perhaps in my name, perhaps in his own—which induced him to do in good faith and honesty, what he had never done before, and to wait about the Bank those two or three nights before he left the town."

"Too plain!" returned the father. "Too plain!"

He shaded his face, and remained silent for some moments. Recovering himself, he said:

"And now, how is he to be found? How is he to be saved from justice? In the few hours that I can possibly allow to elapse before I publish the truth, how is he to be found by us, and only by us? Ten thousand pounds could not effect it."

"Sissy has effected it, father."

He raised his eyes to where she stood, like a *The good fairy* good fairy in his house, and said in a tone of softened gratitude and grateful kindness, "It is always you, my child!"

"We had our fears," Sissy explained, glancing at Louisa, "before yesterday; and when I saw you brought to the side of the litter last night, and heard what passed (being close to Rachael all the time), I went to him when no one saw, and said to him, 'Don't look at me. See where your father is. Escape at once, for his sake and your own!' He was in a tremble before I whispered to him, and he started and trembled more then, and said, 'Where can I go? I have very little money, and I don't know who will hide me!' I thought of father's old circus. I have not forgotten where Mr. Sleary goes at this time of year, and I read of him in a paper only the other day. I told him to hurry there, and tell his name, and ask Mr. Sleary to hide him till I came. 'I'll get to him before the morning,' he said. And I saw him shrink away among the people."

"Thank Heaven!" exclaimed his father. "He may be got abroad yet."

It was the more hopeful as the town to which Sissy had directed him was within three hours' journey of Liverpool, whence he could be swiftly dispatched to any part of the world. But, caution being necessary in communicating with him—for there was a greater danger every moment of his being suspected now, and nobody could be sure at heart but that Mr. Bounderby himself, in a bullying vein of public zeal, might play a Roman part—it was consented that Sissy and Louisa should repair to the place in question, by a circuitous course, alone; and that the unhappy father, setting forth in an opposite direction, should get round to the same bourne by another and wider route. It was further agreed that he should not present himself to Mr. Sleary, lest his intentions should be mistrusted, or the intelligence of his arrival should cause his son to take flight anew; but, that the communication should be left to Sissy and Louisa to open; and that they should inform the cause of so much misery and disgrace, of his father's being at hand and of the purpose for which they had come. When these arrangements had been well considered and were fully understood by all three, it was time to begin to carry them into execution. Early in the afternoon, Mr. Gradgrind walked direct from his own house into the country, to be taken up on the line by which he was to travel; and at night the remaining two set forth upon their different course, encouraged by not seeing any face they knew.

The two travelled all night, except when they were left, for odd numbers of minutes, at branch-places, up illimitable flights of steps, or down wells—which was the only variety of those branches —and, early in the morning, were turned out on a swamp, a mile or two from the town they sought. From this dismal spot they were rescued by a savage old postilion, who happened to be up early, kicking a horse in a fly: and so were smuggled into the town by all the back lanes where the pigs lived: which, although not a magnificent or even savoury approach, was, as is usual in such cases, the legitimate highway.

The first thing they saw on entering the town was the skeleton of Sleary's Circus. The company had departed for another town more than twenty miles off, and had opened there last night. The connexion between the two places was by a hilly turnpike-road, and the travelling on that road was very slow. Though they took but a hasty breakfast, and no rest (which it would have been in vain to seek under such anxious circumstances), it was noon before they began to find the bills of Sleary's Horse-riding on barns and walls, and one o'clock when they stopped in the market-place.

A Grand Morning Performance by the Riders, commencing at that very hour, was in course of announcement by the bellman as they set their feet upon the stones of the street. Sissy recommended that, to avoid making the inquiries and attracting attention in the town, they should present themselves to pay at the door. If Mr. Sleary were taking the money, he would be sure to know her, and would proceed with discretion. If he were not, he would be sure to see them inside; and, knowing what he had done with the fugitive, would proceed with discretion still.

Therefore, they repaired, with fluttering hearts, to the well-remembered booth. The flag with the inscription SLEARY'S HORSE-RIDING was there; and the Gothic niche was there; but Mr. Sleary was not there. Master Kidderminster, grown too maturely turfy to be received by the wildest credulity as Cupid any more, had yielded to the invincible force of circumstances (and his beard), and, in the capacity of a man who made himself generally useful, presided on this occasion over the exchequer—having also a drum in reserve, on which to expend his leisure moments and superfluous forces in the extreme sharpness of his look out for base coin, Mr. Kidderminster, as at present situated, never saw anything but money; so Sissy passed him unrecognized, and they went in.

The Emperor of Japan, on a steady old white horse stenciled with black spots, was twirling five wash-hand basins at once, as it is the favourite recreation of that monarch to do. Sissy, though well acquainted with his Royal line, had no personal knowledge of the present Emperor, and his reign was peaceful. Miss Josephine Sleary, in her celebrated graceful Equestrian Tyrolean Flower-Act, was then announced by a new clown (who humorously said Cauliflower Act), and Mr. Sleary appeared, leading her in.

Mr. Sleary had only made one cut at the Clown with his long whip-lash, and the Clown had only said, "If you do it again, I'll throw the horse at you!" when Sissy was recognized both by father and daughter. But they got through the Act with great self-possession; and Mr. Sleary, saving for the first instant, conveyed no more expression into his locomotive eye than into his fixed one. The performance seemed a little long to Sissy and Louisa, particularly when it stopped to afford the Clown an opportunity of telling Mr. Sleary (who said "Indeed, sir!" to all his observations in the calmest way, and with his eye on the house) about two legs sitting on three legs looking at one leg, when in came four legs, and laid hold of one leg, and up got two legs, caught hold of three legs, and threw 'em at four legs, who ran away with one leg. For, although an ingenious Allegory relating to a butcher, a three-legged stool, a dog, and a leg of mutton, this narrative consumed time; and they were in great suspense. At last, however, little fair-haired Josephine made her curtsey amid great applause; and the Clown, left alone in the ring, had just warmed himself, and said, "Now *I*'ll have a turn!" when Sissy was touched on the shoulder, and beckoned out.

She took Louisa with her; and they were received by Mr. Sleary in a very little private apartment, with canvas sides, a grass floor, a wooden ceiling all aslant, on which the box *Among old friends* company stamped their approbation, as if they were coming through. "Thethilia," said Mr. Sleary, who had brandy and water at hand, "it doth me good to thee you. You wath alwayth a favourite with uth, and you've done uth credit thinth the old timeth I'm thure. You mutht thee our people, my dear, afore we thpeak of bithnith, or they'll break their hearth—ethpethially the women. Here'th Joth'phine hath been and got married to E. W. B. Childerth, and thee hath got a boy, and though he'th only three yearth old, he thtickth on to any pony you can bring againtht him. He'th named The Little Wonder of Thcolathtic Equitation; and if you don't hear of that boy at Athley'th, you'll hear of him at Parith. And you recollect Kidderminthter, that wath thought to be rather thweet upon yourthelf? Well. He'th married too. Married a widder. Old enough to be hith mother. Thee wath Tightrope, thee wath, and now thee'th nothing—on accounth of fat. They've got two children, tho we're thtrong in the Fairy bithnith and the Nurthery dodge. If you wath to thee our Children in the Wood, with their father and mother both a dyin' on a horthe—their uncle a retheiving of 'em ath hith wardth, upon a horthe—them-thelvth both a goin' a blackberryin' on a horthe—and the Robinth a coming in to cover 'em with leavth, upon a horthe—you'd thay it wath the completetht thing ath ever you thet your eyeth on! And you remember Emma Gordon, my dear, ath wath a'motht a mother to you? Of courthe you do; I needn't athk. Well! Emma, thee lotht her huthband. He wath throw'd a heavy back-fall off a Elephant in a thort of a Pagoda thing ath the Thultan of the Indieth, and he never got the better of it; and thee married a thecond time—married a Cheethemonger ath fell in

love with her from the front—and he'th a Overtheer and makin'
a fortun."

These various changes, Mr. Sleary, very short of breath now,
related with great heartiness, and with a wonderful kind of
innocence, considering what a bleary and brandy-and-watery old
veteran he was. Afterwards he brought in Josephine, and E. W. B.
Childers (rather deeply-lined in the jaws by daylight), and the
Little Wonder of Scholastic Equitation, and in a word, all the
company. Amazing creatures they were in Louisa's eyes, so white
and pink of complexion, so scant of dress, and so demonstrative
of leg; but it was very agreeable to see them crowding about
Sissy, and very natural in Sissy to be unable to refrain from tears.
"There! Now Thethilia hath kithd all the children, and hugged
all the women, and thaken handth all round with all the men,
clear, every one of you, and ring in the band for the thecond part!"

As soon as they were gone, he continued in a low tone. "Now,
Thethilia, I don't athk to know any thecreth, but I thuppothe I
may conthider thith to be Mith Thquire."

"This is his sister. Yes."

"And t'other on'th daughter. That'h what I mean. Hope I thee
you well, mith. And I hope the Thquire'th well?"

"My father will be here soon," said Louisa, anxious to pring
him to the point. "Is my brother safe?"

"Thafe and thound!" he replied. "I want you jutht to take a
peep at the Ring, mith, through here. Thethilia, you know the
dodgeth; find a thpy-hole for yourthelf."

They each looked through a chink in the boards.

"That'h Jack the Giant Killer—piethe of comic infant bithnith,"
said Sleary. "There'th a property-houthe you thee, for Jack to
hide in; there'th my Clown with a thauthepan-lid and a thpit,
for Jack'th thervant; there'th little Jack himthelf in a thplended
thoot of armour; there'th two comic black thervanth twithe ath
big ath the houthe, to thtand by it and to bring it in and clear it;
and the Giant (a very ecthpenthive bathket one), he an't on yet.
Now, do you thee 'em all?"

"Yes," they both said.

"Look at 'em again," said Sleary, "look at 'em well. You thee
'em all? Very good. Now, mith;" he put a form for them to sit

on; "I have my opinionth, and the Thquire your father hath hith. I don't want to know what your brother'th been up to; ith better for me not to know. All I thay ith, the Thquire hath thtood by Thethilia, and I'll thtand by the Thquire. Your brother ith one o' them black thervanth."

Louisa uttered an exclamation, partly of distress, partly of satisfaction.

"Ith a fact," said Sleary, "and even knowin' it, you couldn't put your finger on him. Let the Thquire come. I thall keep your brother here after the performanth. I than't undreth him, nor yet wath hith paint off. Let the Thquire come here after the performanth, or come here yourthelf after the performanth, and you thall find your brother, and have the whole plathe to talk to him in. Never mind the lookth of him, ath long ath he'th well hid."

Louisa, with many thanks and with a lightened load, detained Mr. Sleary no longer then. She left her love for her brother, with her eyes full of tears; and she and Sissy went away until later in the afternoon.

Mr. Gradgrind arrived within an hour afterwards. He too had encountered no one whom he knew; and was now sanguine with Sleary's assistance, of getting his disgraced son to Liverpool in the night. As neither of the three could be his companion without almost identifying him under any disguise, he prepared a letter to a correspondent whom he could trust, beseeching him to ship the bearer off at any cost, to North or South America, or any distant part of the world to which he could be the most speedily and privately dispatched.

This done, they walked about, waiting for the Circus to be quite vacated; not only by the audience, but by the company and by the horses. After watching it a long time, they saw Mr. Sleary bring out a chair and sit down by the side-door, smoking; as if that were his signal that they might approach.

"Your thervant, Thquire," was his cautious salutation as they passed in. "If you want me you'll find me here. You muthn't mind your thon having comic livery on."

They all three went in; and Mr. Gradgrind sat down forlorn, on the Clown's performing chair in the middle of the ring. On one of the back benches, remote in the subdued light and the strangeness of the place, sat the villainous whelp, sulky to the last, whom he had the misery to call his son.

In a preposterous coat, like a beadle's, with cuffs and flaps exaggerated to an unspeakable extent; in an immense waist-coat, knee-breeches, buckled shoes, and a mad cocked hat; with nothing fitting him, and everything of coarse material, moth-eaten and full of holes; with seams in his black face, where fear and heat had started through the greasy composition daubed all over it; anything so grimly, detestably, ridiculously shameful as the whelp in his comic livery, Mr. Gradgrind never could by any other means have believed in, weighable and measurable fact though it was. And one of his model children had come to this!

At first the whelp would not draw any nearer, but persisted in remaining up there by himself. Yielding at length, if any concession so sullenly made can be called yielding, to the entreaties of Sissy —for Louisa he disowned altogether—he came down, bench by bench, until he stood in the sawdust, on the verge of the circle, as far as possible, within its limits, from where his father sat.

"How was this done?" asked the father.

"How was what done?" moodily answered the son.

"This robbery," said the father, raising his voice upon the word.

"I forced the safe myself over night, and shut it up ajar before I went away. I had had the key that was found made long before. I dropped it that morning, that it might be supposed to have been used. I didn't take the money all at once. I pretended to put my balance away every night, but I didn't. Now you know all about it."

"If a thunderbolt had fallen on me," said the father, "it would have shocked me less than this!"

"I don't see why," grumbled the son. "So many people are employed in situations of trust; so many people, out of so many, will be dishonest. I have heard you talk, a hundred times, of its being a law. How can I help laws? You have comforted others with such things, father. Comfort yourself!"

The father buried his face in his hands, and the son stood in his disgraceful grotesqueness, biting straw; his hands, with the black partly worn away inside, looking like the hands of a monkey. The evening was fast closing in; and from time to time, he turned the whites of his eyes restlessly and impatiently towards his father. They were the only parts of his face that showed any life or expression, the pigment upon it was so thick.

"You must be got to Liverpool, and sent abroad."

"I suppose I must. I can't be more miserable anywhere," whimpered the whelp, "than I have been here, ever since I can remember. That's one thing."

Mr. Gradgrind went to the door, and returned with Sleary, to whom he submitted the question, How to get this deplorable object away?

"Why, I've been thinking of it, Thquire. There'th not muth time to lothe, tho you muth thay yeth or no. Ith over twenty mileth to the rail. There'th a coath in half an hour, that goeth *to* the rail, 'purpothe to cath the mail train. That train will take him right to Liverpool."

"But look at him," groaned Mr. Gradgrind. "Will any coach——"

"I don't mean that he thould go in the comic livery," said Sleary. "Thay the word, and I'll make a Jothkin of him, out of the wardrobe, in five minutes."

"I don't understand," said Mr. Gradgrind.

"A Jothkin—a Carter. Make up your mind quick, Thquire. There'll be beer to feth. I've never met with nothing but beer ath'll ever a clean a comic blackamoor."

Mr. Gradgrind rapidly assented; Mr. Sleary rapidly turned out from a box, a smock frock, a felt hat, and other essentials; the whelp rapidly changed clothes behind a screen of baize: Mr. Sleary rapidly brought beer, and washed him white again.

"Now," said Sleary, "come along to the coath, and jump up behind; I'll go with you there, and they'll thuppothe you are one of my people. Thay farewell to your family, and tharp'th the word." With which he delicately retired.

"Here is your letter," said Mr. Gradgrind. "All necessary means will be provided for you. Atone, by repentance and better conduct, for the shocking action you have committed, and the dreadful consequences to which it has led. Give me your hand, my poor boy, and may God forgive you as I do!"

The culprit was moved to a few abject tears by these words and their pathetic tone. But, when Louisa opened her arms, he repulsed her afresh.

"Not you. I don't want to have anything to say to you!"

"O Tom, Tom, do we end so after all my love!"

"After all your love!" he returned, obdurately.

The whelp's "Pretty love! Leaving old Bounderby to himself,
farewell and packing my best friend Mr. Harthouse off, and going home just when I was in the greatest danger. Pretty love that! Coming out with every word about our having gone to that place, when you saw the net was gathering round me. Pretty love that! You have regularly given me up. You never cared for me."

"Tharp'th the word!" said Sleary, at the door.

They all confusedly went out: Louisa crying to him that she forgave him, and loved him still, and that he would one day be sorry to have left her so, and glad to think of these her last words, far away: when some one ran against them. Mr. Gradgrind and Sissy, who were both before him while his sister yet clung to his shoulder, stopped and recoiled.

For, there was Bitzer, out of breath, his thin lips parted, his thin nostrils distended, his white eyelashes quivering, his colourless face more colourless than ever, as if he ran himself into a white heat, when other people ran themselves into a glow. There he stood, panting and heaving, as if he had never stopped since the night, now long ago, when he had run them down before.

"I'm sorry to interfere with your plans," said Bitzer, shaking his head, "but I can't allow myself to be done by horse-riders. I must have young Mr. Tom; he mustn't be got away by horse-riders; here he is in a smock frock, and I must have him!"

By the collar, too, it seemed. For, so he took possession of him.

CHAPTER EIGHT

PHILOSOPHICAL

THEY went back into the booth, Sleary shutting the door to keep intruders out. Bitzer, still holding the paralyzed culprit by the collar, stood in the Ring, blinking at his old patron through the darkness of the twilight.

"Bitzer," said Mr. Gradgrind, broken down, and miserably submissive to him, "have you a heart?"

"The circulation, sir," returned Bitzer, smiling at the oddity of the question, "couldn't be carried on without one. No man, sir, acquainted with the facts established by Harvey relating to the circulation of the blood, can doubt that I have a heart."

"Is it accessible," cried Mr. Gradgrind, "to any compassionate influence?"

"It is accessible to Reason, sir," returned the excellent young man. "And to nothing else."

They stood looking at each other; Mr. Gradgrind's face as white as the pursuer's.

"What motive—even what motive in reason—can you have for preventing the escape of this wretched youth," said Mr. Gradgrind, "and crushing his miserable father? See his sister here. Pity us!"

"Sir," returned Bitzer, in a very business-like and logical manner, "since you ask me what motive I have in reason, for taking young Mr. Tom back to Coketown, it is only reasonable to let you know. I have suspected young Mr. Tom of this bank-robbery from the first. I had had my eye upon him before that time, for I knew his ways. I have kept my observations to myself, but I have made them; and I have got ample proofs against him now, besides his running away, and besides his own confession,

which I was just in time to overhear. I had the pleasure of watching
your house yesterday morning, and following you here. I am
going to take young Mr. Tom back to Coketown, in order to
deliver him over to Mr. Bounderby. Sir, I have no doubt whatever
that Mr. Bounderby will then promote me to young Mr. Tom's
situation. And I wish to have his situation, sir, for it will be a
rise to me, and will do me good."

"If this is solely a question of self-interest with
you——" Mr. Gradgrind began.

A mere
question of
self-interest

"I beg your pardon for interrupting you, sir,"
returned Bitzer; "but I am sure you know that
the whole social system is a question of self-
interest. What you must always appeal to, is a person's self-
interest. It's your only hold. We are so constituted. I was brought
up in that catechism when I was very young, sir, as you are aware."

"What sum of money," said Mr. Gradgrind, "will you set
against your expected promotion?"

"Thank you, sir," returned Bitzer, "for hinting at the proposal;
but I will not set any sum against it. Knowing that your clear
head would propose that alternative, I have gone over the calculations in my mind; and I find that to compound a felony, even
on very high terms indeed, would not be as safe and good for me
as my improved prospects in the Bank."

"Bitzer," said Mr. Gradgrind, stretching out his hands as
though he would have said, See how miserable I am! "Bitzer, I
have but one chance left to soften you. You were many years at
my school. If, in remembrance of the pains bestowed upon you
there, you can persuade yourself in any degree to disregard your
present interest and release my son, I entreat and pray you to
give him the benefit of that remembrance."

"I really wonder, sir," rejoined the old pupil in an argumentative
manner, "to find you taking a position so untenable. My schooling
was paid for; it was a bargain; and when I came away, the
bargain ended."

It was a fundamental principle of the Gradgrind philosophy
that everything was to be paid for. Nobody was ever on any
account to give anybody anything, or render anybody help without
purchase. Gratitude was to be abolished, and the virtues springing
from it were not to be. Every inch of the existence of mankind,

from birth to death, was to be a bargain across a counter. And if we didn't get to Heaven that way, it was not a politico-economical place, and we had no business there.

"I don't deny," added Bitzer, "that my schooling was cheap. But that comes right, sir. I was made in the cheapest market, and have to dispose of myself in the dearest."

He was a little troubled here, by Louisa and Sissy crying.

"Pray don't do that," said he, "it's of no use doing that: it only worries. You seem to think that I have some animosity against young Mr. Tom; whereas I have none at all. I am only going, on the reasonable grounds I have mentioned, to take him back to Coketown. If he was to resist, I should set up the cry of Stop Thief! But, he won't resist, you may depend upon it."

Mr. Sleary, who with his mouth open and his rolling eye as immovably jammed in his head as his fixed one, had listened to these doctrines with profound attention, here stepped forward.

"Thquire, you know perfectly well, and your daughter knowth perfectly well (better than you, becauthe I thed it to her), that I didn't know what your thon had done, and that I didn't want to know—I thed it wath better not, though I only thought, then, it wath thome thkylarking. However, thith young man having made it known to be a robbery of a bank, why, that'th a theriouth thing; muth too theriouth a thing for me to compound, ath thith young man hath very properly called it. Contheuently, Thquire, you muthn't quarrel with me if I take thith young man'th thide, and thay he'th right and there'th no help for it. But I tell you what I'll do, Thquire; I'll drive your thon and thith young man over to the rail, and prevent expothure here. I can't conthent to do more, but I'll do that."

Fresh lamentations from Louisa, and deeper affliction on Mr. Gradgrind's part, followed this desertion of them by their last friend. But, Sissy glanced at him with great attention; nor did she in her own breast misunderstand him. As they were all going out again, he favoured her with one slight roll of his movable eye, desiring her to linger behind. As he locked the door, he said excitedly:

"The Thquire thtood by you, Thethilia, and I'll thtand by the Thquire. More than that: thith ith a prethiouth rathcal, and belongth to that bluthering Cove that my people nearly pitht out

o' winder. It'll be a dark night; I've got a horthe that'll do anything but thpeak; I've got a pony that'll go fifteen mile an hour
with Childerth driving of him; I've got a dog that'll keep a man to
one plathe four-and-twenty hourth. Get a word with the young
Thquire. Tell him, when he theeth our horthe begin to danthe, not
to be afraid of being thpilt, but to look out for a pony-gig coming
up. Tell him, when he theeth that gig clothe by, to jump down,
and it'll take him off at a rattling pathe. If my dog leth thith
young man thtir a peg on foot, I give him leave to go. And if
my horthe ever thtirth from that thpot where he beginth a danthing,
till the morning—I don't know him!—Tharp'th the word!"

The word was so sharp, that in ten minutes Mr. Childers,
sauntering about the market-place in a pair of slippers, had his
cue, and Mr. Sleary's equipage was ready. It was a fine sight,
to behold the learned dog barking round it, and Mr. Sleary
instructing him, with his one practicable eye, that Bitzer was the
object of his particular attentions. Soon after dark they all three
got in and started; the learned dog (a formidable creature) already
pinning Bitzer with his eye, and sticking close to the wheel on his
side, that he might be ready for him in the event of his showing
the slightest disposition to alight.

The other three sat up at the inn all night in great suspense.
At eight o'clock in the morning Mr. Sleary and the dog reappeared:
both in high spirits.

"All right, Thquire!" said Mr. Sleary, "your thon may be
aboard a thip by thith time. Childerth took him off, an hour and
a half after we left there latht night. The horthe danthed the
polka till he wath dead beat (he would have walthed if he hadn't
been in harneth), and then I gave him the word and he went to
thleep comfortable. When that prethiouth young Rathcal thed
he'd go for'ard afoot, the dog hung on to hith neck-hankercher
with all four legth in the air and pulled him down and rolled
him over. Tho he come back into the drag, and there he that, 'till
I turned the horthe'th head, at half-patht thixth thith morning."

Mr. Gradgrind overwhelmed him with thanks, of course; and
hinted as delicately as he could, at a handsome remuneration in
money.

"I don't want money mythelf, Thquire; but Childerth ith a
family man, and if you wath to like to offer him a five-pound note,

it mightn't be unactheptable. Likewithe if you wath to thtand a collar for the dog, or a thet of bellth for the horthe, I thould be very glad to take 'em. Brandy and water I alwayth take." He had already called for a glass, and now called for another. "If you wouldn't think it going too far, Thquire, to make a little thpread for the company at about three and thixth a head, not reckoning Luth, it would make 'em happy."

All these little tokens of his gratitude, Mr. Gradgrind very willingly undertook to render. Though he thought them far too slight, he said, for such a service.

"Very well, Thquire; then, if you'll only give a Horthe-riding, a bethpeak, whenever you can, you'll more than balanthe the account. Now, Thquire, if your daughter will ethcuthe me, I thould like one parting word with you."

Louisa and Sissy withdrew into an adjoining room; Mr. Sleary, stirring and drinking his brandy and water as he stood, went on:

"Thquire, you don't need to be told that dogth ith wonderful animalth."

"Their instinct," said Mr. Gradgrind, "is surprising."

"Whatever you call it—and I'm bletht if *I* know what to call it"—said Sleary, "it ith ath-tonithing. The way in whith a dog'll find you—the dithtanthe he'll come!"

Mr. Sleary's canine philosophy

"His scent," said Mr. Gradgrind, "being so fine."

"I'm bletht if I know what to call it," repeated Sleary, shaking his head, "but I have had dogth find me, Thquire, in a way that made me think whether that dog hadn't gone to another dog, and thed, 'You don't happen to know a perthon of the name of Thleary, do you? Perthon of the name of Thleary, in the Horthe-riding way—thtout man—game eye?' And whether that dog mightn't have thed, 'Well, I can't thay I know him mythelf, but I know a dog that I think would be likely to be acquainted with him.' And whether that dog mightn't have thought it over, and thed, 'Thleary, Thleary! O yeth, to be thure! A friend of mine men-thioned him to me at one time. I can get you hith addreth directly.' In conthequenth of my being afore the public, and going about tho muth, you thee, there mutht be a number of dogth acquainted with me, Thquire, that *I* don't know!"

Mr. Gradgrind seemed to be quite confounded by this speculation.

"Anyway," said Sleary, after putting his lips to his brandy and water, "ith fourteen month ago, Thquire, thinthe we wath at Chethter. We wath getting up our Children in the Wood one morning, when there cometh into our Ring, by the thtage door, a dog. He had travelled a long way, he wath in very bad condithon, he wath lame, and pretty well blind. He went round to our children, one after another, as if he wath a theeking for a child he know'd; and then he come to me, and throwd hithelf up behind, and thtood on hith two forelegth, weak ath he wath, and then he wagged hith tail and died. Thquire, that dog wath Merrylegth."

"Sissy's father's dog!"

"Thethilia'th father'th old dog. Now, Thquire, I can take my oath, from my knowledge of that dog, that that man wath dead—and buried—afore that dog came back to me. Joth'phine and Childerth and me talked it over a long time, whether I thould write or not. But we agreed, 'No. There'th nothing comfortable to tell; why unthettle her mind, and make her unhappy?' Tho, whether her father bathely detherted her; or whether he broke hith own heart alone, rather than pull her down along with him; never will be known, now, Thquire, till—no, not till we know how the dogth findth uth out!"

"She keeps the bottle that he sent her for, to this hour; and she will believe in his affection to the last moment of her life," said Mr. Gradgrind.

"It theemth to prethent two thingth to a perthon, don't it, Thquire?" said Mr. Sleary, musing as he looked down into the depths of his brandy and water: "one, that there ith a love in the world, not all Thelf-interetht after all, but thomething very different; t'other, that it hath a way of ith own of calculating or not calculating, whith thomehow or another ith at leatht ath hard to give a name to, ath the wayth of the dogth ith!"

Mr. Gradgrind looked out of window, and made no reply. Mr. Sleary emptied his glass and recalled the ladies.

"Thethilia my dear, kith me, and good-bye! Mith Thquire, to thee you treating of her like a thithter, and a thithter that you trutht and honour with all your heart and more, ith a very pretty thight to me. I hope your brother may live to be better detherving of you, and a greater comfort to you. Thquire, thake handth, firtht and latht! Don't be croth with uth poor vagabondth. People mutht be amuthed. They can't be alwayth a learning, nor yet they can't be alwayth a working, they an't made for it. You *mutht* have uth, Thquire. Do the withe thing and the kind thing too, and make the betht of uth; not the wurtht!

"And I never thought before," said Mr. Sleary, putting his head in at the door again to say it, "that I wath tho muth of a Cackler!"

CHAPTER NINE

FINAL

It is a dangerous thing to see anything in the sphere of a vain blusterer, before the vain blusterer sees it himself. Mr. Bounderby felt that Mrs. Sparsit had audaciously anticipated him, and presumed to be wiser than he. Inappeasably indignant with her for her triumphant discovery of Mrs. Pegler, he turned this presumption, on the part of a woman in her dependent position, over and over in his mind, until it accumulated with turning like a great snowball. At last he made the discovery that to discharge this highly connected female—to have it in his power to say, "She was a woman of family, and wanted to stick to me, but I wouldn't have it, and got rid of her"—would be to get the utmost possible amount of crowning glory out of the connexion, and at the same time to punish Mrs. Sparsit according to her deserts.

Filled fuller than ever with this great idea, Mr. Bounderby came in to lunch, and sat himself down in the dining-room of former days, where his portrait was. Mrs. Sparsit sat by the fire, with her foot in her cotton stirrup, little thinking whither she was posting.

Since the Pegler affair, this gentlewoman had covered her pity for Mr. Bounderby with a veil of quiet melancholy and contrition. In virtue thereof, it had become her habit to assume a woeful look, which woeful look she now bestowed upon her patron.

"What's the matter now, ma'am?" said Mr. Bounderby, in a very short, rough way.

"Pray, sir," returned Mrs. Sparsit, "do not bite my nose off."

"Bite your nose off, ma'am?" repeated Mr. Bounderby. "*Your* nose!" meaning, as Mrs. Sparsit conceived, that it was too developed a nose for the purpose. After which offensive implication, he cut himself a crust of bread, and threw the knife down with a noise.

Mrs. Sparsit took her foot out of her stirrup, and said, "Mr. Bounderby, sir!"

"Well, ma'am?" retorted Mr. Bounderby. "What are you staring at?"

"May I ask, sir," said Mrs. Sparsit, "have you been ruffled this morning?"

"Yes, ma'am."

"May I inquire, sir," pursued the injured woman, "whether *I* am the unfortunate cause of your having lost your temper?"

"Now, I'll tell you what, ma'am," said Bounderby, "I am not come here to be bullied. A female may be highly connected, but she can't be permitted to bother and badger a man in my position, and I am not going to put up with it." (Mr. Bounderby felt it necessary to get on: foreseeing that if he allowed of details, he would be beaten.)

Mrs. Sparsit first elevated, then knitted, her Coriolanian eyebrows; gathered up her work into its proper basket; and rose.

"Sir," said she, majestically. "It is apparent to me that I am in your way at present. I will retire to my own apartment."

"Allow me to open the door, ma'am."

"Thank you, sir; I can do it for myself."

"You had better allow me, ma'am," said Bounderby, passing her, and getting his hand upon the lock; "because I can take the opportunity of saying a word to you, before you go. Mrs. Sparsit, ma'am, I rather think you are cramped here, do you know? It appears to me, that, under my humble roof, there's hardly opening enough for a lady of your genius in other people's affairs."

Mrs. Sparsit gave him a look of the darkest scorn, and said with great politeness, "Really, sir?"

"I have been thinking it over, you see, since the late affairs have happened, ma'am," said Bounderby, "and it appears to my poor judgment——" *Bounderby's judgment*

"Oh! Pray, sir," Mrs. Sparsit interposed, with sprightly cheerfulness, "don't disparage your judgment. Everybody knows how unerring Mr. Bounderby's judgment is. Everybody has had proofs of it. It must be the theme of general conversation. Disparage anything in yourself but your judgment, sir," said Mrs. Sparsit, laughing.

Mr. Bounderby, very red and uncomfortable, resumed:

"It appears to me, ma'am, I say that a different sort of establishment altogether would bring out a lady of *your* powers. Such an establishment as your relation, Lady Scadgers's, now. Don't you think you might find some affairs there, ma'am, to interfere with?"

"It never occurred to me before, sir," returned Mrs. Sparsit; "but now you mention it, I should think it highly probable."

"Then suppose you try, ma'am," said Bounderby, laying an envelope with a cheque in it in her little basket. "You can take your own time for going, ma'am; but perhaps in the meanwhile, it will be more agreeable to a lady of your powers of mind, to eat her meals by herself, and not to be intruded upon. I really ought to apologize to you—being only Josiah Bounderby of Coketown— for having stood in your light so long."

"Pray don't name it, sir," returned Mrs. Sparsit. "If that portrait could speak, sir—but it has the advantage over the original of not possessing the power of committing itself and disgusting others,—it would testify, that a long period has elapsed since I first habitually addressed it as the picture of a Noodle. Nothing that a Noodle does, can awaken surprise or indignation; the proceedings of a Noodle can only inspire contempt."

Thus saying, Mrs. Sparsit, with her Roman features like a medal struck to commemorate her scorn of Mr. Bounderby, surveyed him fixedly from head to foot, swept disdainfully past him, and

ascended the staircase. Mr. Bounderby closed the door, and stood
before the fire; projecting himself after his old explosive manner
into his portrait—and into futurity.

Into how much of futurity? He saw Mrs. Sparsit fighting out a
daily fight at the points of all the weapons in the female armoury,
with the grudging, smarting, peevish, tormenting Lady Scadgers,
still laid up in bed with her mysterious leg, and gobbling her
insufficient income down by about the middle of every quarter, in
a mean little airless lodging, a mere closet for one, a mere crib for
two; but did he see more? Did he catch any glimpse of himself
making a show of Bitzer to strangers, as the rising young man, so
devoted to his master's great merits, who had won young Tom's
place, and had almost captured young Tom himself, in the times
when by various rascals he was spirited away? Did he see any
faint reflection of his own image making a vain-glorious will,
whereby five-and-twenty Humbugs, past five-and-twenty years of
age, each taking upon himself the name, Josiah Bounderby of
Coketown, should for ever dine in Bounderby Hall, for ever lodge
in Bounderby Buildings, for ever attend a Bounderby chapel, for
ever to go to sleep under a Bounderby chaplain, for ever be
supported out of a Bounderby estate, and for ever nauseate all
healthy stomachs, with a vast amount of Bounderby balderdash
and bluster? Had he any prescience of the day, five years to come,
when Josiah Bounderby of Coketown was to die of a fit in the
Coketown street, and this same precious will was to begin its long
career of quibble, plunder, false pretences, vile example, little
service and much law? Probably not. Yet the portrait was to see
it all out.

Here was Mr. Gradgrind on the same day, and in the same hour,
sitting thoughtful in his own room. How much of futurity did *he*
see? Did he see himself, a white-haired decrepit man, bending his
hitherto inflexible theories to appointed circumstances; making his
facts and figures subservient to Faith, Hope, and Charity; and
no longer trying to grind that Heavenly trio in his dusty little
mills? Did he catch sight of himself, therefore much despised by
his late political associates? Did he see them, in the era of its
being quite settled that the national dustmen have only to do
with one another, and owe no duty to an abstraction called a

People, "taunting the honourable gentleman" with this and with that and with what not, five nights a-week, until the small hours of the morning? Probably he had that much fore-knowledge, knowing his men.

Here was Louisa on the night of the same day, watching the fire as in the days of yore, though with a gentler and a humbler face. How much of the future might arise before *her* vision? Broadsides in the streets, signed with her father's name, exonerating the late Stephen Blackpool, weaver, from misplaced suspicion, and publishing the guilt of his own son, with such extenuation as his years and temptation (he could not bring himself to add, his education) might beseech; were of the Present. So, Stephen Blackpool's tombstone, with her father's record of his death, was almost of the Present, for she knew it was to be. These things she could plainly see. But, how much of the Future?

Pictures in the fire

A working woman, christened Rachael, after a long illness once again appearing at the ringing of the Factory bell, and passing to and fro at the set hours, among the Coketown Hands; a woman of pensive beauty, always dressed in black, but sweet-tempered and serene, and even cheerful; who, of all the people in the place, alone appeared to have compassion on a degraded, drunken wretch of her own sex, who was sometimes seen in the town secretly begging of her, and crying to her; a woman working, ever working, but content to do it, and preferring to do it as her natural lot, until she should be too old to labour any more? Did Louisa see this? Such a thing was to be.

A lonely brother, many thousands of miles away, writing on paper blotted with tears, that her words had too soon come true, and that all the treasures in the world would be cheaply bartered for a sight of her dear face? At length this brother coming nearer home, with hope of seeing her, and being delayed by illness; and then a letter, in a strange hand, saying "he died in hospital, of fever, such a day, and died in penitence and love of you: his last word being your name"? Did Louisa see these things? Such things were to be.

Herself again a wife—a mother—lovingly watchful of her children, ever careful that they should have a childhood of the mind no less than a childhood of the body, as knowing it to be even a more beautiful thing, and a possession, any hoarded scrap of which is a blessing and happiness to the wisest? Did Louisa see this? Such a thing was never to be.

But, happy Sissy's happy children loving her; all children loving her; she, grown learned in childish lore; thinking no innocent and pretty fancy ever to be despised; trying hard to know her humbler fellow-creatures, and to beautify their lives of machinery and reality with those imaginative graces and delights, without which the heart of infancy will wither up, the sturdiest physical manhood will be morally stark death, and the plainest national prosperity figures can show, will be the Writing on the Wall,—she holding this course as part of no fantastic vow, or bond, or brotherhood, or sisterhood, or pledge, or covenant, or fancy dress, or fancy fair; but simply as a duty to be done,—did Louisa see these things of herself? These things were to be.

Dear reader! It rests with you and me, whether, in our two fields of action, similar things shall be or not. Let them be! We shall sit with lighter bosoms on the hearth, to see the ashes of our fires turn grey and cold.

THE END

Rinehart Editions

Addison and Steele, SEL. FROM THE TATLER & THE SPECTATOR 87

AMERICAN THOUGHT: CIVIL WAR TO WORLD WAR I 70

ANTHOLOGY OF ENGLISH DRAMA BEFORE SHAKESPEARE 45

ANTHOLOGY OF GREEK DRAMA: FIRST SERIES 29

ANTHOLOGY OF GREEK DRAMA: SECOND SERIES 68

ANTHOLOGY OF ROMAN DRAMA 101

Arnold, SELECTED POETRY AND PROSE 62

Austen, NORTHANGER ABBEY; Walpole, THE CASTLE OF OTRANTO; Radcliffe, THE MYSTERIES OF UDOLPHO (Abridged) 121

Austen, PRIDE AND PREJUDICE 22

Balzac, PÈRE GORIOT 18

Benét, S. V., SELECTED POETRY & PROSE 100

THE BIBLE: SEL. FROM OLD & NEW TESTAMENTS 56

Brontë, Charlotte, JANE EYRE 24

Brontë, Emily, WUTHERING HEIGHTS 23

Brown, C. B., ARTHUR MERVYN 112

Browning, Robert, SELECTED POETRY 71

Bunyan, THE PILGRIM'S PROGRESS 27

Burke, REFLECTIONS ON THE REVOLUTION IN FRANCE 84

Butler, THE WAY OF ALL FLESH 7

Byron, SELECTED POETRY AND LETTERS 54

Chaucer, THE CANTERBURY TALES 65

Chekhov, SIX PLAYS OF CHEKHOV 117

Coleridge, SELECTED POETRY AND PROSE 55

COLONIAL AMERICAN WRITING 43

Conrad, LORD JIM 85

Conrad, NOSTROMO 111

Cooper, THE PIONEERS 99

Cooper, THE PRAIRIE 26

Crane, RED BADGE OF COURAGE, SEL'D PROSE & POETRY 47

Dante, THE DIVINE COMEDY 72

Defoe, MOLL FLANDERS 25

De Forest, MISS RAVENEL'S CONVERSION 74

Dickens, GREAT EXPECTATIONS 20

Dickens, HARD TIMES 95

Dickens, OLIVER TWIST 115

Dostoevsky, THE FRIEND OF THE FAMILY and THE ETERNAL HUSBAND 119

Dreiser, SISTER CARRIE 86

Dryden, SELECTED WORKS 60

Eliot, ADAM BEDE 32

Eliot, SILAS MARNER 114

ELIZABETHAN FICTION 64

Emerson, SELECTED PROSE AND POETRY 30

ENGLISH PROSE AND POETRY 1660-1800: A SELECTION 110

Fielding, JOSEPH ANDREWS 15

FIFTEEN MODERN AMERICAN POETS 79

Flaubert, MADAME BOVARY 2

FOUR MODERN PLAYS: FIRST SERIES, Rev. Ibsen, Shaw, O'Neill, Chekhov 90

FOUR MODERN PLAYS: SECOND SERIES, Ibsen, Wilde, Rostand, Gorky 109

Franklin, AUTOBIOGRAPHY AND SELECTED WRITINGS 12

Frederic, THE DAMNATION OF THERON WARE 108

Frost, SELECTED POEMS OF ROBERT FROST 120

Garland, MAIN-TRAVELLED ROADS 66

Godwin, CALEB WILLIAMS 103

Goethe, FAUST: PART I 75

Goethe, SORROWS OF YOUNG WERTHER, NEW MELUSINA, NOVELLE 13

Gogol, DEAD SOULS 5

GREAT ENGLISH AND AMERICAN ESSAYS 34

Hardy, FAR FROM THE MADDING CROWD 98

Hardy, THE MAYOR OF CASTERBRIDGE 9

Hardy, THE RETURN OF THE NATIVE 39

Hauptmann, THREE PLAYS: The Weavers, Hannele, The Beaver Coat 52

Hawthorne, THE HOUSE OF THE SEVEN GABLES 89

Hawthorne, THE SCARLET LETTER 1

Hawthorne, SELECTED TALES AND SKETCHES 33

Hesse, STEPPENWOLF 122

Howells, THE RISE OF SILAS LAPHAM 19

Ibsen, THREE PLAYS: Ghosts, Enemy of the People, Wild Duck 4

Irving, SELECTED PROSE 41

James, Henry, THE AMBASSADORS 104

James, Henry, THE AMERICAN 16

James, Henry, SELECTED SHORT STORIES 31

Johnson, RASSELAS, POEMS, & SELECTED PROSE 57

Keats, SELECTED POETRY AND LETTERS 50

Lincoln, SELECTED SPEECHES, MESSAGES, AND LETTERS 82

LITERATURE OF THE EARLY REPUBLIC 44

London, MARTIN EDEN 80

MASTERPIECES OF THE SPANISH GOLDEN AGE 93

Melville, MOBY DICK 6

Melville, SEL'D TALES AND POEMS 36

Melville, THE CONFIDENCE-MAN 126

Meredith, THE ORDEAL OF RICHARD FEVEREL 123

Milton, PARADISE LOST AND SELECTED POETRY AND PROSE 35

MODERN AMERICAN LITERATURE 53

Newman, THE IDEA OF A UNIVERSITY 102

Norris, Frank, MC TEAGUE 40

Parkman, THE DISCOVERY OF THE GREAT WEST: LA SALLE 77

PLUTARCH—EIGHT GREAT LIVES 105

Poe, SELECTED PROSE AND POETRY, Rev. 42

POETRY OF THE NEW ENGLAND RENAISSANCE, 1790–1890 38

Pope, SELECTED POETRY AND PROSE 46

RINEHART BOOK OF SHORT STORIES 59

RINEHART BOOK OF VERSE 58

Robinson, E. A., SEL. EARLY POEMS AND LETTERS 107

Roosevelt, F. D., SPEECHES, MESSAGES, PRESS CONFERENCES, & LETTERS 83

Scott, THE HEART OF MIDLOTHIAN 14

SELECTED AMERICAN PROSE, 1841–1900 94

SELECTIONS FROM GREEK AND ROMAN HISTORIANS 88

SEVENTEENTH CENTURY POETRY 124

SEVENTEENTH CENTURY PROSE 125

Shakespeare, FIVE PLAYS: Hamlet; King Lear; Henry IV, Part I; Much Ado about Nothing; The Tempest 51

Shakespeare, AS YOU LIKE IT, JULIUS CAESAR, MACBETH 91

Shakespeare, TWELFTH NIGHT, OTHELLO 92

Shaw, SELECTED PLAYS AND OTHER WRITINGS 81

Shelley, SELECTED POETRY AND PROSE 49

SIR GAWAIN AND THE GREEN KNIGHT 97

Smollet, HUMPHRY CLINKER 48

SOUTHERN STORIES 106

Spenser, SELECTED POETRY 73

Sterne, TRISTRAM SHANDY 37

Stevenson, MASTER OF BALLANTRAE 67

Swift, GULLIVER'S TRAVELS 10

Swift, SELECTED PROSE AND POETRY 78

Tennyson, SELECTED POETRY 69

Thackeray, HENRY ESMOND 116

Thackeray, VANITY FAIR 76

Thoreau, WALDEN, ON THE DUTY OF CIVIL DISOBEDIENCE 8

Thoreau, A WEEK ON THE CONCORD AND MERRIMACK RIVERS 118

Trollope, BARCHESTER TOWERS 21

Turgenev, FATHERS AND CHILDREN 17

Twain, THE ADVENTURES OF HUCKLEBERRY FINN 11

Twain, ROUGHING IT 61

Vergil, THE AENEID 63

VICTORIAN POETRY: Clough to Kipling 96

Wharton, HOUSE OF MIRTH 113

Whitman, LEAVES OF GRASS AND SELECTED PROSE 28

Wordsworth, THE PRELUDE, SEL'D SONNETS & MINOR POEMS, Rev. & Enl. 3